"Mo? You'd better come over here."

She turned to find Brick next to a large pine tree on the mountainside's edge. As she approached she saw the crude heart carved into the pine's bark.

There were two sets of initials at the center: her sister, Tricia's, a plus sign and "JP." Tricia's secret lover had used her maiden-name initial. Wishful thinking on his part? Or was that the last name she'd given him?

"Know anyone with those initials?" Brick asked.

Mo shook her head. "I have no idea who JP is."

The gunshot echoed through the trees, splintering the bark on the tree next to her. Several nearby birds took flight, wings flapping wildly as Brick lunged for Mo, taking them both to the ground.

The second shot ricocheted off the tree where they had been standing, sending bark flying. And then there was nothing but the sound of the breeze in the pines and seemingly hushed roar of the creek. Not even the birds sang...

B.J. Daniels is a *New York Times* and *USA TODAY* bestselling author. She wrote her first book after a career as an award-winning newspaper journalist and author of thirty-seven published short stories. She lives in Montana with her husband, Parker, and three springer spaniels. When not writing, she quilts, boats and plays tennis. Contact her at bjdaniels.com, on Facebook or on Twitter, @bjdanielsauthor.

Books by B.J. Daniels

Harlequin Intrigue

Cardwell Ranch: Montana Legacy

Steel Resolve
Iron Will
Ambush Before Sunrise
Double Action Deputy

Whitehorse, Montana: The Clementine Sisters

Hard Rustler
Rogue Gunslinger
Rugged Defender

The Montana Cahills

Cowboy's Redemption

Whitehorse, Montana: The McGraw Kidnapping

Dark Horse
Dead Ringer
Rough Rider

HQN

Montana Justice

Restless Hearts
Heartbreaker

Visit the Author Profile page
at Harlequin.com for more titles.

B.J.
NEW YORK TIMES BESTSELLING AUTHOR
DANIELS

DOUBLE ACTION DEPUTY
&
HITCHED!

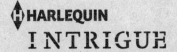

HARLEQUIN
INTRIGUE

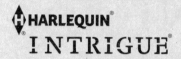

Recycling programs
for this product may
not exist in your area.

ISBN-13: 978-1-335-21399-0

Double Action Deputy & Hitched!

Copyright © 2020 by Harlequin Books S.A.

Double Action Deputy
First published in 2020. This edition published in 2020.
Copyright © 2020 by Barbara Heinlein

Hitched!
First published in 2010. This edition published in 2020.
Copyright © 2010 by Barbara Heinlein

This edition published by arrangement with Harlequin Books S.A.

For questions and comments about the quality of this book,
please contact us at CustomerService@Harlequin.com.

Harlequin Enterprises ULC
22 Adelaide St. West, 40th Floor
Toronto, Ontario M5H 4E3, Canada
www.Harlequin.com

Printed in U.S.A.

CONTENTS

DOUBLE ACTION DEPUTY

This book is for Kay Hould, for all her loving support and encouragement. She is definitely not the gray-haired historical-society woman in my Whitehorse, Montana series. But we first met because of it.

Chapter One

Ghostlike, the woman stumbled out of the dark night and into the glare of his headlights. The tattered bed-sheet wrapped around her fluttered in the breeze along with the duct tape that dangled from her wrists and one ankle.

He saw her look up as if she hadn't heard his pickup bearing down on her until the last moment. The night breeze lifted wisps of her dark hair from an ashen face as she turned her vacant gaze on him an instant before he slammed on his brakes.

The air filled with the smell and squeal of tires burning on the dark pavement as the pickup came to a shuddering halt. He sat for a moment, gripping the wheel and staring in horror into the glow of his headlights and seeing…nothing. Nothing but the empty street ahead just blocks from his apartment.

He threw the truck into Park and jumped out, convinced, even though he hadn't felt or heard a thud, that he'd hit her and that he'd find her lying bleeding on the pavement. How could he have missed her?

If there'd been a woman at all.

In those few seconds, leaving the driver's side door gaping open, the engine running, he was terrified of what he would find—and even more terrified of what he wouldn't.

Could he have just imagined the woman in his headlights? It wouldn't be the first time he'd had a waking nightmare since he'd come home to recuperate. He felt the cold breeze in his face even though it was June in Montana. The temperature at night dropped this time of year, the mountains still snowcapped. He shivered as he rounded the front of the truck and stopped dead.

His heart dropped to his boots.

The pavement was empty.

His pulse thundered in his ears.

I am losing my mind. I hallucinated the woman.

For months, he'd assured himself he was fine. Except for the nightmares that plagued him, something he'd done his best to keep from his family since returning to Cardwell Ranch.

Doubt sent a stab of alarm through him that made him weak with worry. He leaned against the front of the pickup. Why would he imagine such an image? What was wrong with him? He'd *seen* her. He'd seen every detail.

He really *was* losing his mind.

As he glanced around the empty street, he suddenly felt frighteningly all alone as if he was the last person left alive on the earth. This late at night, the new businesses were dark in this neighborhood, some still under construction. The ones that were opened closed early, making the area a ghost town at night. It was one reason he'd taken the apartment over one of the new shops. He'd told his folks that he moved off the ranch for the peace and quiet. He didn't want them knowing that his nightmares hadn't stopped. They were getting worse.

A groan from the darkness made him jump. His heart pounded in his throat as he turned to stare into the blackness beyond the edge of the street. The sound definitely hadn't been his imagination. The night was so dark he couldn't see anything after the pavement ended. The sidewalks hadn't been poured yet, some of the streets not yet paved. He heard another sound that appeared to be coming from down the narrow alley between two buildings under construction.

He quickly stepped back to the driver's side of his pickup and grabbed his flashlight. Walking through the glow of his headlights, he headed into the darkness beyond the street. The narrow beam of light skittered to the edge of the pavement and froze on a spot of blood.

Deeper into the dirt alley, the beam came to rest on the woman as she tried to crawl away. She clawed at the ground, clearly exhausted, clearly terrified, before collapsing halfway down the alley.

She wasn't an apparition. And she was alive! He rushed to her. Her forehead was bleeding from a small cut, and her hands and knees were scraped from crawling across the rough pavement and then the dirt to escape. In the flashlight's glow, he saw that her face was bruised from injuries she'd suffered before tonight. From what he could tell, his pickup hadn't hit her.

But there was no doubt that she was terrified. Her eyes widened in horror at the sight of him. A high-pitched keening sound filled the air and she kicked at him and stumbled to her feet. He could see that she was exhausted because she hadn't taken more than few steps when she dropped to her knees and tried to crawl away again.

She was shivering uncontrollably in the tattered sheet

wrapped around her. He caught up to her, took off his jacket and put it over her, fearing she was suffering from hypothermia. He could see that her wrists and ankles were chafed where she'd been bound with the duct tape. She was barefoot and naked except for the soiled white sheet she was wrapped in.

"It's all right," he said as he pulled out his cell phone to call for help. "You're all right now. I'm going to get help." She lay breathing hard, collapsed in the dirt. "Can you tell me who did this to you? Miss, can you hear me?" he asked, leaning closer to make sure she was still breathing. Her pale eyes flew open, startling him as much as the high-pitched scream that erupted from her.

As the 911 operator came on the line, he had to yell to be heard over the woman's shrieks. "This is Deputy Marshal Brick Savage," he said as he gave the address, asking for assistance and an ambulance ASAP.

Chapter Two

After very little sleep and an early call from his father the next morning, Brick dressed in his uniform and drove down to the law enforcement building. He was hoping that this would be the day that his father, Marshal Hud Savage, told him he would finally be on active duty. He couldn't wait to get his teeth into something, a real investigation. After finding that woman last night, he wanted more than anything to be the one to get her justice.

"Come in and close the door," his father said before motioning him into a chair across from his desk.

"Is this about the woman I encountered last night?" he asked as he removed his Stetson and dropped into a chair across from him. He'd stayed at the hospital until the doctor had sent him home. When he called this morning, he'd been told that the woman appeared to be in a catatonic state and was unresponsive.

"We have a name on your Jane Doe," his father said now. "Natalie Berkshire."

Brick frowned. The name sounded vaguely familiar. But that wasn't what surprised him. "Already? Her fingerprints?"

Hud nodded and slid a copy of the *Billings Ga-*

zette toward him. He picked it up and saw the headline sprawled across the front page, *Alleged Infant Killer Released for Lack of Evidence*. The newspaper was two weeks old.

Brick felt a jolt rock him back in his chair. "She's *that* woman?" He couldn't help his shock. He thought of the terrified woman who'd crossed in front of his truck last night. Nothing like the woman he remembered seeing on television coming out of the law enforcement building in Billings after being released.

"I don't know what to say." Nor did he know what to think. The woman he'd found had definitely been victimized. He thought he'd saved her. He'd been hell-bent on getting her justice. With his Stetson balanced on his knee, he raked his fingers through his hair.

"I'm trying to make sense of this, as well," his father said. "Since her release, more evidence had come out in former cases. She's now wanted for questioning in more deaths of patients who'd been under her care from not just Montana. Apparently, the moment she was released, she disappeared. Billings PD checked her apartment. It appeared that she'd left in a hurry and hasn't been seen since."

"Until last night when she stumbled in front of my pickup," Brick said. "You think she's been held captive all this time?"

"Looks that way," Hud said. "We found her older model sedan parked behind the convenience store down on Highway 191. We're assuming she'd stopped for gas. The attendant who was on duty recognized her from a photo. She remembered seeing Natalie at the gas pumps and thinking she looked familiar but couldn't place her at the time. The attendant said a large motor home pulled in and she lost sight of her and didn't see her again."

"When was this?" Brick asked.

"Two weeks ago. Both the back seat and the trunk of her car were full of her belongings."

"So she was running away when she was abducted." Brick couldn't really blame her. "After all the bad publicity, I can see why she couldn't stay in Billings. But taking off like that makes her either look guilty—or scared."

"Or both. This case got a lot of national coverage for months. Unfortunately, her case was tried in the press and she was found guilty. When there wasn't sufficient evidence in the Billings case to prosecute, they had no choice but to let her go. My guess is that someone who didn't like the outcome took the law into his own hands."

Brick nodded. "It would be some coincidence if she was abducted and held by someone who had no idea who she was." He shook his head, remembering the terror he'd seen in her eyes. "What if she's innocent of these crimes?"

"It seems that all of her nursing care positions involved patients with severe health issues," Hud said. "It's no surprise that a lot of the old cases are being reopened now. All of her patients died before she moved on to her next nursing job."

"So foul play was never considered in most of the other deaths?" Brick said. "But it is now even though she was released. No wonder she ran."

His father nodded. "Several of the Billings homicide detectives are on their way. I get the impression they might have discovered more evidence against her. It's possible they plan to arrest her—or at the least, take her into custody for questioning."

Brick rubbed the back of his neck as he tried to imagine the woman he'd found last night as a cold-blooded killer. "And if they don't?"

"Unless one of the other investigations across the country wants her detained, then, when she's well, she'll be released from the hospital and free to go."

"To be on her own knowing there is someone out there who means her harm?" Brick couldn't help being shocked by that. "Someone abducted her, held her captive for apparently weeks and if not tortured her, definitely did a number on her." He couldn't help his warring emotions. The woman might be guilty as sin. Or not. Clearly, she wasn't safe. He'd seen how terrified she'd been last night. *Someone* had found her. He didn't doubt they would again.

"Once the press finds out who the woman is in our hospital, it will be a media circus," his father was saying. "I know you found her, but I'd prefer you stay out of this. However, I'm sure Billings homicide will want to talk to you. This will have to be handled delicately, to say the least."

"You don't think I can do *delicate*?"

The marshal smiled as he leaned back in his chair. "I think you're going to make a damned good deputy marshal, maybe even marshal, in time." In time. Time had suddenly become Brick's enemy. "You've gotten the training," his father continued, "and once you get the last medical release…"

Brick didn't need the reminder of what had happened to him. The fact that he'd almost died wasn't something he'd forgotten. He had the scars to remind him. Those and the nightmares. But he hadn't just been wounded in the mountains of Wyoming and almost died. He'd killed the man who shot him. He wasn't sure which haunted him the most.

He also didn't need another pep talk on being patient until he got a mental health physician to release him for active duty. Until then, he was sentenced to doing menial desk job work.

"I should get going." No matter what his father said, he had to see the woman again. He wasn't scheduled to work until later. He had plenty of time to stop by the hospital before his appointment with the shrink and his desk job shift. But as he started to get to his feet, his father waved him back down.

"Brick, if you're thinking of going by the hospital, you should know that she can't tell you what happened to her or who is responsible. She's in what the doctor called a catatonic or unresponsive state, something often associated with trauma."

"I know, I already called, but I have to see her." He couldn't forget that moment when she'd appeared in front of his headlights. It haunted him—just as the woman did. "I found her. I almost hit her with my pickup. I feel...connected to her."

Brick knew it was a lot more than that. He was going crazy sitting behind a desk, cooling his heels until the shrink said he was ready to get to work. It left him too much time to think.

Not that he would tell his father or the psychiatrist he was required to see later today, but finding that woman last night *had* brought back his ordeal in Wyoming. That was another reason he wanted—needed—to see this through.

MARSHAL HUD SAVAGE leaned forward to study his son. "How are the nightmares?"

Brick shook his head, not meeting his gaze. "No longer a problem."

He watched his son shift on his feet, anxious to get out the door. "Son, you know how happy I was when you wanted the deputy marshal job that was coming open."

"I can do the job, if that's what you're worried about."

"I believe you can, but not yet."

"I'm healed. Doc cleared me weeks ago."

"I'm not talking about your physical injuries. You need clearance from a mental health professional as well, and I heard you missed your last appointment."

Brick swore. "I'm fine. I had a conflict… Besides, is it really necessary after all this time?"

"It is." He was more convinced of that after seeing how personally involved Brick had become with the woman he'd found last night. Although Brick and Angus were identical twins, they were so different it amazed him. Brick had always been the carefree one, hardly ever serious, ready with a joke when he got in trouble. He was also the one who made his mother laugh the most and that meant a lot to Hud.

Dana was delighted to have her son come home six months ago to recuperate. Hud knew she hoped that he'd be staying once he was well. Brick had always taken wrangling jobs with his brother. That was how he'd ended up down in Wyoming. She'd thought maybe she could convince him, like she had Angus, to stay on the ranch and work it with his twin.

So Dana wasn't as pleased that he wanted to follow his father's footsteps into law enforcement. She blamed Hud for making the profession look too glamorous, which had made him laugh. Her dream was that their children would embrace the ranch lifestyle and return to Cardwell Ranch to run it.

But Brick had always stubbornly gone his own way even as a child.

"It wasn't just your body that went through the trauma," Hud said now to his son. "You need to heal. I suspect one of the reasons you're so interested in this case is that finding that woman in the condition she was in brought back what happened to you in Wyoming."

Brick scoffed. "I was *shot*. I wasn't tied up in some basement and abused."

"I don't think you've dealt with how close you came to dying or the fact that you were forced to take another man's life. It's standard procedure, son. Don't miss today's appointment."

BRICK GLANCED AT the time as he drove to the hospital. There would be hell to pay if he missed his doctor appointment. But he had to at least see the woman again. He felt confused. Not that seeing her lying in the hospital bed would probably help with that confusion.

He still couldn't believe that the woman he'd rescued was the notorious nurse who'd worked as a nanny for a young couple in Billings. The couple's newborn son had multiple life-threatening medical problems. They'd opted to take their son home and be with him for as long as they had.

Natalie Berkshire had sworn that when she came into the nursery she found the baby blue. She'd tried to resuscitate him, screaming for the mother to call 911. But he was gone. An autopsy revealed that the baby had died from lack of oxygen. It wasn't until fibers from the baby's blanket were found in his lungs that Natalie was arrested, and then released when the case against her wasn't strong enough for a conviction.

Now as Brick took the stairs to her floor, he told himself that he was invested in this case whether his father liked it or not. True, he was restless and ached to get back to actively working, but he also wanted to prove to his father that he could do this job.

He knew his dad had had his reservations. All Brick had known growing up on Cardwell Ranch in the Gallatin Canyon was wrangling horses and cattle. He'd never shown an interest in law enforcement before, so he couldn't blame him for being skeptical at first.

After coming home to recuperate after his ordeal in Wyoming, he'd realized it was time to settle down. When he'd heard about the deputy marshal position coming open, he'd jumped at it. He told himself that he wasn't grabbing up the first thing that came along, as his father feared. Somehow, it felt right.

At least he hoped so as he came out of the stairwell on Natalie Berkshire's floor. He was only a little winded by the hike up the stairs, but he was getting stronger every day. Physically, he was recovering nicely, his doctor had said. If it wasn't for the nightmares…

Walking down the hall, he was glad to see the deputy stationed outside her door. He'd been relieved last night when his father had assigned a deputy to guard her after the lab techs had taken what evidence they could gather—including her fingerprints, which ID'd her.

Brick had feared she was still in danger from whoever had held her captive. At the time, he hadn't known just how much danger this woman was in—or what she was running from.

After being raised in a house with his marshal father, he believed in innocence until proven guilty. If this woman was guilty, she deserved a trial. But even as Brick thought it, he wondered if she could get one anywhere in this country after all the publicity.

As he approached her room, he hoped his father hadn't told the guard not to let him in.

"Hey, Jason," Brick said as he approached the deputy sitting outside her door. The marshal department in Big Sky was small, so he knew most everyone by name even though he was new. And everyone knew him. Being the marshal's son was good and bad. He wouldn't get any special treatment—not from his father. If anything, Hud Savage would be tougher on him. But he couldn't have anyone thinking he was special because of his last name.

"That must have been something, finding her like you did," Jason said.

Brick nodded as he looked toward her closed door. "Any trouble?"

"Not a peep out of her."

"No one's come by looking for her?" Brick knew how news traveled in this small canyon town. He feared that whoever had held the woman captive would hear that she'd been taken to the hospital. The hospital was small and busy during the summer season. If someone were determined to get in, they would find a way.

"Nope."

Brick heard a sound inside the room and looked quizzically to the guard.

"Nurse." The deputy grinned. "Good-looking one too. I'd let her take my vitals."

Brick smiled, shaking his head at the man, and pushed open the door. As he did, the nurse beside the bed who'd been leaning over the patient now looked up in alarm.

He took in the scene in that split second as the door closed behind him. The guard was right. The nurse was a stunner, blonde with big blue eyes.

"I didn't mean to startle you," he said as he stepped deeper into the room, sensing that something was wrong.

"You didn't." The nurse began to nervously straighten the patient's sheet before she turned toward him to leave. He realized with a start that the patient had been saying something as he walked in. He'd seen Natalie's lips moving. Her eyes had been open, but were now closed. Had he only imagined that she'd spoken? How was that possible if the woman was catatonic and nonresponsive?

Also, when he'd come in and the nurse had been leaning over the patient, she'd clearly been intent on what Natalie was saying. She'd straightened so quickly as he'd come in. But before that, he'd seen something in the nurse's face…

The hair rose on the back of his neck.

"I heard the patient was catatonic. Any change?" he asked.

"No, I'm afraid not," the nurse said and started toward him on her way out of the room.

"Please don't let me stop you from what you were doing."

"I'm finished." She had to walk right past him to get out the door. As she approached, he looked at her more closely. If he was right and had heard Natalie speak, then the nurse had lied about there being no change. But why would she lie?

Looking past her, he noticed a pillow on the floor where she'd been standing. It had apparently fallen off the bed. It seemed strange that she hadn't taken the time to pick it up and put it back on the patient's bed. But that wasn't half as odd as her apparent need to get out of this room as quickly as possible.

His gaze shot to her uniform. No name tag.

Even as he raised his arm to stop her, he still couldn't be sure of what he'd thought he'd seen—and heard. But he couldn't shake the feeling that something was very wrong here. That he'd walked into something… "Hold up just a minute."

The moment he reached for the woman, she jerked back her arm and spun to face him. Before he could react, she jammed her forearm into his throat. As he gasped for air, she kicked him in the groin.

Even as the pain doubled him over, he grabbed for her, but she slipped through his fingers. He tried to call to the deputy stationed outside the door, but he had no breath, no air, no voice. All he could do for a few moments was watch her push out of the hospital room door.

Limping to the door after her, he found the deputy out in the hall talking to the doctor. The hallway was empty. He tried to speak but nothing came out as he bent over, hands on his knees, and sucked in painful breaths.

The woman in the nurse's uniform was long gone.

Chapter Three

The marshal sat back in his chair and listened as his son told him again what had happened at the hospital. Brick had called it in on his way to his psychiatrist's office. Hud had been glad to see that his son hadn't used what happened to him at the hospital as an excuse to get out of his doctor's appointment.

Hud had been having trouble believing this story. The doctor had insisted that Natalie Berkshire was still catatonic and questioned if the deputy had actually heard her speak. But the description of the nurse Brick had seen didn't match that of any woman who worked at the hospital. Five-foot-five, blonde, big blue eyes, a knockout.

"So you didn't actually witness her doing anything to the patient," Hud said now. He could see how upset his son was. Finding the woman last night had clearly shaken him and now this. As Brick had said, he felt responsible for her, something he admired in his son. But Brick couldn't take on this kind of responsibility every time he helped someone as a deputy marshal. He wondered again if this job was right for him. Or if his son was ready for any of this after what had happened to him.

"No, I didn't actually see her threaten the patient, but there was a pillow on the floor and she was acting…suspicious. Also, I swear, I heard the patient say something to her. If you'd seen the nurse's reaction to whatever Natalie was saying…"

"But you didn't hear the actual words?" Hud asked.

Brick shook his head. "She was whispering and the nurse was leaning over her. My attention was on the nurse and her expression. I'm telling you, the nurse was looking down at the patient as if she wanted to kill her. But whatever Natalie was saying appeared to have… shocked her."

"You got all of this in an instant when you walked into the room?"

His son shrugged. "It was just a feeling I got when I walked in that something was wrong. So maybe I was paying more attention. I know what I saw *and* what I heard. If I hadn't gone in when I did, who knows what the woman would have done."

Hud groaned inwardly. If they arrested every person who acted suspicious there would be no room in the jails for the true criminals. He said as much to his son.

"She was pretending to be a nurse. Not to mention the fact that she attacked me, an officer of the law. Isn't that enough?"

"You said you grabbed her arm as she was starting to leave. Did you announce yourself as a deputy marshal?"

Brick sighed. "No, but I was wearing my uniform, and if you'd seen the way she was looking down at the patient…"

Hud admitted it sounded more than a little suspicious. "Okay, the hospital staff will be watching for her should she try to get into the woman's hospital room again. She could just be a reporter looking for a story. Brick?" He could see how rattled his son was. All the talk in the marshal's department would be about this case. "I want you to take the rest of the week off. I'll talk to your doctor at the beginning of next week. If he gives the all clear…"

His son chuckled and shook his head. "By then, Natalie Berkshire will either be arrested and hauled off for questioning, or gone."

"It's for the best."

BRICK SWORE UNDER his breath. "I know what I saw and what I heard. That woman posing as a nurse was in that room to kill Natalie. But whatever Natalie said to her made her hesitate. Then I walked in… What if this nurse is the one who's been holding Natalie captive?"

"I'll find out the truth," his father said. "I wasn't just suggesting that you take the rest of the week off. It's an order. Go camping. You're too involved in this case. Take advantage of this time off. Hike up into the mountains to a nice lake and camp for a few days. I brought you on too soon and I'm sorry about that."

He was about to argue when his father's phone rang. He wasn't leaving. Not until he convinced the marshal that he couldn't get rid of him that easily.

Then he saw his father's expression as he finished his phone conversation and hung up. What had happened? *Something.* "I'm meeting with a psychiatrist. I'm doing everything you asked. So stop trying to get rid of me. Tell me what's happened. You know I'll find out one way or another anyway. And if you don't want me trying to find out on my own—"

With a sigh, Hud said, "From your description and

surveillance cameras at the hospital, they've been able to make a possible ID of the woman pretending to be a nurse. Her name is Maureen 'Mo' Mortensen."

"She must have some connection to the case," Brick said.

His father nodded. "The baby in Natalie Berkshire's care when he was allegedly murdered was her sister's."

Brick swore. "That would explain why she was standing over Natalie staring down at her as if she wanted to kill her."

"What makes this case more tragic is that Maureen Mortensen's sister committed suicide just days after Natalie was released."

"Tricia Colton," he said. "I remember seeing the husband on the news. He blamed Natalie for destroying his family. His wife had hung herself in the family garage. So Maureen Mortensen is her sister? Is she in the military or something? She attacked me as if she was trained in combat."

"She was a homicide detective in Billings."

"Was?"

"She's been temporarily suspended."

"Why?" Brick asked.

"I suspect it has something to do with her conflict of interest in the case. Apparently, she had been doing some investigating on her own before Natalie was released. She was ordered off the case, but refused to listen." He gave Brick a meaningful look.

Brick ignored it as he thought of what he'd seen at the hospital. "She wasn't the one who abducted and held Natalie Berkshire captive."

"What makes you say that?"

"Just a feeling I got that she hadn't seen Natalie for a while." He felt his father's gaze on him. "What?"

"Always trust your instincts."

He smiled. It was the most affirmation his father had given him since he'd signed on as a new deputy. "Thanks."

"But that doesn't mean that you aren't wrong."

He thought about it for a moment. "This woman, Mo, wants her dead—not tied up and tortured."

"You have no evidence that Mortensen was trying to kill the woman," his father pointed out. "Also, the doctor said that Natalie Berkshire couldn't have spoken to the woman. She's still nonresponsive."

Brick shook his head. "I swear I heard her. What's more, the fake nurse-slash-cop heard her."

"I've put a BOLO out on Mortensen to have her picked up for questioning."

"How about for assaulting a lawman?"

"It's enough to at least hold her for a while. I'm sure Billings PD will want to talk to her once they get here. But I do wonder how it was that she found out Natalie Berkshire was in the Big Sky hospital," his father said. "Unless she's been looking for her since her suspension—and Natalie's disappearance."

"Well, now she's found her," Brick said. "I wouldn't be surprised if she tries to get to her again."

Brick was still trying to process everything his father had told him. He'd been so sure that Natalie Berkshire had been the victim and that Maureen Mortensen was the criminal. Even if his father picked up the blonde cop, his instincts told him that she wouldn't be behind bars long. When she got out, he put his money on her going after Natalie Berkshire.

Maybe his father was right, and Maureen "Mo" Mortensen wouldn't have killed the woman lying in the hospital bed if he hadn't walked in. But from her expression, she'd darn sure wanted to.

"I bet the cop hasn't gone far," he said, wondering where she'd been staying. Probably at one of the local motels. He said as much to his father.

"I know she hurt your ego and you might want to go after her yourself because of it, but you're staying out of this. I shouldn't have put you on the schedule until we had the release from the mental health doctor. Don't argue with me about this. And come to dinner tonight. Your mother would love to see you."

Brick rose and started for the door.

"One more thing," his father said behind him. "I'm going to need your badge, star and weapon."

Brick turned to look at him as he slowly took off his star, pulled his badge and unsnapped his holster and laid all three on his father's desk.

"You can order me to take a few days off, but you can't make me go camping. Just as you can't order me to come to dinner." He turned and walked out, telling himself that becoming a deputy and working under his father was a huge mistake.

MAUREEN "MO" MORTENSEN wiped the steam off the cracked mirror and locked eyes with the woman in the glass, but only for an instant. She didn't like what she saw in her blue eyes. It scared her. Sometimes she didn't recognize herself and the woman she'd become.

Splashing cold water on her face, she thought of what had happened at the hospital. She'd come close to getting caught. But that wasn't all she'd come close to. If that deputy marshal hadn't walked in when he had...

She was still shaken, not just by Natalie's condition. She felt sick to her stomach at the memory. She'd looked down at the woman's bruised face. It had been true, what she'd heard. Natalie had been abducted and held prisoner. She'd thought she couldn't feel sympathy for what the woman must have gone through, but she'd been wrong. She didn't wish that sort of treatment on anyone, even a murderer.

For a long moment, she'd stood next to Natalie's bed, staring down at her. Had she been trying to see the monster behind the skin and bone? When the woman had opened her eyes, it had startled her. She'd read on her chart that she was catatonic. But looking into the Natalie's eyes, she'd seen fear, surprise and then something even more shocking—resignation.

Natalie had known why Mo had sneaked into the hospital dressed as a nurse. Would Mo have gone through with it? She might never know because the woman's words had stopped her cold.

Mo still felt stunned. By the time the words had registered, the deputy had come into the hospital room. She'd wanted to scream because she'd known that her chance to question Natalie had passed. All she could do was clear out of there with the hope that she could get another chance to question Natalie alone.

It surprised her that now she wanted the truth more than she wanted vengeance.

Unfortunately, she also now had the law looking for her. Getting free of the deputy had been instinctive. How could she reach Natalie again, though, with even more people looking for her? That cocky deputy marshal would be after her.

She pushed the thought away. She had more problems than some deputy marshal. Her body ached. Even when she could find the haven of sleep, she often woke bone-weary, more tired than she'd ever been. In her dreams, she'd been chasing Natalie Berkshire for months. In real life, it had only been since the woman had been released from custody—two weeks ago.

Today was the closest she'd come to finishing this. That moment of hesitation had cost her. She remembered looking into those pale hazel eyes. Natalie had known exactly who she was. The words she'd spoken weren't those of a mad woman. Nor of a liar. That was what had made them so shocking.

Natalie had known why Mo was there. She'd been ready to die. Because she knew she deserved it? Or because she knew she couldn't keep running?

In all the time she'd been a cop, Mo had never hesitated when everything was on the line, and yet earlier... If Natalie really had been catatonic... If she hadn't opened her eyes. If she hadn't spoken... The thought chilled her. Would she have gone through with what she'd planned?

Shaking her head at her disappointment in not being able to question Natalie after the woman had dropped that bombshell, she threw what little she'd brought into her suitcase. She didn't have time for introspection or recriminations. Or to try to analyze what the woman said or what it could mean.

She would get another chance to talk to Natalie—hopefully alone. She had to. Natalie had evaded almost everyone—except whoever had abducted her.

Mo thought about the woman's bruises. Whoever had found her didn't want her dead. They wanted to punish her and had.

The thought pained her. It wasn't as if the woman was a stranger. She'd known Natalie. Or at least she thought she'd known her. Mo had spent time at that house with her sister and brother-in-law and their live-in nanny. She'd watched the woman not just with little Joey, but with her sister. Tricia had bonded with Natalie. The three women had become friends. Mo had liked the quiet, pleasant Natalie Berkshire. What's more, she'd seen that her sister had liked the woman as well and vice versa. Natalie, during those months, had become part of the family.

That thought hurt more than she wanted to admit. They'd all trusted the woman—even Mo. She *had* to talk to Natalie again. If there was even a chance that what she'd said might be true…

It surprised her how just a few words from the woman could change everything. When a friend at the police department had called her to say that something had come up on the scanner, she'd driven to Big Sky as fast as she could. The marshal in Big Sky said he'd called Billings PD to let them know that he had Natalie Berkshire after she'd apparently escaped after being abducted. Mo had arrived late last night. When she'd stopped on the edge of Big Sky to get something to eat at an all-night convenience store and deli, she'd overheard a table of nurses talking. One night shift nurse had described the woman who'd been brought in.

Mo had felt a chill ripple through her. From the description, she'd known it was true. The patient was Natalie, no matter how bizarre the circumstances that had landed her in the Big Sky hospital.

She'd listened to the night nurse talking in a low, confidential tone and caught enough to know that the woman brought in had been held captive for an unknown amount of time. She heard the words *duct tape*, *bruises*, *a torn and filthy sheet*.

She'd also heard that a deputy marshal by the name of Brick Savage had found her and gotten her to the hospital—the closest hospital in the area—where she had originally been listed as a Jane Doe. Until her prints had come back.

This morning, Mo had picked up scubs and Crocs at the discount store. She'd walked into the hospital as if she knew what she was doing. The older woman at the information desk only smiled as she went by.

Upstairs, she'd found Natalie's room by looking for the deputy she'd heard had been parked outside it. All she'd had to do was give him a smile and walk right into the room.

One glance toward the bed and she'd known she was about to get her chance for justice. It was Natalie, and given the shape she was in, Mo knew that someone else had caught up to her first. She'd suspected for some time that she wasn't the only one looking for the woman.

She'd thought she'd known exactly what she would do when she found her. She owed it to her sister and to Thomas, her sister's still grieving husband, and to little Joey, their infant son. She'd kept what she was doing from Thomas. He'd been so devastated by the loss of his son and wife that he'd begged Mo to let it go.

"I can't take anymore," he'd cried when she'd argued that she had to find evidence to stop Natalie.

"But she'll kill again," she'd argued.

"For the love of God, Mo. I never want to hear that woman's name again. For months Tricia and I thought we'd get justice. When Natalie was released…" Tricia had killed herself. "I need to make peace with this. I hope you can, too."

She had known that she wouldn't find peace until Natalie was either dead or behind bars. She had been determined that Natalie would not destroy another family.

But then Natalie had opened her eyes and said the only words that could have changed her mind—even temporarily.

Mo moved to the motel room door, suitcase in hand. She looked back to make sure she hadn't left anything behind. She figured that it wouldn't take long, between the deputy who'd gotten a good look at her and the surveillance cameras, before they knew her name. That would definitely make finding her easier since she'd used her real name when she'd checked into the motel.

She wouldn't make that mistake again, she thought. Nor would it be a good idea to stay in any one place too long. Not that she was planning on this taking any longer than necessary. She would get back into the hospital. Security would be tighter. They would be watching for her.

Mo knew that the best thing she could do was wait until Natalie was released, but she had no idea when that would be. Also, she knew that Billings homicide were on their way—because some old cases were now being reopened and other departments were anxious to talk to Natalie. If they didn't arrest her and Natalie was released from the hospital, she would run like a scared rabbit and be all that much harder to catch.

She picked up her purse on the table by the door, swung the strap over her shoulder and, shifting the suitcase in her hand, reached with the other one to open the door. She already had a plan simmering at the back of her mind, a way to get into the hospital again.

She'd go to the store, get some supplies to change her appearance. This time she'd go in not as a nurse, but as a male workman instead. She would bluff her way in and no matter what she had to do, she'd get into Natalie's room. She would get the truth out of the woman and then…

Mo refused to think beyond that point. What she had in mind had never sat easy with her. But she felt she had no choice. She was convinced of what would happen if Natalie was as guilty as she believed and she didn't stop her.

With purse and suitcase in hand, she opened the door and stepped out of the motel room—right into a pair of deputies…and handcuffs.

Chapter Four

Angry and frustrated, Brick was even more determined to find out the truth about Natalie Berkshire. He knew he was taking one hell of a chance, but he drove through town to Highway 191 to the convenience store where Natalie Berkshire had allegedly been abducted. Inside, he bought an ice cream cone and asked the clerk if she'd been on duty that day when the woman had been abducted. She hadn't, but she told him everything the other clerk had told her.

Behind the wheel of his pickup again, he sat and ate his ice cream cone. The appointment with the psychiatrist had gone better than he'd hoped. He liked the man and thought his father was right. Talking about what had happened up on the mountain might get rid of the nightmares. He would gladly see the last of them. They were too vivid and bizarre, a jumble of confusing, frightening images that finally woke him in a cold sweat.

He knew he shouldn't have been surprised, but after talking about it and everything else that had happened in the past twenty-four hours, he felt drained. He had gotten hardly any sleep last night after Natalie Berkshire stumbled into his headlights. He'd been coming from the late shift. Finding her had added even more dark images to his sleep.

Now he couldn't help thinking about her or the blonde cop, Mo. Was Natalie a killer? Or was she innocent? Was Mo a vigilante cop with a need for vengeance? Or was she like a lot of people who feared Natalie had gotten away with murder and would kill again if not stopped?

Two women. One set on escape. The other on closure. But someone else, who was set on dispensing his own brand of justice, had already abducted Natalie Berkshire. Would they have eventually killed her if she hadn't escaped?

And what would the rogue cop do now if she wasn't found and stopped?

Brick knew the answers were out there and he desperately wanted to find them. He still swore that Natalie had spoken to the cop. Said something that had stopped her. Something in addition to continuing to swear she was innocent. The more he thought about it, he realized that the two had known each other before the murder. Natalie had been her sister's nanny. Who knows how close they might have been.

What a complicated, intriguing case. It did make him wonder who was innocent. It also made him want to help solve it more than he'd ever wanted anything.

He sat in his truck for a few minutes after eating his ice cream, trying to decide what to do—if anything. He was exhausted from everything that had happened, not just in the past twenty-four hours. As he shifted in the seat, he felt his harmonica in his pocket and pulled it out. He'd carried the musical instrument from the day his grandfather Angus had given it to him. It had taken him a lot longer than he'd hoped to learn how to play it. But he'd stayed with it until he'd finally mastered a few of his favorite tunes. As was his character, he wasn't one to give up.

That was why it hurt so much to realize that he hadn't played the harmonica since the events up on the mountain in Wyoming. Nor did he want to. He put it back in his pocket and had to swallow the lump in his throat. Maybe he wasn't as well as he thought he was. Not yet. But he would be.

He needed to solve this puzzle for his own sake. It seemed to him that at least two people were after Natalie Berkshire. One was a suspended cop. The other was the person who'd caught up to her, abducted her and abused her. The clerk at the convenience store had said that all the other clerk had seen was a large motor home driven by an elderly man.

Starting his pickup's engine, he realized a place to begin would be finding where Natalie had been held. He'd discovered her on his street, but he knew she could have come from anywhere. All he knew for certain was the first spot she'd appeared.

He drove to his neighborhood. The businesses were all open now, the streets busy since it was June in Montana and the beginning of tourist season. He circled the block, extending his circles further out with each lap.

If he were going to abduct someone he would need a safe place to keep the person. Somewhere away from other people. In a way this could be the perfect neighborhood—at least at night. But during the day, there were too many construction workers around as well as tourists and shop owners and workers. Also, most of the new structures didn't have basements, so where had Natalie been held?

Brick had just turned down another street when he saw that he was running out of town. The landscape around Big Sky was sagebrush before the terrain went up into towering pine-covered mountains. The Gallatin River cut through it, forming the deep, often dark canyon. A sign caught his eye. Campground.

He felt as if he'd been touched with a cattle prod. The clerk at the convenience store had seen a motor home pull in when she'd lost sight of Natalie. He'd at first assumed that the motor home had blocked her view of whoever had taken the woman. But what if whoever had taken the woman had been driving the motor home?

He pointed his truck down the road to the south, but he hadn't gone far when he heard the bleep of a siren. Glancing in his rearview mirror, he saw the quick flash of the light bar on the patrol SUV that was now behind him.

With a curse, he pulled over and got out to walk back to talk to his father.

"I know what you're doing," Hud said with a sigh.

Brick wasn't going to deny it. "I think I know where she was held. That motor home that pulled in. I think she was being held at the campground up the road."

His father shook his head in exasperation before saying, "Get in. I was just headed there. How did I know you'd be going my way?"

Brick grinned at him as he slid in. "You're psychic. I remember when Angus and I were boys. You were always one step ahead of us."

"And you were always the ringleader and the one

that never did what you were told, let alone listened to any advice I gave you."

"Her feet were covered in dirt from walking through soil before she reached my neighborhood."

His father didn't respond, but he saw a small smile curve the man's lips as he drove and Brick buckled up. The campground was just off Highway 191 in stands of pines that offered privacy for campers. It also allowed self-contained rigs to stay for several weeks for free because there were no outhouses or water. Just as there was no campground host. The isolated campsites were large enough to accommodate a motor home.

Even this time of day with the sun high in the sky, the canyon was cold and dark. Brick had been away from home for so long he'd forgotten just how tight the Gallatin Canyon was in places. Highway 191 was a narrow strip of pavement hemmed in on one side by the river and mountain cliffs on the other. It was often filled with deep shadows and stayed cool even in the summer because of a lack of sunshine. During the last widening of the highway, small pullouts had been added for slower vehicles to pull over to let others pass when there was room.

June weather was often unpredictable. It wasn't uncommon for it to snow and end up closing some roads. That was why July and August were the big travel months in this part of Montana. Because of that, the campground would have been relatively empty the past few weeks.

Only two rigs were still parked among the trees. One was a pickup and camper. The other an SUV pulling a small travel trailer.

The marshal pulled in, turned off the engine and

said, "Stay here and try to remember that you're just along for the ride."

Brick watched his father unsnap the weapon on his hip as he climbed out and walked toward to the small trailer. If Marshal Hud Savage was anything, he was cautious, and with reason. They had no idea who had taken Natalie Berkshire prisoner or how many people might be in on it.

Over the patrol SUV radio came a call. Brick picked it up. "Deputy Brick Savage."

The dispatcher said, "Just wanted to let the marshal know that a couple of deputies just brought in Maureen Mortensen."

They'd found the blonde cop already? "I'll let him know." As he got off the radio, he saw his father standing at the trailer door. Sometimes he forgot how large a man Hud Savage was. He had always been broadshouldered and strong as an ox. Even at almost retirement age, he was still a big man, still impressive in not just his size. He'd always been good at what he did as well, Brick thought with a flood of emotion. He wanted so badly to follow in this man's footsteps, but worried he could never fill his boots.

He watched as a rather rotund man answered the marshal's knock.

Popping open his door so he could hear, Brick listened to his father questioning the man before moving on to the next rig.

Brick couldn't hear as well this time, but he saw the man who answered the marshal's knock point to a space at the back of the campground. His father nodded, then headed in that direction.

Brick got out of the patrol SUV and followed him

into a stand of dense pines. If the motor home had been parked here, it wouldn't have been visible from the highway. Nor was it near any other campsite. Even if Natalie had screamed bloody murder, she might not have been heard. But he doubted that whomever had taken her had allowed her to scream at all.

He stopped short when he saw what his father was doing—snapping photographs with his phone of the tire tracks left in the soft earth. This was where the motor home had been. But had Natalie been inside it?

"A call just came in on the radio," he told the marshal. "A couple of deputies picked up Maureen Mortensen." He wasn't sure what response he was expecting, but his father only nodded.

Without a word, they walked back to the patrol SUV and climbed inside before his father said, "You need to learn how to take orders." Hud started the engine. "You always were the stubborn one."

Brick chuckled at that. "Just like my father and grandfather, I'm told."

"Well, at least your namesake grandfather." Brick had heard stories about his grandfather Brick Savage, the former marshal. If half of the stories were true, then his father and the former marshal had butted heads regularly.

"Any update on Natalie?" he asked him now.

"Still catatonic." His father sighed, picked up his radio and called in a description of the motor home that the man in the camper had given him. It sounded like one of those rental motor homes. Older driver. Only description was elderly and gray.

If Natalie had been held in the motor home, the driver could be miles from here by now—or parked at the hospital. His father obviously thought the same thing as he asked that a deputy watch for a motor home at the hospital parking lot and ordered that another deputy go to work calling motor home rentals in the area.

They drove in silence back to where Brick had left his pickup. As he started to climb out, his father said, "Deputy, you want this job? Take a week. I don't want to see you again unless it's at your mother's dining room table. And stay clear of Billings PD's case. Got that?"

"Got it."

As he closed the door, Brick heard a call come in over the radio that all law enforcement available were needed for a three-vehicle pileup in the canyon twenty miles south of Big Sky. His father sped off, leaving him standing next to his pickup.

Brick knew he should go camping. Go back into the mountains and not come out until his next doctor's appointment. But as he watched his father's patrol SUV disappear over the rise, he realized this was his chance to go to the hospital and see Natalie. Maybe she was catatonic. Maybe she wasn't. He knew that he'd heard her say something. There was only one way to prove it.

His father was closing in on the theory that she was abducted by a person driving a motor home. It wouldn't be long before the marshal made an arrest. Meanwhile, the Billings homicide detectives should be arriving at any time—if they hadn't already been to the hospital.

And down at the jail there was a blonde cop with a nasty kick locked up behind bars. He wondered what she'd have to say for herself. His groin still hurt, not to mention his bruised ego. He realized that there was nothing he would enjoy more than seeing her behind bars.

Chapter Five

Mo couldn't believe her luck. She'd been arrested on a charge she could wiggle out of the moment she went before a judge, and these backwoods lawmen had to know that. But how long would that take?

She could feel the clock ticking. Once Natalie was released from the hospital, she would be gone again, only this time, she wouldn't make the same mistakes. She could disappear down a rat hole and might not surface for months, even years. By then she would have had numerous jobs. Which meant numerous victims. Mo couldn't let that happen any more than she could let Natalie get away without having the chance to talk to her one more time.

As it stood now, there was no proof that she'd been at the hospital with any felonious intentions. All they had her on was pretending to be a nurse. Given her connection to Natalie Berkshire, the law could try to make something out of that. But ultimately, they wouldn't be able to hold her on any of it—except for her attack on the deputy marshal, Brick Savage—the man who'd found Natalie after her escape from whoever had abducted her.

Mo paced in her cell. She kept thinking about standing over the woman's bed, hearing the hoarse whisper, feeling the woman's words hit her like a hollow-point slug to her chest. She'd had her right where she wanted her. The truth had been within her reach.

Natalie would run the moment she was released from the hospital. But what was she running from? The law? Her own guilt? Fear? Or this thing she'd kept secret?

At the sound of the door into the cell area opening, she turned to see Deputy Marshal Brick Savage come in and head toward her. She groaned inwardly. Of course he would come to gloat.

When he stopped at her cell door, she warned herself to be cool even as she wanted to wipe that grin off his face. He was enjoying how the tables had turned a little too much. Earlier, she'd felt guilty for attacking him. Right now, not so much.

"Enjoying your stay here?" he asked, shoving back his Stetson to expose a pair of very blue eyes fringed in dark lashes.

"Not really." He was more handsome than she'd taken the time to notice at the hospital. Handsome, well-built and physically fit. And he was clearly looking for a fight. She could tell she'd banged up his ego more than his body.

"You go by Mo?" he asked.

She waited, fairly sure she already knew what had brought him here. She just wondered how long it would take him to get to the point.

Fortunately, it wasn't long. "Look, I know you were planning to kill her earlier in the hospital—just as I know she told you something," he said.

She wanted to say, "Prove it!" but thought better of it. Antagonizing a deputy, let alone the son of the marshal, was probably not in her best interests—even out here in the sticks. Maybe especially out here in the sticks.

"I'm sorry if there was a misunderstanding at the hospital," she said with cavity-inducing sweetness.

He laughed, a beguiling sound. "Oh, I understood you just fine. I saw the way you were looking at Natalie Berkshire. Like you wanted to kill her."

"Fortunately, that's not against the law."

"Attacking an officer of the law is."

She tried not to smile. "I didn't realize you were a lawman."

"The uniform probably threw you," he said sarcastically.

She shrugged. "I thought you were a lecherous security guard."

His blue eyes narrowed, but he smiled.

"You did grab me, and you didn't announce who you were. It was a innocent mistake."

"I doubt there is anything innocent about you," he said.

Mo chuckled at that, thinking how true that was. She was no longer the naive woman who'd believed in the law. That had changed everything about her. She was more daring in every aspect, she realized, as if she had nothing left to lose. In the past, she would have been more careful around a deputy who had her locked up behind bars. Heck, she would have been maybe even a little tongue-tied around a cowboy as handsome as this one. But right now she didn't feel shy or cowed in the least.

She met his Montana-sky-blue gaze, so much deeper and darker than her own. "You're new at this, aren't you? Green as springtime in the Rockies."

His brows furrowed. "Seasoned or not, I'm still a deputy—"

"On medical leave. I also heard that you're the one who found her last night," Mo said. She didn't want to argue semantics. She didn't have time for it.

He eyed her sharply. "Sorry it wasn't you who found her?"

She was, but she wasn't about to admit it to him. "You haven't asked if I was the one who abducted her."

"I don't believe you are. Not your style."

Mo raised a brow and couldn't help but chuckle. "You think you know my style after one…confrontation? I must have made quite an impact on you."

To her surprise, he chuckled, as well. "You could say that. It's why I was anxious to see you—behind bars."

She liked that he could joke. She also liked that he was smart. He'd spotted her quickly for the fraud she was at the hospital. Too quickly. She was curious, though, why he was really here. Just to taunt her? Or did he want something, as she suspected? It was clear that he thought he knew her. That was almost laughable. He had no idea.

"What did she say to you?" he asked.

She felt his gaze on her, a welding torch of heat and intensity.

"She said something to you," he continued. "I heard her."

"I'm not sure what you thought you heard, but the patient, I'm told, is in a catatonic state, unable to speak." She was still dealing with Natalie's words. They'd been private, disarming, horrifying if true. She wasn't about to share them with anyone, especially this half deputy.

"What she said got one hell of a reaction from you,"

he said as if he hadn't heard her denial. "It stopped you from killing her."

She said nothing, surprised to be hearing the truth in his words. She had gone to the hospital to get an answer to one question and then, well, then, she planned to make sure Natalie never destroyed another family again.

"Sorry, but I don't believe you," the deputy said. "You were leaning over her. I saw her lips moving. I heard her whispering something to you. I want to know why her words made you change your mind."

She started to argue that he had no idea what was in her mind—and even if he did, he couldn't prove it, but he cut her off.

"You want out of this cell? Tell me the truth."

"The truth?" she mocked. "The truth is that Natalie Berkshire is guilty as sin."

"You can prove that?"

"It will get proved, but unfortunately, not before someone else dies because our judicial system takes so long."

"I'm still waiting to hear what she said to you," he said, cocking his head to study her with those intense blue eyes of his.

Mo pulled her gaze away first. She didn't want to tell this cocky cowboy deputy anything. She'd overheard the nurses talking about him last night at the deli. The cowboy had reputation with the women and yet women still seemed to be attracted to him, knowing that he might break their hearts. Good thing he wasn't her type.

"I'm guessing that what Natalie said had something to do with your sister." When she said nothing, he added, "Tricia, isn't that right?"

Her pulse pounded in her ears. Had he heard Natalie

say Tricia's name? She groaned inwardly. Natalie Berkshire wasn't just a killer. She was a psychopath who manipulated people. Look how she'd deceived Tricia and her husband, Thomas, and especially Mo herself. Wasn't that the part that kept her up at night?

Trust didn't come easy for her and yet Natalie had gained her trust, and in a very short time. Natalie had walked into their family and become a part of it. Mo had felt as if she'd always known the woman—that was how comfortable she'd been in her presence. Mo didn't make friends easily, but she did make them for life.

When she'd first heard that homicide was being called in, that little Joey was believed to have been smothered, that Natalie was their number one suspect, she hadn't believed it. She'd seen Natalie with Joey. Seen how careful she was with him since his health was so precarious.

But there had been only one other person in that house that afternoon and it was Tricia. According to her sister, she'd been upstairs asleep and had only come down when she'd heard Natalie screaming. It was no wonder the woman had been arrested. Who else could have killed Joey?

That was why Mo had come here to end this nightmare. For weeks she'd rationalized what she had planned, no matter how crazy it seemed most days. Now, she looked the deputy in the eye and told the truth based on what she knew at this moment. "She'll kill again. Unless she's stopped."

"You just know that, right?" he asked, his gaze intent on her. "You have no idea if that is true or not or even if she is the killer." She didn't bother to answer.

"Okay, let's say you're right. How exactly do you plan to stop her?"

"That is the question, isn't it?"

"It seems pretty simple. You're no longer a cop—"

"I'm only suspended," she said in her defense, but wondered how long before they found out what she was up to and fired her.

"My point is," he continued, "you have no authority to take her in, and I understand there are no charges pending against her at this point—only suspicions. So why do this? As a homicide detective you know what will happen if you kill her in cold blood."

"You and I wouldn't have been having this discussion only a few months ago. Since then, things have gotten…complicated."

"You're a vigilante cop upset with the system. Doesn't seem all that complicated. Why take it on yourself? I understand that since Natalie was released, other law enforcement departments are reviewing deaths where the woman might have been involved. If she's guilty, it will be just a matter of time before she's under arrest again and a jury will decide," he said.

Mo let out a snort. "What you say may be true, but there isn't time to prove you wrong." She flipped her hair back and met his gaze, narrowing those tropical-sea-blue eyes on him. "When Natalie gets out of that hospital she'll run. She'll be looking for her next job. Her next victim. Someone has to stop her."

"If she's guilty." He was studying her. She felt the burn of his gaze on her skin. "Admit it. You're having your doubts, especially after what she said to you. I saw your reaction. Tell me and I'll get out of here."

She snorted at that. "You're wrong. Nothing Natalie could ever say would convince me that she isn't a killer. So I guess you and I have nothing more to say to each other." She turned her back on the cowboy deputy.

"You change your mind, you let me know."

BRICK STUDIED THE woman a few moments longer. She had her slim back to him now, her head held high, radiating self-confidence and righteousness. He remembered what the deputy outside Natalie's hospital room door had said about the blonde. At the hospital, he hadn't had the time to get a really good look at her. She was definitely attractive from her thick blond hair that fell over one sea-blue eye before dropping in an asymmetrical cut to her shoulders to her slim, clearly physically fit body. He hadn't known what to expect on actually meeting her, but it was clear to him that she was sharp. She didn't come across as some crackpot on a mission.

Yet while her original intention seemed perfectly clear to him, something had changed when Natalie Berkshire had spoken to her. That intrigued him. Mo hadn't made any bones about her belief that Natalie was guilty. What could the nanny have said to her that would keep her from doing something that she said she was still committed to finishing?

He thought of the pillow on the floor, convinced that his walking into the room wasn't what had stopped her. But he also couldn't imagine what Natalie could have said.

He'd seen the conviction still in Mo's eyes. She wouldn't stop until she found the woman and ended this—one way or another. And like Natalie, soon this woman, too, would be free to do just that.

And that was what had him worried as he left and drove toward the hospital. Mo Mortensen's certainty that Natalie would kill again had him rattled. He was even more anxious to see Natalie Berkshire after talking to the cop. He needed to decide for himself if she was a monster or a victim.

Also, he wanted know exactly what Natalie had said to her, because he no longer believed the woman was catatonic. He could even understand why she was faking it. She was running scared. It was why she'd bailed out of Billings—only to get caught by someone he suspected had been seeking his own kind of justice. Natalie had to know the person would come after her again—or someone like him—not to mention the law now looking for her.

The woman had to know that her house of cards was about to come crashing down on her at any moment— whether she was guilty or not. Wasn't there still the chance, though, that she wasn't?

As he walked down the hall toward Natalie's room, he noticed the deputy leaning back in his chair outside her door, legs outstretched. The deputy appeared to be asleep. As he got closer, he saw that the man's hat was pulled down low over his eyes. His heart began to race. Things might be dull on the floor, but there was no way a deputy would fall asleep on the job.

He rushed to him, touched his shoulder. The deputy keeled over onto the floor. Brick felt his chest constrict as the man's hat fell away and he saw the blood and the large goose egg on the deputy's forehead. He quickly checked the man's pulse in his neck—strong—before rushing into Natalie Berkshire's room.

Just as he'd known, the bed was empty. He swore.

Hadn't he known she wasn't catatonic? Just as he'd known that she'd spoken to Mo. He quickly looked around. The bathroom door was closed. "Natalie?" He stepped to the door and grabbed the knob. "Natalie?" No answer.

He opened the door. Of course the room was empty. Because Natalie Berkshire was gone.

He started to pull out his phone when he heard a moan coming from somewhere in the room. The sound froze his blood. He wasn't alone in here after all?

Brick spun around. The room was still empty. Another moan. He caught movement under the bed and rushed to push the bed aside. The nurse lay on the floor, gagged and bound with IV tubing. She was attired in nothing but panties and a hospital gown.

As he pulled off the gag and began to untie her, she said, "She jumped me. She took my uniform, my bra, my socks and shoes. She…" The nurse began to cry. "She threatened me. Said if I made a sound…"

"How long ago did she leave?" Brick asked as he freed her.

"Five minutes, maybe more."

At the sound of the deputy regaining consciousness out in the hall, Brick rushed out. "Take care of the nurse and call this in."

"The nurse?" The deputy touched the bump on his head gingerly. His eyes widened as if he realized at last what had happened. "The patient. Is she…?"

"Gone."

"I don't know what happened."

"Say that to my father," Brick called as he ran down the hall.

He told himself that the woman might not have gotten out of the building yet. She was wearing scrubs—just like every other nurse.

Brick took the stairs three at a time and burst out on the lower floor to race for the front door. After pushing out through it, he stopped to glance around the parking lot. He didn't see her.

At the growl of a motorcycle, he spun around and saw a woman in scrubs roar past. Her hair was a dark wave behind her as Natalie Berkshire sailed away.

Brick ran to his pickup and went after her. But he hadn't gone two blocks when he realized he'd lost her. He called it in, but didn't hold out any hope that she would be caught. The dispatcher told him that a young man who'd been in the hospital parking lot was calling to say that a nurse had shoved him off his motorcycle and taken it.

Brick pulled over, slamming his fist down on the wheel. Natalie was in the wind. What were their chances that they could find her? At the moment, she wasn't wanted by the law for anything but questioning. Her life was in danger, though, and she had to know that. Without money or transportation other than a stolen motorcycle, where would she go? Her car had been impounded. And considering what was found in her car, she'd already been running scared before she was abducted. What would she do now?

His cell phone rang.

"I get only one call so don't make me waste it." He recognized the voice at once, a little sultry, definitely direct. "I just heard the news here at the jail," Mo said. "Natalie has taken off. I suspected she'd pull something like this. But I can help you find her if we hurry."

He scoffed. "Too bad you're behind bars."

"Listen," Mo said. "I *know* this woman. I knew she would run when she was released from jail. I knew she'd take off the way she has. You'll never find her without my help. You want the blood of her next victim on your hands? Give it some thought. Then get me out of here." She hung up.

Brick shook his head as he disconnected. He was on a forced medical leave and she was suspended. Neither of them had any authority to go after Natalie. Mo really thought he would spring her?

He knew she'd be out by morning, once she went before a judge. But at least for the moment she was locked up. Unfortunately, that didn't make Natalie safe. Who knew who all was after the woman?

He sat in his pickup for a moment, his mind a rabbit warren of thoughts. What if Mo was right? What if the real person in danger was Natalie's next client?

Starting the pickup, he drove to his apartment. On the way, he half expected to see Natalie in his neighborhood. He knew it wasn't logical. Just as he knew he would always be expecting to see her somewhere until she turned up again. If she ever did. He still hadn't decided if she was a victim or a possible serial killer.

Mo Mortensen thought she knew, but she was too personally involved. He couldn't trust her judgment any more than his own.

At his apartment, he walked in, closing the door behind him. He stood just inside looking around the studio apartment as if seeing it for the first time. Nothing about the space reflected him in any way. It was as if no one lived here. Clearly, it was a hiding place, not a home.

He sighed as he pulled off his Stetson and raked a hand through his hair. His father was right. He wasn't healed. Nor did he have any idea how to put himself back together again. He felt unsure of everything—except the steady beat of his heart. He was alive. He'd survived a bullet. Maybe he could survive the rest. Maybe. But not here in this colorless, empty apartment.

Brick walked over to the wardrobe, pulled it open and began to dump what he might need into a backpack. Swinging it over his shoulder, he took one last look around before he walked out.

Chapter Six

"Took you long enough," Mo said as she held on to the bars of her cell as if trying to bend them. "We've lost valuable time."

Brick shook his head. "You were that sure I was coming for you?" he asked as he held up the keys that would free her.

She smiled in answer, and if he hadn't realized that this woman might be trouble, he was beginning to. "Well?" she demanded. "Did you come to taunt me or get me out where we can find Natalie before it's too late?"

"I'm not unlocking your cell until you tell me what she said to you and why you reacted the way you did." He could see the internal battle going on inside her. For a moment, he thought she would simply move away from the bars, go sit on her bunk, tell him to go to hell. He wouldn't have been surprised.

Except for one thing. She was desperate to find Natalie. He had to know why. He no longer thought it was to harm her. But then again, he could be wrong about that, too. He could be letting another kind of monster free.

"Tell me why her words hit you so hard," he said, and when she didn't answer, he said, "Fine, then stay where you are. I'll find Natalie on my own."

"You won't," she snapped as he started to turn away. "I know how she thinks. You, on the other hand, are convinced that she is some innocent, helpless creature who needs you." She reminded him that Natalie had played him after he'd tried to help her.

"Okay," he conceded, keeping his back to her. "Maybe she wasn't as traumatized as she appeared."

"You think? You'd better hope we find her before whoever held her captive does. I'm betting he's also looking for her and will try to abduct her again. You need me."

He smiled to himself as he turned back to her. "And you need me. So…"

"She said Tricia didn't kill herself."

He felt the weight of words fall on him. *What the—?* "What does that mean?"

"Natalie was probably lying. Trying to save her own skin. But if there is a chance she was telling the truth…"

Brick shook his head. "That explains why you looked so shocked. You must have thought there was more than a chance she was telling the truth. But if so—"

"Then someone killed her."

"Why would someone kill your sister?"

"That's what I have to find out. So, are you going to help me or not?" Mo let go of the bars and met his gaze. "I'll tell you everything. Just get me out of here so I can find her—before someone else gets to her."

Her last words shook him more than he wanted to admit. Natalie had already been abducted and held captive. He didn't doubt that there were others who were determined to see that the woman paid for what they believed she'd done. Mo had been one of them, he knew. Had a few words from Natalie really changed that?

"*We* find her." He waited for her to agree. "We do this together or you stay where you are. I posted your bond. I keep my investment safe by not letting you out of my sight."

"Fine." She motioned impatiently for him to unlock the cell.

He hoped he wasn't making a huge mistake as he inserted the key. "I already picked up your belongings."

"My car?"

"You won't be needing it. My truck's outside," he said as he turned the cell door key.

"My car would be more comfortable, not to mention, I'm an ace driver."

"I'm sure you are. That's why I can just see you leaving me high and dry."

"Have you always been so suspicious?" she asked as they headed out of the building.

"Apparently, since I spotted you for the fake you were quickly enough at the hospital."

She rolled her eyes as they walked together toward the parking lot. "I thought I made a pretty believable nurse." Her gaze locked with his for a moment. "Until I had to kick your butt."

He laughed. "Yes, there is that score to settle yet."

"Until next time."

"Only next time I'll see you coming."

She chuckled. "Just keep telling yourself that," she said over her shoulder as she continued down the sidewalk.

"MAUREEN?"

They were almost to the parking lot when she turned to see the man who'd called her name coming down the sidewalk toward her. She was as shocked to see her brother-in-law here as he sounded to see her.

"It *is* you," Thomas said as he reached her and Brick. "I saw you coming out of the jail..." His gaze sharpened. "What are you doing in Big Sky?"

"I could ask you the same thing," Mo said, taken off guard by seeing him here of all places. Since her sister's funeral, she'd been avoiding him and felt guilty about it. But Thomas reminded her of all Tricia's hopes and dreams now gone forever. He'd also made it clear that he wanted to put Natalie and the rest behind him, something she couldn't do. "What are you doing here?"

He raised an eyebrow. "I'm here on business. Life does go on, Maureen. But it seems you know that. You're back at work?" He shot a glance at the law enforcement building. He thought she was here also working—certainly not just being released from jail.

She didn't answer as she looked past him to the cute brunette with him. Her eyes narrowed.

Following her gaze, he turned and drew the young woman into the conversation. "This is Quinn Pierson. We work together." He sounded defensive.

Mo instantly regretted making him feel that way. Thomas had been through enough with the loss of his son and wife. Surely she didn't resent that he was here on business with a colleague, probably attending some seminar since she knew that many of them were held here at the resort each year. But she did resent that he'd gone on with his life when she couldn't.

"I'm sorry," she said, meaning it. She saw that he was staring at Brick with the same questioning look she'd given the brunette. "This is Brick Savage. A...friend."

Thomas seemed to turn the name over in his mouth

as if trying to place it. Brick's name was unusual enough that she knew he was bound to eventually tie it to Natalie since the deputy's name had been in all the news as the man who'd rescued the distraught woman in the middle of the night. Once Thomas did figure out who Brick was, he'd know what she was up to. Unless he'd already heard about Natalie being in the hospital here before making her daring escape.

But now he merely lifted a brow at her before he stuck out his hand to shake Brick's. "I'm also a friend of Mo's," he said, making her feel worse, if that was possible. He'd made his position clear after the funeral, the last time they'd talked.

"I really don't care what happens to Natalie Berkshire," he'd said. "I never want to hear her name again."

"You don't want justice?" Mo had demanded.

"Justice? My son is dead, my wife is dead. Tracking down Natalie won't bring either of them back."

"But she'll kill again, she'll destroy other families, she'll—"

"I can't do anything about that."

"Well, I can," Mo had snapped. "And I will."

Thomas had begun to cry. "Please, for my sake, if not your own, let it go, Maureen. I can't bear anymore. I'm begging you. Let your sister and the rest of us find some peace."

Had he found that peace? She sure hadn't.

"We really should get going," Quinn said, dragging Mo back from the past. "We're already running late for the seminar." She gave Mo an apologetic shrug and held out a flyer. "I don't know if you're familiar with Palmer's seminars. They're enlightening."

Mo took the sheet of paper without looking at it.

"It was nice to meet you," Quinn said. She really was pretty. And young. The word *fresh* came to mind.

"You, too," Mo said automatically as she wished she hadn't run into them now of all times. As the two walked away, she saw Thomas turn to Quinn and say something. The brunette's soft laugh filtered back, making Mo uncomfortable. She thought about Tricia. Something had been wrong in that house. Natalie had tried to tell her, but Mo hadn't wanted to hear. Now she regretted it.

"You going to tell me what that was about?" Brick said once the two were out of earshot.

"That was my brother-in-law." She realized she hadn't introduced Thomas by his last name. "Thomas Colton. Tricia's husband."

Brick had to catch up to her since she'd turned and taken off, wanting to put that entire scene behind her. Sometimes she spoke before she thought. Change that to *often*. It got her into trouble. She wouldn't be suspended right now if she were capable of keeping her mouth shut.

"He knew Natalie well, I'm assuming?" Brick said as he caught up to her and motioned to where his pickup was parked. She nodded and slowed, no longer cringing, but glad to have put distance between her and Thomas and his…associate.

Once in his pickup, he reminded her that she hadn't finished her story.

She realized she was still holding the flyer the woman had given her. Wadding it up, she tossed it on the floor. "Drive and I'll tell you everything. Natalie already has a huge head start."

He hesitated, but only a moment before he started the truck. "We need to establish some ground rules," he said as he pulled away from the jail. "We do this together. You take off, you go back behind bars. You help me find her, but then she's going to be returned for questioning about her abduction and any other deaths under her employ. Is that understood?"

"Whatever you say."

"I'm out on a limb here. Don't saw it off, because I don't want to be hunting you next."

"We don't have time to argue," she said, dismissing his concerns. "Tell me how she got out of the hospital."

He told her about Natalie taking the nurse's clothing and leaving her gagged and bound half-naked under the bed before stealing a motorcycle and escaping. "She probably got the idea from you."

Mo seemed to ignore that. "She'll be looking for different clothing first. Which way did she go when she left the hospital?" He told her. "Then take that street."

"There are no stores that way."

"She has no money. She'll be looking for clothing she can steal."

Brick wondered if she was talking about what she would do under the same circumstances—or about Natalie. But he didn't argue. He drove through the residential area as Mo craned her neck down each side street they passed.

"So," he said. "Tell me."

She sighed. Clearly, it was a story she'd condensed, having lived with it for so long. "I stopped by Tricia's that day. She was sleeping so I didn't want to disturb her. She'd been struggling with everything—postpartum depression, the baby's health issues, who knows what else? Anyway, I decided to just look in on Joey. I was worried about him because of all his medical problems and even more worried for Tricia. She'd had trouble conceiving. It looked like she and Thomas weren't going to be able to have children, something Tricia had wanted desperately. Then, out of the blue, she'd gotten pregnant. I'd expected her to be over-the-moon happy, but she seemed anxious all the time. Then, when Joey was born with all the medical problems and the doctors said he probably wouldn't make a year..." Her voice trailed off for a moment.

"That day I sensed something being...off. Joey was fine. He was such a beautiful baby. If you didn't know about his health problems... As I started to leave, Natalie stopped me by the front door. She was trying to tell me something when Tricia came down the stairs. I could tell Natalie was upset. I knew she was worried about Tricia. I was, too."

Brick thought about this for a moment, seeing how upset Mo had become just retelling it. "Natalie never told you what she had to talk to you about?"

Mo shook her head. "We never spoke after that. Natalie was arrested, and evidence was coming out about her. Even if she told me what might have been going on in that house."

"What do you mean, about what was going on in that house?"

Mo looked away for a moment.

"I realize this is hard for you—"

"Thomas and Tricia were my family. I hate talking about personal details of their lives. I hate that because of what happened, their personal lives have become media fodder."

"They were having problems," he guessed. "I would imagine the stress…"

She nodded, some of her anger visibly evaporating. "I think it might have been more than the pregnancy and even Joey's health."

"You don't think Thomas and the nanny were—"

"Having an affair?" She shook her head adamantly. "But something was wrong. Tricia wouldn't talk about it and neither would Thomas—not that I tried very hard. I was so intent on proving Natalie guilty and getting justice that I wasn't there for my sister when she needed me the most."

"That's why you want to believe that she didn't kill herself," he said. "Could there have been another man?"

Mo hesitated a little too long. "She and Thomas had been together since college. They were the perfect couple." As if sensing his skepticism, she said, "He idolized her. He was so excited about the baby. He was a wonderful father."

Brick kept driving, wondering what he'd gotten himself into, when she cried, "Stop! Down there."

Backing up, he drove down the side street until she told him to stop again. By then she was out of the truck. He swore, threw the pickup into Park and went after her, thinking she was already breaking their deal.

Instead, she rushed over to an older house with a long three-wire clothesline behind it. The day's wash flapped noisily on the line except for the spaces where it appeared someone had removed items randomly.

A woman came out of the house brandishing a broom. "Don't even think about it. What is this, some kind of scavenger hunt?" she demanded. "You're not taking any more of my clothing."

Brick quickly introduced himself. "We're looking for the woman who stole the clothes off your line. Was she dressed like a nurse?"

The woman nodded. "I couldn't imagine why a nurse would be stealing my clothes."

"Can you tell me what she took?" Mo asked. "And describe the items?"

The woman lowered her broom and thought about it for a moment. "A pair of my black active pants, my favorite flowered shirt, a pair of jeans and my husband's hooded sweatshirt. It's navy. The flowered shirt is mostly red."

"Thank you. Did you see her leave? What she was driving? Which way did she go?"

The homeowner shook her head. "I saw her taking the clothes and ran outside but she disappeared around the side of the house. Wait. I did hear what sounded like a motorcycle engine. Does that help?"

Brick nodded. "It does, thanks. How long ago was that?"

"Thirty minutes ago, maybe longer."

"We'll do our best to get your clothes back for you," he said and turned toward the pickup.

They were back in the pickup when Mo said, "She'll ditch those clothes as soon as she gets some money. I hope that woman doesn't hold her breath about getting them back. She'll dump the motorcycle first—if she hasn't already. She'll be looking for a vehicle. One that won't be missed for a while."

Brick shot a look at Mo as he started the truck. "You make her sound like a hardened criminal. What if she's innocent and now has people chasing her who want to do more than hurt her? Maybe she's just trying to stay alive as best she can."

"That's exactly what she's trying to do. She's running for her life."

Brick's cell phone rang. He thought it would be his father. He'd already ignored three calls from him. Instead, it was the deputy from the hospital.

"I heard you're looking for the patient that got away," the deputy said. "I hope you find her. The marshal wants to have my head over this." He explained that while he was getting examined for the wound on his head, he heard that an attendant's purse had gone missing about the same time that Natalie took off. "She thinks the patient who escaped took it."

Brick told Mo.

"Ask how much money was in the purse," she said.

He did and hung up. "Just over a hundred and fifty dollars."

"So Natalie has some money. Now all she needs are wheels," Mo said. "If I were her, I'd be looking around bars, cafés, places where everyday people work and don't worry about their vehicles being stolen."

"Anyone ever mention that you think like a criminal?"

Mo smiled. "Thanks. There's a bar up ahead. Pull in."

As Brick did, his cell phone rang again. This time it was his father.

HUD STARTED TO leave another voice mail on his son's phone when, to his surprise, Brick answered. He'd come back to the office to find out that not only had Natalie Berkshire taken off before the Billings homicide detectives arrived, but his son had broken suspended homicide detective Mo Mortensen out of jail.

"What the hell are you doing?" he demanded the moment his son answered the call. "You spring a woman you don't know from Adam. A woman who is in our jail because she attacked you? Are you trying to end your career before it even starts?"

"I'm on leave, remember."

The marshal swore. "What is that noise in the background?"

"I'm standing outside a bar waiting for Mo."

Hud wanted to scream. "Mo, is it now? Brick…" He let out an angry breath. "I hope the bar doesn't have a back door. Why did you bust her out of jail?"

"She's going to help me find Natalie."

"Are you crazy? You said this woman wants to kill Natalie."

"Maybe she wants to, but she won't. And even if she still did, I won't let her."

He swore under his breath. "Do I have to tell you again that Natalie Berkshire isn't wanted for anything other than questioning at this point? Or that you don't have the authority to go after her, let alone arrest her, even if there was a warrant out for her? Worse, Natalie might not be the woman you have to fear. You could be with the real criminal right now. How do you know she wasn't involved with Natalie Berkshire's abduction?"

"She wasn't. Which means that she isn't the only one on this woman's trail. We need to find her first. I was right about what happened at the hospital. Natalie did say something to her, just as I thought I heard. She said that Tricia, Mo's sister, didn't kill herself."

"What?"

"Apparently there was more going on with that family than anyone—other than Natalie, who lived in the house—knew. If Tricia didn't kill herself, if Natalie didn't take that baby's life, then who did?"

"Brick," his father snapped. "What are you going to do with her if you find Natalie? Maybe more to the point, what is Mo going to do? Even if you find Natalie, you can't restrain her in any way or you'll find yourself behind bars for kidnapping. Clearly the woman was well enough to escape the hospital. Letting the cop who's chasing her out of jail is just asking for trouble."

"Maybe Natalie lied about all of it. But what if she didn't?" Hud heard the music in the background change. Then his son said, "I think I see the motorcycle she stole. I have to go."

He swore as Brick disconnected. He tried to call him back, but the phone went straight to voice mail. He debated putting a BOLO out on both his son and Mo. Natalie already had one out on her. Along with being wanted for questioning, she was wanted for tying up a nurse and stealing a motorcycle and a purse at the hospital. Also at this point, Hud had no doubt that the woman would be safer behind bars.

The marshal looked up to find a deputy standing in his doorway. "Anything more on the motor home?"

"So far I haven't found any that have been returned in the past twenty-four hours that might have been damaged as if someone had broken out of it," the deputy said, clearly unhappy with this assignment.

Hud waved him away, saying, "Keep trying." As the deputy left, he wondered if it wasn't a waste of manpower. Maybe whoever had rented the motor home would be smart enough not to turn it in anywhere nearby. That was if he was right and there'd been damage to it when Natalie had escaped.

HERBERT LEE REINER could feel sweat running down the middle of his back. He watched the two men in the glassed-in vacation rental vehicle office. Whatever they were discussing, it looked serious.

He thought about walking out. The car rental agency was just down the road. He could get there quickly enough. But it would mean leaving behind his reimbursement check. His deposit was a hefty amount—even after the repair bill had come out of it.

He glanced toward the motor home sitting where he'd parked it, then back at the men in the RV rental office. It was hot in here. He wanted to push back the sleeves on his shirt, but then the scratches would show. The clerk, a young man named Gil, had been suspicious enough when he'd seen the damage done to the door in the motor home's one bedroom. Now Gil was in the office talking to his older boss.

His throat dry as dust, Herb spotted the drinking fountain off to the side and walked over nonchalantly, hoping he looked like a man without a care in the world. He turned it on and took a long drink even though the water wasn't quite cold enough. It also had a funny taste. But at his age, everything was either tasteless or strange. Aging taste buds, though, were the least of his worries right now.

Glancing at his watch, he felt time running out. As he took another drink and straightened, Gil came out of the glass enclosure holding his paperwork. Herb felt his heart drop as he saw that the man's boss was now on the phone.

"I really need to get going," Herb said. "Is there a problem?"

"No," the clerk said a little too quickly. "I'm just new at this and I want to do it right."

He tried not to be impatient as he watched the clerk tap at his computer keys. Had Gil been told to stall Herb until the police arrived?

Glancing toward the outside door, he considered making a run for it. But his legs felt as if they'd turned to blocks of wood. He hadn't run anywhere in years and there was his bad knee to consider. He shifted on his feet, looked down and frowned. There was a spot of blood on his right sneaker. The sight elevated his heart rate. He felt his chest tighten.

"I think I have it now," Gil said. The printer began to grind out more paperwork. How much paperwork did it take to un-rent a motor home anyway?

Gil moved to the printer, pulled out the papers and began sorting through them. Through the glass window into the office, Herb saw that the boss was off the phone and looking in his direction.

But the man's gaze dropped the moment it connected with Herb's. His heart was pounding now, making breathing more difficult. If he didn't get out of here—

Gil handed him a stack of papers. On the top was a check for both his deposit and his refund since he was turning the motor home in earlier than he planned. He signed where Gil pointed and picked everything up with trembling fingers.

"Thank you," he said automatically and turned toward the door, trying not to rush.

"I thought you needed a ride?" Gil called after him. "If you can wait just a few minutes—"

He couldn't wait. He burst out the door, expecting to hear sirens in the distance. Breathing in the fresh, cool air, he turned left and began walking toward the car rental agency.

All of the rental places were along a frontage road not far from the airport. He kept walking, checking behind him every few minutes. He was limping a little, the bad knee, as he listened for the crunch of gravel behind him. He was that sure that a patrol car would be pulling up any minute.

He'd thought he was being so smart renting the motor home. But he'd seen Gil's expression when he'd seen evidence of the violence that had destroyed the bedroom door. Fortunately, Gil hadn't noticed where the duct tape had taken the paint off the bed frame.

At the car rental agency, Herb stopped and looked behind him. Cars whizzed past. No cop cars. He hurriedly stepped inside, closing the door, and took a deep breath, trying to quiet his pounding pulse. At this place at least the air conditioning was working, he thought as he moved to the counter.

Had he cleaned up any evidence he might have left in the motor home? That was the question that nagged at him as he again filled out paperwork and produced a credit card and Arizona driver's license.

It wasn't that he worried about being caught. He knew that was going to happen soon enough. He just couldn't get caught until he'd fulfilled his promise to his wife of fifty-two years.

The paperwork took just enough time that he was sweating profusely even in the air-conditioned building. But eventually, he walked out with the keys to a white panel van. The clerk had asked him if he was moving.

"Getting rid of a few things," he'd said.

Once behind the wheel, he drove down the highway to the small coffee shop where he'd left his wife. Dorie was sitting by the window, staring down into her coffee cup as he pulled up. He hit the horn twice. For a moment he thought she hadn't heard.

Then slowly, she raised her head. He figured the sun was glinting off the windshield because it took her a minute to recognize him before she smiled. He was used to her slack-jawed empty stare. Just as he was her confused frowns. Often it was hard to get her attention.

While those times felt like a knife to his chest after all these years together, it was her gentle, sweet smile that was his undoing. In that smile he saw the accumulation of both her pain and his. Their loss was so great they no longer cared what happened to either of them.

Dorie rose slowly from the table inside the coffee shop. As she lifted her head, she changed before his eyes. He saw the young woman she'd been the first time he'd seen her. She didn't look frail. She didn't look like a woman who was dying. He knew all that was keeping her alive was the promise he'd made her.

A part of him had thought Dorie might not be strong enough to go on. He'd told her he would go alone, but she'd insisted that like him, she would see this through. Dorie climbed into the van without looking at him. Instead, she noticed something on her sleeve. As if sleepwalking, she picked a long, dark hair off her sweater and held it up to study it for a moment, her face grim, before she whirred down her window and threw it away.

Finally, she turned to him. "Can you find her again?"

He nodded, knowing that he would go to the ends

of the earth for this woman he'd spent the better part of his life with. "I'll find her."

Dorie reached over and placed her small, age-spotted hand on his arm for a moment before she looked toward the mountains, that distant stare returning to her beautiful eyes as she absently ran her fingers down the sleeve of her sweater as if looking for another strand of Natalie Berkshire's dark hair.

Chapter Seven

The light was dim inside the bar. At this hour, the place was packed. Mo stood just inside the door, letting her eyes adjust as she did a quick scan for Natalie. She didn't see her. Behind her, Brick came into the bar, closing the door and the afternoon out. "There's a motorcycle beside the bar. It looks like the one she stole from the hospital parking lot."

Mo nodded. "I'll check the restroom. If you see her—"

"Don't worry, I won't let her get away."

Mo headed for the ladies' room, the smell of beer and nachos seeming to follow her. Her stomach growled and she realized she couldn't remember the last time she'd had something to eat. Brick had broken her out of jail before she'd been fed.

Pushing open the bathroom door, she saw two women at the sinks. One was putting on lipstick, the other drying her hands and talking a mile a minute about some guy she'd met at the bar. Three of the stalls' doors stood open. Two were closed.

As Mo started toward the closed doors, one came open and a dark-haired woman stepped out in a red shirt. For a split second, Mo thought it was Natalie, but then the woman turned. She moved past and took the stall next to the one with the closed door.

Bending down, she glanced under the neighboring stall. No nurse's Crocs, but that didn't mean that Natalie hadn't changed into the fairly new-looking sneakers in the stall next door. She'd had plenty of time to find a change of footwear.

Mo sat down on the toilet fully clothed and waited. The talkative woman at the sink left with her friend. She could hear water running, then the grind of the paper towel machine. The bathroom door made a whooshing sound and the room fell silent.

Next to her, the woman in the stall hadn't moved. Hadn't reached for toilet paper, hadn't flushed. Mo knew she could be wasting valuable time. Natalie could have already stolen a car from the bar lot and was now miles from here.

She cleared her voice. "I'm sorry, but could you hand me some paper?" she asked the woman in the next stall. "I'm all out over here."

Without a word, the woman pulled off some paper and handed it under the side of the stall. Mo saw the freshly painted fingernails as she took the rolled up paper. Nothing like the chipped ones she'd seen on Natalie's hands in the hospital.

"Thanks," she said, dropped it into the toilet and flushed before she pushed open her door. She was washing her hands when the woman came out of the stall and swore.

Mo saw her looking around. "Lose something?"

"My purse. I left it right there." She shook her head, exasperated. "I hope my friend picked it up for me."

"Any chance you had your car keys in it?" Mo asked. The woman's eyes widened in answer.

As they walked out of the bathroom, she told Brick what had happened. He stepped outside with the woman who'd lost her purse—and her car, as it turned out. He called it in to the marshal's department.

Mo was considering getting a drink while she waited for Brick to return when a male voice said, "Bartender, give that woman a beer on me." She turned in surprise as she recognized the voice.

"Shane, what are you doing here?"

Shane Danby laughed. "Same thing you are, I would imagine. Thought we had come to take Natalie Berkshire back to Billings. But got here too late. The nurse nanny got away. You wouldn't know anything about that, would you? Maybe it had something to do with you being on the wrong side of the law?"

His laugh told her that he knew about her being arrested. "Sorry, but I'm not interested in discussing it with you."

"Not interested in discussing it with me?" he mocked, his voice rough with anger. "You always thought you were better than the rest of us, didn't you, Mo? Well, you aren't the only one looking for Natalie. There's a bounty on her head. That's right, some father of a kid she killed is offering a reward to anyone who brings her in—dead or alive. Everyone in four states is looking to collect. If I find her first I'm going to shoot and ask questions later."

Mo feared it might be true. "And what if she's innocent?" she demanded. She realized that she was starting to sound like Brick. But she couldn't bear the thought that some trigger-happy lawman killed Natalie before she could get to the truth when it hadn't been that long ago that she'd thought that was exactly what she'd wanted. "She deserves a trial."

Shane scoffed. "The crazy psycho deserves the same treatment she gave those patients under her care."

"No wonder you didn't make Homicide." She started past him, but he grabbed her arm and dragged her into an alcove away from the people at the bar. When she started to fight back, he grabbed her by the throat and shoved her against the wall, holding her there with his body.

"Assault, Shane?" she asked around the pain in her throat. "I'm still a homicide cop."

"Are you? That's not what I hear. I heard you went after Berkshire to put her down like a mad dog. Now I'm wondering if you're trying to help her slip the noose."

Just the reminder of how her sister had died brought up a low growl from her throat. "I suggest you let me go."

"Oh, really? Is that what you would suggest?" he said with a laugh. "I can tell you'd like to kick my ass right now." He was so close she could see the dark spots among the brown in his eyes and smell the onions he'd had on his burger for lunch. "The only reason you got Homicide over me is because you're a woman. Gotta meet their quotas." He turned his head to spit on the floor. His hand on her throat tightened. "It's all bullsh—"

The rest of his words were lost as he was grabbed from behind and slammed into the wall next to her. Brick had several inches in height on Shane and was in better shape. He grabbed him by the throat—just as Shane had held her.

"I'm the law, you idiot!" Shane cried and swore.

"You're not the only one," Brick said. "Deputy Marshal Brick Savage. You think you're tough, being rough with a woman?"

As much as she wouldn't mind seeing Brick kick his butt, she stepped in. "Let him go. Trust me, he isn't worth it."

Brick let go of him so quickly, Shane stumbled and almost fell. As Brick started to turn away, Shane picked up an empty bottle someone had left in the alcove and went for him—just as Mo knew he would. She put her foot out, and the lowlife cop went sprawling. The bottle shattered in his hand. As he started to get up, Brick stepped on his hand, pressing it to the glass-strewn floor and making him cry out.

"We done here?" Brick said, lifting his boot to free the cop's bleeding hand.

"Need a man to fight your battles, Mo?" Shane yelled as he sat back to cradle his cut hand.

She stepped around the corner to grab a rag off the bar and tossed it to him. "Shane, you just don't learn." As she started to turn, he kicked out, catching her in the shin. She spun on him and kicked back, catching him in the thigh. He doubled over, writhing on the floor. "Don't ever grab me by the throat again or next time, it won't be my boot toe. It will be a bullet."

"That man is dangerous," Brick said as they walked away. "From what I heard, he has a grudge against you."

"Shane has a grudge against the world. You can't take him seriously."

"Mo, you need to watch your back around him."

She couldn't help being touched by his concern.

"While I appreciate you coming to my rescue, now you have to watch your back as well when it comes to him."

"You could have taken him." He was studying her as they walked.

Mo nodded. "I could have that time because I saw him coming. That's the problem with men like Shane Danby. When he's most dangerous is when you don't see him coming. But he told me something disturbing." Mo told him about the bounty. "It might be a lie. But it also might be true, in which case we have to find Natalie before anyone else does."

"WELL, AT LEAST WE know what Natalie is driving," Brick said as they left the bar. A deputy from the department was taking down the information on the stolen car. He and Mo hadn't needed to hang around to listen to the description of the thief the woman from the car was giving the deputy. "There's a BOLO out on the car. I wouldn't be surprised if she's picked up within the hour."

Mo snorted as she and Brick left. "Have you ever noticed how large Montana is?" She shook her head. "There isn't enough law enforcement to cover it all. But more important, Natalie grew up here. She knows the state. She'll know where to go."

He glanced over at her. "You really have no faith at all in the law, do you?"

Mo was busy calling up a map on her phone. "If you wanted to go to the closest small town, which one would you chose?"

"West Yellowstone. Or cut across to Ennis. They're both small. She'd be harder to find in Bozeman, though."

"Ennis," she said emphatically. "Let's go."

Ennis wouldn't have been his choice, but he didn't argue. Mo said she knew Natalie. He headed south down the canyon toward the cut-across to Madison Valley and Ennis. "I'm curious. How did your sister find Natalie?"

"Through the hospital. Natalie had left her information there. She had a great résumé. She seemed perfect since she specialized in patients with special needs and she'd worked as a nurse nanny."

"Did your sister get references on her?"

Mo nodded. "She made a few calls, but once she met Natalie, she liked her so much she didn't bother checking the rest of the references."

Brick thought of the woman he'd seen on television and photographed in the newspaper. Slightly built, Natalie was a plain, nonthreatening young woman with what he would have thought of as an honest face.

"It was for such a short time since Tricia planned to stay home full-time, but had to tie up loose ends at her job. Also, Natalie didn't mind the short-term employment. Mostly, Tricia was just so grateful to find someone so experienced. But I know a lot of it was that she liked Natalie right away. I did too when I met her. She had this way of making you feel at ease around her. It's no wonder that she's fooled so many people."

"If she's guilty," he said, and she grunted.

As he drove past the turnoff to his family ranch, he glanced in that direction. A cold chill ran up his spine to lift the hair on the nape of his neck. He had the worst feeling that he might not ever see it again. It was a crazy premonition that something bad would happen and he'd never make it home again. He didn't believe in premonitions. He wondered what the shrink he saw would make of it. But it still shook him.

"You know anything about her background?" he asked to clear his own thoughts.

"Trying to profile her? Good luck with that. It's pretty boring. She was raised on a ranch in eastern Montana, two hardworking parents, an only child. She was valedictorian and president of her senior class. Got top grades in nursing school and excelled at the two hospitals where she worked before going into in-home care."

"Was she ever arrested before?" he asked as he drove down the canyon. The sun dropped behind the mountains and twilight began to cast long shadows in the canyon.

"No. Not even for a parking ticket. But who knows about her other nursing jobs? Apparently the patients all had life-threatening medical problems. Most of them weren't expected to live, so when they died…"

"But she was never a suspect before, right?"

"That doesn't mean that she's not guilty," Mo said defensively. "Maybe this time she wasn't as careful. Or the medical examiner was more qualified."

He glanced over at her. "But now any deaths where she was the nurse are in question." He drove in silence as he thought about the woman he'd seen in his headlights not even twenty-four hours before. "I'm sorry, but I keep thinking, what if she really is innocent? We hear about babies dying of SIDS or doctors being unable to pinpoint what caused a death. Maybe she wasn't responsible for any of them. Maybe it's just bad luck on her part. And if what she told you is true…"

"If it's true, why didn't she tell the police?"

"Maybe she did. I doubt they were apt to believe her. You're still not sure you do."

She shot him a look before she said, "Let me know

when we reach Ennis or if you need me to drive." Then she turned away from him and a few minutes later, he heard her slow, rhythmic breathing and realized she'd fallen asleep.

Mo CAME OUT of the nightmare fighting.

"Whoa! Take it easy," Brick cried as he held up a hand to ward off her blows while keeping the pickup on the road with the other.

She sat up blinking as she fought off the remnants of her bad dream. She could feel Brick's questioning gaze on her. She ignored him. No doubt he'd seen and heard enough as she was coming awake to know it had been a nightmare. She didn't want to talk about it and hoped he wouldn't ask.

Through the pickup's windshield she could see lights ahead illuminating the small Montana town on the horizon. "Ennis?" she asked, sitting up straighter, still trying to shake off the dream. It was a familiar one. Some things changed, but the feeling was always the same. She was trapped in a small, dark space all alone and yet there was someone nearby. She could hear them breathing. Then she heard something rattle. Whoever was out there wasn't content to leave her to die. They were coming in for her.

"Ennis," he said, stealing glances at her. Fortunately, he didn't ask, but she knew he was wondering about her—as he should be. "What now?" he asked as he drove into the tiny Western burg.

"Food and then somewhere to sleep."

That surprised him. "I thought we were in a hurry to catch her."

"We are. If I'm right, she's already here. She won't leave until she is forced to."

He seemed surprised, but only said, "Well, I could definitely eat something," as he pulled into a space in front of a log cabin café.

But neither of them moved for a moment as if happy not to be in motion after hours on the road.

HERB LICKED HIS praline ice cream before it melted down the cone and watched the couple that had just driven up in the pickup. He recognized the man behind the wheel. Deputy Marshal Brick Savage had been pointed out to him as the man who'd discovered the abducted woman.

"Enjoying your cone, Dorie?"

She smiled over at him, chocolate ice cream on her lips.

They'd gotten ice cream on their very first date fifty-three years ago. He'd known then that he was going to marry her. Their future had been so bright. There'd been a few bumps in the road over the years, but nothing they hadn't been able to overcome together.

Until the death of their youngest grandchild, the first boy out of six. Their daughter had named him Herbert after his grandfather, an honor that had brought tears to Herb's eyes. He'd been so happy and had gladly offered to pay for a full-time nanny to live in the house and help their youngest daughter with her first child, since the baby had some special medical needs.

He wiped at an errant tear and noticed that his ice cream was melting. He quickly turned his attention back to his cone—and the pickup. The occupants hadn't gotten out. He could see the woman sitting on the passenger side. Another cop? The hospital had been in pandemonium over what had turned out to be a suspended homicide detective pretending to be a nurse, he'd heard when he'd stopped by. The woman had gotten into Natalie Berkshire's room—right past the deputy stationed outside the door.

Herb wondered what the cop had been planning to do. Or if she was merely trying to find out who had taken Natalie captive. That was when he'd decided it was time to get rid of the motor home.

Seeing the two law officers here in Ennis, he knew he'd been right about where he could find Natalie again. He realized that they might be able to help him. He glanced over at Dorie. She'd almost finished her cone. She looked content for the moment and that alone made him happy.

Unlike him, he thought she had moments when she didn't remember what had happened to their only grandson. What a blessing for her and one that he just assumed he wouldn't have until he died, which wasn't that far off given the way he'd been feeling lately.

But first, he intended to take the woman who'd killed his grandson with him as soon as he found her again. It was time.

HUD WALKED INTO the old two-story house on Cardwell Ranch, hung his Stetson on the hook by the door and dropped onto the bench to take off his boots.

"You look exhausted," Dana said as she hurried to help him with his boots, an offer she'd given him most nights since they'd married. Tonight, though, he seemed glad for her help as if he needed it badly. For months, she'd been encouraging him to retire. Their children were raised, and she suspected it wouldn't be that long before they had grandchildren.

"It was one of those days," the marshal admitted as he gave her a wan smile. "You're going to hear about it soon enough anyway…" He seemed to brace himself. "Brick…" He raked his fingers through his graying hair.

Sometimes it hit her how much they'd both aged. Like now. Normally when she looked at her husband, she saw the young, big strong man he'd been when she'd fallen in love with him. She was still desperately in love with this man, looking past the gray and the wrinkles and the slight stoop of his broad shoulders.

"Brick has gotten himself involved in a case that could blow up in all of our faces," Hud said finally.

"I thought he was technically still on medical leave?"

"Tell that to him. I told him until I got the release from the head doctor…" He met her gaze. "He's still having the nightmares, I know he is. He thinks he's fine. You know him."

"Is this about the woman he found?"

Hud nodded. "She escaped from the hospital after taking a nurse's clothing and leaving the woman tied up under the bed."

Dana gasped. "This is the same woman that someone had abducted and held?" He nodded. "Why would she do something like that?"

"I suppose she's scared. Or she heard Billings homicide was on its way to question her. But what complicates it is this cop who's after her…"

"The one who attacked our son?"

For a moment, he looked surprised that she'd heard that detail through the grapevine. He shouldn't have been. He had to know how talk moved down this canyon.

Hud sighed. "We had her behind bars, but Brick broke her out. Now the two of them have gone after the woman who escaped the hospital. Brick to save her and…who knows what Mo has planned."

"Mo?"

"Maureen 'Mo' Mortensen, the suspended cop who your son is now mixed up with."

Dana had to bite her tongue. She'd been against Brick going into law enforcement from the beginning. For years she'd worried about Hud's safety every time he left the house to go to work. She didn't want to have to worry about one of her sons, as well.

"He was born to do this," her husband said as if seeing her expression. She met his gaze, too upset to speak. "I didn't encourage him. And I certainly didn't approve of this. But you know how he is."

"He wants to please you," she said, her voice breaking. "He idolizes you, so of course he wants to follow in your footsteps." Hud said nothing. Clearly he had to know there wasn't much he could say. She saw how difficult this was for him. He was worried and upset. She felt her anger vanish as quickly as it had appeared.

Stepping to him, she wrapped her arms around him. He pulled her down on his lap and buried his face into her neck. "Brick will be fine," she whispered. "He's enough like you, he'll be fine."

Hud nodded against her shoulder, and she tightened her arms around him as she hoped it was true. His cell phone rang, making her groan. That was another reason she was anxious for him to retire. They deserved peace and quiet at this age—not the constant sound of a phone ringing at all hours and Hud having to go take care of marshal business.

She stepped from his arms so he could take the call. But she didn't go far. If this was about Brick... She listened to her husband's side of it, something about a motor home being found. So *not* about Brick.

Turning away, she headed toward the kitchen to bake something, anything. That was what she did when she was upset—bake. She didn't want to know about the dark things her husband dealt with daily. She didn't want to think about what Brick had involved himself in or how dangerous it might be.

She turned on the oven, anxious to smell something sweet filling up the old ranch house kitchen.

"I CAN'T BELIEVE Natalie would stop this soon," Brick said as he looked around at the busy main street as people were enjoying the warm summer night. Everywhere there were tourists with their campers and sunburned kids, fishermen wearing fly vests, an older couple sitting outside eating ice cream cones and watching all the activity. "But I can see where she could blend in here since the locals seem to be outnumbered."

His comment rated him one of Mo's smiles. This one actually reached her blue eyes. He felt himself grow warm under the glow of it and warned himself to be careful. If she turned it on him too much, he might find himself feeling close to her and that would be a mistake, especially given his reputation—and hers.

"Natalie knows this area. She went to college in Bozeman so she's floated the Madison River on tubes, drunk beer in Bogert Park's old band shell and sledded Pete's Hill. There are just some things you do when you attend Montana State University. Or at least we did back in the day."

He turned toward her. "You went to MSU?" She nodded. "Did you know—"

"Natalie?" She shook her head. "But we were there about the same time. I wouldn't be surprised if we crossed paths and didn't know it." She seemed to be studying the activity on the main street.

He followed her gaze to all the people dressed in shorts and sandals. It made him think of a summer when his parents took them to Yellowstone Park. Growing up on the ranch, there was no such thing as a lazy summer. There was always work to do. It was why he used to sneak away and find a place in the shade to take a nap, but his mother always found him. She would scold him and before she was through, she'd suggest they all go down to the creek for a swim.

That summer in Yellowstone he'd felt like one of the tourists. It had been a great summer with his twin, Angus, brother Hank, sister Mary and cousins Ella and Ford. He realized Mo was staring at him.

"Nice memory?" she asked. "Let me guess. There's a girl involved."

He laughed. "As a matter of fact, there is. My mother." He told her what he'd been thinking about and the picnic lunch they'd had in Yellowstone, swimming in the Firehole, watching Old Faithful go off at sunset before pitching tents at Lake Campground and sitting around a campfire roasting marshmallows. Ranch kids often didn't get those kinds of trips. Too many animals that needed tending to. "The whole trip was my mother's idea."

She didn't say anything for a moment. "She sounds like a great lady."

He smiled. "She is. Not that Dana Cardwell Savage

isn't tough when she has to be. She's one strong, determined woman." He met Mo's gaze. "A lot like you."

"She doesn't want you doing this, does she."

Brick leaned back behind the wheel, watching tourists stream past for a moment. "She doesn't want me doing a lot of things, including becoming a deputy marshal."

He could feel Mo openly studying him. "Maybe you should listen to her."

He turned so he was facing her. "You don't think I have what it takes?"

"I didn't say that."

"But it's what you were thinking."

She shook her head. "Don't assume you know what I'm thinking." They both grew quiet. "I just don't want to be responsible for your mother having to attend your funeral."

"Then you'd better make sure nothing happens to me," he said and laughed. "Look, it's nice to know you care, but I'm not your responsibility. This is my choice and I can take care of myself."

He followed her gaze. Mo was watching the older couple down the street. They were taking all day to eat their ice cream cones. "And you aren't responsible for me. If the only reason you're here is to stop me, well, I just hate to see you risking your life for nothing."

"What was your nightmare about?" he asked.

"I don't remember." She opened her door. "I thought you said you were hungry?"

Brick knew a nightmare when he saw one. He found himself watching Mo out of the corner of his eye as they took a booth inside the café.

After the waitress brought them menus and water, he

opened his, but found himself distracted by what had happened in the pickup earlier. Mo had been sleeping soundly when she began whimpering. He'd asked if she was all right, but hadn't gotten an answer. Her whimpering had become louder and stronger and she began to quiver until he'd reached over and touched her arm.

She'd come unglued, swinging her fists at him, her blank blue eyes filled with terror. Did this have something to do with Natalie and her fears that the woman was telling the truth and Tricia didn't take her own life? Or was there more about Maureen Mortensen that he had to worry about?

"I'll take the special, the chicken-fried steak," Mo was saying. "Mashed, white gravy and the salad with blue cheese."

He hadn't realized that the waitress had come back until Mo spoke. He closed his menu. "I'll take the same." He could feel her staring at him.

"I wish you wouldn't," she said, when the waitress had picked up the menus and moved away.

"Wouldn't order what you did?"

She mugged a face. "Wouldn't ask."

He nodded sagely. "Wouldn't ask about your nightmare. I'm guessing it isn't your first. I say that because I've had a few of my own lately."

Mo seemed surprised to hear that.

Brick looked away. "Supposedly I almost died after being shot. But I don't think that's what's causing the nightmares. I killed a man after he shot me."

"Your first." It wasn't a question. She picked up her fork and her napkin and began to polish the tines.

"What about you? Have you had to kill someone as a cop?"

She put down the fork and picked up the knife and began polishing it. "Why did you order the same thing I did?"

The woman was anything but subtle when it came to changing the subject. "I wasn't paying any attention to what was on the menu. I was more concerned about you."

"Having doubts about coming with me now because I had a bad dream?"

He shook his head. "I had doubts about going anywhere with you long before that." Their gazes met across the expanse of the table and held for a long moment. He felt heat race along his veins.

The waitress put down their salads, breaking their connection. Mo laid her knife down and picked up her fork again. He watched her eat her salad, wondering if she'd felt that flutter at heart level that he had just moments ago. The waitress brought the rest of their food and Mo dug in, avoiding his gaze. He was hungry too and happy to just eat in the companionable silence that fell between them.

"You're a cowboy, right?" she asked halfway through the meal. "So why follow your dad into law enforcement?"

"I grew up on Cardwell Ranch, yes. But I never wanted to just be a rancher." He shrugged. "When I heard that a deputy marshal position was opening up, I thought, why not? I found out that I could do a lot of my year at the police academy online. The rest I'll do once I get my medical release." He looked up and met her blue eyes and again felt as if he was falling down a deep well before she shifted her gaze back to her plate. "When Natalie stumbled out into the street in front of my pickup that night…" He shook his head. "The more I learned about this case, the more I wanted to know what happened."

"You want to solve it."

"Don't you?"

She shrugged and continued eating for a moment. "Law enforcement isn't for everyone. It can be dangerous and soul-stealing. It can take you to places you never wanted to go and can never forget." She looked up, locking eyes with him. "It can change you into a person you no longer recognize."

"Was it law enforcement that did that? Or Natalie Berkshire?"

Mo said nothing as she finished her meal. But her words were still haunting him as they left the café. As they climbed into the pickup to drive to the closest motel, he saw her freeze for a moment.

"What's wrong?" He followed her gaze up the street.

"Nothing. I thought I saw… Never mind. I just imagined it. Let's go."

But he noticed how quiet she was as they checked into a room with two beds. Had she thought she'd seen Natalie? Or someone else?

"And yes, I got us just one room *because* I don't trust you, in case you're wondering," he said as she looked at the two queen beds that took up most of the space.

"If I wanted to get away from you, I could."

"So why haven't you?"

She seemed to study him. "I either like your company or I think you might come in handy."

He raised a brow. "Let's be clear. I'm here to keep you from doing anything stupid when we find Natalie."

Mo smiled as she closed the distance between them.

"I asked around the jail about you. I know about your reputation with women. You're a heartbreaker."

He started to object, but she placed a finger against his lips to silence him.

"You won't be breaking my heart, and please don't take that as a challenge." She had a great smile. Her lips turned up at one corner a little more than the other. It was cute. She was more than cute. She was adorable, but also dangerous if the pounding of his heart was any indication.

He pulled her finger from his lips. "Like I said—"

"Right, you're just here to protect Natalie and me from myself." She moved within a breath of her lips touching his lips. "Then I should be able to rest peacefully tonight knowing you will keep me from doing anything…stupid."

As she stepped away, he let out the breath he hadn't realized he'd been holding.

EARLY THE NEXT MORNING, Hud looked up from his desk to see his deputy standing in front of him, grinning. "You found the motor home we're looking for."

"Well," he said, his grin shrinking some. "I think so. It was returned yesterday, and it did have damage to one of the bedroom doors."

The marshal got to his feet. "Tell me it hasn't been cleaned or the damage repaired."

"It hasn't. It was rented by a man named Herbert Lee Reiner out of Sun Daisy, Arizona."

Arizona? Hud recalled one of the inquiries he'd gotten about Natalie Berkshire was from Arizona. "Send a forensic team." He frowned. If the man had used his real name to rent the motor home, then maybe this wasn't the right one.

As the deputy left his office to notify the team, the marshal returned to his computer to gather what information he could about Herbert Lee Reiner. Married to Doris Sue Thompson for fifty-two years. Herbert had been a postman until his retirement. That meant his fingerprints would be on file.

It didn't take long before their names began coming up in newspaper articles. The articles read much like the ones that had run in the Billings newspaper. The older couple were the grandparents of an infant with health problems born to their youngest child. The other name that came up in the baby's death was Natalie Berkshire.

BRICK WOKE TO the sound of the shower. He looked around the motel room, then at the queen-sized bed he lay in. The covers weren't overly disturbed. He hadn't had a nightmare. That alone surprised him.

He stretched, feeling better than he had in weeks. That too surprised him. Maybe what he'd told his father was true. Maybe this was exactly what he'd needed, something he could sink his teeth into, he thought as Mo came out of the bathroom in nothing but a towel.

"Oh, good you're awake." She dug in her suitcase, pulled out jeans, a T-shirt and white panties and bra. "I thought you might want a shower," she said pointedly when he hadn't moved.

He'd been doing his best not to look at her since the towel was pretty skimpy. "You think I need one?"

"I just don't want to have to try to dress in that dinky bathroom." She cocked her head toward the open bathroom door. "Do you mind?"

He threw back the covers and swung his legs over the side. Last night he'd slept in his boxers and nothing else. He hesitated.

"I've seen men in a lot less," Mo said, shaking her head with obvious amusement.

As he strutted past her into the bathroom, he heard her chuckle. He stepped into the bathroom and opened his palm to remove the keys to the pickup he'd grabbed before coming in here. He tucked them under a towel and turned on the shower, smiling to himself. If Mo was planning to leave in his pickup this morning, she was in for a surprise.

He recalled last night when she'd told him he wasn't going to break her heart. It had sounded way too much like a challenge, he thought. But that was the old Brick. He hadn't been serious about any woman—at least not for long. That apparently was how he'd gotten the reputation—news to him.

When he thought about Mo, about the look they'd shared at the café, about how his body had reacted with her standing so close last night and again this morning in that towel… The woman had been taunting him. Well, if she thought for a moment that he was going to make a move on her…

Brick turned the shower to cold for a few moments before climbing out. He wasn't going to let this woman distract him. In the mirror, he ran his fingers through his dark hair. It was a lot longer than he usually wore it, he thought. Also, he had a day's stubble. He rubbed his jaw, but decided to leave it, not wanting to take the time to shave. Grabbing a towel, he dried off, then pulled on his boxers. He stepped back out of the bathroom.

Mo was gone.

Chapter Eight

Mo looked up as she came out of the local grocery store. From the expression on Brick's handsome face, he'd thought she'd left him for good. She could see that he was upset and trying to hide it—now that he'd found her. She felt almost guilty for giving him a scare. Also for giving him a hard time last night. She had seen first-hand that the man definitely had a way with women. But then, she'd known that the moment she'd laid eyes on him.

He was too good-looking, too cocky, too full of himself, she'd told herself. And yet since they'd hooked up, so to speak, she'd seen another, more vulnerable side of him. Not that she was going to let that fact weaken her resolve to keep everything between them professional.

"You could have left a note," he said, walking up to her.

She laughed. "You sound like we're a thing. If you must know, I went out to get us some doughnuts and coffee," she said, indicating the bag she was holding in one hand and the to-go tray with two coffees in the other. She handed him the bag, then took one of the coffee cups from the tray and handed it to him. "Also,

I looked for an apartment." He blinked. "Not for us, sweetie. For Natalie."

The morning was sunny and just starting to warm up. She could smell pine and river scents drifting on the breeze. There was a picnic table on the lawn in front of the small motel. She walked to it and sat down. To anyone watching, they might look like a married couple on vacation.

She opened the bag of doughnuts and offered one to Brick as he joined her.

He took a glazed one and said, "An apartment for Natalie?"

"If you were her, what would you do? She can't keep running. We know she has limited funds. She has to look for a job. Why not a small tourist town where people with money have built huge summer homes and would love a nanny? Most are probably from out of state and have never heard of Natalie Berkshire—not that she will use her real name, I would imagine. It would only be for the summer or maybe just a few weeks. Exactly what she's looking for."

He shook his head. "I'm still surprised she'd stop so close to where she was caught."

"Because she knows that we expect her to run farther," Mo said and took a sip of her coffee. "She needs to find a job, and if I'm right, disappear into a family with her next victim. She's getting desperate. I believe that's why she made the mistake she did."

"What mistake was that?" he asked and took a bite of his doughnut, chasing it with a sip of coffee. He frowned at the cup in his hand.

"You do take your coffee with sugar and cream, right?" she asked.

He looked up in surprise. "How did you—"

"It's no mystery. You had an old cup in your pickup. It was written on the side along with your name and the logo of your favorite coffee shop." She grinned.

"Okay, you're observant. I'll give you that. What mistake did Natalie make?"

"She let her guard down and got caught. She'll want to do what comes naturally to her, which isn't running. She's here in this town. I feel it." Mo saw his skepticism and reached into her pocket to take out a scrap of paper. She handed it to him. "The apartment comes with a garage where she can hide the stolen car—if she hasn't had a chance to get rid of it already."

"Where did you get this?" he asked as he turned the strip of paper over in his fingers. He had nice hands, she noticed. Long fingers. Strong, tanned hands. A man's hands. She felt a shiver at even the thought of those hands exploring her body.

"You want my jacket?" Brick asked, thinking she was chilly. He was already starting to take off his jean jacket.

She shook her head. "It was on a bulletin board in the only grocery store in town advertising a studio apartment cheap with the telephone number on the slips of paper on the bottom. Only one other slip of paper had been pulled off so I figured the ad hasn't been posted for long."

"That doesn't mean Natalie took the other one."

She nodded in agreement. "But there is one way to find out." She pulled out her phone and called the number. No answer. She left a message saying that she was looking for a long-term rental and hoped the apartment was still available.

When she looked up at Brick, she expected to see disapproval in his expression because of how easily the lie had come to her lips. Instead, he was rising to his feet, his eyes fixed on his pickup parked in front of their motel unit. She watched him walk over to the truck and pull what appeared to be a folded sheet of paper from under the passenger-side windshield wiper.

As he unfolded the paper and read what was written there, his gaze shot to her. Mo felt her heart begin to pound.

BRICK HANDED Mo the note he'd found on his pickup's windshield. He watched her quickly unfolded it and read the words neatly printed there.

> Chasing me won't give you the answers you want. You should be looking for the man Tricia had been seeing. I don't know his name. I only saw him once. Blond with blue eyes, about six-two or six-three. I swear I didn't hurt the baby. But if Joey was her lover's baby… By the way, someone is following you.

He watched her refold the note and put it into her pocket without a word. He could tell that she was upset, but what was written on the note didn't seem to come as a shock compared to what Natalie had already told her at the hospital. Was it why she hadn't let Natalie tell her that day at the house before Joey died? She hadn't wanted to hear it, still didn't want to believe it.

"We going to discuss this?" he asked when she still said nothing.

Mo opened her mouth, but closed it as her cell phone

rang. She checked the phone and then took the call, listening for a few moments before she said, "That's too bad. I'm one of the new teacher aides at the elementary school." Brick's eyebrows shot up. The woman was a born liar. "Do you have any other units?" If Mo were right, Natalie would have only taken the apartment short-term, apparently now making the landlord regret renting it. "I'm moving here soon and anxious to get settled into a place." Again she listened before she smiled. "I'd love to see it." If Natalie had rented the apartment, she would have already been moved in, he thought.

Mo gave the man her number again and disconnected. "He's going to call the new renter to see if she's home and he can show the apartment. She only rented it for a few weeks." When the phone rang, he started and saw Mo take a breath before she picked up. "Hello? Yes? Oh, that's too bad. But could you at least tell me where it is? I could drive by. If I like the area, I'll get something temporary until it opens up."

He saw her nod before she disconnected. "Let's go," she said and started for her side of the pickup. "She's at the apartment. But the call from her landlord will probably spook her."

"You're that sure the woman who rented the apartment is Natalie?" he said, wondering if Mo was ever wrong about anything. She didn't bother to answer, her gaze on the street ahead as she repeated the directions to the apartment that the landlord had given her.

Brick felt his pulse jump. This could be it. They could be about to confront Natalie. Ennis was already busy, the traffic slow and congested until they got away from the main street in town. He tried to remain calm, uncertain how this would go down. He could see Mo tapping the edge of her side window with her finger-tips, clearly impatient. Clearly anxious. He was glad he was driving instead of her. She wore an expression that told him she would have plowed through the cars and pedestrians, horn blaring.

The apartment was in an older area of town. He drove down the street slowly, looking for the stolen silver SUV in a state that had hundreds of silver SUVs.

"The apartment is on the third floor, a small one-bedroom with stairs off the back," Mo said. "That's it." She pointed at a tall white building with navy trim that had clearly once been a single dwelling, now made into three apartments. Two bikes were chained to the front porch. A small pickup was parked out front along with a smaller compact car next to the two-car garage.

He pulled over. "I don't see a silver SUV, but I suppose it could be in the garage."

"She probably ditched it and picked up something else." Mo opened her door, climbed out and started across the street.

"We're taking her back to Big Sky for questioning," he reminded Mo.

"You wouldn't have found her if it hadn't been for me," she said under her breath as they approached the apartment house. "You'd be looking as far away as Spokane."

"Mo—"

"I just need to talk to her, so let's find her before we debate what to do with her."

He knew she was right. It felt as if they were chasing a ghost. He glanced behind them, thinking about the note. Was someone really following them? Look how easily Natalie had found them. He remembered Mo thinking she saw someone last night. Natalie? If so, the woman had seen them and could have followed them to the motel.

"I'll take the back stairs," Mo said now. "You go in the front door. Bleeding heart or not, try to remember that this woman is dangerous." She took off at a run around the back.

He headed for the front door, determined to get to the woman before Mo did—if Natalie was in this building. Brick tried the front door, not surprised when it opened into a small foyer. There were two doors and stairs.

He took the stairs two at a time, no longer worrying about making too much noise. If Natalie had rented this apartment, if she was still up there…he had to get to her and fast.

At the top of the stairs, he found a door and quickly stepped to it to knock. He thought he heard a sound on the other side of the door and for a moment, he thought about drawing his weapon. Mo had warned him that Natalie was dangerous. But he remembered the terrified woman he'd seen in his headlights. The woman lying in the hospital bed. He still wanted to believe that she was a victim, an innocent victim. He left his gun holstered and tried the door.

It opened, startling him.

"Come in," Mo said on the other side of the doorstep. "She's gone."

"Natalie?" Mo didn't answer as she turned back into the apartment. He followed, a little stunned. Had she been right about Natalie renting this place? "How do you know for certain it was her?"

She shoved a copy of a local shopper at him. It was

folded so that the want ads were on top. Several positions had been circled. His heart slammed against his ribs as he saw they were for nanny positions. One of them for an infant that needed special care.

Mo had moved into the bedroom, where she was standing at the end of the unmade bed.

"Are you all right?" he asked her. She wasn't moving, hardly appeared to be breathing. He realized that his heart was still thundering in his chest. Mo hadn't just been right about the apartment. She'd been right about Natalie looking for another job. A possible new victim.

"Maybe she'll come back," he said.

Mo shook her head. "She's gone. I found something interesting in her trash in the bathroom. She's changed her appearance, cut her hair and colored it red." He could hear regret in her voice. They'd come so close. They couldn't have missed her by more than a few minutes.

Her gaze met his, but only for an instant as she pushed past him and left.

He stood for a moment looking at the room. From what he could see, it appeared that the renter had left in a hurry. One of the drawers in the bureau stood open and empty. The door to the small closet was open, the metal hangers bare. That was if Natalie had even had time to pick up more clothing. He suspected she was traveling light.

They'd gotten close. Just not close enough.

He found Mo outside, leaning against the side of his pickup. She appeared to be looking up at the snow-capped mountains. But as he drew closer, he saw that her eyes were closed, her chest heaving as if she was having trouble breathing.

As he approached her, her eyes opened. A lock of

blond hair fell over one blue eye as she turned to him abruptly. "You still think she's innocent?" She sounded angry and upset and disappointed, he realized. Disappointed not just because they hadn't caught up to Natalie. He had a feeling she was even more disappointed in herself for not wanting to hear what Natalie had tried to tell her that day at the house.

"You can't second-guess yourself," he said quietly. "You can't change what happened."

She shook her head and looked away. "No, but I can find out what happened to my sister. I can make sure Natalie doesn't hurt anyone else."

Did he still think Natalie was innocent? Did he think the circled job openings were about her needing to get back to work because she needed money? Or as Mo said, a woman looking for her next victim?

He squinted toward the mountains. "I want to find her as much as you do."

Mo shook her head. "You don't. Which is why you need to go back to Big Sky and your job before you lose it. Don't throw your career away like I did. This isn't about you."

"It's about justice. Without it, we're nothing but outlaws. And if I went back, I'd have to take you with me. I'm not sure I can trust you to appear at your hearing."

She met his gaze and held it. "Fine, stay. Just remember, I warned you."

Her cell phone rang. She pulled it out of her pocket and looked at the screen before she stepped away to take the call.

Mo HEARD THE anger in Thomas's voice and groaned inwardly. "That man you were with the other day," her brother-in-law said without preamble. "Deputy Marshal Brick Savage? He's the one who found Natalie—and lost her again. Maureen, what are you doing?"

She realized it always bothered her that he'd never called her by her nickname. It had always been Maureen. "Thomas, why have you never called me Mo?"

"What?"

"I just realized that you've never called me by my nickname."

"Are you drunk? Or have you just completely lost your mind?"

"Thomas—"

"What are you doing, *Mo*?" He sounded more pained than angry now. "I begged you at the funeral to let it go. Joey is gone. Tricia is gone. Why are you destroying your life, too? I called the police station. They said you've been suspended. Please, Maureen, Mo, whatever. *Stop*." His voice broke.

She felt a painful tug at her heart. She'd met Thomas at college when her only eighteen months older sister had started dating him. They'd hung out with the same crowd. He was like a brother to her. She'd been maid of honor at their wedding.

"I can't talk to you about this," she said. "It doesn't have anything to do with you."

"How can you say that?" he asked, raising his voice. "Joey was my son, Tricia was my wife. Natalie was like a member of our family. This has been a nightmare. One I just want to put behind me."

"I wish I could, but I can't."

"So, what are you going to do?" he demanded.

She looked back at Brick leaning against his pickup, waiting for her. They needed go after Natalie. She was getting away. Again. She thought about telling Thomas about the note, about Natalie saying that Tricia hadn't taken her own life, but didn't. Like he said, he was trying to put it all behind him. Until she had even a shred of proof that it was true, she needed to keep it to herself. She didn't want to hurt him any more than she already had. "I don't know what I'm doing." She could almost see him shaking his head.

"The cops let her go, Maureen."

"That doesn't mean she was innocent."

"But it could, couldn't it?" He sounded as if he was pleading. "Isn't it possible Joey just died? The doctor had said he might die. If he'd lived, he was going to have to have all those surgeries and even then, the doctor said he might never..." His voice broke again. She could hear him crying.

She'd done this. "I'm so sorry. This is why I didn't want to tell you."

"Then don't do this. Go back to work. It's the only thing I've found that helps. I'm sure you can get back on at your old job if you leave all of this behind. You know you being obsessed over this is the last thing Tricia would want."

She didn't know what to say because she knew it was true. But then again, she questioned if she'd ever known her sister at all. Tricia was having an affair? It seemed impossible. She still didn't believe it, but knew she had to find out the truth no matter where it led her.

"You and I shouldn't have any secrets, Maureen. We're..." His voice broke again. "Family."

Her heart clinched. The worst thing about this was lying to Thomas. His losses were so much greater than hers. And now she had him worrying about her.

"I need you to be all right," he'd told her at Tricia's funeral. "I can't bear losing anyone else."

The anguish in his voice now broke her heart all over again. "I'll be okay," she said, wondering if it would ever be true. She'd told herself that she would be fine as soon as she got the justice her sister and Thomas deserved. But she wasn't even sure of that anymore.

"I know I can't stop you, but promise me this. That you'll call every few days, Maureen. I need to hear your voice. I need to know that you're okay."

"I'll call," she said. "Thomas?" She searched for something to say that would help them both. "It's going to get better." At least she hoped so.

Chapter Nine

"Your brother-in-law?" Brick asked as Mo pocketed her phone and walked toward him and his pickup. She nodded without looking at him. "You all right?"

He watched her look away to hide her raw emotions. "You don't have to worry about me."

"I wish that were true." When she met his gaze, he reached over to brush a lock of her hair back from her face. "You're having second thoughts."

She shook her head. "You have no idea what I'm thinking."

"I see more than you think. You're conflicted about all of this."

"Of course I am," she snapped and tried to step past him, but he blocked her way. She sighed. "What is it you want me to say? That maybe you're right and I'm wrong? Don't you think I wish that were true?"

"What if it is?"

She glared at him, clearly losing her patience. "Here is the problem. When we find her, and we will, you'll still be debating it all in your mind. She will use that against you and you'll end up dead."

"You've made her into a monster with powers that don't exist."

She scoffed at that. "This woman's greatest advantage is that she doesn't look or act the part. It's her strongest defense and most dangerous attribute." She pulled out the folded note he'd found on his pickup's windshield. "You think I don't want to find out if this is true? You think I don't want to believe that my sister didn't take her own life?"

"Why would Natalie lie?" Brick asked.

"It's nothing but a distraction. So instead of going after Natalie, I chase my sister's death only to find out it was all a lie. But by then, Natalie is long gone. She's living in someone else's house, taking care of a patient for a family who has no idea what horror has walked through their door." She pushed past him. "We need to get moving."

Mo felt close to tears. She couldn't help being upset. She hated hurting Thomas more than he was already suffering. Add that to her disappointment. They'd come so close to catching Natalie. She could feel the note in her pocket, the words burned into her brain. Tricia was having an affair. She didn't want to believe it. Just as she didn't want to believe any of this was happening.

And yet, it was happening. It had happened. What if Tricia really did have another man in her life? Did that really change anything? Unless it was true and Tricia hadn't taken her own life. All Mo could think was, why hadn't she known? She and Tricia used to be so close. How had she not known what was going on with her own sister?

"Where to now?" Brick asked as they climbed into the pickup cab again and he started the engine.

She pulled out her phone to call up a map and tried

to get her emotions under control. Thomas's phone call had gutted her. She kept thinking of the wedding. Her sister had been so happy. The two had been in love since college. Everyone said they made the perfect couple. But after trying so many times to have a child and failing... Is that when everything changed?

"Take 287 north," she said to Brick and pocketed her phone. "We'll watch the truck stops, the convenience stores." In truth, she had no idea what Natalie would do now. "She'll be wanting to get rid of the vehicle she's driving."

"While you were on the phone, I spoke to one of the neighbors. He said she left in a hurry, driving a tan older model two-wheel-drive pickup, so she's already dumped the car she stole in Big Sky," Brick said.

She looked over at him. "Nice work."

"This one sounds like it might have been cheap enough that she bought it with the money she's stolen so far."

Mo nodded. "I suspect Natalie's been living on the run for a long time, afraid to stay anywhere for too long. She's at the point now that she'll do whatever she has to do to survive." A part of Mo felt that way, as well. She'd given up everything—her job, the life she'd made for herself, her savings—to find this woman.

What am I doing? Chasing a possible killer and if so, when and how would it end? She feared the answer.

FROM DOWN THE STREET, private investigator Jim Cameron slid down behind the wheel as he watched the two climb into the pickup. He held the phone tighter to his ear.

"I'm looking at them as we speak," he said into the phone. "The female cop and the deputy marshal."

"Did they find Natalie?"

"No. Apparently she went out the back before I got here."

"Stay on it. This has to end."

He thought about the elderly couple that had cruised by in a sedan earlier—before the cop and the deputy had arrived. He'd noticed the way they'd stared at the three-story house.

"There's this old couple," Jim said. "I've seen them too many times and they drove by, both of them staring at the house."

"I'm not worried about some old couple. Stay on the cop and the deputy. Make sure they don't find Natalie first."

Jim shook his head. As many people as there appeared to be after this woman, himself included, none of them had gotten their hands on her except for whoever had abducted her in Big Sky. And the woman in question had managed to escape.

"Keep me informed." The line went dead.

Jim disconnected and sat up a little. The cop and the deputy had been sitting in his pickup unmoving so far. This had seemed like a simple enough job when he'd taken it on. If he wasn't getting paid so well…

He tried not to question what exactly was going on. It seemed to him that Natalie Berkshire was doing her best to crawl into a hole and stay there. Why roust her out? Why keep forcing her to run? Why not let her land somewhere and then throw a net over her?

The pickup with the cop and deputy was moving again. He waited a few moments before he fell in behind it.

BRICK DROVE THROUGH the residential area toward the center of town. Mo was lost in her own thoughts. What would Natalie do now? Run! What choice did she have? This time, she might run farther and be harder to find.

They were almost to the main drag in town when Mo saw the lights of police cars and what appeared to be a wreck in the middle of the intersection. As they drew closer, an officer waved him around the two-vehicle accident. She saw that a sedan had been involved—and a tan older model two-wheel-drive pickup.

"Isn't that the couple we saw eating the ice cream cones last evening?" Mo asked as he started to drive past the couple the police were talking with.

"Maybe, but that definitely looks like the description of the pickup Natalie was driving," Brick said.

"Stop." Mo threw her door open and she was out, slamming it behind her. She heard the cop order Brick to keep moving as she disappeared into the crowd gathered at the scene.

"Did you see what happened?" she asked several people on the street.

"That older couple T-boned that pickup with the woman inside," a man told her. "I swear that elderly driver sped up just before they collided."

"What happened to the woman in the pickup?" Mo asked. From where she stood, she could see that the driver's side of the pickup was caved in—and the passenger door was hanging open.

"She got out of the passenger side and limped off before the cops arrived," a woman said. "She was hurt, bleeding, but she took off down that way. The police are looking for her. Maybe she thought the accident was her fault and she wanted to get away. Or she was so shaken up that she didn't even know what she was doing."

"How badly hurt was she?" Mo asked.

"She was limping," one of the bystanders told her. "And bleeding."

"I bet she doesn't get far," someone said.

Mo wouldn't have taken that bet.

She continued down the street until she spotted Brick. He'd pulled over into the first parking space he'd found and now stood next to his truck, waiting. That he knew she'd find him made her realize how much their relationship had changed. Only this morning he'd thought she had taken off. She didn't know what had changed or when—just that it had. Smiling to herself, she realized she was actually glad to see him and had to swallow the lump in her throat as she joined him and told him what she'd learned.

As BRICK CLIMBED behind the wheel, he pulled out his phone. "There's something I want to check." He called his father's cell. The marshal answered on the first ring. "Brick—"

"Before you start in, didn't you tell me that the woman at the convenience store said the man in the motor home was elderly?" He knew he'd hit on something when all he heard for a moment was silence.

"We found the motor home," his father said. "A forensic team found evidence that it was the one where Natalie Berkshire was held captive."

"And the elderly driver?"

"Herbert Lee Reiner and his wife, Doris Sue, out of Sun Daisy, Arizona. They're grandparents of a woman whose baby died. Natalie was the nanny. I have a BOLO out on them."

Brick felt his stomach drop as his father described the two. "They just tried to kill Natalie in Ennis. She's on the run again, although injured after her vehicle was rammed by their car. I just thought you'd want to know." He disconnected before his father could lecture him and turned to Mo to tell her what he'd learned.

"So we head up Highway 287 north?" he asked as he started the pickup and glanced in his rearview mirror. He'd seen a dark SUV earlier. But now he saw nothing suspicious.

"Change of plans," Mo said. "What would you do if you'd just lost everything again and were now injured?"

"Go to the hospital?"

"Not just any hospital. You'd go to where your ex-husband the doctor worked. He's a surgeon at the hospital in the state capital—and not that far from here."

Chapter Ten

On the drive to Helena, Mo seemed to relax. He respected how she seemed to bounce back from disappointment quickly.

"Tell me about Brick Savage," she said out of the blue.

He glanced over at her for a moment before turning back to his driving. "Not much to tell," he said, wondering if she was just bored or if she were really interested.

"I doubt that's true since your reputation with women precedes you. Apparently you like to lasso them, but you always set them free."

"I wouldn't believe everything you hear." He cleared his throat. "You want to hear my life story or just the raunchy parts?"

She laughed. "I want to hear it all," she said, settling into her seat for the drive.

"Okay. I was born and raised in the Gallatin Canyon, grew up on a ranch with a mother who ran day-to-day operations and a father who was the local marshal. My whole family lives in that canyon. Ranching and wrangling is all I've ever known."

"And yet you're a deputy marshal," she said. "Or will be if I don't get you fired before you even start."

He ignored that. "I guess in the back of my mind I always thought I would follow in my father's footsteps."

"Will working with me ruin that for you?" she asked, sounding actually concerned.

"Don't worry about me." Brick had to admit, he'd always been impulsive, going with what felt right at the moment. He'd never felt rooted to the ranch the way his siblings had. He'd always been a free spirit.

Then again, he'd always had his twin brother, Angus, the solid, steady one, to help steer him out of trouble—until recently. Not to mention, he'd also had his very wise cousin Ella. But now he was on his own since both of them had moved on with their lives.

And now here he was. On his own. Two rogue lawmen. He couldn't depend on Mo to steer him into anything but trouble.

"So you said you were shot. An angry husband?"

"I've made a habit of steering clear of married women. My brother and I and my cousin Ella were helping a rancher in Wyoming on a cattle drive. Her husband, who she was divorcing, was giving her a hard time. I just got in the way of a bullet."

"That explains a lot. It was all about rescuing a woman in distress. You just can't help yourself, can you?"

He shook his head and sighed as they reached the Helena hospital where they would find Natalie's ex. "You just like giving me a hard time, don't you?"

Mo grinned. "Now that you mention it…"

THE TALL, DARK-HAIRED doctor came into the room on a gust of air-conditioned breeze. He closed the door and went straight to his desk, sitting down behind it before he considered the two of them. Clearing his voice, he glanced at his watch and asked, "I don't have a lot of time before my next surgery. What is this about?"

"We're here about your ex-wife Natalie," Mo said, trying to see the woman she'd known with this man. In the time she'd spent time around the woman, Natalie had never mentioned her ex.

"Natalie and I are no longer married."

"We are hoping you'd seen her today," Brick said.

Dr. Philip Berkshire shook his head. "Why would I? I haven't even seen her in years." He started to rise.

"She contacted you for bail money when she was arrested," Mo said.

He slowly lowered himself into the chair. "I said I hadn't seen her. I didn't say I hadn't heard from her."

"She didn't call you today?" Brick asked.

"No. She called when she needed bail money, and I turned her down."

"Why?" Brick asked.

"Why?" the doctor seemed shocked by the question. "Because I don't owe her anything."

"Or because you believe she's guilty?" Mo asked. "The two of you worked together. That's how you met and married, right?"

"That was a long time ago. I know nothing of the kind of woman she is now."

"What kind of nurse was she?" Mo asked.

"She was a fine nurse, a devoted, compassionate nurse."

"Why did she quit nursing to become a nanny?"

"You would have to ask her that."

Brick shifted in his chair. "I would love to, but since she's not here and you are…"

"We divorced."

"Why?"

Berkshire shot Brick a narrowed look. "That's personal."

"Look, we're trying to find her. Her life is in danger," he said. "Also, she might have information that we need in another death."

The doctor closed his eyes and slowly shook his head. "She had this thing about babies, sick babies. I'm sure you already know this," he said, opening his eyes and turning his attention on them again. "She had a younger sister who was born very sick. The doctor had given the infant only weeks to live. Natalie told me that she couldn't bear the child's suffering and was relieved when the baby passed. That is what you're looking for, isn't it? A reason?"

"You think she put her sister out of her pain and suffering?" Mo asked, feeling sick to her stomach. What if it had begun when Natalie was only a child herself?

"I think she wanted to. Whether or not she did… I believe it's why she became a nurse and why when we divorced, she left the hospital to become a nanny for fatally ill children."

"Is she capable of killing a suffering infant?" Brick asked.

Berkshire steepled his fingers in front of him, studying them for a moment before he spoke. "Not without causing herself great harm. If Natalie is anything, it is too caring. She was incapable of keeping any distance between herself and her patients. I could see how it was eroding her objectivity. She was too involved, too compassionate."

"Does she have a close friend that she might turn

to?" Mo asked, hoping for some clue where the woman might be headed now that she was injured.

He shook his head and then shrugged. "I have no idea."

Brick leaned forward in his chair. "She was injured in a car accident in Ennis. I thought maybe she might have come to you for help."

"No. Natalie wouldn't come to me. Not after I wouldn't give her the bail money. Her pride wouldn't allow that."

"What about her family?" Mo asked. "Would she go to them?"

"Her mother's dead and she had a falling out years ago with her father when her mother got sick. Look, I'm sorry, but I'm scheduled for a surgery," he said as he rose to leave.

Mo asked for directions to Natalie's father's house and the doctor told her. "What kind of falling out?" she asked as he headed for the door.

The doctor stopped but didn't turn around. "Her mother asked Natalie to help her die." With that, he was gone.

BRICK FOLLOWED A long dirt road that cut across arid country bare of little more than sagebrush. They'd been driving all day across Montana, from Ennis to Helena and now to the eastern portion of the huge state. He was wondering if they'd taken a wrong road when they came over a rise and he saw an old farmhouse in the distance.

As they grew closer, he could see that the two-story stick-built house was once white. Over the years, the paint had faded and peeled until now it was a windswept gray. The yard resembled other ranch and farmyards he'd seen across Montana. Ancient vehicles rusted in the sun along with every kind of farm implement. An old once-red barn leaned into the breeze. A variety of outbuildings were scattered like seeds over the property.

As they pulled down the driveway, an equally weathered looking man came out the screen door. Shading his eyes, he watched the pickup approach as if he hadn't seen anyone this far out in a very long time.

Brick parked, killed the engine and got out. He heard Mo exit the pickup and wondered what she was thinking as she took in this place. This was where Natalie had grown up?

"You lost?" the man asked. His voice and on closer inspection, his face, though weathered, was closer to fifty than eighty. Brick realized he was probably looking at Natalie's father.

"We're looking for Natalie Berkshire," Mo said.

Before she could get the words out of her mouth, the man was shaking his head. "Never heard of her," he said, already turning back toward the house.

"She's your daughter," Mo snapped.

The man stopped, his back to them. "Not anymore."

"She's on the run from people who want to hurt her," Brick said quickly. "She's injured and scared and probably has no one else to go to. Why wouldn't she come here?"

The man let out a deep-rooted bitter sound and slowly turned to face him. "Because she knows better than to come here."

"You wouldn't help her?" Brick asked, finding it hard to believe that blood wouldn't help blood.

"I wouldn't throw water on her if she was on fire."

"I don't believe that," Mo said.

"What do you know about anything?" the man demanded.

"I know she's your only child and if there is something wrong with her, then you have to share in that blame."

The man narrowed his eyes, anger making his nose flare. "Leave my property before I get my gun and run you off. That girl was a bad seed from birth." His voice broke. "Her mother tried to save her with love and look where that got the woman. Dead and buried." There were tears in his eyes as he went back inside, slamming the screen door behind him.

Mo WATCHED THE arid landscape sweep past as they drove back to the two-lane highway. Neither of them had spoken as if they didn't know what to say. As Brick pulled up to the stop sign, he glanced over at her.

"Which way?" he asked.

For a moment, she didn't know how to answer. They could drive to the closest town, where Natalie would have gone to school, find someone who knew her when she was young, maybe even find out why the woman's father hated her so much.

But Mo realized that none of that would help. For all she knew, the car crash could have caused internal bleeding and Natalie could be lying in a ditch somewhere, dying or already dead. Or she could have appropriated another vehicle and stolen some cash, and was on her way to her next job in another city, even in another state.

Mo had to make a choice. She felt as if she was at a crossroads. Maybe Natalie had nowhere to go, no one to help her. If she wasn't badly injured, she would keep going. Maybe Brick was right and it wasn't Mo's job to stop the woman—even if she could.

So what did that leave? Keep chasing Natalie or face a possible truth about her sister? If she wanted answers, she was going to have to find them herself without Natalie's help. A part of her still believed that Natalie was lying. But if she wasn't… It was a chance she couldn't take.

Brick was still waiting. "South to Billings," she said. "If it was true and Tricia was seeing another man, I need to find out who he is and what part he might have contributed to all of this." She kept having nightmares about that day and what role she may have played herself. Maybe if she'd listened to what Natalie had to tell her then…

He turned onto the highway headed south. Mo leaned back in the seat and closed her eyes for a moment. She feared sleep, especially after meeting Natalie's father. If that didn't bring on more nightmares, she didn't know what would.

She could tell that man had shaken Brick, as well. When Natalie told her that she grew up on a ranch, Mo had pictured rail fencing, horses running around a green pasture, a large house with a mother baking in the kitchen. She realized that Natalie had let her picture that, wanting Mo to believe that she was a born and bred Montana girl as open and honest as the big sky.

Victim or monster? Mo still couldn't say. Brick wanted to believe the best. But even if Natalie was the murderer Mo believed she was, it didn't mean that she'd killed Joey. Who was this woman and how much of what she'd told her was true?

"I believe that Natalie knows more than she told the

police," she said. "More than she's told me. She was trying to warn me that day. She seemed worried about Joey. Worried…" She looked over at him and felt tears fill her eyes. She was fighting to make sense of all of this.

She looked away as he voiced her worst fear.

"Worried that Tricia might have harmed her own baby?"

Mo quickly wanted to argue that Tricia wouldn't, couldn't. But in truth, given the condition her sister had been in the last time she'd seen her, she didn't have an argument in response. Fortunately, Brick didn't give her a chance.

"Natalie was living in that house, right? Of course she would have seen things, overheard things… If she didn't kill Joey, then someone else with access to that house did. If there was another man…"

Mo felt the weight of his words and hated that he was right. "It's time to find out if anything the woman has told me is the truth." Whether she wanted to hear it or not.

Chapter Eleven

Brick couldn't help but question how far he would go to see this finished as he drove toward Billings. He'd been hell-bent on saving Natalie Berkshire, convinced that she was a victim. He still was determined to see that she got a trial. With all the evidence he feared was coming out against her, a trial, it seemed, would only land her in prison for the rest of her life.

And yet not even Mo was now convinced that she'd hurt Joey. Unless Natalie was lying. Was she lying about everything else, as well?

As he glanced over at Mo, he knew that no matter what, he would see this through. Mo needed him, even if she didn't think so. He smiled to himself at the thought as he listened to the sound of the tires on the highway as the miles swept past. And he had needed her. He felt himself getting stronger. Not just physically but emotionally, as well.

Whatever happened now, he and Mo were in this together. As they crossed high prairie, the sun setting behind the Little Rockies, he kept thinking about Natalie's ex and her father. Was the young woman a bad seed?

He thought of that old couple that had rammed her pickup and injured her. Guilty or not, she deserved better. He hoped that old couple got the book thrown at them, then remembered what his father had told him. The couple had lost their grandchild and believed Natalie was responsible. Not that it gave them the right to take the law into their own hands.

"So if Natalie is the person you suspect she is, how long do you think she's been doing this?" he asked, realizing that his greatest fear was that Mo was right and Natalie would kill again.

"I wouldn't be surprised to find out that this started a lot longer ago than we know. I'm sure there has always been a lack of evidence. Maybe she wasn't even a suspect in most of the cases. Natalie seems to have the ability to be whatever she thinks other people need. Her father aside, I do believe there is something very wrong with her and that her childhood played a part in making her the woman she is now." Mo looked over at him. "Or maybe she is completely innocent of not just Joey's death but the others that are now being reinvestigated."

"Maybe," he said, though no longer sure of that. He realized that he was tired of thinking about it. Right now he was more interested in the woman sitting in the pickup cab next to him. "What about you?"

"What about me?" she asked, sounding surprised by the question.

"I've told you my life story—"

"Hardly."

"And you haven't told me anything about you."

She shook her head. "You know everything that is of any interest."

He scoffed at that. "So, where did you grow up?"

"Really?" She sighed. "Southern California."

He waited, but of course she wasn't forthcoming with more. "A surfer girl."

She scowled. "What is it you're looking for?"

"Maybe just polite conversation."

She gave him a look that said he'd come to the wrong place for that. But after a moment, she said, "My aunt raised me after my parents divorced and couldn't hold it together long enough to raise a child."

He hadn't been expecting that and he was sure his expression showed it. "What about your sister?"

"She was eighteen months older, so she went to live with our grandmother who said she could use the help." Mo shrugged. "Gram was a sour old woman but Tricia got along with her fine, I guess."

"So how was it living with your aunt?"

"I loved my aunt and uncle. They were wonderful to me. My uncle was from Mexico and they owned an authentic Mexican restaurant. I worked there from the time I was nine. I loved it. In fact, my happiest memories are of hanging out in the kitchen as they cooked. There was always music playing and laughter. My uncle cooked the best mole sauce you have ever tasted." She kissed her fingers. There were tears in her eyes.

"Are they still—"

"They were both killed in a drive-by shooting when I was weeks away from eighteen. Before you ask, yes, it is probably why I studied criminology in college and became a cop. I'd already gotten a scholarship so I headed to the same college where my sister was enrolled, Montana State University. Enough?"

"I'd ask about your love life—"

"But you're way too smart for that," she said. "Stop up here. I need something to eat."

As he pulled into a convenience store on the edge of a very small town, his cell phone rang.

"Want me to get you something?" she asked.

"Surprise me." As she climbed out of the cab, he took the call.

"Where are you?" his father asked without preamble.

He felt his pulse jump. "What's happened?" he asked, hearing something in his father's marshal voice.

"Natalie Berkshire has been found. She's dead. She died of her injuries from the car accident."

The breath he'd been holding came in a whoosh as he watched Mo moving around inside the convenience store. He wondered how this would impact her. He felt shaken.

"Herbert Lee Reiner and his wife Doris have been arrested in Ennis for her abduction and her death."

Brick didn't know what to say. "Maybe if we hadn't gone after her—"

"Son, there have been more investigations being re-opened. It appears there were a lot of suspicious injuries and deaths at her past jobs."

"You're telling me that she was guilty."

"She might have seen them as mercy killings."

Brick shook his head. He'd wanted to believe she was a victim. He'd wanted to believe he could save her. Or at least keep her safe until she could have a proper trial. His father was right. He'd gotten too involved. Maybe he wasn't cut out for law enforcement after all.

"It's over. You need to come home."

Brick couldn't speak for a moment as he thought of the night Natalie had stumbled into his headlights and how that had led to this moment and the blonde homicide cop standing at the register inside the convenience store.

"It's not over. Not yet. If Natalie was telling the truth then she wasn't responsible for the baby's death and Mo's sister was murdered."

His father swore. "You have no idea what you're getting yourself into. Even if you don't get killed, you could end up in jail."

"That's a chance I have to take. Mo needs my help."

The marshal swore. "You've always led with your heart instead of your head."

"And that's a bad thing?" he joked as he watched Mo finish paying inside the store.

"Not according to your mother," his father said with a sigh. "I wish you'd come home."

"Pretend I'm up in the mountains camping until you see me again." Mo headed out of the store. "Thanks for letting me know."

"Brick? Promise me you'll be careful. Maybe especially with your heart."

As he disconnected, Mo looked up at him, stopping in midstride as if seeing the news etched on his face.

He got out of the truck and went to her. "That was my father. They found Natalie. She died of her injuries from the car crash. The older couple has been arrested."

Her expression didn't change as she nodded. And then she was in his arms, sobbing against his shoulder. He held her, unsure if her tears were of relief or of grief. Like she'd said, she'd known the woman, she'd liked her. But she'd been terrified that Natalie would kill again if not stopped. Now, though, there was no chance of finding out anything more from Natalie. They were on their own.

As quickly as she'd thrown herself into his arms, Mo stepped out of them and wiped her tears before climbing into the cab of his pickup.

"I'm sorry," he said as he slid behind the wheel, not sure of his own feelings. It wasn't what he wanted for Natalie. He wanted justice, but that might have been years of waiting for numerous trials where she was found guilty. She might have ended up on death row in one of the states or merely spent the rest of her life behind bars. If truly guilty, she might have been saved from all that by dying from her injuries.

"I'll understand if you want to stop this," he said to Mo, realizing that this might change everything.

She'd been sitting, holding a convenience store bag on her lap, and staring out the truck windshield. But now she turned to look at him in surprise. "I can't stop now. I have to know the truth. All of it. But you don't have to—"

"I'm in this with you. All the way."

She smiled through fresh tears for a moment before opening the bag in her lap. "I brought you doughnuts. If you're going to be a cop…"

"So… Billings?" She nodded and handed him a doughnut. He took a bite and shifted into gear.

Several hours later, they were on the outskirts of the largest city in Montana. They approached from the north, giving Brick a different view than he normally had approaching the city. He could see the bands of rock rims that ran on each side of the Yellowstone River— and the city. From this vantage point, higher than the city itself, it appeared to be lush green. The bowl between the rims was a canopy of treetops and a green ribbon of Yellowstone River.

And somewhere in Montana's largest city hopefully were the answers Mo so desperately needed.

EARLIER, MO HAD insisted on driving part of the way, letting Brick sleep. They'd stopped in Roundup at the convenience store to use the restroom and get something more to drink, and Brick had taken the wheel again.

"Where do we start?" he asked now as he drove through what were known as The Heights before dropping down into Billings proper.

"Tricia had a friend from high school and college who she still saw. If anyone knows what might have been going on with my sister it will be Hope."

He shot her a look, hearing something in her tone. "A friend you don't like."

She looked over at him in surprise. "It isn't that I don't like her—not exactly." She mugged a face. "Fine, I don't like her. I never trusted her. I always thought Tricia felt sorry for her. Hope is one of those people who demands a lot of sympathy. I swear she makes her own bad luck just for the attention."

"You were jealous of her relationship with your sister."

Mo rolled her eyes but didn't argue the point since he was right. She gave him directions to the woman's house. The house was small and located in an older neighborhood that had seen better times. Weeds grew tall in the yard and the siding could have used a coat of paint years ago.

"You think she's back from work?" he asked as he pulled up out front and checked the time.

Mo snorted. "If she had a job," and opened her door to get out, but stopped.

BRICK COULD TELL she was about to tell him he didn't have to come with her. But apparently changed her mind, adding, "On second thought, she'll take to you right off."

He wasn't sure he liked that, but followed her up the walk nonetheless.

The thin, dark-haired woman who answered the door wore a tank top and shorts. Her feet were bare. She had a plain face made plainer by her straight shoulder-length hair.

She frowned at Mo, clearly questioning what she was doing on her doorstep. But when her gaze took him in, she smiled and gave him a more welcoming look.

"I didn't expect to see you," Hope said as she jammed her hands on her hips and glared at Mo. "You weren't exactly friendly at the funeral."

"It was a *funeral*, not a party you were invited to." Brick could tell Mo was wishing she didn't need this woman's help. He thought Mo might want to try sugar rather than vinegar in this instance, but kept his mouth shut.

"Look, Hope, I didn't come here to argue with you about some past slight or misunderstanding," Mo said.

"What? You didn't come by to apologize?"

As if seeing that her tactics weren't working, Mo said, "Hope, could we please come in? I need to ask you something about Tricia."

The woman in the doorway hesitated, her gaze going back and forth from one to the other of them before she stepped back with obvious reluctance.

Once inside, Hope didn't offer them a chair. Instead, she stood just inside the door, arms crossed waiting.

"Thanks, we'd love to sit down," Mo said and walked

into the living room to perch on the edge of the couch. She looked at Hope and snapped, "Could you drop the drama queen act? I need to know if Tricia had a lover."

Brick had moved to the fireplace and stood waiting to see how all of this was going to shake out. Hope looked pointedly at him without moving.

"This is Deputy Marshal Brick Savage. He's helping me investigate Joey's death," Mo said.

"Wait, *you're* investigating? I heard you got kicked off the force and aren't a cop anymore."

"I was suspended, not fired. Are you going to answer my question or just give me a hard time?" Mo sounded tired and weary. Brick knew the feeling. It had been another long day.

Hope must have decided to cut Mo some slack because she dropped her belligerent stance and moved away from the door to take a chair at the edge of the living room.

"If Tricia had wanted you to know what was going on in her life, she would have told you," Hope said haughtily.

Mo swore. "Tell me who the man was."

"Tell me why I should? Tricia's dead. I promised her I wouldn't tell anyone ever, especially *you*."

"How long had she been seeing him?"

Hope looked away for a moment. "Over a year."

Brick heard Mo emit a painful sound that made Hope smile. But he knew what Mo had to be thinking. There was the possibility that the baby had been her sister's lover's and not Tricia's husband's—just as Natalie had questioned.

"Was she in love with him?" Mo asked.

Hope shrugged. "At first it was just a fling. She

didn't think it would last. I think she realized that she'd gotten married too young and she wanted to see if she'd missed out on something. Apparently she had. It was thrilling, she said. I think it was fun because it was a secret. No one knew but me. Your sister knew what you'd say if she told *you*."

Mo seemed to ignore that. "Did you meet him?" Brick saw the answer. "So you never met him."

"They had to keep it secret. Billings may be the largest city in Montana, but it isn't so large that you can have an affair and people don't find out," Hope said.

"So you don't know his name," Brick said, making the woman look over at him. He got the feeling she'd forgotten all about him until then.

"I didn't need to know his name," Hope said irritably. "But why should I tell you even if I did know?" she demanded of Mo.

"Because I have reason to believe Tricia didn't kill herself."

The woman's eyes widened. *"Seriously?"*

"Seriously."

"So…" Hope was frowning again. "You think someone killed her?" Mo said nothing. "You can't think it was Andy."

"Andy?"

Brick saw that Mo's eyes had widened in surprise. "Who is Andy?" he asked.

"A friend of Thomas's."

Mo COULDN'T BELIEVE THIS. "Andy? It's Andy?"

"She never told me it was Andy," Hope said quickly, backpedaling. "Just that it was someone from college, someone she'd had a crush on."

With relief, she realized that if Natalie had been telling the truth, the man Tricia had been having the affair with was blond and more than six feet tall. Andy was short and dark-haired.

She looked at Hope, wanting to throttle the woman. "So you never saw him, never met him. I'm beginning to wonder if Tricia even confided in you."

"She did!" the woman cried. "She was in love and heartbroken because she didn't want to hurt Thomas."

"She was in *love*?" This wasn't adding up. "I thought it was just a fling?"

"At first. She thought it was just for fun, but then it turned into something else and then…" Hope looked away.

"And then she got pregnant," Mo guessed. All those months of trying to get pregnant with Thomas's child and suddenly she had an affair with another man and got pregnant. "Whose baby was Joey?"

Hope shook her head. "She didn't know. She was in a panic. I tried to get her to take a DNA test before the baby was born."

"Did she?"

The woman shook her head. "She was determined that it was Thomas's. She broke off the affair. She told me her boyfriend was really upset."

Mo thought about the emotional roller coaster Tricia had been on during her pregnancy. No wonder she'd been all over the place. "Did her boyfriend not want the baby?"

"Oh, no, he wanted it. He wanted her to leave Thomas and marry him, but she was having second thoughts, regrets, you know. Thomas had found out that she was pregnant and was so happy that she convinced herself that it was his and lied to her boyfriend about taking the test. She said the baby was her husband's and that the affair was over."

"But she didn't know who Joey's father was?"

Hope shook her head. "Then when he was born with so many medical problems and the doctor said he probably wouldn't live…"

Mo knew her sister. "She blamed herself."

"I told her it was stupid. That it was just bad luck."

Mo sat back on the couch. This explained so much. Natalie must have seen how out of control Tricia had been. Once she saw Tricia with the other man… "If you think of anything she might have said about the man that might give me a clue who he was…"

"Like I said, she didn't tell me that much about him. Mostly she talked about the way he made her feel. He was like her. He loved animals." Mo thought about her sister's disappointment that she couldn't have a dog because Thomas was allergic. "And he was romantic," Hope was saying. "One time he carved their initials into a tree."

Mo pulled out of her thoughts to look at the woman. "Where was this?"

"On a camping trip they took some weekend when Thomas was at one of his seminars. Their inside joke was how taken Thomas was with the Jeffrey Palmer seminars." She looked over at Brick. "Jeffrey Palmer is a self-made millionaire. He gives leadership seminars that he charges a fortune for so others can believe they might one day be rich, too. Thomas idolizes him and never misses one of his seminars, especially since his company sends him along with his associates so they can become leaders."

"The carving on the tree," Mo said pointedly. "Where was it exactly?"

Hope seemed to give it some thought. "I think it was near Red Lodge by a creek." She shrugged. "I just remember how happy Tricia was."

"Until she wasn't."

"I hope you find him. I do remember that when Tricia told me about breaking up with him over the pregnancy, she didn't come out and say it, but I could tell that she'd been worried about how he was going to take it. She said he was so angry, she'd never seen him like that, and she was sure that she'd done the right thing by breaking it off, but then later he called. She sat right here and cried her heart out. I think she really loved him."

Mo felt her heart ache for her sister. "She kept seeing him, didn't she?" Hope looked away, answer enough. Mo got to her feet, thanked her and started for the door.

Brick asked behind her, "Where was this photo taken?" She turned to see that he was pointing at a snapshot that had been stuck into the edge of a framed photograph on the mantle.

It appeared to be one of Tricia. In the photo, her sister was smiling at the person taking the photo. She did look happy. Behind her was a stream and pines.

"Oh, I forgot all about that photo," Hope cried. "Tricia left it here since she couldn't take it home. It was her favorite from their camping trip. He said it was his favorite photo of her and gave her a copy of it. I'm sure there were others of the two of them but she never showed them to me. That reminds me." Hope got to her feet. "She left some stuff here. I thought you might—"

"I'd like it, please," Mo said and they waited as the

woman disappeared through a door and returned moments later with a large manila envelope.

"I don't know what's in it. I never looked." She handed it to Mo. "Tricia said I should give it to you if anything happened to her."

"Are you serious?" Mo demanded. "When were you going to tell me about this?" She clutched the envelope to her chest and glared at the woman.

"If you hadn't been such a bitch at the funeral—"

"I'm curious. Why the secrecy?" Brick interrupted. "Why wouldn't Tricia tell you the man's name since she told you everything else?"

Hope shrugged again. "I wondered about that, too. I think he was somebody, you know? A name that either I would know or would have heard of. She was so worried that Thomas would find out and maybe do something to him."

"Or she thought you wouldn't have been able to keep her secret," Mo said, still clearly angry.

Hope glared back at her. "At least I knew what was going on." She raised a brow as if to say, *and she was your sister.*

Brick surreptitiously pocketed the photo he'd taken from the mantel and quickly got them both out of there.

Once in the pickup and driving again, Brick said, "This makes me wonder if Natalie wasn't telling the truth about all of it. You knew her. You liked her. She was worried about your sister, worried about Joey. She tried to warn you about what was going on. She was even convinced that Tricia didn't commit suicide and swears that she didn't harm Joey."

"What is the point of debating it now? She's dead." All she could think was that caught in this heartbreaking triangle and filled with guilt over Joey's paternity and health, her sister could have been in such an emotional state that she had killed herself.

"She wasn't lying about Tricia having an affair," he pointed out. "I don't think she was lying about your sister not killing herself."

"I don't know," Mo said, the manila envelope resting unopened in her lap. She saw him check his rearview mirror and not for the first time. "What is it?"

"We're being followed and have been since we left Hope's house."

Chapter Twelve

"You were right," the PI said into his hands-free device. "She went by the house. She was in there a good half hour. I'm following her and the deputy now."

He swore as he realized that he'd been spotted. "I'm going to have to let them get ahead of me." He turned at the next street. He was pretty sure where he could catch up to them again.

"How did they seem when they came out of the house?"

"Hard to say." He got paid to spy on people, photograph them, follow them. He didn't get paid to analyze their feelings, but he was smart enough not to say that. "Subdued." He could hear that the answer didn't make his client happy.

Ahead, he saw the pickup, but this time he stayed back. "They've pulled into a motel and are going inside the office." He told his employer the name of the downtown Billings motel as he pulled over to wait. "What would you like me to do? It appears they have booked a room and are now carrying their bags there."

"One room?"

"Yes, they both went into the same room." Jim listened for a moment. "Right, I can do that. I'll put the tracking device on the pickup tonight." Now that they knew they were being followed, he couldn't let them see him again.

"Once I can track them myself, I think it would be best if I took it from here."

"You're the boss."

"I'll stop by your office and pay you in cash when I pick up any file you might have made on this."

The man was worried that hiring a private detective to follow a homicide cop and a deputy marshal might come back on him?

"I understand." He hung up, telling himself he was glad to be done with this one. But just to cover his own behind, he'd keep a digital copy of his work and the man's requests. Hopefully, he would never have to use it, he thought as he waited for it to get dark enough to go back to the motel and attach the tracking device to Deputy Marshal Brick Savage's pickup.

"I'M NOT SURE I'm up to understanding any of this," Mo said once they were settled into the motel room and she'd taken a peek inside the envelope. She was exhausted—and still upset. Her sister had told Hope to give it to her in case anything happened to her. What had Hope been thinking? Clearly the woman didn't have a brain the size of a pea.

But what scared her was the realization that Tricia had known there was a chance that something *would* happen to her. So she'd left whatever was in this envelope for Mo. If only Hope had given it to her right away.

"What is it?" Brick asked as he pulled back the curtain to look out into the street.

"A stack of photocopied financial reports," she said.

"I can't make heads or tails of them, not tonight." She wasn't sure what she'd hoped to find in the envelope. A diary. Photos. A suicide note. Something personal to Mo to explain what it was that she'd left for her. It made her question if Tricia had been in her right mind. Wasn't that her fear? That Natalie hadn't killed the baby? The only other person in the house that day was Tricia.

"I'm tired, too," Brick said as he checked outside again.

"Have you seen the vehicle that you thought was following us?" she asked, putting the manila envelope into her suitcase.

"No, maybe I was just being paranoid."

"Or letting Natalie get to you," Mo said with a sigh. "I'll wash up and go to bed."

Brick moved away from the window and stretched out on top of his bed.

By the time she came out of the bathroom, he was sound asleep. She crawled between the sheets in the matching queen bed. She couldn't quit thinking about her sister. Had Tricia fallen in love with the mystery man? That she would even have an affair was so unlike her, it was hard to believe. Tricia had always been the good one. It was one of the reasons she had gone to their grandmother's instead of Mo.

She closed her eyes, desperately wanting to put the day behind her. Natalie was dead. Whatever secrets the woman had refused to give up would go to the grave with her. She felt sleep tugging at her. Her last thought was that she hadn't gotten a chance to tell her sister goodbye.

Mo came out of the dream screaming. She felt hands

on her and fought to shove them off, but the fingers were like steel.

"Mo. *Mo?*" The hands gave her a shake, and she opened her eyes, startled and instantly embarrassed because she knew she'd had another one of her dreams.

Brick released her and she sat up, backing against the headboard as she chased away the last of the darkness. They'd hardly spoken after renting the motel room. Mo didn't remember falling asleep but it must have been quickly.

She gulped air and tried to still her pounding heart. A chill in the room dried the perspiration on her skin, but her nightshirt still felt damp. As the light on in the room chased away the dark shadows that followed her sleep, she began to breathe easier.

"Better?" Brick asked now. He was sitting on the edge of the bed, but no longer touching her.

She nodded, unable to look at him. The nightmares were terrifying and embarrassing. They made her feel weak. Worse, vulnerable.

"A bad one, huh? I've had a few that followed me into daylight," he said quietly. "The worst ones don't go away easily. They always make me afraid to close my eyes again because I know the terror is waiting for me."

She glanced in his direction and saw that he was looking at the hideous mountain painting on the opposite wall instead of at her. Her heart seemed to fill. He understood what she was going through because he'd not only had the bad dreams, but also he'd felt the weakness, the vulnerability, the embarrassment of them.

"If it helps, I can leave the light on," he said when he finally did look at her.

Mo shook her head. As he started to get up from her

bed to turn off the lamp next to them, she touched his hand. She hadn't meant to reach for him. It was as if an inner need was stronger than she was. She hated needing anyone and yet she did.

"I can turn out the light and stay here, if you want me to," he said quietly.

She nodded, tears filling her eyes. She wiped at her the wetness on her face, heard him turn off the light, then felt his weight settle in next to her on the bed. She took a few calming breaths before she slid down in the bed to lie next to him.

Staring at the ceiling in the ambient light coming through the motel room's curtains, she felt him take her hand in his large warm one. Until that moment, she hadn't realized that she was trembling. But as he held her hand, she felt his warmth move through her until she quit shaking, until she was no longer afraid to close her eyes.

BRICK WOKE WITH Mo snuggled against him and his arm around her. He didn't dare move, not wanting to wake. Not wanting to let her go just yet. He wondered about her bad dreams and was glad she hadn't had another one later last night.

With a shock he realized that he hadn't had one since the two of them had joined forces. Maybe he really was getting better. He smiled to himself and felt her shift in his arms. He held his breath.

"I know you're awake," she whispered.

"How can you tell?" he asked.

"Because your hand isn't on my breast anymore."

Brick withdrew his arms as she turned to face him. "I'm sorry, if I did anything—"

"I was joking," she said smiling. "You were a perfect gentleman." She eyed him as if surprised by that. And maybe…disappointed? "Should I be insulted?"

He chuckled. "Trust me, it's not because I haven't wanted to."

She laughed and turned to get up on the opposite side of the bed. "Trust you?" she said, her back to him. "Won't that be the day. I'm going to get a shower." She stopped and turned. "Have you ever carved your initials into a tree along with the name of one of your… women?"

"No."

Mo nodded and smiled. "I'm anxious to find that tree. I'm assuming you'll want to go along?" She said it over her shoulder as she headed for the bathroom.

"I'm stuck to you like glue," he said before she closed the door.

They spent the morning canvassing the neighborhood around Tricia and Thomas's house. Brick knew Mo was hoping that one of the neighbors might have seen a man going into the house who wasn't Thomas over the weeks that Tricia had been having the affair— or on the day she'd died.

When they came up empty, they stopped for lunch and then headed toward Red Lodge in hopes of finding the campsite where Tricia's lover had left their initials carved in a tree.

THEY ARRIVED AT the forest service campground midmorning. Most of the sites were open. A few occupants in tents and small trailers were packing up to leave as he drove slowly through the pines higher up the mountain.

He had the photograph that Tricia's alleged lover had taken on their camping trip.

On the way to the campground, Mo had been looking through the envelope her sister had left for her. Now she put it away, apparently still not understanding why Tricia wanted her to have it.

"I'm still shocked that we are looking for the identity of my sister's lover," Mo confided. "Tricia was always the rule follower, the voice of reason. For her to do this…"

"People fall in love," he said. "At least that's what I've heard."

She swung her gaze on him. "You've never been in love?"

He seemed as surprised by the question as she was shocked that he hadn't been in love. He slowly drove through another loop of the campground. "Why? Have you?"

"Middle school, my science teacher. High school, this sweet boy who wrote me these awful poems. A couple of times in college. Several since then."

He laughed. "That's your love life?"

"Apparently, it's better than yours. You've really never been in love?"

He could feel her gaze on him as he pulled over and cut the engine in an empty campsite. "There's a tree down," he said in explanation for stopping. "We're going to have to walk to see the upper end of the campground, where we should have a view of the creek that's in the photo."

"You didn't answer my question," she said, keeping him from exiting the truck cab. "You weren't in love with even one of the women you dated?"

"I cared about all of them. Maybe you and I have a different definition of love. When I tell a woman that I love her it will be right before I propose marriage." With that, he climbed out of the pickup and closed the door.

Mo exited the truck as well, still looking surprised by his answer. They started up the mountain road, climbing over downed trees and limbs. "Looks like they had a storm up this way," he said. This high up the mountain, there were only the sounds of birds, the breeze high in the tops of the pines and the whisper of the stream. As they climbed higher, though, the sound of a roaring creek grew louder.

"Seriously, you've never felt…love?" she asked.

"The head over heels kind?" He shook his head and glanced at her. "I'm assuming you haven't, either. It's probably why you can't understand what happened to your sister."

She seemed to consider that. "You're probably right. It seems…reckless, something Tricia never was. At least I thought that was true. Let me see the photo." He handed it to her. "I think that's it up there," she said excitedly. "See that mountain in the distance?" She held up the snapshot.

"Lead the way," he agreed as they quickened their pace. Now all they had to do was find a tree up here with Tricia and her lover's initials carved in it.

As THEY REACHED the campsite, Mo stopped to check the photo again. "This is the campsite." She turned to see Brick already checking trees.

For a moment, she merely stood looking at this beautiful sight. The creek cut a green swath through the rocks and pines to fall away down the mountainside below them. She breathed in the rich, sweet scent of pine and caught a hint of someone's campfire smoke trailing up from a site below.

She thought of her sister, the last person she could imagine enjoying camping. That Tricia might have slept up here in the blue tent in the photo… It boggled the mind. She tried to imagine the man who could sweep her sister off her feet.

"Mo? I think you'd better come over here," Brick said.

She turned to find him standing next to a large pine tree at the edge of the mountainside, overlooking the roaring of the creek. As she approached, she saw the crude heart carved into the bark of the pine.

There were two sets of initials at the center of the heart. TM, a plus sign, and JP. Tricia's lover had used her maiden name initial. Wishful thinking on his part? Or was that the last name she'd given him? This man had understood from the beginning that Tricia was married, hadn't he?

"Know anyone with those initials?" Brick asked.

Mo shook her head. "I have no idea who JP is."

The gunshot echoed through the trees, splintering the bark on the tree next to her. Several nearby birds took flight, wings flapping wildly as Brick lunged for her, taking them both to the ground.

The second shot ricocheted off the tree where they had been standing, sending bark flying again. And then there was nothing but the sound of the breeze in the pines and seemingly hushed roar of the creek. Not even the birds sang for a moment as Mo tried to catch her breath.

Chapter Thirteen

In the distance, Brick heard an automobile engine start up. Through the trees he caught a flash of silver as the vehicle sped off, the sound dying as whoever had taken the potshots at them drove away.

Mo was on her feet as quickly as he was, the two of them running back down the road to where they'd left the truck. They had to slow down to climb over the downed trees and limbs, but finally reached the pickup.

Brick started it and drove as fast as he could out of the campground. By the time they reached the highway, there was no sign of the vehicle they'd glimpsed through the pines.

"Whoever that was, wasn't driving the black SUV that had been following us yesterday," Brick said. "What I want to know is how they knew we were going to the campsite?"

"Hope? You think she lied about knowing the man's name. She could have called him to tell him what she'd told us? That would be pretty stupid of her, wouldn't it? Especially if Tricia's lover is the one who just shot at us."

Brick pulled off his Stetson and raked a hand through his hair. "Then how did anyone know where to find us?"

"She must have told someone, unless..." Mo met Brick's gaze across the cab of the pickup. "You don't think..."

"I do think." He pulled the pickup to the side of the road and they both got out to search the undercarriage. They found the tracking device quickly enough. Brick was about to destroy it when Mo stopped him.

"Let's give whoever did this something to follow," she said, pointing to the freight train moving slowly along the tracks on the other side of the road.

Brick smiled and spotted a dirt road that ran beside the train track. Back in the truck, he drove along a narrow road along the tracks. Heading off the slow-moving freight train, he jumped out of the truck and waited for it to catch up to him. He was back to the pickup within minutes.

"All done." His gaze locked with hers. He was still shaken by the close call on the mountain. "Any idea what is going on?"

"I think we're getting close to the truth." She shook her head. "But I'm nowhere near figuring out who JP might be or what these documents are that Tricia left me."

"I need to go back up the mountain to get that one slug that lodged in the tree," he said. "That is, if we're going to take this to the police."

Mo shook her head. "It's a long shot we could ever track it to the gun, but at least we will have the evidence."

He drove back up the mountain. "Why don't you wait here? I won't be long." He pulled his spare pistol out from under the seat of his truck and handed it to her. "Fire a shot if you need me."

She smiled. "You just handed me a loaded gun. I think I'll be able to take care of myself."

He wasn't gone long before he returned with the slug he'd dug out of the tree with his pocketknife.

"Do you think the person who shot at us was trying to kill us or just scare us?" she asked.

Brick smiled. "If he was trying to kill us, then he was a piss-poor shot. I think he was trying to send us a message."

"To quit looking for the man Tricia was involved with? Or stop looking for her killer?"

"Could be one and the same," Brick said.

Mo made a disgruntled sound. "All he did was make me more determined—and more convinced that what Natalie told me was true. Tricia didn't kill herself."

"He? The shooter could be a woman."

"My money is on her boyfriend. Who else would be worried about us finding out his identity?"

He could tell that Mo had been racking her brain, trying to figure out who JP could be while he was up on the mountain getting the slug.

"I can't even imagine how Tricia crossed paths with him between taking care of her house and her day job, though," she said.

"What is it?" Brick asked as he saw her freeze and then hurriedly pull out her phone.

"Something Hope said." She scrolled on her phone for a moment before she looked up. "My sister volunteered every other Saturday at a nonprofit dog shelter. I remember Thomas complaining that she spent more time there than at home and had to shower before he could get near her."

"Any luck?" he asked as he watched her thumb through the shelter site.

She shook her head. "No one on the board with those initials. I'm going to call Hope. Maybe the initials mean something to her." When Hope answered, she put the cell on speakerphone.

"We found the campsite and the carving on the tree of the heart with their initials in it. Do you remember anyone from college with the initials JP?"

"*JP?* No. Honestly, I've always thought it was Andy. He's such a sweetie and he's always liked her."

"Think. Do you know anyone by those initials?"

Hope was quiet for a moment. "Sorry, I don't. Tricia always referred to him as her special friend."

Mo HUNG UP and put her phone away, irritated with Hope and even more irritated with herself. If she'd let Natalie tell her what was going on that day, she could have talked to Tricia. At least she would have tried to help her rather than hiding her head in the sand, not wanting to hear that anything was wrong.

"I'll call my partner at homicide when we get back to Billings," she said. "We can give him the slug you dug out of the tree—although I doubt it will lead us to the shooter. But I want to get everything I can on my sister's death."

An hour later, Mo introduced Brick to her partner, Lou Landry, outside the diner around the corner from Billings PD. A little gray around the edges and highly seasoned after thirty-five years at this, Lou was more like a father figure than a partner. Mo knew she'd been placed with him so he could keep her out of trouble. It had worked—until the Natalie Berkshire case.

"You are opening up a can of worms," Lou said after she told him what she needed. "Are you sure you want to do this?"

"I have to know if what Natalie Berkshire told me was true."

"Mo, I probably shouldn't be telling you this, but we are getting inquiries from all over the state and even the country about Natalie. It's much worse than we first thought. People are demanding the cases be reopened. They want answers and quite frankly it appears there is only one answer. Natalie Berkshire was a serial murderer."

"She swore she didn't kill Joey." She saw his pitying look.

"Just as she swore that your sister didn't kill herself?"

"At least I know that Natalie didn't have anything to do with Tricia's death. She was behind bars when Tricia hung herself."

Lou shook his head. "I'll get you the autopsy report, but I don't think you're going to find any answers in it. The coroner ruled it a suicide. If there had been anything suspicious—"

"I want to see the photos taken at the scene, as well."

He sighed. "Why put yourself through that?"

"Because I can't close that door until I'm sure."

"All right. I'll meet you back here in thirty minutes."

"Lou…thank you."

"What are partners for?" His expression saddened. "You're not coming back to the force, are you?"

"I don't know."

He nodded. "Thirty minutes." And he was gone.

She looked at Brick.

"He seems like a nice guy."

"He is."

"Are you really never going back?"

She shrugged. "Buy me a cup of coffee?" As they entered the diner, she saw Shane Danby and several of his friends leaving. Her stomach dropped, half expecting him to make a scene. To her surprise, he merely nodded and left.

Thirty minutes later, Lou entered the coffee shop and handed her a paper sack. "I hope you know what you're doing," he said and left.

Mo glanced into the sack and saw a copy of the autopsy report and the photos taken at the scene. She closed the bag and turned to Brick. "I thought we could take these back to the motel. But first I need to use the ladies' room."

"I'll be waiting for you outside," he said, looking worried. Like Lou. Both knew that seeing the report and the photos was going to hit her hard. But she had to know. Since her sister's death and Joey's, she'd been having the nightmares. She had to believe that the reason for them was that justice hadn't been meted out. Not yet anyway.

Brick stepped outside the coffee shop into the summer sun. He was worried about Mo with good reason, he thought as he started down the street to where he'd parked his pickup. The threat against her was real. Someone had taken potshots at them. And now she was looking into her sister's death. Had they been followed to the campsite outside of Red Lodge?

He'd watched for a tail and hadn't spotted one. Who else knew about Tricia having been there? Who else knew about the carving on the tree with the initials on it? Tricia's lover.

"Well, look who it is?" said a male voice as he walked past an alley near where he'd left his truck. He'd been so lost in thought that he hadn't seen the man. Turning, he saw cop Shane Danby and two other men. Clearly, the three had been waiting for him. "Guess we meet again."

"What a coincidence," Brick said. "And you're looking for trouble just like last time, only this time you brought your friends to help you."

Shane's jaw muscles bunched along with his fists as he took a step closer. "You should have stayed out of it with me and Mo. You messed with the wrong man." He took a swing, but Brick easily sidestepped it.

"Get him!" Shane cried and charged, head down. Brick caught him in an uppercut that knocked the man to his knees, but then Shane's buddies were on him. One slammed a fist into his lower back, knocking the wind out of him, as the other grabbed him in a headlock from behind.

He tried to fight them off as Shane got to his feet again and attacked with both fists before the cop's friends threw Brick to the ground. As he tried to get to his feet, Shane kicked him in the side, then the stomach, then in the head.

Brick heard the sound of sirens as he fought not to black out.

"He's a cop, man," one of his friends said as he pulled Shane away to keep him from kicking Brick again.

"I didn't know he was a cop," Shane said as he stumbled over to him and pulled his wallet out. "I was just walking by and the bastard attacked me. The two of you saw it. I didn't know he was some deputy marshal until I pulled his ID and by then, I had arrested him."

"That's your story?" one of Shane's friends demanded.

"That's *our* story," Shane snapped.

"You are going to get us into so much trouble," his friend complained.

"I already called in the attack," Shane said with a laugh. "A disturbance in an alley near Henry's Bar. Might need medical attention. Cops attacked."

As the cop car came roaring up, siren blaring and lights flashing, Shane said, "Just stick to the story." Walking past Brick, the cop got in one more kick.

Just before he passed out, Brick heard Mo's angry voice and then she was taking his truck keys as he was being carried to the cop car. The last thing he heard was her saying, "Don't worry, I'll get you out."

MO HAD WANTED TO attack Shane herself. Instead, she demanded that Brick be given medical attention, promising to bail him out as quickly as she could.

"Shane, you best watch your back," she warned him quietly as Brick was loaded into the back of the ambulance behind the police cruiser.

"You aren't threatening an officer of the law, are you, Mo?" He smirked at her. "Careful, or you'll end up behind bars, as well."

She'd already been behind bars, so she kept her mouth shut. This was all her fault. If she hadn't involved Brick in this… If he hadn't come to her rescue at the bar… Through her anger, she told herself that there was nothing else she could do for Brick. He wouldn't be arraigned until tomorrow at the earliest. All she could do was wait and then get him out on bail—just as he'd done for her.

In the meantime, she had the autopsy report and the photos, and she knew the initials of Tricia's lover. It wasn't much, but there had be something in them to prove that Tricia hadn't taken her own life. Once she did that, she wouldn't let it go until her sister's murderer was caught.

Storming over to Brick's pickup, she climbed in and tossed the paper sack Lou had given her onto the seat. It toppled over, spilling some of the contents onto the floor.

Mo saw one photo of her sister, the noose around her neck, and burst into tears. She leaned over the steering wheel, letting it all out. For weeks, she'd used her anger keep her from releasing the pain inside her. Now it overflowed with chest-aching sobs, the dam breaking.

After a few minutes, she gulped and wiped furiously at her face. Finally under control, she leaned down to pick up everything that had fallen. She was shoving it all back into the paper sack when she realized the paper in her hand hadn't come out of the bag Lou had given her.

She stared down at the sheet of paper. It took her a moment to realize what she was looking at—the flyer Thomas's associate Quinn had handed her outside the jail. Something caught her eye. She smoothed out the sheet of paper.

Jeffrey Palmer, the self-made man and seminar speaker. JP. She remembered Thomas talking about the wonderful speakers his company always managed to book. Hadn't Tricia gone to one of these with her husband?

The multimillionaire's list of accomplishments was a mile long. She stared at his photograph. He had to be pushing seventy with thick gray hair and bushy gray eyebrows. This man couldn't have been Tricia's lover, could he?

Jeffrey Palmer was hosting a cocktail party the last night of the conference at his home in Big Sky. She was telling herself that it was just a coincidence that the man had the same initials as Tricia's lover when she turned the flyer over and froze.

In this photograph, Jeffrey Palmer Sr. stood next to his son, Jeffrey "JP" Palmer Jr. Her gaze dropped to the cutline under the photograph. Palmer and his son had received the governor's award for a nonprofit corporation they'd started called My Son's Dream, an animal sanctuary.

Her heart began to pound harder. My Son's Dream. MSD, Inc. The animal shelter where Tricia had volunteered. Mo remembered a baseball cap with MSD, Inc., on it that her sister had worn to a picnic last summer.

She looked closer at the photo of JP. According to his bio, he was just a year older than Mo. The closer she looked at him, she realized she recognized him. He'd changed considerably since college. He'd filled out, no longer wore thick dark-rimmed glasses, and his dull brown hair was now blond. In college, he'd gone by Junior.

Like Hope, Jeffrey junior had always been at the periphery of the group that she and Tricia had hung out with. So Hope would have known Jeffrey junior, but probably wouldn't have remembered him by JP any more than Mo had.

Was it possible this was Tricia's lover? It had to be.

It was his animal shelter that Tricia had worked at. She recalled Thomas complaining about how much time she spent down there. That had to be where they'd met, and hadn't Hope said that Tricia and her lover had shared a soft spot for animals?

Her heart was a drum in her chest. She recalled Hope saying that Tricia and her lover had joked about how much Thomas loved Jeffrey Palmer's seminars. The pieces of the puzzle fit.

"I've got you, JP," she said as she started the pickup. Now all she had to do was find out why her sister had wanted her to have the papers she'd left for her. They must have meant something to Tricia. Mo had a friend, Elroy, in finance.

Thirty minutes later, she dropped off the papers. Elroy promised to get back to her. She thought about waiting until she got Brick out on bail before she confronted JP, but that would be so not like her, she thought as she drove out to the animal shelter.

Chapter Fourteen

Brick sat on the cot in the cell, worrying about Mo. He knew she could take care of herself. But he also knew how emotionally involved she was in finding out the truth about her sister's death. That alone could put her off her usual guard. Not to mention, they'd already been shot at. He no longer doubted that they had been on the trail of a killer. A killer who now knew that Mo was after him.

At the rattle of his cell door, he looked up to find a guard standing there. "Phone call," the man said, not sounding happy about it as he unlocked the door. "Come on."

In a small office off the cell block, he took the phone that was handed to him. "Hello?" He was hoping to hear Mo's voice. But his gut told him there could be only one person calling. He closed his eyes at the sound of his father's voice.

"What the hell, Brick?"

He turned his back to the guard, keeping his voice down. "I was jumped in the alley by three cops. Believe me, I didn't start this."

Marshal Hud Savage sighed. "Maybe it's the best place for you right now."

"It's not." He glanced at the cop standing by the door. "Mo is out there trying to find her sister's murderer. I'm worried about her."

"I'm worried about *you*."

"Mo will get me out once I see a judge."

"Brick, if you're serious about keeping your job—"

"I'll take care of this." There were witnesses at the bar when Shane attacked Mo and he had hopes that the other two cops would tell the truth when push came to shove. But this wouldn't look good on his record if he couldn't convince a judge of his innocence.

Mo REALIZED THAT she would have never connected JP with the young man she remembered from college. Seeing this version of the man, she could understand how Tricia might have fallen for him. He had broad, well-developed shoulders and had apparently traded the glasses for contacts, and his face was ruggedly handsome, all sign of his bouts of acne long gone under his tan.

But the shyness was still there. Mo could see where Tricia would have found it charming. She watched him move through the crowd, greeting people as he went. Apparently the shelter was having a fund-raiser this evening. Mo thought of all the organizations father and son were involved in, including MSD, Inc. But it was the shelter that would have helped steal Tricia's heart.

When he reached her, she saw the sparkle of surprise in his blue eyes. She hadn't expected him to remember her. But then again, if he'd been having an affair with her sister...

"Maureen," he said and reached for her hand, cupping it in both of his large ones. "It is so good to see you. I didn't realize you were an animal lover."

"Not as much as my sister, Tricia, I'm sure."

His eyes narrowed slightly, but his smile remained in place. "Let's step into my office." She followed him down a thick-carpeted hallway lined with framed professional photographs of adorable animals.

Everything about this part of the shelter felt lavishly done so she wasn't surprised when he opened the door to his office. It had the same polished, rich look to it from the shine of the huge mahogany desk to the well-appointed other furnishings.

"We're having a little thank-you party for some of our donors, so I don't have much time to spare." He closed the door behind him. "Please have a seat," he said as he motioned to one of the chairs in front of the desk. He took his seat behind the desk. "Can I get you some coffee, water, champagne?"

"I'm good, thanks," she said as she sank into the soft leather. "It's been a long time." She considered him. "You've changed."

He chuckled. "Just on the outside. I'm still that shy, tongue-tied awkward guy I was in college."

She highly doubted that and said as much.

Leaning back, he seemed to study her. "I didn't think you ever knew who I was at college."

She knew that Tricia would have been impressed by these surroundings. JP, like his father, had made something out of himself and he was saving animals. It would have been a deadly combination.

"But my sister would have remembered you," she said. "When the two of you ran into each other here at the shelter."

His eyes lost some of the blue twinkle. "She told you about us?"

"No, *you* did. The heart you carved in the tree at the campground above Red Lodge. You used her maiden name initial. TM plus JP. Instead of *C* for her married name, Colton. You did know she was married, right?" She saw the answer in his expression. "Mortensen was the name you'd known her by in college, but I guess I don't have to tell you that."

"She didn't pay any more attention to me in college than you did, but we realized we knew some of the same people."

Was that bitterness she heard in his voice? "Is that why you decided to ruin her marriage and ultimately her life?"

He sat forward so abruptly it startled her. "I *loved* her. I still love her." His voice broke and tears flooded his eyes. "It just happened. Working here together, we fell in love. We didn't mean for it to happen."

She looked around his posh office for a moment. "Did your father know about you and Tricia?"

He sat back again. "Why would you ask that?"

She said nothing and waited, her gaze coming back to him.

Finally, he said, "My father wasn't happy about my falling in love with a married woman, no. But I didn't care and I told him as much. I was going to marry her and we were going to raise our son together."

"*Your* son?" She stared at him. "Joey was your son?"

"I don't know that he was mine biologically. It didn't matter. As far as I was concerned, he was ours no matter what."

"That's very noble," she said, unable to keep the sarcasm out of her voice.

"I told you. I loved her. I would have done anything for her. *Anything.*"

"Where did the two of you get together besides here?" she asked, having seen the inviting leather couch off to one side of the room.

He sighed. "Does it really matter?"

She narrowed her gaze on him. "It does to me."

"My father has a cabin outside of Red Lodge." She could just imagine what Jeffrey Palmer Sr.'s *cabin* was like. "Are these questions really necessary? Your sister is—"

"Dead. Yes, I know. When did Tricia break it off?" She waited and when he didn't answer, she said, "She did break it off, right? You must have been upset."

"Of course I was upset. She told me she was pregnant with Thomas's son. I knew she couldn't know that for sure. But it was clear she wanted Joey to be his. She was determined to make her marriage work as if she had to pay penitence for falling in love with me."

"But even after she broke it off, the two of you were still seeing each other," Mo said.

He looked away for a moment. "We couldn't stay away from each other. I wanted her to tell Thomas. I was sick of lying and hiding in the shadows. I wanted everyone to know how much I loved her."

"You must have been angry when she wouldn't."

JP groaned. "What are you getting at? You think me putting pressure on her drove her to suicide?"

"Do you think she killed herself?"

He went stone cold still, his eyes widening. "I... I was told that she did. Are you telling me she didn't?"

She didn't take her gaze from his face. "I think there's a chance someone murdered her."

JP looked as if he was in shock. He stood up, but then sat back down. His gaze ricocheted around the room before falling on her again. "She was *murdered*?" He seemed genuinely shocked.

"I don't have any proof. Yet."

He stared at her. "Then why would you say something like that?"

"Natalie. She told me it wasn't suicide."

"How would Natalie know?" When she said nothing, he continued as if trying to work it out himself. "Tricia didn't accidentally hang herself. Though Natalie certainly isn't the most reliable source." Mo realized that JP hadn't heard about Natalie's death. He'd just referred to her in the present. "But if Natalie is telling the truth…" His gaze locked with hers. "I always feared what Thomas would do when he found out."

"But he wasn't going to find out—not unless you told him," Mo said. She thought of what Natalie had written in the note. "After Joey was born, she refused to see you again, didn't she? Natalie witnessed your argument."

Mo watched his expression sour. She could see the answer in the hard glint of his blue eyes. He tapped his freshly manicured nails on the edge of the desk for a moment before balling his hands into fists. She could see him fighting to get control again.

"Tricia was a mess. She blamed herself for Joey's medical problems. She thought it was karma, payback. I tried to reason with her… We were so right for each other. We loved each other. We belonged together." He looked down, saw his tightly fisted hands and quickly relaxed them.

Mo thought of how stubborn her sister could be. "I take it she wouldn't listen to reason?"

He scoffed. "She didn't want to break Thomas's heart. My heart was another story." His hands had fisted again and his blue eyes had gone dark. He met her gaze, and in that moment she saw a man capable of murder.

Chapter Fifteen

Back in downtown Billings, Mo went to work to free Brick. She canvassed the neighborhood near the coffee shop until she found what she was looking for—a surveillance camera that had caught everything that happened in the alley.

"I'd prefer to handle this in-house," the chief of police told her after he'd watched the surveillance video she'd copied to her phone. He'd watched it twice before swearing and handing her phone back. She knew this wasn't the first time there had been complaints against Shane Danby. "Email me that," he said gruffly. "We should talk about you coming back to work."

Mo got to her feet. "I appreciate everything you've done for me—"

"I'm not accepting your resignation if that's what you're about to say. Mo, I know how hard all this has been on you. You need time, so take as much as you want. Please, don't make a hasty decision."

She nodded. "Thank you. Can you release Deputy Marshal Brick Savage for me?"

He groaned. "What the hell was Shane thinking? A deputy marshal whose father is the marshal at Big Sky?" Shaking his head, he picked up the phone and called down. Hanging up, he turned to her again. "He's all yours."

She smiled at that.

"By the way, I'm not sure what the two of you are up to…" He waited as if he'd hoped she would fill in the blanks.

"We're just friends enjoying a Montana summer together."

Her boss groused. "Have it your way."

Downstairs, Mo was waiting as Brick was brought out. She grimaced at his swollen black eye, the bandaged cut on his temple, a split lip and the bruise on his cheek. She could tell from the way he was moving that his ribs were bruised. She hoped she didn't run into Shane in a dark alley because she knew it would take a half-dozen men to pull her off him.

Not wanting Brick to see how shocked she was by his injuries or how furious it made her, she joked, "We really have to quit meeting like this."

He smiled even with his cut lip. "Good to see you, too."

"This is all my fault," she said. "If I hadn't got into it with Shane—"

"Nothing about this is your fault. He's a bad cop. You already knew he was dangerous and he's worse when he has two friends with him."

"Well, all charges against you have been dropped. A surveillance camera on one of the businesses across from the alley caught it all. Shane will be lucky to keep his job, and the other two…" She shook her head. "Fools that they are, hopefully they'll wise up and put some distance between themselves and Shane. But I have good news."

"Sounds like you already gave me the good news," he said as she handed him his keys.

"I found JP," she said.

"You FOUND HIM?" Brick grinned at her as they walked out of the police station. She just kept amazing him. He couldn't believe how glad he was to see her—and not just because she'd gotten him out of jail. The moment he'd spotted her coming toward him, he'd felt his pulse kick up. When she smiled at him… What was it about this woman? She was often prickly as a cactus, annoyingly stubborn and impossible to reason with much of the time. But just the thought of this being over and never seeing her again…

He tried to concentrate on what she was telling him.

As she finished filling him in on her meeting with JP at the animal shelter, he felt sick. While he was behind bars, she'd risked her life. "You shouldn't have gone there alone. If there is even a chance that he's responsible for your sister's death—"

She laughed at that as they exited the building. "You keep forgetting that I'm a cop. I can take care of myself. Protecting me, well, that's not why I need you."

He felt heat rush to his veins and smiled as he stopped to face her. "You need me?" He locked eyes with her for a few breathless moments.

She laughed. "You're growing on me, okay?"

He'd been fighting the urge to take her in his arms and kiss her for too long. He pulled her to him, his mouth dropping to hers. She melted into him as if she'd been made to fit there. Her lips parted as he pulled her closer, deepening the kiss and completely forgetting where they were until he heard cheering and clapping.

They pulled apart as a group of cops came out of the police station and headed for his pickup.

He opened her passenger-side door for her before he walked stiffly around to climb behind the wheel. When he looked over at Mo, he saw that her cheeks were flushed. "About the kiss—"

She cut him off. "I liked it, okay? Let's leave it at that for now."

He couldn't help his grin as he punched the key into the ignition. "So," he said, clearing his throat. "Do you think JP might be responsible for your sister's death?" Brick heard her settle into her side of the pickup cab. He wondered if her heart was pounding as hard as his was.

"I don't know. I think JP's life of privilege and his unrequited love for my sister makes him capable of murder. I want to talk to his father. The elder Jeffrey Palmer was not happy about the situation. I'm wondering what he might have done about it."

Her cell phone rang. She checked to see who it was and quickly picked up. "Elroy, tell me you made sense of those papers I gave you." She listened, nodding, then smiling over at Brick. "If you're sure that's what needs to be done. Just keep a copy of them for…insurance." She chuckled. "No, I don't trust anyone. And thanks again." As she disconnected, she looked like the cat who'd eaten the canary. "We definitely should talk to Jeffrey Palmer Sr."

"You aren't going to tell me?"

She merely smiled. "Let's see what Jeffrey says first."

He liked that there was no question about them not working together anymore. They were in it to the end. He just didn't like thinking about it ending.

"Jeffrey Palmer Sr. has a lodge near Lone Peak Mountain outside of Big Sky. I thought we could pay him a surprise visit."

Brick smiled over at her as he started the pickup. "Lucky me, I know the way."

"THE TRACKING DEVICE isn't working."

The PI sat up in bed, blinking as he tried to wake up. He'd been on an all-night surveillance trying to get the goods on a cheating husband and had just gotten to sleep when his cell phone had rung.

He started to ask, "Who is this?" but then he knew. He'd thought it was the last he'd be hearing from this client. "I put it on the deputy's truck."

"Well, you must have not gotten it right because I show the truck is on its way to the Midwest."

Jim groaned. "He must have discovered it." That could mean only one thing. "He must have caught you following him." Silence. He closed his eyes, cursing silently. This is why he hated to have clients take over the surveillance. They thought they could do this, but often learned the hard way that it wasn't that easy. Now his client had blown it.

"What can we do now?"

He opened his eyes, having been here before. "I might be able to find them but it will take time and money."

"Find them. I don't care what it costs."

The PI smiled. This was why he always put a second tracking device on the vehicle that only he could access on his phone. He knew it wouldn't be found because the first device was where it couldn't be missed. Once they found the first one, they never looked for a second.

"I'll do what I can." He hung up and reached for his phone to check the device. It appeared the deputy was headed home to Big Sky. Turning off the phone, Jim lay back down and closed his eyes. He would let the client stew for at least a few hours before he called to inform him of the cost before he told him where he could find the deputy.

A THUNDERSTORM MOVED across the tops of the mountains, smothering the sunlight and throwing the canyon in deep shadow as they neared Big Sky.

"I don't know about you, but I'm hungry," Brick said. He'd had breakfast in jail, but hadn't eaten since.

"I'm starved," Mo said and glanced around, surprised they were almost back to Big Sky. She realized she must have fallen asleep—and not had a nightmare. That alone surprised her almost as much as the earlier kiss. Oh, she'd known that Brick was going to kiss her. She'd been expecting it for some time.

What had come as a shock were the emotions the kiss had evoked. Not just desire. The deputy was drop-dead sexy. But the close feeling she'd felt. The safe, protected...loving feeling that had filled her. Was that why she hadn't had the nightmare?

That she'd even come close to thinking the *L* word scared her. She knew his reputation and she wasn't about to fall for him. Maybe she hadn't had the nightmare because she knew she was close to getting justice for her sister—if not for Joey.

"I know a great place to eat," Brick said and pulled out his phone. "I'll get us a reservation."

"Reservation?" She looked down at what she was wearing. "I'm not dressed for somewhere fancy."

"Trust me, you're dressed perfectly for this place." He grinned at her and even the approaching thunderstorm couldn't dampen the moment.

She smiled back at him, enjoying his enthusiasm. How easy it would be to fall for this man. She shook her head at that stray thought and realized the time. It was almost five in the afternoon. Whatever restaurant he called must have just opened for the evening.

"Great, we'll be there in about twenty minutes," he said into the phone and disconnected. "The special tonight is roast beef with mashed potatoes, freshly picked carrots in a butter sauce and chocolate cake for dessert."

She groaned. "You are making my mouth water."

"And what a mouth it is."

She felt heat rush to her cheeks and looked away, telling herself not to get caught up in his flirting. At the same time, she was glad to have Brick distracting her. For so long her mind had been dominated by getting justice. She was looking forward to a meal with this man. She'd actually missed him while he was locked up in jail—not that she'd admit it to him, she thought with a smile.

As he passed the exit to Big Sky, she wondered where this restaurant was that he was taking her to. A few miles later, he turned off the highway. The pickup bounced along the dirt road, over a bridge spanning the Gallatin River, and came to a stop in front of a large two-story ranch house. She saw barns and outbuildings, corrals and horses. Up on the mountain was a series of small cabins.

"Brick?" she asked as she took in the house again. This didn't look like a restaurant. As the front door opened and an older woman stepped out wearing an apron, Mo saw the resemblance immediately. "Is that your mother?"

"Best cook in four counties," he said, smiling as he got out of the pickup and came around to her side to open the door for her as if this was a date. She realized that to Brick, it was. Worse, he'd taken her home to meet his mother? And if that patrol car parked on the other side of the ranch pickup was any indication, it wasn't just his mother.

Mo cursed him under her breath. She was having dinner with the marshal and his wife? What had Brick been thinking?

Chapter Sixteen

"Mom, this is Mo," Brick said and quickly added, "Maureen Mortensen."

Dana smiled and reached for Mo's hand. "When my son called and asked about bringing a guest for dinner, I was delighted. I don't see enough of him and it is always wonderful to meet a friend of his."

Mo started to correct her about their relationship, but Brick cut her off as he put his arm around her and said, "I was just telling Mo that my mother is the best cook in four counties."

"Oh, you quit that," Dana said, letting go of Mo's hand to swat playfully at him. She frowned as she took in his injuries, but didn't say anything. No doubt she'd already heard he'd been in jail. "In case you haven't noticed, my son tends to exaggerate."

"I've noticed," Mo said and turned to gaze up at him, her blue eyes hot as a laser. "He's just full of surprises."

His mother cocked her head at him as if wondering about his relationship with this woman, but she was smiling as she ushered them both inside. "Your father should be here shortly. He's checking the new foal. I thought it would be nice to just have dinner with the four of us."

"Where's Angus and Jinx?" he asked as they entered the farmhouse with its wood floors, Native American rugs and antlers on the walls. The place never changed and that was what he loved about it. Coming here always felt like home. The house was cool even on the hot summer evening and rich with the scent of roast beef cooking in the kitchen.

"Your brother has Jinx up on the mountain, helping him at the house," Dana said and turned to Mo. "Angus and his wife are building a home on the ranch. I assume you haven't met either of them yet?" She looked to her son.

He shook his head. "We've been busy."

"So I've heard."

"Angus is my twin brother. I'm the charming one," Brick said. "I'm also the handsome one."

"Don't believe anything Brick says," his mother chided. "He just can't help himself." At the sound of the front door opening, she insisted they have a seat in the dining room while she saw to his father.

Brick knew what that meant. The marshal was unaware of their dinner guests.

"This was a very bad idea," Mo said under her breath as he steered her toward the huge table that took up most of the equally huge dining room.

"It's fine, trust me."

"There you go again thinking I'm going to trust you." She stopped short of the table and turned to face him. "And why are you letting your mother think that we're…"

"Lovers?"

Her eyes flared even hotter. "Involved."

"We *are* involved. And last night we slept together."

He grinned to show that he was joking. "What does it matter what she thinks about our relationship?"

"It's not honest. And I like her. I don't want to lie to her."

He cocked an eyebrow at her. "I had no idea you were so straight-laced," he said, leaning close to whisper the words. "I'm beginning to wonder just about your relationships with those men you said you thought you had fallen in love with before."

"If you're asking what I think you are…" She gave him a shove. Brick chuckled, seeing her face redden charmingly before he realized they were no longer alone.

"Marshal," Mo said.

Brick turned to face his frowning father. "I guess Mom warned you that you have dinner guests."

"Everyone, please sit," his mother said, rushing into the room. "Brick's been bragging up my cooking, so I'd better get that roast out before it's overdone."

"Let me help you," Mo said and left Brick alone with his father, which he realized was her plan.

"I hate to even ask," Hud said.

"Then don't. I promised Mo a good meal with lively conversation."

His father harrumphed at that. "Not from me."

"Never from you," Brick said and laughed.

As the marshal moved toward his seat at the head of the table, he placed a hand on his son's shoulder and gave it a squeeze. "Glad to see you're still alive and not in jail."

"Me, too," he admitted as he hurried to help his mother with the huge platter of roast beef. She always cooked as if for an army so he'd known there would be plenty. Mo brought out bowls of towering fluffy mashed potatoes and freshly snapped and cooked green beans from his mother's garden as well as the buttered carrots.

As Brick pulled out a chair for Mo to sit, his mother ran back into the kitchen for the homemade rolls still warm from the oven, along with butter and honey.

"Brick, if you would pour the iced tea," she said as she took her seat on her husband's right. She always sat close to the kitchen in case anyone needed anything. He knew that one of the reasons she stayed in such good shape was that she kept so busy taking care of all of them.

And yet as the food was passed around and his mother kept the conversation going, he was reminded that both of his parents were at the age where they had started to slow down. He was glad that he'd come home to stay and could help out more.

"Interesting how you two met," his mother was saying.

"I sprung her from jail," Brick said. "Will make a fun story to tell our children."

Mo KICKED HIM under the table and said, "He is such a kidder, isn't he?"

"Isn't he though?" the marshal agreed, joining the conversation for the first time. "Are you about done with your…investigation?"

"We're getting it narrowed down," Brick said. "Tonight we're going to a cocktail party up on the mountain. Jeffrey Palmer Sr. is putting it on. Are you familiar with him?" he asked his father.

"Only by reputation."

Mo noticed that this part of the conversation had definitely piqued the marshal's interest, though.

"He's a very powerful man," the marshal said. "I hope—"

"That we'll be well behaved?" Brick said and laughed. "Always."

"Brick," Dana began, but was cut off.

"I've had the charges against Mo dropped," Hud to his son. "I believe the charges against you in Billings have also been dropped? I was hoping that would be the last of your combined jail times."

"Our hope, as well," Brick agreed.

Mo saw that the marshal's gaze was on her. "You still believe that your sister was murdered?"

She nodded, sorry that the conversation had taken this turn. She was enjoying the wonderful meal and pleasant conversation with Dana. She had liked her at once. What a warm, loving woman. No wonder Brick was the man he was.

"And where does Jeffrey Palmer fit into this?" the marshal asked.

"His son, JP, was having an affair with my sister," Mo said.

Hud sighed. "He's a suspect, but his father…?"

"His father knew about the relationship and disapproved," Mo said. "If he wanted my sister out of his son's life badly enough…" She didn't add what Elroy suspected about the financial papers Tricia had left for her. He was having a friend look at them and would get back to her.

The marshal leaned back in his chair, pushing his nearly empty plate away. "You two are scaring me. If you really believe either of these men is capable of murder..."

"We'll be careful," Brick said.

His mother rose to take their plates, announcing that there was chocolate cake for desert. Mo could see how nervous she was with this kind of talk. After all the years her husband had been in law enforcement, Mo would have thought that she'd gotten use to it. She got up to help with the cake.

"It's a cocktail party," Mo said, trying to relieve her concerns as she came into the kitchen. "There will be lots of people there. I'm sure there won't be any trouble."

Dana turned to look at her. "You know that I'm not delighted with Brick joining the marshal's department."

Mo nodded, seeing that she also wouldn't be delighted with having another cop in the family. "Brick and I aren't...in a romantic relationship."

The ranch woman smiled at her, the skin around her eyes crinkling with humor. "I was going to say that I've accepted that Brick wants to follow the path his father took. I'll never get used to the discussions we've had around my dining room table, but I've also never seen Brick happier. Thank you." Dana reached for her hand and squeezed it. "We'd better get this cake out there and save my son from his father's interrogation."

Mo wanted to tell her that she wasn't responsible for Brick's happiness, but before she could, the woman pushed four dessert plates into her hands. Dana picked up the most beautiful chocolate layer cake Mo thought she'd ever seen before leading the way back into the dining room.

It wasn't until after dessert that Mo found herself alone with the marshal. She felt she had to say something into the heavy silence that had fallen over the room in Brick's and his mother's absence.

"I'm sure you're angry at me for getting your son involved in this," she said and waited.

Hud studied her openly for a moment, then shook his head. "Brick is his own man. He's always been determined to finish what he started. What worries me is that he's never brought a woman home. That he brought you home for one of his mother's meals... He's falling for you." He must have seen her surprise. "He jokes around, yes, but I know my son. All I ask is that you not break his heart since this is a first for him."

Their conversation ended abruptly as Brick and his mother returned from helping his mother with the dishes, something he'd insisted on. Clearly the two had been in silent alliance.

Mo had trouble following the rest of the conversation before she and Brick left for the cocktail party at Jeffrey Palmer Sr.'s. She kept thinking about what the marshal had said and wanting to deny—even to herself—how close she and Brick had gotten.

THE PI MADE the call earlier than he'd planned when another case took precedence. After the client wired him the extra fee, he said, "She returned to Big Sky." He held the phone away from his ear as his client let out a thunderbolt of curses.

"Why would she do that?"

Jim had to assume it was a rhetorical question since he didn't know the woman.

"Is she still with that deputy?"

"I can only suppose so. I just know that they returned to Big Sky. If you want more information—"

"I'll get it myself," the client snapped and disconnected.

The PI also disconnected and checked to see where the pickup was now. It appeared to be on the opposite side of the river from the town of Big Sky. He looked closer. It appeared to be at a ranch of some sort.

As he put away his cell phone, he realized that he knew where the deputy's pickup was, but he couldn't be sure that the female was still with him.

He shook his head as if to clear his thoughts. The client was determined to take it from here. He considered what he'd been hired to do over the past few days and tried to make sense of it before he stopped himself.

He often didn't understand why people did what they did. In all the years he'd been a private investigator, he'd found they often did the one thing they shouldn't because it was going to get them into trouble. But they still did it.

He had a feeling his client was about to do something that he would regret.

Jim was just glad he'd gotten his final payment before the fool either ended up dead or in jail. But he had to wonder why the man was so obsessed with the woman cop.

Chapter Seventeen

Jeffrey Sr. ushered them into his den, closing the door behind him before striding around to sit behind his desk. "I was surprised to hear that the two cops who crashed my cocktail party now want to speak to me in my office. Deputy Marshal Brick Savage and Homicide Detective Mo Mortensen?" He pretended to tip his hat to them each. "To what do I owe this honor since one of you is suspended and the other is on inactive duty, as I understand it?" Mo thought it interesting that the man had taken the time to check on both of them first. "So can I assume this isn't a professional visit?"

"Assume whatever you like," she said as she took a seat even though he hadn't offered her one. Brick remained standing next to her chair. "Your son was having an affair with my married sister."

The senior Jeffrey showed no reaction to her statement. She reached out and stroked the wings on the large sculpture of an eagle that graced his desk.

"I'm sure you were aware they were using your residence outside of Red Lodge for their…clandestine rendezvous." To her surprise, she saw that he hadn't been aware of that. His face clouded, eyes darkening, but he quickly recovered.

"If you're asking if I sanctioned such a…relationship, I did not."

"I believe it was at your Red Lodge home that Tricia learned something she shouldn't have. Something about one of your nonprofits that you didn't want the public to know." Still no response. "Knowing Tricia, she would have taken her concerns directly to you. I would imagine you alleviated her fears, but you couldn't trust that she might say something, so you went to her house that day. You knew Thomas wasn't there because he was at work. You're a big strong man. It wouldn't have taken much to see that she never talked. Although Tricia would have fought you. I suspect you drugged her, but that will come out once toxicology tests are run."

"Wasn't her body cremated?"

That this man knew that chilled her to the bone. "I guess you haven't heard. A scientist found a way to get evidence from a cremated body. I've turned Tricia's remains over to Forensics."

Did Jeffrey look paler? He wiped a spot on his upper lip that had turned shiny.

"The police had no reason not to believe it was a suicide after Tricia lost her baby—and maybe a hint that her marriage was on the rocks," Mo said. "How am I doing so far?"

"It's your tale," the man said, looking bored.

"Basically, you killed two birds with one stone. You weren't happy about your son and Tricia's relationship, especially with a baby involved. So that took care of that as well as making sure your secret never came out."

Jeffrey chuckled. "I'm much smarter than I thought since apparently I also got away with it because all of this is simply conjecture. If you had any proof, the *real* police would be here, right?"

"I can't prove that you killed her, but you definitely had motive."

Jeffrey sighed. "I really have no idea what you're talking about. What is it you want from me? I'm a busy man and my guests are waiting."

Mo pushed to her feet. "Nothing. I believe I'll have what I've come for soon. Justice for my sister."

She started to turn to leave but stopped. "By the way, those incriminating papers Tricia found in your study at the Red Lodge cabin? She made copies. She loved dogs and when she realized what you were using the nonprofit facility to do, she planned to stop you. But she must have told you that." She hesitated for a couple of beats. "Or maybe she only told your son. That kind of information could destroy you and JP if he knew about it. But I'm sure he denied everything to her— unless she didn't believe him. Oh, and the evidence? I put it somewhere safe with instructions that if anything should happen to me or anyone around me, it would be released to the FBI and the media—and not just locally."

With that she headed for the door. Behind her, she heard Jeffrey pick up the eagle sculpture from his desk. It shattered just feet from them as she and Brick walked out.

ONCE OUT IN the hallway, Brick swore as he spotted his father moving through the crowd. "My father is here. I need to see why—other than worrying about us."

"I could use some fresh air," Mo said. "I'm going to step out on the patio. Holler if you need me."

He chuckled at that. He would always need her, he

thought, and quickly stepped away before he was fool enough to say it.

"Tell me you didn't follow us," Brick said as he stepped up behind his father.

The marshal turned, pretending surprise to see his son there. "I just came for the champagne."

Brick laughed. "Sure you did. Seriously," he said, lowering his voice. "What are you doing here?"

"It has nothing to do with you."

"Right."

"But I do wish that you and Mo would get out of here soon," his father said, glancing around.

Brick felt the hair prickle on the back of his neck. "You're here for a bust? *And arrest?* Is it—"

The marshal shot him a look that made him swallow back the words. He thought about what Mo had said to Jeffrey Sr. Did she really have some kind of evidence on him that would be worth killing to keep secret? Or had she been bluffing? The woman could craft a lie faster than anyone he'd ever met and yet...

He met his father's gaze. "I'll find Mo and we'll go."

AFTER BRICK LEFT to talk to his father, Mo had started for the doors out to the patio when she'd heard a voice directly behind her. She'd instantly tensed as she'd recognized it.

"We should step out on the patio." JP had placed his hand in the center of her back, his touch gentle but insistent.

Mo didn't put up a fight as he'd pushed open the patio doors and they exited the cocktail party. The patio was large, hanging over the side of the mountain, and the view was spectacular. The patio was also empty since the breeze was a reminder that the mountains around them were still snowcapped. Or maybe she felt the chill because she suddenly found herself alone on the edge of a precipice with a man who very possibly was a killer.

Jeffrey steered her to the edge, as far from the party as possible. "What are you doing here?" he demanded. He was dressed in formal attire and couldn't have been more handsome and distinguished. Her heart ached at the thought that if Tricia had seen him like this, she would have fallen instantly in love with him. He would have been everything she didn't have in her life with Thomas, everything she'd apparently yearned for and maybe hadn't even realized it.

Unlike Mo, her sister wouldn't have seen beyond the veneer and the money and prestige. "I wanted to talk to your father."

He frowned. "Why?"

"To tell him that I knew what was going on at your nonprofit animal shelter and probably all you and your father's other businesses—and so did Tricia."

"What are you talking about?"

Did he really not know? No, Tricia would have told him, wouldn't she? She would have given him a chance to explain.

"I'm talking about the reason the woman you say you loved is dead."

He shook his head, looking confused. "You think it has something to do with the shelter?" He raked a hand through his blond hair. "You can't possibly think that I... I loved her," he said with both conviction and what sounded like pain. "I would have done anything for her. Anything."

"You said that before. What *did* you do for her?" Mo asked as she hugged herself against the night chill and the knowledge that she was taking a chance with her life being here with him. She glanced toward the house. She doubted anyone but Brick knew she was coming out here.

"What are you trying to accuse me of?" he demanded, some of that anger she'd seen before surfacing.

"You said she wouldn't leave Thomas, or was it the baby that was the problem?"

He stared at her as if in disbelief.

"What happened between you and Tricia at the end?"

He shook his head. "I told you. She broke it off."

"And you never saw her again. You never tried to change her mind. You never went by her house."

His gaze narrowed as he settled it on her again. "The nanny saw us, didn't she?" He let out a bitter chuckle. "I thought at least she would have told you or Thomas what she'd overheard, but I guess she was busy with her own…problems."

"I know you were angry, much as you are right now."

He seemed to catch himself and draw back, pulling in his ire as he dropped his voice again. "She did break it off, but then she changed her mind. We were going to raise Joey together. She was going to tell Thomas but then Joey was killed, Natalie was arrested…"

"She never told Thomas."

Jeffrey shook his head. "You know Tricia. She was devastated by all of it, but Thomas was inconsolable. She couldn't do it. She begged me to give her time."

"And when you didn't—"

"Why are you so determined to make me the villain?" he demanded. "I told her she could have all the time she needed. I was a mess, too. I'd been looking forward to us being a family. With Joey gone..." He looked away. "She wasn't sure she wanted to risk having another child. I told her we could adopt. We were planning a future together. Why would I kill her?"

Mo studied him in the faint light coming from the house and realized that he at least believed every word of it. And she believed that he'd loved Tricia as she saw his eyes fill. He hastily wiped at them as the glass doors into the house opened and his father called his name.

"I have to go," he said and cleared his throat. His watery gaze met hers. "I loved her. If I'd had any idea that she might..." He shook his head, reached for her hand and squeezed it. "I miss her so much."

With that, he walked back toward the house and his waiting father.

Mo stood at the edge of the patio, looking out across the mountaintops into the darkness beyond. Lost in her thoughts, she started when she felt a hand on her arm and spun around to find Brick.

"We need to get out of here."

ON THE WAY off the mountain, Mo told Brick what Elroy had told her.

"Money laundering?" He shook his head. "And your sister knew?"

"Apparently. Why else would she copy the financial records? Tricia was a whiz at math and loved all that stuff, while just the thought makes my head hurt. She either recognized what was going on or at least suspected."

"Your theory is that she told JP?" He heard Mo hesitate.

"She was in love with JP. I believe she found the papers at his father's home outside of Red Lodge. I think she went to the old man."

He shot her a look. "Then he killed her to keep her from coming forward?"

"Also from telling his son. According to the lecture series flyer that Quinn gave me that day, the animal shelter was something he did for his son. If JP knew how it was really being used…"

Brick shook his head. "JP has to know. Whoever came by Tricia's house that day was someone she knew and trusted. Otherwise she wouldn't have opened the door to him." He saw that Mo hadn't wanted to believe it.

She put her face in her hands for a moment. "How could a man who professed his undying love for her kill her?"

"You're a homicide detective. You know. She'd hurt him. He could have lied about this rosy future the two of them had planned. It could be a case of *if I can't have her, neither will Thomas*."

"That isn't love," she said, removing her hands to look over at him.

"No. But love and hate can be two sides of the same coin…"

"I guess I've never been in love."

He considered her for a moment as he drove down from the mountain into Meadow Village. "Never, huh? Maybe we have that in common."

She didn't look at him and asked, "Where are we going?"

He hadn't really known where he was headed. After everything she'd told him, he had to assume that Tricia wasn't the only one who'd suspected something was going on with Jeffrey Palmer's nonprofit businesses. The self-made man could be in handcuffs by now—and so could his son. "I hadn't thought—"

"Let's go to your apartment."

"To my apartment?" He must have misheard her. "Are you sure about that?" She shot him a look. He held up one hand in surrender. "My apartment it is."

He could feel her gaze on him. As he pulled into the parking spot behind his apartment, he asked, "Are you sure about this?"

She chuckled. "It's the only thing I've been sure about for a very long time."

Brick met her gaze in the glow of a streetlamp up the block. "You know my reputation. I don't want to hurt you."

Mo smiled. "You won't because whether you know it or not, you're as crazy about me as I am about you."

He laughed. "You think?"

"I *know.*" Her words came out a whisper, as light as a caress.

He studied her in the dim light, realizing that he was a captive to everything about her—and had been since the moment he broke her out of jail. "Are you ever unsure about anything?"

"*Everything*, but this." She leaned toward him, cupping his face in her hands, and kissed him gently on the lips.

He drew her to him, buried his face in her hair and whispered, "Do you know how badly I want you?"

"As much as I want you," she whispered as she leaned

her head back to let him trail kisses down her throat. He felt her shudder, his desire spiking, as his kisses reached the rise of her breasts. He could see her hard nipples through her bra and the fabric of her blouse.

"You are so dang sexy. I want to take you right here."

"What's stopping you?" she asked, her voice cracking with emotion.

He chuckled. "Bucket seats," he said and drew back to look into those blue eyes of hers. He took a breath, suddenly terrified. He didn't just want this woman. He *wanted* this woman, all of her, for keeps. He'd never felt like this and it scared the hell out of him.

"You ready to see my apartment?" he asked. "It's not much to look at."

"I doubt we'll be looking at the decor." She reached to open her door.

He caught her before she could get out, and opened his mouth to say what? He'd never know because she put a finger over his lips and shook her head.

A low, seductive chuckle rose from her lips. "We're acting as if this is the scariest thing we'll ever do. It just might be because I suspect there's no coming back from it." With that, she exited the pickup.

Brick sat for just a moment before he opened his door and followed her. He actually fumbled opening the door. He felt tongue-tied and uncertain as if this was his first time. In so many ways, it was.

He held the apartment door open and Mo stepped through. The moment he entered and closed the door behind him, she turned to him and, stepping forward, she began to slowly unbutton his shirt. She looked up at him with those big blue eyes and he was overcome with a longing for something he'd never experienced before. He lowered his mouth to hers and knew he was lost.

Mo lay in Brick's arms. They'd finally made it to the bed. Earlier, the moment the door had closed, they were tearing at each other's clothing. They had been headed here for some time, she knew, but she hadn't expected the kind of passion they'd inspired—and neither had Brick, it seemed from the dazed look on his face.

After their crazed lovemaking, they'd lain on the floor, unable not to laugh as they stared up at the ceiling and tried to catch their breaths. After a few minutes, they looked over at each other. She remembered looking into those deep blue eyes of his and feeling... love and desire, hotter than a Fourth of July firecracker.

They'd made love again, slower this time, but with no less passion.

It was crazy, no doubt about it. They hadn't known each other but for a few days. Mo thought of her sister. Tricia would have said that they didn't know each other, that they needed to take some time, that they didn't even know where this was headed.

But then again, Mo thought, maybe her sister wouldn't have said any of those things. Tricia had fallen in love with a man who wasn't her husband. That she could do something like that given how straight-laced she was... Well, Mo smiled to herself. Maybe Tricia would have understood, maybe even approved since the only two people who could get hurt were Mo and Brick.

Mo started at the pounding on the door. She shot a look at Brick. "Your father?"

He shrugged and got up from the bed to pull on his jeans. She grabbed what she could find of her clothing and hurried into the bathroom and closed the door. She could hear voices. The marshal?

She was dressed pretty much by the time Brick tapped on the door.

"There's someone who needs to see you," he said.

She opened the door and looked out. Her brother-in-law, Thomas, stood just inside the door—which was almost in the middle of the tiny studio apartment.

"Thomas?" she asked, stepping from the bathroom. Out of the corner of her eye, she saw Brick pull on a shirt. They were both barefoot and she hadn't been able to find her bra. Her body still tingled from their lovemaking and she knew her cheeks had to be flushed. "What are you doing here?" she asked, catching the tumble of covers on the unmade bed out of the corner of her eye.

"I have to talk to you," he said, a muscle jumping in his jaw as he looked from her to Brick. "I had a feeling you'd be here." He didn't sound approving, which instantly got her hackles up.

"We should step outside." She moved toward him even as he glanced pointedly at her bare feet. "This won't take long," she said to both him and Brick. Once out on the outdoor second-story landing, she demanded to know what he wanted.

As if seeing her ire, he said, "I'm sorry, but I had to talk to you. I came up after Jeffrey called me, but when I got there, he and JP were being arrested. Do you have any idea what is going on? Does it have something to do with Tricia's death?"

His words stopped her cold. Did he know about Tricia and JP? "Why would you ask that?"

"Because she worked at that animal shelter they owned."

"Remember, I was suspended. I don't know what charges are being brought against them," she said truthfully.

"It's not just that," Thomas said. "I found something in Tricia's closet, hidden in the back."

"Why were you digging in—"

"It's a box with a note on top that says I am to give it to you."

She took a breath and let it out slowly. "Did you look inside?" Of course he would look. Any normal person would.

"There were some papers in a manila envelope. I couldn't make heads or tails out of them."

Mo nodded. "She left some other ones for me, as well. You don't need to worry about it. I'm taking care of it." She started to turn back to the door inside. The night air was chilly. Brick's warm arms called to her. She hadn't let herself admit it, but she felt safe with him. Safe and protected in a way that didn't take away her own strength, her own ability to take care of herself.

"It wasn't just paper," Thomas said. "There was also a key to what appears to be bank security box in the bottom of the envelope. I wasn't able to open the box at the bank, but I thought with your police connection..."

She stopped midstep. A safety deposit key? Maybe Tricia had left something even more important. Mo still wanted a letter or a note from her sister. She knew Thomas did, as well.

"Give it to me and I'll see what I can do," she said, holding out her hand.

"I don't have it. I locked it up in my desk at work

until I saw you. I didn't expect to find you here in Big Sky or I would have brought it."

She studied him in the faint starlight. "Why are you here if you hadn't known I was?"

"Jeffrey. He called to say he needed to see me."

"About what?"

"He wouldn't say. I just assumed it had something to do with one of his seminars. He had approached me about working for him if I ever thought about leaving my pharmaceutical job."

This surprised her. "Were you thinking of leaving it to work for him?"

Thomas let out a laugh. "Not now that he's been arrested. Listen, I'll let you get back to…" He waved a hand toward the apartment door. "I'm helping lock up Jeffrey's house after the FBI are finished."

"I didn't realize you and Jeffrey were that close." She could tell the question irritated him.

"It's not just me. There's a group of us who have volunteered to help. I'm sure he'll be out within hours once he calls his lawyer." Mo wasn't so sure about that, but she kept her thoughts to herself. "I plan to drive back to Billings tomorrow afternoon," he was saying. "If you're back by then, why don't you stop by my office?"

"Tomorrow's a Sunday. You normally don't work—"

"I like working on the weekends. It gives me something to keep my mind off everything." He must have seen her hesitation. "Or you can wait until Monday or whenever to get the key. Up to you."

He had to know how anxious she was to find out what Tricia had left for them. "I'll drive over tomorrow. I'll call when I get to town." In the meantime, she wanted to spend the rest of this night with Brick.

BRICK'S CELL PHONE brought him swimming up from the wonder of deep, nightmare-less sleep. For a moment, he couldn't find his phone, he was so wrapped up in Mo's warm body. His hand snaked out. He felt around on the table beside the bed and finally found it by the fourth ring. "Hello?" His voice was rough with sleep and the remnants of a night of lovemaking.

"Brick?"

His mother's voice brought him fully awake. "Mom?" Through a crack in the curtains he could see daylight just breaking behind the mountains. He untangled himself from Mo to sit up. She sat up as well, concern in her expression as she turned on the night-light. "What's wrong?"

"It's your father," his mother's voice broke. "He's had a heart attack. I'm at the hospital with him." The words hit him like thrown stones. "Your uncle Jordan is here with me. We're waiting to hear word on his condition. The rest of the family is on the way."

"Mom, is he…" Brick realized he couldn't say the words. But she wasn't listening. He could hear voices in the background. He felt his heart drop. What was happening? "Mom? Mom?"

"The doctor says they're flying him down to Bozeman to the ICU. I have to go. You can meet us there."

Brick disconnected and looked at Mo.

"I HEARD," MO SAID quickly, squeezing his arm. "Go."

He turned to pull her into a hug for a long moment before he released her and swung his legs over the side of the bed. "Come with me?"

"Brick, I'm the last person your father would want to see—let alone right after a heart attack."

"You know that's not true," he said as he pulled on his jeans and looked around for his boots.

"I'll follow you to the hospital for an update. Then I have to go to Billings. Until I have those papers and that key in my hand…" When she'd come back into the apartment last night, she'd told him everything Thomas had said. He'd insisted that the two of them would go to Billings first thing this morning.

"I know," he said, turning to look at her. "I just don't like you going alone. Even with the Jeffrey Palmers under arrest, they can still get word out to their…associates. You're in danger if they fear the evidence your sister found is more damning than what the feds already have."

She shuddered, well aware of how powerful the men were—and what kind of friends they must have made in the money laundering business. Also, she didn't want Thomas figuring out a way to get into the box without her. She had a bad feeling that she needed to be there when the box was opened.

"Once I have the papers and whatever was in that safety deposit box…"

"I know. Just be careful and call me as soon as you have everything and are safe," he said.

"I will." She climbed out of bed to kiss him, pressing her body against his as if to memorize the feel of him. He groaned and kissed her hard, bunching the fabric of the sheet she had wrapped around her as he held her to him. She didn't want him to let her go and that told her how afraid she was that something would keep them apart. "I'll call you later to find out how your father is," she said.

He gave her another kiss and released her, though with obvious reluctance.

"What are you doing?" she asked as he pulled out his phone and called the marshal's office to inquire about her car. "You don't have to do that."

He smiled at her and mouthed, "Yes I do," as he asked that one of the deputies bring her vehicle to his apartment. "Just leave the keys under the mat. Thanks." He disconnected. "I'm not leaving you high and dry without your car."

"Stop worrying about me and go. I know how anxious you are to get to your father."

Brick nodded as he pulled on his boots. "Be careful and hurry back to me." His voice sounded rough with emotion.

She swallowed the lump in her throat. "I will." She touched the tip of her tongue to her lower lip, remembering their night of shared intimacy as he recovered his shirt.

As he started for the door, he stopped to look back at her as if hating to leave her. She knew the feeling. Being in his arms, she'd felt free of pain, her heart lifting, her blood a welcoming hammer in her veins. She would have given anything to never leave this bed, never leave this man.

What surprised her even more were the tender feelings she felt for Brick. She'd gotten close to him in a matter of days, something completely unheard of for her, especially with a man. Now he didn't want to leave her any more than she wanted him to.

"Don't worry," she quickly assured him. "I can handle this on my own. You just worry about your dad. I'll call later to see how he's doing. Once I have whatever

Tricia left, I'll be back. My prayers are with your dad and the rest of your family. Call me if you need me."

His gaze softened in the early-morning light as he opened the door. "I suspect I am always going to need you." He looked as if he wanted to say more.

"Don't worry. We're not done. Whatever it is you want to say to me, there'll be time."

Brick picked up his Stetson. "I forget that you're always right. Hope you are about this."

"I am." And he was gone.

She stared at the closed door until she could no longer hear the sound of his pickup engine. Even then, she didn't want to move. She still felt wrapped in last night's lovemaking. Brick had been a generous, thoughtful lover. He'd made her feel things she'd never felt before. Afterwards, they'd lain in each other's arms, needing no words.

They'd been spooned together when he whispered next to her ear, "You were right. I'm crazy about you."

She'd smiled and reached back to touch his stubbled cheek. "You're going to get tired of saying that." He'd chuckled and pulled her closer and she'd closed her eyes, drifting off into a sleep free of nightmares.

Still warm with the memory, she headed for the shower.

SITTING NEXT TO the hospital bed in ICU, Brick held his father's large, sun-browned hand in his two hands. He studied the scars and brown spots as if all the man's secrets were hidden there. The doctor said Hud was out of the woods. He'd been lucky that it had only been a mild heart attack.

There would have to be some changes, the doctor had

said. Less stress, more dietary restrictions. Brick had seen the relieved look on his mother's face, the tears in her eyes at the good news.

"He has to retire," she'd said. "But will that kill him?"

Brick had shaken his head and hugged her. "He can live vicariously through me, if he lets me back on the force."

"It won't be easy," his mother had said, worry etched on her still pretty face.

"Dad's tough. There isn't anything he can't handle. He'll handle retirement. Maybe there'll be a few grandkids for him to chase around."

She'd smiled. "He would love that and so would I. Thinking of anyone in particular?"

"Angus and Jinx," he'd joked. He would imagine his twin would be all for a passel of kids.

"What about you?" Dana had asked.

"If I found the right woman…"

She'd swatted playfully at him. "You can't fool your mother."

Now he thought about the future for not just his father and mother and the rest of his family. He was worried about Mo and what she would find in that safety deposit box at the bank. He knew how anxious she was to get the key. Maybe, now that his father was out of the woods, he'd drive down to Billings and—

"Brick."

His head jerked up and he looked into his father's eyes.

"You're awake." He let go of his father's hand. "I need to get Mom. She made me promise—"

"Just a moment. I need to say something to you."

"Dad—"

"I'm proud of you."

Brick chuckled. "I know that."

"Do you? Of all my children I've given you the hardest time. It's because you are so much like me and yet also like your mother. What a deadly combination of our free spirits. I realized that I've never told you…" He coughed.

"You really don't have to do this now."

"I do. When I felt that pain in my chest…" His father's eyes filled with tears. "I thought I might not get a chance…" His dad coughed before he added, "I like her."

Brick frowned at him, not sure who he was referring to.

"Mo. She suits you. Don't let her get away."

He laughed and patted his father's hand on the bed. "I don't intend to. But if I don't let Mom know that you're awake she will never forgive me." And yet he didn't want to leave his father. "Thanks, Dad."

His father's eyes closed again. He stepped out into the hall to see his mother headed in his direction. She looked alarmed at first until she saw him smiling. She handed him the cup of coffee she'd brought him and hurried to her husband's side.

Brick thought he'd give them a minute and walked down the hallway away from his dad's room. As he did, his cell phone rang. He stepped into the stairwell to take the call. He'd thought it would be Mo and he really needed to hear her voice.

"Deputy Savage?" The voice was that of an elderly woman. "This is Ruth Anne Hager." The name meant nothing to him at first. The elderly woman had to remind him that he was the one who had approached her.

"I live kitty-corner from the woman who died."

"Oh, yes, Mrs. Hager, I'm sorry."

"It's Miss, but you can call me Ruth Anne."

"All right, Ruth Anne." He waited.

"You said to call if I thought of anything. The other day I was busy with my grandson when you stopped by and didn't have time to even think, let alone recall what happened weeks ago. But since then, I got to thinking. I did see someone go into the back of the house that day. I recall because I was waiting for my trash to be picked up. I'd made some cookies for the men and didn't want to miss them. They're partial to my toffee cookies and they do such a good job, I like to make treats for them."

"You saw someone go into the back of Tricia's house," he gently prodded.

"I was surprised to see the husband return," the woman said. "He never came home at this time of the day, let alone park behind the house. I thought he must be ill."

Brick held his breath for a moment. "You're sure it was her husband?"

"Yes. He was always so punctual on when he came and went. Same time every morning, home same time every night all week long. I liked that about him. Seeing him in the middle of the afternoon on a workday, I was worried."

"What did he do?"

"He went into the house. I'd seen the nanny come out not thirty minutes before that as if headed for the store. That nice-looking young woman. I can't believe what they are saying on the news."

"How long was her husband inside?"

"Well, the two men who pick up my trash came by. I went out to take them their cookies. They always comment on how nice my backyard looks and how neat I keep the area around my trash containers."

"So you visited for a while. Did you hear any noise coming from the house?"

"Their truck was still running so I wouldn't have heard anything but maybe the other neighbors might have. Did you talk to them?"

He and Mo had. "They didn't hear anything."

"I'm sure everything was all right because I saw him when he left. He did seem a little upset, but he wouldn't have just gone back to work if he'd found her. He wouldn't have left her, now, would he?"

The moment Brick got off the phone, he called Mo. Her cell went straight to voice mail. "I need to talk to you before you see Thomas. It's urgent." He left the message, then thought it more likely she would see a text.

T went home day Tricia died.

He sent it and then hurried into his father's room, where his mother was sitting next to the bed. He quickly told them his suspicions.

"I'm afraid she might not get the message before she sees Thomas," he said.

"Call the Billings police," his father said.

Brick shook his head. "I can't trust them after what happened with me."

"Then go," Hud said and reached for the phone beside the bed. "I'll get you a patrol car so you can use the lights and siren. It will get you there much faster."

Mo THOUGHT ABOUT her sister, missing her, as she rode up the elevator to the top floor of the office building. As she stepped out, she had to wipe her tears. Looking around, she caught a glimpse of the Billings skyline through the floor-to-ceiling windows. The rim of rocks the city was famous for gleamed golden in the lights from the city.

She'd never been to Thomas's office. She walked to the wall of glass and tried the door. Then she heard a click and the door opened into a room full of tiny cubicles. Mo realized that she'd never asked Thomas if he enjoyed his work. When he and Tricia had gotten engaged, Thomas had been on his way to medical school. So how had he ended up working for a pharmaceutical company in one of these small cubicles?

The office, she noticed, was empty, most of the overhead lights dark. She started toward the area where there was light when her phone lit up and a notification pinged from her shoulder bag, indicating an incoming text. She started to check it when Thomas called out, "Over here."

She wound her way toward him, thinking of her sister. Had Tricia been unhappy with her choice in a husband? Had nothing turned out the way she thought? Or had she just fallen in love with JP, something she hadn't seen coming? Something that had turned her life upside down and ended in her death?

Mo still had so many questions and feared she might never get all the answers. But at least the paperwork from the animal shelter had helped bring down Jeffrey and JP. She knew the feds had been building a case for a long time. But after Elroy had taken the papers to the FBI, they had moved quickly.

"Hey," Thomas said as he turned in his chair to look at her.

She took in his cubicle, the small desk, the stacks of paperwork, a few sticky notes on his bulletin board to remind him of meetings. A framed photograph of Tricia sat in the corner. She stared at her sister's smiling face and remembered the day the photo was taken. They'd all been at a family picnic not long after Thomas and Tricia were engaged. Her sister looked happy.

"Are you all right?" Thomas asked, bringing her out of her thoughts.

She nodded distractedly. "Were you happy?"

He blinked. "You mean married to Tricia?" She waited for his reply, not sure why she'd asked. "She was the only woman I ever loved."

"But were you happy?" She motioned to their surroundings.

Thomas looked around as if seeing his office space for the first time.

"I remember when you wanted to be a doctor."

He swallowed and looked away. "Dreams change. We were going to start a family. Medical school would have taken so long and been too expensive and Tricia wanted a home and…" His voice died off. "Why are we talking about this now?"

She knew he was right. She cleared the lump in her throat. "You said you found more papers and a safety deposit box key?"

He nodded and rose. She could see that her earlier questions had upset him. "I need a cigarette."

"I didn't know you smoked."

"I hadn't for years until… It's a terrible habit, but right now I need one. Do you mind?"

She did. The drive had been long. She was tired and wanted to get this over with. Tomorrow her partner had said he would go with her to the bank to get the safety deposit box opened.

"If you could just give me the key and papers…"

"Maureen, can't we just step outside for a few minutes? Please?"

The empty office felt eerie and the last thing she wanted to do was breathe in secondhand smoke. But what was one cigarette? "Sure. But after that, I need to go." She wanted to get back to Brick. Once she got the safety deposit key, she would drive back to be with him and his family.

Thomas was rummaging around on his desk for his pack and lighter. "This will just take a minute. I hardly ever see you anymore. I've missed you." She watched him dig around nervously in the drawer.

Something shiny caught her eye on his desk. A lethal-looking silver letter opener. She tried to make out the design, moving the stack of papers until she could see the logo: MSD, Inc. The name of the corporation that ran the nonprofit animal shelter when Tricia met JP? Her heart bounced in her chest.

"Got it." Thomas said as he pocketed his cigarettes and lighter. "We can go outside."

Mo heard her phone ping with another text. She started to check it when Thomas took her phone out of hand.

"You can do without this for a few minutes. I'd like

your undivided attention for once," he said, putting the phone down on his desk next to his computer.

As he turned out of the cubicle, she impulsively picked up the letter opener, tucking it into the back waistband of her jeans and covering it with her shirt and jean jacket.

"Coming?" he asked, looking back at her.

She saw something in his gaze. Suspicion? She was sure he hadn't seen her pick up the letter opener. But he did glance at the desk as if he couldn't remember what was on it. Important papers he hadn't wanted her to see? Or something else?

She felt foolish for taking the letter opener. Did she really think taking it would be any less of a reminder of Tricia's betrayal once her affair with JP came out? And she feared it would come out now that he'd been arrested. Tricia had known something was wrong. Would she have blown the whistle had she lived?

Nor was it necessarily strange that Thomas had the letter opener. Tricia could have picked it up at the animal shelter and given it to him before the affair.

Or maybe he'd gotten it from Jeffrey Palmer Sr. The man probably gave them away at his seminars. Thomas having it didn't mean anything. And yet her heart was pounding like a war drum in her chest. She was so sick of all the secrets and lies and worse, the suspicions. Thomas was making her nervous.

"I just need a quick cigarette," he said as he unlocked a door at the end of the long, dimly lit room. It opened onto a set of stairs that rose to another door. He motioned for her to lead the way.

The stairs were even more dimly lit. Their footfalls

echoed as they climbed up to the next door. Thomas opened it.

Mo stepped out onto the dark rooftop, Thomas right behind her, and felt a chill that had nothing to do with the summer night air.

Chapter Eighteen

Mo hesitated on the rooftop. She'd never been that fond of heights.

"Come on, you have to see the city from over here." Thomas moved past her, leading the way to a corner of the roof where there were a couple of benches and a planter. She could smell stale cigarettes and see a can filled with butts.

Thomas lit a cigarette and stepped to the edge. "Quite the view, don't you think?" He took a drag. From where she stood, she could see that his hand was shaking as he put the cigarette to his lips again.

Mo moved closer to look out over the city. The view really was breathtaking. But she felt anxious and more nervous than she wanted to admit.

Thomas exhaled and squinted through the smoke as he looked over at her.

Mo felt a frisson of apprehension move through her. From the look in his eyes, he'd brought her up here for more than a cigarette.

"There's something I've been meaning to ask you," he said quietly. "How long have you known Tricia was cheating on me?"

She felt as if the air had been knocked out of her. Any

doubt she had about whether or not Thomas knew was answered in that heartbeat. There was also an alarming sharp edge to his question, accusation as jagged as a hunting knife's blade.

"I didn't know. Until a few days ago." She met his gaze. "Tricia didn't tell me. I never would have suspected. I didn't believe it at first."

He let out a hoarse laugh. "I know what you mean." His eyes narrowed again. "You and Tricia were always so close. I thought if anyone knew what was going on with her, it would be you." He waited a beat, then added, "So you know about JP."

"I figured it out."

Thomas nodded. "Have you narrowed it down to which one of them killed her? She must have confronted JP and his father and they had to stop her from going to the cops."

It still hurt that her sister hadn't come to her. Mo felt her aching heart break a little more. Tricia hadn't trusted her. Not until it was too late. She pressed her hands to the top of the short parapet wall and stared out at the city, the lights blurring through her tears.

"It had to be someone Tricia trusted, otherwise she wouldn't have let him into her house—let alone accepted a drink from him." Still she didn't look at Thomas.

"A drink?" he asked, sounding confused.

"Her ashes. I took some to the lab. It's amazing how far forensics has come. There was a time when a person could have a body cremated to cover a crime. Not anymore." At least that much was true. "She was drugged." It amazed her sometimes how easily she could lie.

Thomas angrily snuffed out his cigarette and lit another, his hands shaking so violently that it took several tries. "Drugged?"

"How else would the killer have been able to put a noose around her neck without her fighting back?" The image turned her stomach along with the acrid scent of Thomas's cigarette smoke.

"How did you find out about Tricia's affair?" she asked.

He made a guttural sound. "Jeffrey called me."

Mo closed her eyes, imagining the pain Thomas had felt to have the man he idolized be the one to tell him that his wife was having an affair with the man's son. She turned to look at him. "I'm so sorry."

"Tricia and Thomas, the perfect couple, isn't that what everyone said?" His gaze hardened before he broke eye contact to look out over the city. "And after everything we went through, Tricia finally getting pregnant. We were going to be a little family. Only something was wrong with our baby. *Our baby.* What a laugh."

She could hear the pain and anger in his voice, the night growing colder as a breeze moved like a specter across the rooftop.

Thomas let out a stream of smoke and looked over at her. "Guess how I felt when the doctor told me that they wouldn't be needing my blood for my son's first operation because it wasn't a match?" He nodded, smiling a monster's twisted smile. "I knew Joey wasn't mine. What I didn't know was that Tricia was no longer mine, either. Everything I'd believed was a lie."

"I didn't know about Joey," Mo said quietly.

"No one did." He let out a laugh that sounded more like a sob. "I kept it to myself, still hoping that however Joey had come into existence, it wouldn't destroy our lives. Do you have any idea what it is like to carry a burden like that?"

She couldn't imagine the kind of hell he'd gone through learning of Tricia's deception, her betrayal, and said as much. But it was her sister who made her heart ache. She tried not to think of her last minutes on earth, balancing on a chair with a noose around her neck, knowing that her husband was going to kill her.

Mo tried not to glance past Thomas for the exit. She didn't want to estimate about how far she might get before he caught her. She could feel the letter opener digging into the flesh at her back. All her excuses as to why she'd picked it up, she knew it hadn't been impulsive. It had been instinct. She was a born cop. She calculated how many seconds it would take to reach for it under her jacket and shirt, get her fingers around the handle and pull it. Too long.

She told herself that she had a better chance reasoning with Thomas. But when she met her brother-in-law's gaze, all hope of talking him down fled. He planned to end this up here on this roof tonight.

Chapter Nineteen

Brick sped into downtown Billings, the rim rocks around it glowing in the lights from the city. He turned off the lights and siren a few blocks before the building where Thomas worked. He didn't want him to know he was coming. Mo had told him that it was where Thomas had said he had the papers and key locked in his desk drawer. She was meeting him there to pick them up.

He told himself that there was no cause for alarm. That Mo would have gotten the papers and already left. But he'd tried her phone a half-dozen times. Each time it had gone straight to voice mail. Each time, he'd left a more urgent message. Each time, she hadn't called back.

In his gut, he knew. Mo had realized that her brother-in-law was the killer. As he pulled up in front of the building, he saw Mo's car parked on the almost empty street and felt his heart drop. Mo was in there with a killer.

The front door opened onto a small entry. He ran to the elevator and the information sign next to it. The pharmaceutical company was on the top floor. In the elevator he pushed the button again and again until the doors finally closed and he felt the lift begin to climb.

His heart was pounding. He tried to tell himself that

she could take care of herself. If she saw it coming. But the fact that she was still here, that she hadn't called, that she wasn't taking any calls told him she was in trouble.

The elevator finally came to a stop, the door sliding open. Brick rushed off only to find a deserted office full of cubicles behind a wall of glass. He tried the door. Locked. He looked around, frantic to get inside. He could see a light on deep inside but saw no one.

Spying a fire extinguisher at the end of the hall, he pulled his weapon and using the butt end, smashed the cover and lifted the fire extinguisher out. Moving to the glass door into the office, he swung the heavy fire extinguisher and let it go, shielding his eyes as the glass shattered.

He shoved his way through the shattered glass, felt a shard bite into his arm and catch on his long-sleeved shirt. But he ignored the pain as he rushed in toward the only area that was lit.

"Mo!" he called as he ran, his pistol he'd taken from the patrol car drawn. "Mo!" His voice echoed through the emptiness, sounding hollow. He knew before he reached the last set of cubicles that Thomas and Mo weren't here.

But a suit jacket lay over the back of a chair nearest the exit. Brick stepped to the desk and saw Mo's cell phone sitting beside the computer. She was here and hadn't gone far. Where was Thomas? Brick picked up the scent of cigarette smoke from the jacket and looked toward the exit. A hardcore smoker couldn't go long without one, which meant there was no way he went all the way down to the ground floor every time he took a break.

He ran toward the exit door and shoved it open to a set of stairs that led up. Taking them, he followed the scent of cigarette smoke as if it were a bread crumb trail.

As he burst out the door onto the roof, he didn't see anyone. But he heard the murmur of voices. His instincts had him closing the door quietly behind him as he moved toward the sound, his weapon drawn.

MO NEVER THOUGHT she'd find herself on a rooftop fourteen floors above the city with a killer. What made it more surreal was that she *knew* this man. She'd loved Thomas like a brother.

"I knew you would figure it out if you kept at it long enough," Thomas said, his gaze locked on her. "Tricia used to say that you were like a dog with a bone when you got something into your head. How could I forget that you're a cop, through and through? Her ashes, huh?"

"When did you realize that I knew?" Mo asked as Thomas lit another cigarette, never taking his eyes off her.

"You forget. You and I go way back, Maureen. I met you even before I met your sister. I know you. What I don't understand is why you would come here alone tonight to meet me, knowing what I'm capable of doing." He started as if it finally hit him. *"You didn't know."*

She felt the fine hairs stand up on the back of her neck. "You're not a killer."

His laugh sounded full of glass shards. "I wouldn't have thought so not all that long ago, but now…" His expression soured. "But maybe you haven't noticed, I've changed."

She shook her head. "You killed Tricia in a fit of

passion, I would imagine. Killing me would be in cold blood."

"It's not all that much different, I don't believe. It's about survival. I don't want to go to prison. I want to live."

She knew in that instant. "Quinn."

He smiled, his teeth looking sharp in the glow of the city below them. "You picked up on that right away, didn't you?"

"So you and Quinn—"

"I wasn't having an affair at the same time my wife was, if that's what you're asking. I got to know Quinn after Tricia died—"

Mo felt a stab of anger at how blasé he was about her sister's death. "She didn't *die*. She was *murdered*."

His gaze narrowed. "You want to hear this or not?"

She didn't really want to. Was she that sure that he wouldn't hurt her? Or that sure that she could take care of herself?

Right now both seemed foolish. Thomas had fallen in love again. He had even more reason to want to be free of the past and that meant being free of his sister-in-law, as well.

"I got to know Quinn. She's sweet."

"You thought Tricia was sweet."

His eyes narrowed dangerously again. "But I never thought of you that way, Maureen."

His words actually hurt. "You're confusing sweet with vulnerable." Mo had forgotten that her sister had been in love with another boy at college before she'd met Thomas. The boy had broken it off. Had she not realized how vulnerable Tricia had been when she'd met Thomas? Had he recognized it, though, and preyed on her?

She'd thought she had such a clear picture of the past, but now it wavered as if for years she'd remembered only what she wanted to. Thomas and Tricia, the not-so-perfect couple.

Even in the beginning, hadn't she seen tiny flaws in their relationship? Red flags that her sister had ignored. She suspected that Thomas had never let Tricia forget that he'd given up medical school for her. Add to that Tricia's problems getting pregnant—until she met JP.

She told herself she could talk him off this roof. Talk them both off. "I was surprised when you had her cremated."

He finished his cigarette, brutally stubbing it out with the others. "You think she deserved a nice burial?" He snorted. "When I confronted her, she told me that she had planned to tell me. Leave me, is what she meant, but then she realized she was pregnant. Apparently her lover wasn't interested in fatherhood so she broke it off. Or so she said. But often I smelled him on her skin." His eyes swam with tears. "That's right, your precious sister wasn't just an adulteress, she was going to pass off another man's son as mine." He made a swipe at his tears with the back of his sleeve. "It was just one betrayal after another."

She considered her options. He was standing only inches away. If she made any kind of sudden move, he could grab her before she took a step. He was a good foot taller and sixty pounds heavier. He worked out almost every day. She didn't stand a chance against him even with her training.

"If you turn yourself in—"

He laughed. "And go to prison for the rest of my life? I don't think so. Just tell me this. Does your deputy friend know?"

"No," she said quickly. Maybe too quickly because Thomas smiled.

"When I caught you at his apartment, I couldn't believe it was like that between the two of you. I never thought you'd find a man who you felt was your equal."

"Who said I think Brick is?"

Thomas laughed. "Sorry, *sister*, I don't believe you. I know how distraught you've been over your sister's death. But I never expected you to jump off the roof of my office building."

"I'm not jumping, Thomas." She didn't move even when he pulled the pistol from under his shirt behind him and pointed it at her. She wasn't the only one who had a weapon tucked in her waistband, it seemed.

She met his gaze and saw both desperation and determination. One way or another, she was going off the roof of this fourteen-story building.

BRICK MOVED ACROSS the dark rooftop. The glow of the city illuminated a portion of the roof at the corner. He spotted the two figures silhouetted against the city lights—the radiance bouncing off the weapon in Thomas's hand. The barrel of the gun was pointed at Mo's chest. She was talking quietly, cajoling, but the figure opposite her was tense and on alert.

Brick worked his way closer, staying to the shadows. The sound of traffic fourteen floors below drowned out his footfalls. He wanted to rush Thomas, but didn't dare. He couldn't take the chance that the man would get a shot off before he tackled him to the rooftop.

He was within a half-dozen yards now. He could see that Thomas's hand holding the gun was shaking. The man was about to do something stupid, but then he'd already done that when he'd killed his wife.

Unfortunately, Brick couldn't get a shot from where he was without jeopardizing Mo's life. He had to get closer because he could feel time was running out.

MO SAW BRICK out of the corner of her eye. She wanted to call to him, to warn him, but as he stealthily approached, she knew he must have seen the gun Thomas was holding on her. She didn't dare look straight at him for fear Thomas would see and turn and fire.

"You don't want to do this."

"No, I don't. But you've given me no choice, Maureen. I begged you to let it go." His voice broke. The gun in his hand wavered just enough to tempt her.

Taking it away from him was dangerous, but he was getting more anxious by the minute. She had to do something. She could still feel the letter opener digging into her back. "We can both walk away from this."

He shook his head. "Even if Tricia hadn't been your sister, you couldn't forget this. It's that cop in you. You just couldn't leave it alone. That damn Natalie had to open her mouth…" He shook his head. "Did she say how she knew that Tricia hadn't killed herself?"

"No. I never got to talk to her before she died. Maybe she was just suspicious."

Thomas made a sound like a wounded animal. "That would be just like her. She was always watching us, couldn't keep her nose out of our business. I hated having her living in our house. I could see how close Tricia was getting to her. I would see them with their heads together. I'd walk into a room and they'd both shut up as if they'd been talking about me. I'm sure they were. I'd failed Tricia over and over. I couldn't even give her a child."

She had to keep him talking. Brick was edging closer. Once he was close enough... "Tricia loved you. That's why she broke off the affair. She wasn't leaving you."

"Is that supposed to make me feel better?" he scoffed. "Do you really think I wanted anything to do with her after she'd been with him? After she'd had *his* baby? That was supposed to be *our* family. *Our family.* Not his."

Mo felt a shock race like fire through her veins. Joey. "Thomas, the baby, you didn't..." She couldn't breathe as she saw the answer in his eyes. "You killed him."

"He was going to die anyway."

She felt bile rise to the back of her throat. She was going to throw up. "You let Natalie take the blame."

"She would have done it if I hadn't. Don't you think I watch the news? She's under investigation for other murders. You know how badly I wanted a family. I gave up my dreams. I gave up everything." His gaze hardened. "Why haven't you tried to get away or take the gun away from me, Mo?"

"And give you an excuse to coldcock me with the gun and throw me over this wall?"

Thomas took a step toward her. She stepped back and he advanced again, this time pinning her in the corner of the rooftop.

She reached back, supporting herself with one hand, pulling out the letter opener with the other. "Thomas, don't do this."

"You've left me no choice. I begged you…" His voice broke. "Climb up on the ledge, Maureen. I don't want to hit you. Make this easy on yourself."

"On you, you mean."

BRICK SAW THAT time had run out. He was close now. But not close enough. Thomas had Mo trapped in the corner at the edge of the roof.

"Thomas!" he called out, making the man jump and begin to turn. He'd seen Mo reach behind her as if to steady herself on the short wall an instant before he caught the glint of something long and lethal in her hand.

As Thomas saw Brick, he must have also seen Mo's movement out of the corner of his eye. He swung the gun toward her. The weapon in his hand arced in a circle as she ducked the blow aimed at her head.

The gun caught her in the back, doubling her over on the narrow short roof wall. Turning, Thomas got off a couple of wild shots before he grabbed Mo, lifting her to push her over the wall.

Brick charged, watching in horror as she was lifted up. He saw the flash of the object in her hand as she drove the weapon into Thomas's side. He let out a scream of pain. She struck him again as Brick grabbed him from behind and brought him down to the rooftop. But Thomas didn't release Mo, taking her down with him at the edge of the roof.

Belatedly, Brick saw that Thomas hadn't lost his grip on his gun. The man grabbed Mo and put the barrel against her temple.

"You both should have stayed out of it," Thomas spat and pulled the trigger. As he did, Mo stabbed the man in the throat with what appeared to be a letter opener at the same time Brick fired his own weapon. Thomas's shot was so close, it had to be deafening for Mo. But fortunately, the bullet missed. Brick's, though, had found its mark. Thomas crumpled to the ground next to her.

Brick quickly pulled Mo up into his arms. He held her, refusing to let her go as he called 911.

Chapter Twenty

There was nothing more wonderful than a summer day in the Gallatin Canyon of Montana. Unless of course it was a warm summer night on the Fourth of July with everyone on the Cardwell Ranch gathered to celebrate.

Brick found Mo down by the creek. She'd spent most of the morning in the kitchen with his mother and aunts, preparing the picnic feast they'd had earlier. He'd loved watching Mo with the other people he loved. His mother had taken to her, and his father seemed pleased that Brick hadn't let her get away. It made his heart swell to see how easily she had fit into the Cardwell-Savage clan. The two of them had moved into a larger apartment in Big Sky. Though anxious, Brick had known to give Mo time.

So much had happened, maybe not even the worst of it on that rooftop in Billings. Mo had lost so much. But if the woman was anything, she was resilient. He'd never met anyone stronger or more determined. In the weeks since, everything had come out about Tricia's and Joey's murders. Jeffrey and JP Palmer were still behind bars, both denied bail because they were flight risks. Jeffrey had money stashed all over the world. Passports with new identities had been found for both of them, although JP swore he had no idea what his father had been doing.

Thomas's body had been cremated, his ashes dumped in the Yellowstone River. Brick had stood beside Mo as they watched the last of him wash away. Once the slug from the campground tree was compared to the bullets in Thomas's gun, they'd known who'd taken the potshots at them outside of Red Lodge. Nor had it taken much to find out that Thomas had hired a private investigator to track Mo. He had known that Mo wouldn't stop until she got justice.

Once the dust had settled, Brick had gotten his mental health clearance and gone back to work as a deputy marshal. With his father retiring, there was going to be an opening for marshal. Hud had suggested Mo might be interested. Brick had encouraged her to apply for the position.

"You really wouldn't mind me being your boss?" Mo had asked, sounding surprised.

"Of course not. You have the experience. I think you would make a good marshal. I'd be honored to work with you. Or for you," he added with a grin. "Just so long as when we walked through our apartment door, you remember who is really boss." He'd laughed just in case she hadn't realized he was joking, and she'd stepped to him and kissed him.

"Are you all right?" he asked now as he joined her. Moonlight played in the water's ripples, the sky overhead a canopy of stars.

Mo nodded and turned to smile at him. "I was just making a wish on that star." She pointed at a bright one sitting just over the top of Lone Peak Mountain.

"I know that star. I've made a few wishes on it myself." He met her gaze. "Your sister?"

"I wish none of that had happened, but I can't change any of it. That wasn't what I wished for."

"No?" he asked, eyeing her more closely. "What did you wish for?"

"If I tell, it won't come true."

He looked at the star and made a wish before he turned to her. "I'm glad I found you down here. There's something I need to tell you."

She turned her face up to him and waited as if not sure what to expect.

"I love you."

Mo laughed. "I gathered that."

"I don't just love you. I've never told a woman that I love her because, as I once told you, if I did, it would be only if I then asked her to marry me."

She smiled. "You were serious about that?"

He pulled her to him. "I've never been more serious about anything. I want to marry you. I want you to be my wife."

Mo LOOKED AT this handsome cowboy and felt her heart swell. Tricia used to tease her, saying she was too picky when it came to men, and no wonder she hadn't gotten married. It was true.

But she'd never thought she'd ever meet a man like Brick Savage. She doubted the Lord had made more than one. She laughed in delight as she looked at him, wondering how she could have gotten so lucky.

"I love you, Brick Savage, and I would be honored to be your wife."

He grinned and kissed her as the fireworks show at the ranch began with a boom that exploded over their heads. Twinkling lights showered down to expire before hitting the ground around them. The summer breeze stirred nearby pines as the creek next to them was bathed in moonlight.

For so long, she'd been looking back. But as Brick pulled her close, she looked to the future. She'd already fallen for his family and this amazing ranch life here in the canyon. Cardwell Ranch felt like home.

The other night, she'd found Brick sitting on the porch after dinner with his parents. He'd been playing a song on a harmonica and she hadn't wanted for him to stop. But he must have heard her approach, because he'd finished the song and turned to her.

"I didn't know you played," she'd said, realizing she had so much to learn about this man and how much she was looking forward to it.

"I didn't play for a long time," he'd said. "For a while, I wondered if I ever would again. But then you came along. You filled my heart with music again."

She'd smiled and whispered, "If that's a line to get me into your bed—"

He'd grabbed her and pulled her onto his lap. "If that's all it takes…"

She'd known long before that moment, sitting out there on his family's porch swing, that she was in love with this man.

"Come on," she said now. "Let's go celebrate with your family."

As they headed arm in arm back to the festivities, more fireworks exploded over their heads. Mo felt as if he were leading her out of the darkness. Ahead was a bright future that she couldn't wait to share with the man she loved.

* * * * *

HITCHED!

This one is for E-Dub. You are always an inspiration!

Chapter One

Jack hadn't seen another person in miles when he spotted the woman beside the road. He was cruising along Highway 191, headed north through the most unpopulated part of Montana, when he saw her.

At first he blinked, convinced she had to be a mirage, since he hadn't even seen another car in hours. But there she was, standing beside the road, hip cocked, thumb out, a mane of long, ginger hair falling past her shoulders, blue jeans snug-fitting from her perfect behind down her impossibly long legs.

Jack slowed, already having doubts before he stopped next to her in his vintage, pale yellow Cadillac convertible. Just the sight of her kicked up the heat on an already warm May day.

She had a face that would make any man look twice. He watched her take in the restored convertible first then sweep her green-eyed gaze over him. He thought of warm, tropical sea breezes.

Until he looked closer. As warm as the day was, she wore a jean jacket, the collar turned up. He caught a glimpse of a stained T-shirt underneath. Her sneakers looked wet, like her hair. Her clothes were dusty and the cuffs of her jeans wet and muddy.

He'd seen an empty campground in the cottonwoods as he passed the Missouri River, but it was still early in this part of Montana to be camping, since the nights would be cold. It was especially too early to be bathing in the river, but he had to assume that was exactly what she'd done.

"Going any place in particular?" he asked, worried what she was doing out here in the middle of nowhere all alone. Assuming that was the case. He glanced toward the silky-green pine trees lining the road, half-expecting her boyfriend to come barreling out of them at any minute. But then, that was the way his suspicious mind worked.

"Up the highway." She leaned down to pick up the dirty backpack at her feet. It appeared as road worn as she was.

All Jack's instincts told him he'd regret giving this woman a ride. But it was what he glimpsed in her eyes that made up his mind. A little fear was normal for a woman traveling alone in the middle of nowhere. This woman was terrified of something.

He saw her glance back down the highway toward the river, that terror glittering in all that green.

"Then I guess you're going my way." He smiled, wondering what the hell this woman was running from and why he was opening himself up to it. Any fool knew that a woman on the run had trouble close at her heels. "Hop in."

She swung the backpack to her shoulder, straightened the collar of her jean jacket and shot another look back down the lonesome highway.

Jack glanced in his rearview, half-afraid of what had her so scared. Heat rose from the empty two-lane blacktop. He caught a glimpse of the river below them, the dark surface glistening in the morning sunlight. A hawk squawked as it soared on a current coming up out of the river. A cloud passed overhead, throwing the rugged ravines and gullies choked with scrub juniper and pine into shadow.

As he turned back, she was apologizing for her muddy sneakers.

"Don't worry about that," he said, figuring this woman had a lot more to worry about than getting his car dirty.

As he reached across to open her door, she dropped her backpack onto the passenger-side floorboard and slid into the seat, closing the door behind her.

Jack tried to shove off his second thoughts about picking up a total stranger on the run from beside the road in such a remote, isolated place as he watched her settle into the soft leather.

He couldn't miss the way she pulled her bulging backpack protectively between her feet. The backpack, like her T-shirt, was stained with dirt and splattered with something dark the color of dried blood.

"Name's Jack. Jack Winchester." Then he asked, "I'm on my way to the Winchester Ranch. You don't happen to know the Winchesters, do you?"

"I don't know a living soul in Montana." She took his outstretched hand. Her skin was silky smooth and just as cool. "Josey." Her eyes widened a little, as if that had just slipped out. "Josey Smith."

She'd stumbled on the last name, a clear lie. It made him wonder again who or what was after her. "Nice to meet you, Josey." He told himself he was just giving her a ride up the road as far as the turnoff to the ranch.

Shifting the Caddie into gear, he took off. As they topped the mountain and left the river and wild country of the Breaks behind, he saw her take one last look back. But the fear didn't leave her eyes as they roared down the long, empty highway.

JOSEY FOUGHT TO still the frantic pounding of her heart. She didn't want this man to see how desperate she was. She was still shaking inside as she turned up the collar on her jean jacket and lay back against the seat.

She needed time to think. It still wasn't clear to her what had happened back there on the river.

Liar. She closed her eyes, trying to block it all out. But the memory was too fresh. Just like the pain. She could still see the car breaking the dark green surface and sinking, hear the gurgling sound as water rushed in, see the huge bubbles that boiled to the surface.

She'd stumbled and fallen as she scaled the rocky bluff over the river, then worked her way through the pines, not daring to look back. She'd only just broken out of the trees and onto the highway when she'd heard the growl of an engine and spotted the Cadillac coming up the hill. It was the first vehicle she'd seen or heard in hours.

Holding her breath and reining in her urge to run, she'd stuck out her thumb—and prayed. Her only hope was to get as far away as she could. She'd been scared the driver of the Cadillac wouldn't stop for her. She could just imagine the way she looked.

But he had stopped, she thought. That alone made her wary. She tried to concentrate on the warm spring breeze on her face, telling herself she was alive. It seemed a miracle. She'd gotten away. She was still shaking, though, still terrified after the horror of the past two days.

She opened her eyes, fighting the urge to look back down the highway again, and glanced over at the man who'd picked her up. Under normal circumstances she would have thought twice about getting into a car with a complete stranger, especially out here where there were no houses, no people, nothing but miles and miles of nothing.

Jack Winchester looked like a rancher in his jeans, boots, and fancy Western shirt. His dark blond hair curled at his nape under the black Stetson. She glanced down at her own clothing and cringed. She looked as if she'd been wallowing in the dirt. She had.

Furtively, she brushed at her jeans and, unable to refrain any longer, turned to look back down the highway.

Empty.

She felt tears sting her eyes. He wasn't coming after her. He couldn't ever hurt her again. She shuddered at the thought.

Not that it was over. By now California criminal investigators would have put out an all-points bulletin on her. Before long she'd be wanted in all fifty states for murder—and they didn't know the half of it.

AHEAD, THE LITTLE ROCKIES were etched purple against the clear blue sky of the spring day. As the land changed from the deep ravines and rocky ridges of the Missouri Breaks to the rolling prairie, Jack watched his passenger out of the corner of his eye. She chewed at her lower lip, stealing glances in the side mirror at the highway behind them. She had him looking back, as well.

Fortunately, the two-lane was empty.

As he neared the turnoff to the ranch, Jack realized he couldn't just put her out beside the road. He couldn't imagine how she came to be hitchhiking, but his every instinct told him she was in danger.

He could only assume it was from some man she'd hooked up with and later regretted. Whoever was after her, Jack didn't want him or her to catch up with his passenger.

He knew it was crazy. The last thing he needed was to get involved in this woman's problems. But he also didn't want her blood on his hands.

A thought crossed his mind. He prided himself at thinking on his feet. Also at using situations to his advantage.

And it appeared fate had literally dropped this woman into his lap. Or at least dropped her into his Caddie. Josey couldn't have been more perfect if he'd ordered her from a catalog. The more he thought about it, the more he liked his idea, and he wondered why he hadn't thought of it before he'd agreed to this visit to the "family" ranch.

He glanced over at her. She had her eyes closed again, her head back, her hair blowing behind her in a tangled wave of sun-kissed copper. She was stunning, but beyond that his instincts told him that this woman wasn't the type who normally found herself in this kind of position beside a road, and possibly running for her life.

Jack reminded himself that his instincts had also warned him not to pick her up back there.

He smiled to himself. Taking chances was nothing new to him, nor was charming his way to what he wanted. He'd been told that he could talk a rattlesnake out of its venom without even a bite. He knew he could talk this woman into what he had in mind or his name wasn't Jack Winchester.

But he didn't figure it would take much charming. He had a feeling she'd go for his proposal because she needed this more than he did.

"So, Josey, how do you feel about marriage?" he asked as they cruised down the vacant two-lane headed toward Whitehorse, Montana.

"Marriage?" she asked, opening one eye.

Jack grinned. "I have a proposition for you."

Chapter Two

Josey had been taken aback, instantly suspicious until he explained that he was on his way to see his grandmother, who was in her seventies.

"She has more money than she knows what to do with and lives on a huge ranch to the east of here," Jack said. "You'd be doing me a huge favor, and I'd make it worth your while. The ranch is sixty miles from the nearest town and a good ten from the nearest neighbor."

A remote ranch. Could she really get this lucky? He was offering her exactly what she needed, as if he knew how desperate she was. Was it that obvious?

"What do you get out of it?" she asked, wary.

"Your company as well as a diversion. Since we're on our honeymoon I have the perfect excuse to spend less time at my grandmother's bedside."

"I take it you aren't close."

He laughed at that. "You have no idea."

Still, she made him work for it. This wasn't her first rodeo, as they said out here in the West, and Jack Winchester was definitely not the first con man she'd come across in her twenty-eight years.

He was good, though, smooth, sexy and charming as

the devil, with a grin that would have had her naked—
had she still been young and naive.

She was neither. She'd learned the hard way about
men like Jack Winchester back in her wild days.

But she also knew he would be suspicious if she
gave in right away.

"One week," she said, hoping she wasn't making a
huge mistake. Jack had showed up just when she needed
him and this marriage charade. No wonder she was feeling this was too good to be true.

But given her lack of options…

He flashed her a sexy grin, and she told herself all
she had to do was resist his cowboy charm for a week.
No problem.

She closed her eyes and dozed until she felt him
slowing down on the outskirts of what appeared to be
a small Western town nestled in a river bottom.

"Welcome to Whitehorse," Jack said with a laugh
as they crossed a narrow bridge. "I thought we'd buy a
few things for you to wear this week. I'm guessing you
don't have a lot of clothing in that backpack."

That almost made her laugh as she pulled the backpack closer. "I definitely could use some clothes and a
shower before I meet your grandmother."

"No problem. Just tell me what you need. I'm sure
there's a truck stop at one end of this town or another.
It's the only town for miles up here."

She looked over at him. He was making this too
easy. Was he thinking that with a wife his grandmother
would give him twice the inheritance? "You're sure
about this? Because I'm really not dressed to go into
a clothing store," she said, sliding down in the seat as
they entered town.

JACK FELT A CHILL as Josey turned up the collar on her jean jacket and slid down in her seat. *Who the hell is after her? And what the hell have I got myself into?*

Still, the gambler in him told him to stick to his plan. He couldn't throw this woman to the wolves. "My wife can have anything she wants or needs," he said. "Just name it."

And she did, including hair dye and a pair of sharp scissors. He hadn't even lifted a brow, but he'd hated the thought of what she planned to do to that beautiful hair of hers.

It definitely brought home the realization that he'd underestimated just how much trouble this woman was in. "I'll tell you what. Why don't I drop you at the truck stop? You can get a hot shower, get out of those clothes and I'll come by with everything else you need."

"You don't know my size."

"I'm good at guessing." He saw her hesitate. "Trust me."

Like a dog that'd been kicked too many times, her look said, *When hell freezes over.*

She told him what else she needed, which turned out to be just about everything. He had to wonder what *was* in that backpack. It looked full. But apparently there wasn't much clothing in it.

Whatever was in the backpack, it was something she wasn't letting out of her sight. She kept the backpack close, taking it with her when he dropped her at the truck stop.

Jack watched her walk away, her head down as if trying to go unnoticed, and told himself he was going to regret this.

JOSEY DIDN'T EXPECT to see Jack Winchester again as he drove away from the truck stop. She wouldn't have blamed him. She'd caught the look that crossed his handsome face when she'd asked for the dark hair dye and scissors.

Only a fool wouldn't get the implication of that and Jack, she suspected, was no fool. By the time she'd showered, she'd found the items she'd asked for waiting for her just outside the shower door.

She took the scissors to her hair, surprised by how painful it was. It was just hair. It would grow back. But she knew she wasn't upset about her hair. It was all the other losses in her life.

She let the dye set in her short hair as she avoided looking in the mirror, then took another shower, wondering if she would ever feel truly clean again. In the bags he'd left for her, she found jeans, shirts, a couple of summer dresses, sandals, undergarments, a robe and nightgown, and even a pair of cowboy boots.

Josey shook her head, amazed that he would make so many purchases including the two scarves she'd asked for. He really was good at guessing. He'd not only guessed her sizes right down to her shoe size, but he'd chosen colors and styles that she might have chosen for herself.

She'd been so touched, it had choked her up, and she realized how long it had been since someone had been nice to her.

Jack was waiting for her in the shade outside beside the Cadillac. It surprised her that she'd been dreading his reaction to the change in her appearance. She'd worn the boots, jeans and Western shirt he'd bought her, as well as a scarf tied around her neck that went with the shirt.

He smiled when he saw her. His gaze took in her hair first, then the rest of her. "I see the clothes fit."

"Yes, thank you." She felt strangely shy.

"I like your new look," he said, nodding, as they climbed into the car.

"You do?" she asked, and braved checking herself in the vanity mirror. It startled her, seeing herself as a brunette with short curly hair that framed her face. Her green eyes appeared huge to her. Or maybe it was the dark shadows under them. She didn't even recognize herself.

"It suits you," he said.

"Thank you." She snapped the visor up. Who was she kidding? Changing her hairstyle wasn't going to save her. Nothing would. It was just a matter of time before the rest of her world came crashing down.

She saw Jack looking at her backpack again, even more curious. She'd put her dirty clothing and sneakers into one of the shopping bags, and had to stuff the second bag with the new clothing.

She'd have to watch him closely until she had an opportunity to hide the backpack's contents for safekeeping during the week at the ranch.

If she lasted the week. If there was even a ranch, she thought, as Jack drove south on a highway even less traveled than the last one they'd been on.

She no longer trusted herself to separate the good guys from the bad.

JACK STUDIED JOSEY as they left town. The new hairstyle and color only made her more striking. A woman like her couldn't go unnoticed, if that was what she was hoping. So far, he thought she was safe. The truck stop hadn't been busy, and the clerk there hadn't given either of them a second glance. She'd been too busy watching the small television behind the counter.

Jack had noticed that when Josey came out to the car she'd carried both bags of clothing he'd purchased for her as well as that backpack she refused to let out of her sight. With her dirty clothes in one bag and the other bag overstuffed with her new clothes, he was even more concerned about what was in her backpack.

"You didn't have to buy me so much," Josey said now as he drove east out of town.

"I wouldn't want my grandmother to think that I'm cheap when it comes to my wife and her wardrobe."

His expression sobered at the thought of his grandmother, Pepper Winchester. He didn't give a damn what she thought, but he *did* want her to believe this marriage was real. It hadn't crossed his mind to bring a "wife" along. Not until he'd picked up Josey beside the road and had this overwhelming desire to help her. *No good deed goes unpunished,* he could hear his father say.

Jack admitted that his motives hadn't been completely selfless. Having a wife would allow him more freedom on the ranch, freedom he would need.

He thought of his mother and told himself he was doing this for her. It wasn't about revenge. It was about justice.

As he glanced over at Josey, he knew he would have to be careful, though. Josey was a beautiful woman. He couldn't afford to get involved in her trouble and lose sight of why he was really going to the ranch.

He reminded himself Josey had gone along with the

"marriage" because she needed to hide out somewhere safe for a week—just as he'd suspected. What was there to worry about?

"I hope we've got everything we need," he said, glancing back at Whitehorse in his rearview mirror. The tiny Western town was only about ten blocks square with more churches than bars, one of the many small towns that had spouted up beside the tracks when the railroad had come through.

"A few more miles and it will be the end of civilization as we know it," Jack said. "There are no convenience stores out here, nothing but rolling prairie as far as the eye can see."

"It sounds wonderful," she said.

"I should probably fill you in on my grandmother," Jack said, as the road turned to gravel and angled to the southeast. "She's been a recluse for the past twenty-seven years and now, according to her attorney, she wants to see her family. The letter I received made it sound as if she is dying."

Josey looked sympathetic. "I'm sorry. A recluse for twenty-seven years? I can understand why you might not have been close."

"I was six the last time I saw her." But he remembered her only too well. Her and the ranch and those long summer days with his mother, all of them living a lie.

As JACK DROVE out of Whitehorse, Josey felt a little better. She'd been nervous in town, trying hard not to look over her shoulder the whole time. At the truck stop, she'd just about changed her mind. She desperately needed to put more distance between her and her past. But the only other option was hooking a ride with a trucker passing through, since there appeared to be no place in this town that she could rent a car or even buy one.

Also, why chance it when she could hide out for a week at some remote ranch? She was anxious to do the one thing she needed to do, but it would have to wait just a little longer. She certainly couldn't chance walking into a bank in this town. It was too risky.

But then again, how risky was it pretending to be a stranger's wife? Even as desperate as she was. Even as good-looking and normal as Jack Winchester appeared.

Who was this man? And what was the deal with his reclusive grandmother? She reminded herself how bad her judgment had been lately, her hand going to her neck beneath the scarf and making her wince with pain. She hoped she hadn't just jumped from the frying pan into the fire.

As the Cadillac roared down the fairly wide gravel road through rolling grasslands and rocky knolls, she tried to relax. But Jack Winchester had her confused. He seemed like a nice guy, but nice guys didn't fool their grandmothers with fake wives.

Even though she'd fought it, Josey must have dozed off. She woke as the Cadillac hit a bump and sat up, surprised to see that the road they were on had narrowed to a dirt track. The land had changed, becoming more rough, more desolate.

There were no buildings, nothing but wild country, and she had the feeling there hadn't been for miles.

"Is the ranch much farther?" she asked, afraid she'd been duped. Again.

Sagebrush dotted the arid hills and gullies, and

stunted junipers grew along rocky breaks. Dust boiled up behind the Cadillac, the road ahead more of the same.

"It's a bit farther," Jack said. "The ranch isn't far from a paved highway—as the crow flies. But the only way to get there is this road, I'm afraid."

Josey felt a prickle of fear skitter over her skin. *But come on, what man would buy you clothes just to take you out in the middle of nowhere and kill you?* She shuddered, thinking she knew a man exactly like that.

"You thought I was kidding about the Winchester Ranch being remote?" Jack asked with a laugh.

When he had told her about where they would be spending the week, she had thought it perfect. But now she doubted there was even a ranch at the end of this road. It wouldn't be the first time she'd been played for a fool, but it could be the last. Josey had a bad feeling that she'd used up any luck she'd ever had a long time ago.

She shifted in her seat and drew the backpack closer, considering what she was going to do if this turned out to be another trap. Jack didn't look like a deranged madman who was driving all this way to torture and kill her. But then RJ hadn't looked like a deranged madman, either, had he?

She stared at the road ahead as Jack drove deeper into the wild, uninhabited country. Occasionally she would see a wheat field, but no sign of a house or another person.

As the convertible came over a rise in the road, Jack touched his brakes, even though all she could see was more of the same wild landscape. He turned onto an even less used road, the land suddenly dropping precariously.

"Are you sure you're on the right road?" Her hand went to her backpack, heart hammering in her chest as she eased open the drawstring and closed her hand around the gun handle, realizing she had only four shots left.

"I'm beginning to wonder about that myself. I asked for directions back at a gas station in town before I picked you up, so I'm pretty sure I'm on the right road." The car bumped down the uneven track, then turned sharply to the right. "There it is." He sounded as relieved as she felt.

Josey looked up in surprise to see a cluster of log buildings at the base of the rugged hills behind it. A little farther down the road Jack turned under a huge weathered wooden arch, with the words *Winchester Ranch* carved in it.

Her relief was almost palpable. Josey released her hold on the pistol, trying to still her thundering heart as the Cadillac bumped down the narrow dirt road toward the ranch buildings.

She frowned, noting suddenly how the grass had grown between the two tracks in the road, as if it hadn't had much use. As they grew closer, she saw that the cluster of log buildings looked old and…deserted.

Josey reminded herself that the grandmother had been a recluse for the past twenty-seven years. At least that was what Jack had said. So she probably hadn't had a lot of company or use on the road.

After what she'd been through, Josey thought she could handle anything. But she suddenly feared that wasn't true. She didn't feel strong enough yet to be tested again. She wasn't sure how much more she could take before she broke.

As they rounded a bend in the road, her pulse quickened. This place was huge and creepy-looking. Sun glinted off a line of bleached white antlers piled in the middle of a rock garden. She noticed other heads of dead animals, the bones picked clean and hanging on the wood fence under a row of huge cottonwoods. As she looked at the house, she thought of the "big bad wolf" fairy tale and wondered if a kindly grandmother—or something a lot more dangerous—was waiting inside.

Jack parked in front and killed the engine. A breathless silence seemed to fill the air. Nothing moved. A horse whinnied from a log barn in the distance, startling Josey. Closer a bug buzzed, sounding like a rattlesnake. She felt jumpy and wondered if she'd lost her mind going along with this.

"Are you all right?" he asked. He looked worried.

She nodded, realizing she was here now and had little choice but to go through with it. But this ranch certainly wasn't what she'd expected. Not this huge, eerie-looking place, that was for sure.

"I know it doesn't look like much," Jack said, as if reading her mind.

The house was a massive, sprawling log structure with wings running off from the main section and two stories on all but one wing that had an odd third story added toward the back. The place reminded her of a smaller version of Old Faithful Lodge in Yellowstone Park.

At one time, the building must have been amazing. But it had seen better days and now just looked dark and deserted, the grimy windows like blind eyes staring blankly out at them.

"Don't look so scared," Jack said under his breath.

"My grandmother isn't that bad. Really." He made it sound like a joke, but his words only unnerved her further.

As the front door opened, an elderly woman with long, plaited salt-and-pepper hair filled the doorway. Her braid hung over one shoulder of the black caftan she wore, her face in shadow.

"Showtime," Jack said as he put his arm around Josey and drew her close. She fit against him, and for a moment Josey could almost pretend this wasn't a charade, she was so relieved that at least part of Jack's story had been true. An old woman lived here. Was this the grandmother?

Jack planted a kiss in her hair and whispered, "We're newlyweds, remember." There was a teasing glint in his blue gaze as he dropped his mouth to hers.

The kiss was brief, but unnervingly powerful. As Jack pulled back he frowned. "I can see why we eloped so quickly after meeting each other," he said, his voice rough with a desire that fired his gaze. This handsome man was much more dangerous than she'd thought. In at least one way, she had definitely jumped from the skillet into the fire.

She gave Jack a playful shove as if she'd just seen the woman in the doorway and was embarrassed, then checked to make sure the scarf around her neck was in place before opening her door and stepping out, taking the backpack with her. *Showtime,* she thought, echoing Jack's words.

No one would ever find her here, wherever she was. She had to pull this off. She was safe. That was all she had to think about right now, and as long as she was safe her mother would be, as well. One week. She could do this.

Jack was by her side in a flash, his arm around her, as they walked toward the house. An ugly old dog came out growling, but the elderly woman shooed him away with her cane.

Josey studied the woman in the doorway as she drew closer. Jack's grandmother? She didn't have his coloring. While he was blond and blue-eyed, she was dark from her hair to her eyes, a striking, statuesque woman with a face that could have been chiseled from marble, it was so cold.

"Hello, Grandmother," Jack said, giving the woman a kiss on her cheek. "This is my wife—"

"Josey Winchester," Josey said, stepping forward and extending her hand. The woman took it with obvious surprise—and irritation. Her hand was ice-cold, and her vapid touch sent a chill through Josey.

"I didn't realize you were married, let alone that you'd be bringing a wife," his grandmother said.

Jack hadn't planned on bringing a wife. So why had he? Josey wondered. It certainly hadn't ingratiated his grandmother to him. And as for money…was there any? This place didn't suggest it.

"This is my grandmother, Pepper Winchester," Jack said, an edge to his voice.

The elderly woman leaned on her cane, her gaze skimming over Josey before shifting back to Jack. "So, you're my son Angus's boy."

Wouldn't she *know* he was her son's child? The woman must be senile, Josie thought. Or was there some reason to question his paternity?

"I remember the day your mother showed up at the door with you," Pepper said. "What were you then?"

"Two," Jack said, clearly uncomfortable.

His grandmother nodded. "Yes. I should have been suspicious when Angus involved himself in the hiring of the nanny," Pepper said.

So Jack was the bastard grandson. That explained this less than warm reception.

Jack's jaw muscle tensed, but his anger didn't show in his handsome face. He put his arm around Josey's waist and pulled her closer, as if he needed her as a buffer between him and his grandmother. Another reason he'd made her this phony marriage offer?

When he'd told her about his grandmother and this visit, Josey had pictured an elderly woman lying in bed hooked up to machines, about to take her final gasp.

This woman standing before them didn't look anywhere near death's door. Josey had speculated that this was about money. What else? But if she was right, then Jack had underestimated his grandmother. This woman looked like someone who planned to live forever and take whatever she had with her.

"Since I didn't realize you had a wife," Pepper Winchester was saying, "I'll have to instruct my housekeeper to make up a different room for you."

"Please don't go to any trouble on my account," Jack said.

The grandmother smiled at this, cutting her dark gaze to him, eyes narrowing.

Be careful, Josie thought. *This woman is sharp.*

JACK HESITATED AT the door to the huge ranch lodge. This place had once been filled with happy memories for him, because he'd lived here oblivious to what was really going on. Ignorance had been bliss. He'd played with the other grandchildren, ridden horses, felt like a Winchester even before his mother had confessed that he was one and he realized so much of their lives had been lies.

"Coming, dear?" Josey called from the open front doorway.

He looked at his beautiful wife and was more than grateful she'd agreed to this. He wasn't sure he could have done it alone. Josey, so far, was a godsend. His grandmother was a lot more on the ball than he'd thought she would be at this age.

Grandma had disappeared into the musty maze of the lodge, leaving them in the entryway. Jack was surprised that he still felt awe, just as he had the first time he'd seen it. This place had been built back in the nineteen forties and had the feel of another era in Western history.

He stared at the varnished log stairway that climbed to the upper floors, remembering all the times he'd seen his mother coming down those stairs.

"Mrs. Winchester said you are to wait down here." Jack swung around, surprised to see the gnarled, petite elderly woman who had managed to sneak up on them. To his shock, he recognized her. "Enid?" She was still alive?

If she recognized him, he gave no indication as she pointed down the hallway then left, saying she had to get their room ready. She left grumbling to herself.

Behind them, the front door opened, and an elderly man came in carrying Jack's two pieces of luggage from the trunk of the Cadillac. Alfred, Enid's husband. Amazing.

He noticed that Josey still had her backpack slung over one shoulder.

Alfred noticed, as well. "I'll take that," the old man said, pointing to it.

She shook her head, her hand tightening around the strap. "I'll keep it with me, thank you."

Alfred scowled at her before heading up the stairs, his footsteps labored under the weight of the bags and his disapproval.

"I can't believe those two are still alive," Jack whispered to Josey, as he led her down the hallway. "I remember them both being old when I was a kid. I guess they weren't that old, but they sure seemed it." He wondered if his grandmother would be joining them and was relieved to find the parlor empty.

Josey took a seat, setting her backpack on the floor next to her, always within reach. Jack didn't even want to speculate on what might be in it. He had a bad feeling it was something he'd be better off not knowing.

Chapter Three

Deputy Sheriff McCall Winchester had been back to work for only a day when she got a call from a fisherman down at the Fred Robinson Bridge on the Missouri River. Paddlefish season hadn't opened yet. In a few weeks the campground would be full with fishermen lined up along the banks dragging huge hooks through the water in the hopes of snagging one of the incredibly ugly monstrous fish.

This fisherman had been on his way up to Nelson Reservoir, where he'd heard the walleye were biting, but he'd stopped to make a few casts in the Missouri as a break in the long drive, thinking he might hook into a catfish.

Instead he'd snagged a piece of clothing—attached to a body.

"It's a woman," he'd said, clearly shaken. "And she's got a rope around her neck. I'm telling you, it's a damned noose. Someone hung her!"

Now, as McCall squatted next to the body lying on a tarp at the edge of the water, she saw that the victim looked to be in her mid-twenties. She wore a thin cotton top, no bra and a pair of cutoff jeans over a bright red thong that showed above the waist of the cutoffs.

Her hair was dyed blond, her eyes were brown and as empty as the sky overhead, and around her neck was a crude noose of sisal rope. A dozen yards of the rope were coiled next to her.

McCall studied the ligature marks around the dead woman's neck as the coroner loosened the noose. "Can you tell if she was dead before she went into the water?"

Coroner George Murphy shook his head. "But I can tell you that someone abused the hell out of her for some time before she went into the water." He pointed to what appeared to be cigarette burns on her thin arms and legs.

"Before he *hung* her."

"What kind of monster does stuff like that?" George, a big, florid-faced man in his early thirties, single and shy, was new to this. As an EMT, he'd gotten the coroner job because Frank Brown had retired and no one else wanted it.

"Sheriff?"

McCall didn't respond at first. She hadn't gotten used to being acting sheriff. Probably because she hadn't wanted the job and suspected there was only one reason she had it—Pepper Winchester.

But when the position opened, no one wanted to fill in until a sheriff could be elected. The other deputies all had families and young children and didn't want the added responsibility.

McCall could appreciate that.

"Sheriff, we found something I think you'd better see."

"Don't tell me you found another body," the coroner said.

McCall turned to see what the deputy was holding.

Another noose. Only this one was wrapped around a large tree trunk that the deputies had pulled up onto the riverbank.

As McCall walked over to it, she saw two distinct grooves in the limb where two ropes had been tied. Two ropes. Two nooses. The thick end of the dead branch had recently broken off.

She looked upriver. If the limb had snapped off under the weight of two people hanging from it, then there was a good chance it had fallen into the river and floated down to where the deputy had found it dragging the second noose behind it.

"Better go upriver and see if you can find the spot where our victim was hung," McCall said. "And we better start looking for a second body in the river."

PEPPER WINCHESTER RUBBED her temples as she paced the worn carpet of her bedroom, her cane punctuating her frustration.

The first of her grandchildren had arrived—with a new wife. She shouldn't have been surprised, given Jack's lineage. None of her sons had a lick of sense when it came to women. They were all too much like their father, suffer his soul in hell. So why should her grandsons be any different?

Her oldest son Worth—or Worthless, as his father had called him—had taken off with some tramp he met in town after Pepper had kicked him out. She would imagine he'd been through a rash of ill-conceived relationships since then.

Brand had married another questionable woman and had two sons, Cordell and Cyrus, before she'd taken off, never to be seen again.

Angus had knocked up the nanny and produced Jack. She shuddered to think how that had all ended.

Trace, her beloved youngest son, had gotten murdered after marrying Ruby Bates and producing McCall, her only granddaughter that she knew of.

Pepper stepped to the window, too restless to sit. When she'd conceived this plan to bring her family back to the ranch, she wasn't sure who would come. She'd thought the bunch of them would be greedy enough or at least curious enough to return to the ranch. She didn't kid herself that none of them gave two cents for her. She didn't blame them, given the way she'd kicked them all off the ranch twenty-seven years ago and hadn't seen one of them since.

So why was she surprised that Jack wasn't what she'd expected? The same could be said for his wife. She wasn't sure what to make of either of them yet.

She pulled back the curtain and stared out at the land. *Her* land. She remembered the first time she'd seen it. She'd been so young and so in love when Call had brought her back here after their whirlwind love affair and impromptu marriage.

He hadn't known any more about her than she had him.

How foolish they both had been.

It had been hard at first, living on such an isolated, remote ranch. Call had hired a staff to do everything and insisted no wife of his would have to lift a finger.

Pepper had been restless. She'd learned to ride a horse and spent most of her days exploring the ranch. That was how she'd met neighboring rancher Hunt McCormick.

She shivered at the memory as she spotted movement in the shadows next to the barn. Squinting, she saw that it was Enid and her husband, Alfred. They had their heads together and their conversation looked serious. It wasn't the first time she'd caught them like that recently.

What were they up to? Pepper felt her stomach roil. As if her family wasn't worry enough.

JOSEY STUDIED JACK. He seemed nervous now that they were here at the ranch. Was he realizing, like her, that his grandmother had gotten him here under false pretenses?

"As you've probably gathered, my mother was the nanny here as well as the mistress of Angus Winchester, my father," Jack said distractedly, as he moved to look out the window. "According to my mother, they had to keep their affair secret because my grandmother didn't approve and would have cut Angus off without a cent." He turned to look at her. "As it was, Pepper cut him and the rest of her family off twenty-seven years ago without a cent, saying she didn't give a damn what they did. When my father died, my grandmother didn't even bother to come to his funeral or send flowers or even a card."

"Why would you come back here to see your grandmother after that?" Josey had to ask.

He laughed at her outraged expression. "There is no one quite like Pepper Winchester. It wasn't just me, the bastard grandson, she washed her hands of after her youngest son disappeared. Trace Winchester was her life. She couldn't have cared less about the rest of her offspring, so I try not to take it personally."

Shocked, she watched Jack study an old photograph

on the wall. "If the only reason you came here is because you thought she was dying—"

"It isn't the only reason, although I've been hearing about the Winchester fortune as far back as I can remember." Jack smiled as he glanced at her over his shoulder. "She looks healthy as a horse, huh? I wonder what she's up to and where the others are."

"The others?" she asked.

"My grandmother had five children. Virginia, the oldest, then Worth, Angus, Brand and Trace."

"You haven't mentioned your grandfather."

"Call Winchester? According to the story Pepper told, he rode off on a horse about forty years ago. His horse came back but Call never did. There was speculation he'd just kept riding, taking the opportunity to get away from my grandmother."

Josey could see how that might be possible.

"When Trace disappeared twenty-seven years ago, it looked like he was taking a powder just like his father," Jack said. "I would imagine that's what pushed my grandmother over the edge, and why she locked herself up in this place all the years since."

"So what changed?"

"Trace Winchester's remains were found buried not far from here. Apparently he was murdered, and that's why no one had seen him the past twenty-seven years."

"Murdered?"

"Not long after his remains were found I got a letter from my grandmother's attorney saying my grandmother wanted to see me." Jack walked over to the window again and pushed aside the dark, thick drape. Dust motes danced in the air. "It was more of a summons than an invitation. I guess I wanted to see what the old gal was up to. Pepper Winchester never does anything without a motive."

His grandmother had suffered such loss in her lifetime. To lose her husband, then her youngest son? Josey couldn't even imagine what that would do to a person. She could also understand how Jack would be bitter and angry, but it was the underlying pain in Jack that made her hurt for him. She knew only too well the pain family could inflict.

The last thing she wanted, though, was to feel anything for Jack Winchester.

Nor did she want to get involved in his family drama. She had her own problems, she reminded herself. She pulled her backpack closer, then with a start realized there was someone standing in the doorway.

The housekeeper Jack had called Enid. Josey wondered how long the woman had been standing there listening. She was one of those wiry old women with a scornful face and small, close-set, resentful eyes.

Enid cleared her throat. "If you'll come with me." She let out a put-upon sigh before leading them back to the staircase.

As they climbed, Josey took in the antique furniture, the rich tapestries, the thick oriental rugs and the expensive light fixtures. She tried to estimate what some of the pieces might be worth. Maybe there was money here—if the ranch wasn't mortgaged to the hilt. She feared that whatever had brought Jack here, he was going to be disappointed.

Jack looked around as they climbed the stairs, his face softening as if he was remembering being a boy in this place. There must be good memories along with bittersweet ones during his four years here.

Josey felt a sudden chill along with a premonition. She tried to shake it off. Why would there be any reason to be afraid for Jack?

They were led down a long, dark hallway to an end room. "Since you're newlyweds," Enid said. "This way you won't disturb the rest of the household."

Jack arched a brow at the old woman behind her back.

"I'm sure you'll ring me on the intercom if you need anything." Enid let out an irritated snort. "Dinner is served at seven on the dot. I wouldn't be late if I were you." With that she left them standing outside the room and disappeared into the dim light of the hallway, her footfalls silent as snowfall.

"That woman is scary," Josey whispered, making Jack chuckle.

"Let's do this right," he said, surprising her as he swung her up into his arms. "In case anyone is watching," he added in a whisper.

She let out a squeal as he carried her over the threshold, making him laugh. His laughter was contagious and she found herself caught up in the moment as he kicked the door shut and carried her into the bedroom.

The room was huge, with a sitting area furnished with two chintz-covered chairs in front of a stone fireplace. Josey caught a glimpse of a large bathroom done in black-and-white tile, sheer white drapes at the open French doors to a small balcony and, at the heart of the room, a large canopied bed.

Jack slowed at the bed, and as he gently lowered her to the cool, white brocade spread his gaze met hers. The sheer white curtains billowed in, bringing with them the sweet scent of clover and pine.

She felt as if she'd been saved by a white knight and brought to the palace for safekeeping. It would have been so easy to lose herself in the deep sea-blue of his eyes as he leaned over her. Jack was incredibly handsome and charming. Everything seemed intensified after what she'd been through. The hard feel of his chest against her breasts, the slight brush of his designer stubble against her cheek, the oh-so-lusty male scent of him as he lowered her to the soft bed.

She wanted desperately to blot out everything but this. It would have been so easy, with her gaze on his sensual, full mouth, to bury her fingers in his a-little-too-long blond hair and drag him down until his lips, now just a breath away from hers, were—

"You're not thinking about kissing me, are you?" he asked, sounding as breathless as she felt. "Because that wasn't part of the bargain. Unless you want to re-negotiate?"

Josey realized that he'd been about to lose himself as well, and, for whatever reason, he'd stopped himself. And her. She shouldn't be feeling safe. She should be thinking of the consequences of losing herself even for a little while in the arms of this man. Jack was making it clear what was going to happen if she opened that door.

She squeezed her hands between their bodies, pressing her palms to his muscular chest, but she didn't have to push. Jack eased slowly back to a safer distance, though it seemed to take all of his effort.

"Didn't Enid say something about dinner at seven?" she asked, her voice sounding strange even to her ears. "I have just enough time to take a bath first."

Jack glanced toward the bathroom. He must have

been wondering why she needed another bath since she'd had a shower in town.

"I can't resist that tub." A huge clawfoot tub sat in the middle of the black-and-white tiled floor.

His blue eyes darkened again with desire, and she saw both challenge and warning as he glanced from the tub to her. They were alone at this end of an empty wing pretending to be husband and wife. Unless she wanted the marriage *consummated,* she'd better be careful what signals she sent out.

Josey slid from the bed, grabbed her backpack and stepped into the bathroom, closing and locking the door behind her. The room was large. Along with the tub there was an old-fashioned sink and dressing table, and enough room to dance in front of a full-length old-fashioned mirror.

Josey set down her backpack and stepped to the tub to turn on the faucet. Enid had left her a bottle of bubble bath, bath soap and a stack of towels. As the tub filled, bubbles moved in the warm breeze that blew in from an open window in the corner and billowed the sheer white curtains.

She stripped off her clothing and, with a start, caught her reflection in the full-length mirror behind her. She looked so different. Slowly, her heart in her throat, she studied her face, then the bruises she'd been able to hide under her clothing. The raw rope burn on her neck made her wince at just the sight of it. What had she been thinking earlier with Jack? Had she lost herself in him, he would have seen—

She shuddered at the thought. She couldn't let that happen. It wouldn't be easy to keep her injuries covered so no one saw them until she had a chance to heal.

But that would be easier than trying to explain them if she got caught.

Josey turned away from her unfamiliar image, anxious to climb into the tub of warm, scented water. She knew she couldn't wash away her shame any more than she could wash away the memory of what had happened.

As she stepped into the tub and slowly lowered herself into the bubbles and wonderfully warm, soothing water, she listened for Jack. Had he left the room? Or was he just on the other side of the door?

Against her will, her nipples hardened at the thought. She reminded herself that Jack was just a means to an end. A safe place to hide out until she could decide what to do. As Jack had said, the Winchester Ranch was in the middle of nowhere. Her past couldn't find her here.

Once she knew her mother was safe...

She lay back in the tub, the breeze from the window nearby stirring the bubbles, but the chill Josey felt had nothing to do with the warm spring air coming through the window.

Was she really safe here? There was something about this place, something about Jack's grandmother, definitely something about the Hoaglands, that gave her the creeps.

Josey shivered and sank deeper in the tub, realizing the most dangerous person in this house could be the man she'd be sleeping in the same room with tonight.

VIRGINIA WINCHESTER STOOD at the window where she'd watched the Cadillac convertible drive up earlier. She hadn't been sure which nephew it was and hadn't cared. All she knew, and this she'd had to get from Enid since her mother wasn't apt to tell her, was that three nephews had confirmed that they would be arriving over the next few weeks.

She wouldn't have recognized any of them. The last time she'd seen them they'd been sniveling little boys. She'd had no more interest then than she did now.

By now there could be more. She shuddered at the thought.

She did, however, wonder why her mother hadn't just invited everyone back at the same time. Pepper had her reasons, Virginia was sure of that.

She herself was the fly in the ointment, so to speak. The letter had specified the time her mother wanted to see her. She assumed everyone else had also been given a specific time to arrive.

Virginia wasn't about to wait. She wasn't having it where her mother invited her favorites first. Virginia planned to be here to make sure she wasn't left out. So she'd come right away—to her mother's obvious irritation.

Growing up on the ranch, she'd felt as if their mother had pitted them all against each other. The only time she'd felt any kind of bond with her siblings had been their mutual jealousy, distrust and dislike of their younger brother Trace—their mother's unequivocal favorite.

Now Virginia worried that just because two of her brothers had produced offspring—at least that she knew of—the Winchester fortune would be divided to include them.

As the only daughter and oldest of Call and Pepper Winchester's children, she deserved her fair share, and she said as much now to her mother.

Pepper sighed from her chair nearby. "You always were the generous one. Of course you would be the first to arrive and completely ignore my instructions."

"I came at once because…" Her voice trailed off as she caught herself.

"Because you thought I was dying."

The letter had clearly been a ruse to get them all back to the ranch. Virginia saw that now. Pepper Winchester didn't even look ill. "The letter from the attorney…" She floundered. There had never been anything she could say that had pleased her mother.

She'd been torn when she'd received the letter from the attorney on her mother's behalf. Her mother was dying?

The thought had come with mixed emotions. It was her *mother*. She should feel something other than contempt. Pepper had been a terrible mother: cold, unfeeling, unreachable. Virginia hadn't heard a word from her in twenty-seven years. What was she supposed to feel for her mother?

"I'm just asking that you be fair," Virginia said.

"I suppose you'd like me to cut out my grandchildren?"

Like her mother had ever been a loving grandmother. "Those of us without children shouldn't be penalized for it. It's not like you would even recognize your grandsons if you passed them on the street," Virginia pointed out.

"I also have a *granddaughter*."

Virginia turned from the window to stare at her mother.

"McCall. Trace's daughter. She's with the sheriff's department. She's the one who solved your brother's murder and was almost killed doing so."

"McCall?" That bitch Ruby had named her kid after Virginia's father? Why wasn't Pepper having a conniption fit about this? She should have been livid. "Surely you aren't going to take the word of that tramp that this young woman is a Winchester."

Her mother's smile had a knife edge to it. "Oh, believe me, she's a Winchester. But I knew the rest of you would require more than my word on it. I have the DNA test results, if you'd like to see them."

Virginia was furious. Another person after the Winchester fortune. No, not just another person. *Trace's* daughter. Virginia felt sick.

"So I have four grandchildren I don't know," her mother corrected with sarcasm. "And there could be more, couldn't there?"

Virginia swore silently. "Why did you even bother to get the rest of us home?"

Pepper raised a brow. "I knew you'd want to see me one last time. Also I was sure you'd want to know the whole story about your brother Trace. You haven't asked."

"What is there to ask?" Virginia shot back. "His killer is dead. It was in all the papers." Trace was dead and buried. "I would think that you wouldn't want to relive any of that awfulness."

She didn't mention that Pepper had kept her other children away from Trace when he was young, as if afraid they might hurt him. Her protectiveness, along with her favoritism and love for Trace, was why they had no great love for their little brother. He'd come into their lives after they'd heard their mother couldn't have anymore children. Trace became the miracle child.

"You weren't at his memorial service," her mother said.

Virginia couldn't hold back the laugh. "Are you kidding? I didn't think I was invited." She started for the door, unable to take any more of this. "You should have warned us in the letter from your lawyer that this visit was really about Trace."

"Your brother was *murdered!* I would think something like that would give even you pause," her mother said, making Virginia stop in midstep on the way to the door.

Even her? As if she had no feelings. Her mother didn't know. Her mother knew nothing about what she'd been through. As if Pepper was the only one who'd lost a child.

"I was sorry to hear about it," Virginia said, turning again to face her mother. "I already told you that, Mother. What about your children who are still alive? The ones you *didn't* protect when they were young? Aren't we deserving of your attention for once, given what you let happen to us?"

The accusation hung in the air between them, never before spoken. Pepper's expression didn't change as she got to her feet. If Virginia hadn't seen the slight trembling in her mother's hand as she reached for her cane, she would have thought her words had fallen on deaf ears.

"You are so transparent, Virginia," her mother said, as she brushed past. "Don't worry, dear. Your trip won't be wasted."

McCall stood in the dust, staring at the makeshift camp, hating the feeling this place gave her. Her deputies had gone only a few miles along the riverbank before they'd come across it and the tree where the limb had broken off and fallen into the water.

This was where they had camped. From the footprints in the mud and dirt around the area, there'd been three of them. One man, two women.

A breeze blew down the river, ruffling the dark green water. She caught the putrid odor of burned grease rising from the makeshift fire pit ringed in stones. Someone had recently cooked over the fire. A pile of crumpled, charred beer cans had been discarded in the flames and now lay charred black in the ash. Little chance of getting any prints off the cans, but still a deputy was preparing to bag them for the lab.

"We followed the tire tracks up from the river through the trees," one of the other deputies said, pointing to the way the campers had driven down the mountainside to the river. "They came in through a farmer's posted gate on a road that hadn't been used in some time."

"You think they lucked onto it or knew where they were going?" she asked. The narrow dirt road had led to this secluded spot, as if the driver of the vehicle had wanted privacy for what he had planned. If he'd just wanted to camp, he would have gone to the campground down by the bridge.

"If he knew about the road, then that would mean he could be a local," the deputy said. "I say he lucked onto the road, figuring it ended up at the river."

Like him, she didn't want to believe whoever had hung two people was from the Whitehorse area. Or worse, someone they knew. Who really knew their neighbors and what went on behind closed doors?

McCall had learned that there were people who lived

hidden lives and would do anything to protect those secrets.

She watched as a deputy took photographs of the dead tree with the broken branch at the edge of the bank, watched as another made plaster casts of both the tire prints and the footprints in the camp.

"Sheriff?"

She was starting to hate hearing that word. She turned to see the deputy with the camera pointing into the river just feet off the bank.

"I think we found the missing car."

Chapter Four

Jack listened to the soft lap of water, fighting the image of his "wife" neck deep in that big old tub just beyond the bathroom door.

This definitely could have been a mistake. He felt a surge of warring emotions. A very male part of him wanted to protect her and had from the moment he'd stopped to pick her up on the highway.

But an equally male part of him was stirred by a growing desire for her. Josey was sexy as hell. To make matters worse, there was a vulnerability in her beautiful green eyes that suckered him in.

His taking a "wife" had been both brilliant and dangerous. The truth was he didn't have any idea who this woman in the next room was. All he knew was that she was running from something. Why else agree to pretend to be his wife for a week? The thought worried him a little as he glanced toward the bathroom door.

The sweet scent of lilac drifted out from behind the closed and locked door. But nothing could shut out the thought of her. After having her in his arms, it wasn't that hard to picture her lush, lanky body in the steamy bathroom: the full breasts, the slim waist and hips, the long, sensual legs.

The provocative image was almost his undoing. He groaned and headed for the door. He couldn't let her distract him from his real reason for coming back to Montana and the Winchester Ranch—and that was impossible with her just feet away covered in bubbles.

Opening their bedroom door, he headed down the hallway toward the opposite wing—the wing where he and his mother had lived twenty-seven years ago.

Jack had expected to find his mother's room changed. As he opened the door, he saw that it looked exactly as he remembered. The only new addition was the dust. His boots left prints as he crossed the floor and opened the window, needing to let some air into the room.

The fresh air helped. He stood breathing it in, thinking of his mother. She'd been a small, blond woman who'd mistakenly fallen in love with a Winchester. She'd been happy here—and miserable. He hadn't understood why until later, when he'd found out that Angus Winchester was his father.

His jaw tightened as he considered the part his grandmother had played in destroying Angus Winchester, and that reminded him of the reception she'd given him earlier when he and Josey had arrived.

He shouldn't have been surprised. When he was a boy, Pepper hadn't paid him any mind, as if he were invisible. They'd all lived in some part of the huge old lodge, but seldom crossed paths except at meals.

It wasn't that she'd disliked him. She just hadn't cared one way or the other, and finding out he was Angus's child hadn't changed that.

He stood for a moment in the room, promising his mother's memory that he'd see that Pepper Winchester paid for all of it, every miserable day she'd spent in this house or on Earth. Then he closed the window and left the room, anxious to get back to Josey.

Who knew what a woman on the run with a trail of secrets shadowing her might do.

From the tub, Josey glanced over at her backpack resting on the floor of the bathroom. Just the sight of it turned her stomach, but she was pretty sure she'd heard Jack leave and she had no idea how long he might be gone.

She quickly climbed from the tub and didn't bother to towel off. Instead, she grabbed the robe he'd bought her and avoided looking in the mirror at her battered body. She also avoided thinking about how she'd gotten herself into such a mess. She was sick to death of all the "if only" thoughts.

As the saying went, the die was cast.

All she knew was that she couldn't keep carrying her backpack around like a second skin. She'd seen the way Jack had eyed it. He was more than a little curious about what was so important in it that she wouldn't let it out of her sight, and he'd eventually have a look.

Which meant she had to find a safe place for its contents.

She listened. No sound outside the bathroom door. Hefting the backpack, she cautiously opened the door a crack. The room appeared to be empty.

She shoved the door open a little wider, not trusting that he hadn't returned.

No Jack. She wondered where he'd gone. She wondered a lot of things about him, but mostly why he'd wanted her to masquerade as his wife. He'd have to have seen she was in bad shape when he'd picked her up on the highway.

So what was in it for him? After meeting his grandmother, Josey was pretty sure it couldn't be money. She just hadn't figured out what Jack was really after.

Josey reminded herself it had nothing to do with her. All she had to do was play her part, hide out here on this isolated ranch until the heat died down. No one could find her here, right?

She quickly surveyed the room. She couldn't chance a hiding place outside this room for fear someone would find it.

Across the room, she spotted the old armoire. The wardrobe was deep, and when she opened it she saw that it was filled with old clothing.

Strange. Just like this huge master suite. Who had it belonged to? she wondered, as she dug out a space at the back, then opened her backpack.

The gun lay on top. She grimaced at the sight of it. Picking it up, she stuck the weapon in the robe pocket. What lay beneath it was even more distressing. The money was in crisp new bills, bundled in stacks of hundreds. Over a million dollars splattered with blood.

Hurriedly she dumped the bundles of cash into the back of the wardrobe, hating that she had to touch it. Blood money, she thought. But the only way to save her mother. And ultimately, maybe herself.

She quickly covered it with some old clothing. Then, grabbing some of the clothing still on hangers, she stuffed the clothes into the backpack until it looked as it had.

Straightening, she closed the wardrobe and looked around to make sure Jack wouldn't notice anything amiss when he returned.

Footsteps in the hallway. She started. Jack? Or some-one else?

As she rushed back into the bathroom, closed and locked the door, she stood for a moment trying to catch her breath and not cry. Seeing the gun and the bloody money had brought it all back.

She heard the bedroom door open and close.

"You all right in there?" Jack asked. Her heart pounded at how close a call that had been.

Discarding the robe, she quickly stepped back into the tub. "Fine," she called back, hating that she sounded breathless.

"We're going to be late for supper if you don't move it."

The water was now lukewarm, the bubbles gone. She slid down into it anyway and picked up the soap. Her hands felt dirty after touching the money. Her whole body did. She scrubbed her hands, thinking of Lady Macbeth. *Out, damned spots.*

Suddenly she remembered the gun she'd stuffed into the robe pocket. She rinsed, stepped from the tub and pulled the plug. The water began to drain noisily as she looked around for a good place to hide the weapon.

There were few options. Opening a cabinet next to the sink, she shoved the gun behind a stack of towels on the bottom shelf. It would have to do for now until she could find a better place to hide it.

She intended to keep the weapon where she could get to it—just in case she needed it. That, unfortunately, was a real possibility.

WHEN JOSEY CAME out of the bathroom, she wore another of the Western shirts he'd bought her in town and the new pair of jeans that fit her curves to perfection. Jack had also picked her out a pair of Western boots, knowing she would need them to horseback-ride during their week on the ranch.

Jack grinned, pleased with himself but wondering why she hadn't worn the two sexy sundresses he'd picked out for her. He'd been looking forward to seeing her in one of them, and he said as much.

"Maybe I'm a jeans and boots kind of girl," she said.

She looked more like a corporate kind of girl who wore business suits and high heels, he thought, and wondered where that had come from. "You look damned fine in whatever you wear."

She appeared embarrassed, which surprised him. The woman was beautiful. She must have had her share of compliments from men before.

As he smiled at her, he couldn't help wondering who she was—just as he had from the moment he'd spotted her on the highway with her thumb out. Josey carried herself in a way that said she wasn't just smart and savvy, she was confident in who she was. This woman was the kind who would be missed.

Someone would be looking for her. If they weren't already.

Jack warned himself not to get involved, then laughed to himself at how foolish that was. He could have just dropped her off beside the road. Or taken her as far as the town of Whitehorse, given her some money and washed his hands of her and her troubles. He should have.

But something about her...

Jack shook his head. He'd played hero and sold himself on the idea of a wife for this visit with his grandmother, and now he worried he'd bought himself more than he could handle as he looked at her.

Her face was flushed from her bath, the scent of lilac wafting through the large bedroom. The Western shirt she'd chosen was a pale green check that was perfect for her coloring and went well with the scarf that she'd tied around her neck. The two scarves had been her idea.

She looked sweet enough to eat and smelled heavenly. It was going to be hell being around her 24/7 without wanting more than a pretend marriage.

Worse, their charade required a modicum of intimacy with her. As he led her down to dinner, he put his hand against the flat of her back and felt the heat of her skin through the thin cotton of her shirt. The touch burned him like a brand.

She looked over at him. Her smile said she knew what he was up to. He smiled back. She had no idea.

"Finally," said a woman impatiently from the parlor where they'd been shown in earlier.

Jack looked in to see his aunt Virginia, a glass of wine in her hand and a frown on her less than comely face. The years hadn't been kind to her. The alcohol she'd apparently already consumed added to her overall disheveled look.

Her lipstick was smeared, her linen dress was wrinkled from where she'd been perched on the arm of one of the leather chairs and there was a run in her stockings.

"We eat at seven sharp," she snapped, and pointed to the clock on the wall, which read several minutes after.

Josey started to apologize, since it was her fault for staying in the tub so long, but the other woman in the room cut her off.

"You remember Virginia," Pepper Winchester said drily.

"Of course, Virginia," Jack said, extending his hand.

His aunt gave him the weakest of handshakes. "Mother says you're Angus's son?" Like his grandmother, Virginia had also missed her brother's funeral. *Nothing like a close-knit family,* Jack thought.

Virginia was studying him as if under a microscope. Her sour expression said she saw no Winchester resemblance. "The nanny's child." She crinkled her nose in distaste. "Dear Angus," she said, as if that explained it.

Jack tried not to take offense, but it was hard given the reception he and his pretend wife were getting here. He reminded himself that this wasn't a social visit. Once he got what he'd come for, he would never see any of them again.

"This is my wife, Josey," he said, glad as hell he hadn't come here alone. All his misgivings earlier about bringing her were forgotten as he slipped his arm around her slim waist and pulled her close.

JOSEY FELT JACK'S ARM tighten around her as Virginia gave her a barely perceptible handshake.

It was hard not to see the resemblance between mother and daughter, Josey thought. Both women were tall, dark-haired and wore their bitterness on their faces. Virginia was broader, more matronly and perhaps more embittered as she narrowed her gaze at Josey, measuring her for a moment before dismissing her entirely.

"Can we please eat now?" Virginia demanded. "I'm famished. Little more than crumbs were served for lunch. I hope dinner will prove more filling." She turned on her heel and headed down the hall.

Josey turned to Pepper, who was reaching for her cane. "I do apologize. I'm afraid I enjoyed your wonderful tub longer than I'd meant to. That is such a beautiful bathroom. I especially like the black-and-white tiles."

Pepper seemed startled. "Enid put you in the room at the end of the south wing?" She quickly waved the question away. "Of course she would. Never mind."

Grabbing her cane, she followed her daughter down the hallway. Josey noted that Pepper Winchester was more feeble than she let on. Maybe she really was dying. Or maybe just upset.

"I knew it," Josey whispered to Jack, as they followed Pepper at a distance toward the dining room. "That room must have been your grandmother's and grandfather's. Wouldn't Enid know that putting us in there would upset your grandmother?"

"I would bet on it," he said.

Josey followed his gaze to where Enid stood in the kitchen doorway, looking like the cat who ate the canary. "She must have shared that room with your grandfather. I wonder why she moved out of it?"

Jack chuckled and slowed, lowering his voice as they neared the dining room. "I doubt it was for sentimental reasons. My mother told me that according to Winchester lore, Pepper didn't shed a tear when my grandfather rode off and was never seen again. She just went on running the ranch as if Call Winchester had never existed—until her youngest son Trace vanished."

Dinner was a torturous affair. Jack had known it wouldn't be easy returning to the ranch, but he hadn't anticipated the wellspring of emotions it brought to the surface. As he sat at the dining room table, he half expected to see his mother through the open kitchen doorway.

It was at that scarred kitchen table that he and his mother had eaten with the Winchester grandchildren and the staff. In the old days, he'd been told, Pepper and Call had eaten alone in the dining room while their young children had eaten in the kitchen.

But Call had been gone when his mother came to work here, and Pepper had eaten with her then-grown children in the dining room. When Trace was home, his mother had heard Pepper laughing. After Trace eloped with that woman in town and moved in with her, the laughter stopped. Jack's mother said she often didn't hear a peep out of the dining room the entire meal with Pepper and her other children.

"The animosity was so thick in the air you could choke on it," his mother had told him. "Mrs. Winchester took to having her meals in her room."

"Well, Mother, when are you planning to tell us what is really going on?" Virginia demanded now, slicing through the tense silence that had fallen around the table. She sat on her mother's right, Jack and Josey across from her. Her face was flushed; she'd clearly drunk too much wine. Most of dinner she'd complained under her breath about Enid's cooking.

Jack had hardly tasted his meal. He'd pushed his food around his plate, lost in the past. Josey had seemed to have no such problem. She'd eaten as if she hadn't had a meal for sometime. He wondered how long it had been.

Pepper had also seemed starved, cleaning her plate with a gusto that didn't go unnoticed. For a dying woman, she had a healthy appetite. Almost everyone commented on it, including Enid when she'd cleared away the dishes before bringing in dessert.

"Well, Mother?" Virginia repeated her demand.

Enid had stopped in midmotion and looked at Pepper, as if as anxious as any of them to hear why the family had been invited back to the ranch.

"Isn't it possible that I wanted my family around me after receiving such horrible news about your brother?" Pepper asked, motioning for Enid to put down the cake and leave the room.

Virginia scoffed at the idea. "After twenty-seven years you suddenly remembered that you had other family?"

"Does it matter what brought us together?" Jack spoke up. "We're here now. I assume some of the others will be arriving, as well?" he asked his grandmother.

She gave him a small smile. "A few have responded to my invitation. I knew it would be too much to have everyone here at the same time, so the others will be coming later."

"Well, I know for a fact that my brother Brand isn't coming," Virginia said unkindly. "He's made it perfectly clear he couldn't care less about you or your money." She poured herself the last of the red wine, splashing some onto the white tablecloth. "In fact, he said he wouldn't come back here even if someone held a gun to his head."

"How nice of you to point that out," Pepper said.

Enid had left, but returned with a serving knife, and saw the mess Virginia had made. She set the knife beside the cake and began to complain under her breath about how overworked she already was without having to remove wine stains from the linens.

"That will be enough," Pepper said to the cook-housekeeper. "Please close the kitchen door on your way out."

Enid gave her a dirty look, but left the room, slamming the door behind her. But Jack saw through the gap under the door that Enid had stopped just on the other side and was now hovering there, listening.

"I only mention Brand to point out that not everyone is so forgiving as I am," Virginia said. She glanced at her mother, tears welling in her eyes. "You hurt us all, Mother. Some of us are trying our best to forgive and forget."

"Let's not get maudlin. You're too old, Virginia, to keep blaming me for the way your life turned out."

"Am I? Who do *you* blame, Mother?"

A gasp came from behind the kitchen door.

Pepper ignored both the gasp and her daughter's question as she began to dish up the cake. "I've always been fond of lemon. What about you, Josey?" she asked, as she passed her a slice.

Josey seemed surprised at the sudden turn in conversation. "I like lemon."

Pepper graced her with a rare smile that actually reached the older woman's eyes. "I don't believe you told me how you and my grandson met."

"I was hitchhiking and he picked me up," Josey said.

Jack laughed, as he saw Josey flush at her own honesty. "It was love at first sight." He shot her a look that could have melted the icing on her cake.

Her flush deepened.

"She climbed into my car and, as they say, the rest is history," Jack said.

Pepper was studying Josey with an intensity that worried him. The elderly woman seemed to see more than he had originally given her credit for. Did his grandmother suspect the marriage was a ruse?

"Well, how fortunate," Pepper said, shifting her gaze to Jack. "You're a lucky man." Her smile for him had a little more bite in it. "You have definitely proven that you're a Winchester."

Jack chuckled, afraid that was no compliment. It didn't matter. He could tell that his grandmother liked Josey and he would use that to his advantage. But it wouldn't change the way he felt about his grandmother.

He'd spent most of dinner secretly studying his beautiful "wife." Josey continued to surprise him. Her manners and the way she carried herself made him realize she must have come from money—probably attended a boarding school, then some Ivy League college. She seemed to fit in here in a way that made her seem more like a Winchester than he ever could. So how did she end up on the side of the road with nothing more than a backpack? And more importantly, why would a woman with her obvious pedigree be sitting here now, pretending to be his wife?

"You've hardly touched your food."

Jack dragged his gaze away from Josey as he realized his grandmother was talking to *him*. "I guess I'm not really hungry."

Pepper nodded. "You probably have other things on your mind."

"Yes. I should apologize for making this trip into a honeymoon. It wasn't my intention when I answered your letter."

"No, I'm sure it wasn't," his grandmother said with a wry smile. "But what better place than the family ranch? I assume you remember growing up here. You loved to ride horses. Surely you'll want to ride while you're here and show Josey the ranch. You were old enough to remember your uncle Trace, weren't you?"

Virginia didn't bother to stifle a groan.

Her mother ignored her. "You must have been—"

"Six," Jack said, and felt all eyes at the table on him. Beside him, he sensed that even Josey had tensed.

"Then you remember the birthday party I threw for him?"

Jack nodded slowly. It wasn't likely he would forget that day. His mother told him years later that Pepper had been making plans for weeks. Everything had to be perfect.

"I think she really thought that if she threw him an amazing birthday party, Trace would come back to the ranch," his mother had told him. "Of course the only way he was welcome back was without the woman he'd eloped with, the woman who was carrying his child. Or at least he thought was carrying his child. Pepper didn't believe it for a moment. Or didn't want to."

"I had a cake flown in," Pepper said, her eyes bright with memory. "I wanted it to be a birthday he would never forget." Her voice trailed off, now thick with emotion.

Instead it had been a birthday that none of the rest of them had ever forgotten. His grandmother, hysterical with grief and disappointment when Trace hadn't shown for the party, had thrown everyone off the ranch, except for Enid and Alfred Hoagland.

"I bought all the children little party hats," she was saying. "Do you remember?"

From the moment he'd received the letter from his grandmother's attorney, Jack had known she wanted something from him. He just hadn't been sure what. But he had an inkling he was about to find out.

"I recall sending all of you upstairs so you wouldn't be underfoot," Pepper said. "I believe you were playing with my other grandchildren at the time." Her gaze locked with his, and he felt an icy chill climb up his spine and settle around his neck. "Whose idea was it to go up to the room on the third floor? The one you were all forbidden to enter?"

THIS FAR NORTH it was still light out, but it would be getting dark soon. Deputy Sheriff McCall Winchester listened to the whine of the tow truck cable, her focus on the dark green water of the Missouri River.

Déjà vu. Just last month, she'd watched another vehicle being pulled from deep water. Like now she'd feared they'd find a body inside it.

A car bumper broke the surface. The moment the windshield came into view, McCall felt a wave of relief not to see a face behind the glass. Which didn't mean there still wasn't someone in the car, but she was hoping that bizarre as this case was so far, it wouldn't get any worse.

The tow truck pulled the newer-model luxury car from the water to the riverbank, then shut off the cable motor and truck engine. Silence swept in. Fortunately they were far enough upriver on a stretch of private ranch land away from the highway, so they hadn't attracted any attention.

McCall stepped over to the car as water continued to run out from the cracks around the doors. She peered in, again thankful to find the car empty of bodies. Snapping on latex gloves, she opened the driver side door and let the rest of the water rush out.

Along with river water, there were numerous fast food containers, pop cans, empty potato chip bags.

"Looks like they were living in the car," a deputy said.

McCall noticed something lodged under the brake pedal.

"Get me an evidence bag," she ordered, and reached in to pull out a brand-new, expensive-looking loafer size 10½.

"The driver got out but left behind his shoe?" a deputy said as he opened the passenger-side door. "But did he make it out of the water?"

"See if you can find any tracks downstream," Mc-Call said. "The current is strong enough here that he would have been washed downriver a ways."

"Should be easy to track him since he is wearing only one shoe," the deputy said.

"Let's try to find out before it gets dark," McCall said. Otherwise they would be dragging the river come morning for a third body.

On the other side of the car, a deputy pulled on a pair of latex gloves and opened the passenger-side door to get into the glove box. McCall watched him carefully check the soaking wet registration.

"The car is registered to a Ray Allan Evans Jr., age thirty-five, of Palm City, California. Looks like he just purchased the car three days ago."

Chapter Five

Josey felt the air in the dining room tremble with expectation as she waited for Jack to answer his grandmother. What was this about a room that he'd been forbidden to enter?

"What would make you think I've been in that room?" Jack said, meeting his grandmother's gaze with his cold blue one.

His grandmother's look was sharp as an ice pick. She knew, just as Josey sensed, that he was evading the question. But why would he care about something that happened when he was six?

And why would his grandmother care after all these years?

"Those cute little party hats you were all wearing when you went upstairs," his grandmother said. "I found them in the room."

"Really?" Jack said, forking the piece of the cake Pepper had passed him. "I'm afraid I don't remember anything about some party hats."

"Is that right?" His grandmother's tone called him a liar. "Are you going to also tell me you don't remember that day?"

"Oh, I remember that day. I remember my mother

losing her job and us having to leave the ranch, the only home I'd ever known," Jack said in a voice Josey barely recognized. "I remember my mother being terrified that she wouldn't be able to support us since Angus had been cut off without a cent and didn't have the skills or the desire to find a job. I remember looking at the Winchester Ranch in the rearview mirror and you standing there, making sure we all left and didn't come back."

"Oh, my," Virginia said, clearly enjoying Jack's rancor at her mother.

"I remember Angus losing himself in the bottle and my mother struggling to take care of us while she tried to make us a family," Jack said, his voice flat and cold. "I remember the toll it took on her. But nothing like the toll being exiled from here took on Angus."

"Your mother. Is she…?" Virginia asked.

"She died a year before Angus drank himself to death."

Pepper looked down at her untouched cake. "I didn't know."

"Really? Then you didn't know he left a note?" Jack reached into his pocket and took out a piece of folded, yellowed paper. Josey saw that it was splattered with something dark and felt her stomach roil.

Jack tossed the note to his grandmother. "It's made out to you." With that he got to his feet, throwing down his cloth napkin. "If you'll excuse me."

MCCALL SAT IN her patrol car, studying the screen. The moment she'd typed in Ray Allan Evans Jr.'s name, it had come up. Ray Jr. was a person of interest in a homicide in Palm City, California. The murder victim was his father, Ray Allan Evans Sr. He'd been killed two days ago—just a day after his son had purchased a very expensive luxury automobile.

She put through a call to the detective in charge of the case in the Palm City homicide department, Detective Carlos Diaz. She told him that she'd found Ray Jr.'s car and that he was wanted in Montana for questioning in another homicide case.

She asked what they had on the Evans murder so far.

"A neighbor can place Ray Jr. at the house at the time of the murder. But he wasn't alone. His stepsister was also there. Her car was found on the property. No staff on the premises, apparently, which in itself is unusual. This place is a mansion with a full staff, at least a couple of them live-in."

"I'm sorry, did you say his *stepsister?*" McCall asked, thinking of the young Jane Doe the fisherman had hooked into.

"Josephine Vanderliner, twenty-eight, daughter of Harry Vanderliner, the founder of Vanderliner Oil. The father is deceased. The mother married Evans two years ago, was in a car accident shortly afterward, suffered brain damage and is now in a nursing home. The stepdaughter had been in a legal battle over money with Evans Sr. Her fingerprints were found on the murder weapon. Neither Vanderliner or Evans Jr. has been seen since the night of the murder."

"What's the story on Ray Jr.?"

"Goes by RJ. Thirty-four, no visible means of support, lives with his father."

And yet he'd purchased himself a new expensive car on the day his father was murdered?

"The housekeeper found Ray Sr.'s body—and the safe—wide-open. She says she saw Ray Sr. putting a large amount of cash into the safe just that morning. According to the eyewitness, RJ and his stepsister left together in a large, newer-model black car at around the time of death estimated by the coroner. Didn't get a make and model on the car."

"Sounds like the one we just pulled from the Missouri River."

McCall filled him in on what they had so far—one female victim in the same age range as Josephine Vanderliner and a car registered to Ray Allan Evans Jr., driver missing and suspected drowned. "We're dragging the river now for a possible third body," she told him.

Detective Diaz sent her photographs of both Ray Jr. and Vanderliner.

McCall watched them come up on her screen. Ray Evans Jr. first. A good-looking, obviously rich kid from the sneer on his face. She thought of the abuse her Jane Doe had suffered before being hanged and drowned. Did he look like a man capable of that? Or was he also a victim of foul play?

McCall held her breath as she clicked on the photograph of Josephine Vanderliner.

JOSEY TOUCHED HER napkin to the corner of her mouth, then carefully placed it beside her dessert dish before rising to follow her "husband" outside.

"That was awkward," she heard Aunt Virginia say, as Josey left the dining room. "So what does the note say?"

"Not now, Virginia."

"He killed himself because of you, didn't he?"

As Josey reached the front door she heard what sounded like a slap followed by a cry and glass break-

ing. She didn't look back as she pushed open the door
and stepped out into the fresh air.

Spotting Jack down by the barn, she walked in that
direction, just glad to be out of the house. She figured
Jack wanted to be alone and certainly wouldn't want her
company. For appearance's sake, she had needed to go
after her husband. She hadn't wanted to feel his pain,
but her own emotional pain was so near the surface and
had been for too long. She knew family drama and how
it could tear you apart from the inside out.

Josey slowed as she neared. He stood with his back
to her, his head high as if he were gazing out across the
ranch. The sun hung over the Little Rockies in the far
distance, the sky ran from horizon to horizon, so wide
and deep blue, she could understand why Montana was
called Big Sky Country.

Jack didn't look at her as she joined him at the corral fence. He'd opened himself up back there at dinner, and even though she hadn't known him long, she
was sure he regretted it. He'd exposed how vulnerable
he'd been, still was, when it came to his grandmother
and the past.

Against her will, Josey felt a kinship with him. Life
hadn't been kind to him, and yet she sensed a strength
in him born of hard times. Jack might have taken a
beating, but he wasn't down for the count, she would
bet on that.

"Did you enjoy my sad tale?" he asked, still without
looking at her.

She sensed the last thing he needed right now was
her sympathy. "It was a real heartbreaker. Was any of
it true?"

He looked over at her and grinned. "It almost brought a tear to the old bat's eye, don't you think?"

"I could tell it broke your aunt Virginia's heart."

He laughed and slipped his arm around her, his gaze going back to the sunset. "I can't believe how lucky I was to find you."

She might have argued that, but she was smart enough to keep those thoughts to herself. As long as no one discovered where she'd gone, they were both lucky.

"Have you ever seen anything more beautiful?" he asked, looking toward the horizon.

"No." She studied the wild landscape, broken only by a few outcroppings of rock and the dark tops of the cottonwoods. Between the ranch and horizon was a deep ravine that seemed to cut the place off from the world.

"The Winchester Ranch is the largest ranch in three counties," Jack said.

"So it's the money you're after?"

He smiled. "Who says I'm after anything?" He pulled her closer as he turned them back toward the ranch lodge.

Josey had seen how upset he'd been at dinner. Maybe he wasn't after his grandmother's money, which was just as well because Josey doubted he would be getting any. But he was after something, and that something felt more like settling a score with his grandmother.

She felt a chill as they walked arm in arm back to the lodge, wondering what his grandmother was after and why she was bringing the family back to the ranch.

Whatever Jack was up to, his grandmother had her own agenda, Josey thought. Out of the corner of her eye she saw a face at one of the lodge windows.

Pepper Winchester's face appeared for an instant before the curtain fell back into place.

THE PHOTOGRAPH OF Vanderliner was several years old, but there was no mistake. She wasn't the Jane Doe now lying in the county morgue.

So who was the victim they'd pulled from the river?

"Our Jane Doe isn't Vanderliner," McCall told Detective Diaz. She promised to get back to him as soon as they were able to run the dead woman's prints.

Back down at the river, the surface golden with the last of the sun's rays, McCall listened to the sound of the boat motor as her fiancé, Game Warden Luke Crawford, helped drag the river for the bodies.

Because of the lack of manpower in a county sheriff's department, game wardens were often called in, since they had the same training as other law enforcement in the state.

Normally crime in and around Whitehorse was mostly calls involving barking dogs, noisy neighbors or drunk and disorderlies. Occasionally there would be a domestic dispute or a call to check on an elderly person who wasn't answering her phone.

Murder was rare, but not unheard of. McCall knew that firsthand. She'd had more than her share of bloodshed recently. The last thing she wanted was another homicide.

"So if the driver of the vehicle was able to swim to safety, he's on foot," George said.

McCall nodded, glancing down river toward Highway 191.

"You're thinking someone picked him up," George said with a nod. He sounded exhausted. "Makes sense.

He would probably need medical attention. I'll call the hospital emergency rooms." He headed for his vehicle.

"You don't have to stick around. I can call you if we find another body."

He shook his head. "I want to be here."

"Thanks." McCall turned back to the river. If RJ wasn't in the river, he'd be on the hunt for shoes, dry clothing, a vehicle and possibly medical attention, as George had said.

So what would he do? Head for the highway. The nearest town was Whitehorse to the north, but she doubted he'd be picky if he could catch a ride. If he was headed south he'd probably have to go clear to Billings to get what he needed. Or cut over to Lewistown, which was closer.

George came back to tell her that a man matching RJ's description or a woman matching Josephine Vanderliner's hadn't come into emergency rooms in Whitehorse or Lewistown.

"So either he wasn't hurt that badly or he hasn't gotten to a place where he can get medical attention," McCall said, glancing behind her into the tall pines. Vanderliner, she could only assume, was in the river.

She heard one of the search-and-rescue volunteers call her name. "Got something down here," the volunteer called.

McCall worked her way down the river to where the volunteer stood next to something caught in a limb beside the water. She shone her flashlight on the object. A leather shoulder bag.

Squatting down and pulling on her latex gloves, she dragged the bag to her and opened it. A wallet. She focused her flashlight beam on the driver's license inside—and the photograph of a pretty, ginger-haired young woman. The name was Josephine Vanderliner.

PEPPER STEPPED BACK from the window, trembling inside with rage and embarrassment. How dare they condemn her? Couldn't they understand how devastated she'd been to lose Trace?

She brushed angrily at her tears. She wasn't looking for their sympathy. Nor their understanding. And it was a damned good thing, because clearly she would get neither.

She felt the note she'd stuffed into her pocket and eased it out. The paper was yellowed. The dark splatters made her recoil. Angus's suicide note. She didn't have to open it to know that he was blaming her even from the grave.

What about the failings of his father? Where was their anger toward the man who had gone to such extremes, spoiling them rotten one moment and then punishing them by locking them in that third-floor room?

She thought of the young wife she'd been. The foolish young woman who'd let Call Winchester rule all their lives for way too long.

Funny, she was still acutely disappointed in him even after all these years. Her anger had eased as did her fear of him, she thought with no small amount of irony, but not her disappointment.

Was it any wonder that she had never trusted another man? Even Hunt McCormick. How different her life would have been if she'd run off with him like he'd wanted her to.

She shook her head at the very thought. She hadn't been able to leave because of her children, children she should have protected from Call. All her children, not just Trace. But the older ones had always been Call's children from the time they were born, and she'd felt so helpless against him back then.

The truth was she'd loved Call, trusted him to do what was best for all of them, even when it came to how their children should be raised.

She'd been blinded by that love.

Until Trace was born.

Pepper would never know what had changed. Maybe she'd finally seen Call for what he was, a bully. Or maybe she'd finally fallen out of love with him.

Either way, she'd been determined to save Trace from him. That struggle had definitely killed any love she had for her husband and had cost her the rest of her children.

Pepper knew that some people thought she was cold and heartless. They pointed to her reaction when Call hadn't come back from his horseback ride more than forty years ago. She hadn't been able to hide her relief that he was gone.

But her secret shame was that a part of her still loved the Call she thought she'd married. Just as a part of her still loved Hunt McCormick.

She started to unfold the note, bracing herself, but changed her mind and dropped the paper into the wastebasket. For a long moment she stood there, staring down at Angus's last cry for help. The one thing she'd never been was a coward. At seventy-two, she couldn't start now. She bent down to retrieve the note and carefully eased the paper open.

The words were scrawled and almost illegible. The handwriting of a child. Or a terrified, sick man.

*I'm so sorry, Mother. Forgive me. I forgive you.
Angus.*

She crumpled the note in her fist, suddenly unable
to catch her breath or stem the flow of tears. Her body
jerked with the shuddering sobs that rose up in her. It
was all she could do not to scream out her anguish.

Pepper didn't hear the door open behind her.

"I thought you might need something," Enid said,
making her spin around in surprise. Enid held a tea-
cup and saucer.

Pepper could smell the strong tea, strong to cover
up the drugs her housekeeper had been systematically
and surreptitiously giving her for years. At first Pepper
hadn't noticed, she'd been so grateful for the oblivion.
She assumed it made Enid's job easier having Pepper either out like a light or so docile she wasn't any
trouble.

But after learning about Trace, things had to change.
She needed her wits about her. She also needed to be
more careful when it came to Enid.

She quickly turned her back to Enid, stepping to
the window to hastily dry her tears and pull herself
together. Enid was the last person she wanted seeing
her like this.

She heard the elderly housekeeper set down the cup
and saucer on the end table by the bed and move to join
her at the window. Enid pulled back the curtain wider
to see what Pepper had been looking at out the window.

She smiled smugly as she saw what Pepper did—
Jack and Josey walking arm in arm toward the house.

"I brought you up some chamomile tea to help you

sleep." Enid motioned toward the cup she'd put down beside Pepper's bed.

"You are so thoughtful," Pepper said, not bothering to hide the sarcasm in her tone.

"Yes, aren't I," Enid said and turned to leave. "Good night."

"Good night," Pepper repeated, just wanting the woman to leave her room.

"Drink your tea while it's hot."

She bristled. "Please close the door behind you." Pepper didn't turn until she heard the door close.

The smell of the strong tea made her nauseous as she stepped to the door and locked it, then she picked up the cup of tea and carried it into the bathroom, where she paused before pouring it down the drain.

Tonight she could have used the mind-numbing effect of whatever drug Enid had put in it. But she could no longer allow herself that escape.

She dumped the tea and rinsed out the sink. The cup she left by her bed before going to the window to look out across the deep ravine to the rocky point in the distance.

It was over there, just across from the ranch, that her precious son had been murdered. Pepper thought of the third-floor room, the binoculars she'd found, and the feeling lodged deep in her heart that someone in her own family was involved.

Nothing else mattered but finding out the truth. It was why she'd made sure her granddaughter McCall had become acting sheriff. While they had never discussed it, Pepper had seen something in McCall's expression. She didn't believe, any more than Pepper did, that the alleged, now-deceased killer had acted alone.

And McCall, who was so like her grandmother, would never let a killer go free. Pepper was counting on her.

As THEY ENTERED the house, Jack discovered his aunt Virginia had been waiting for them.

"I'd like to speak to my nephew," she said, looking pointedly at Josey. *"Alone."*

"Anything you have to say, you can say in front of my wife," he said indignantly.

"It's okay," Josey said, touching his arm. "I'd like to take a look around the ranch."

"Don't go far," Jack said.

Josey looked amused.

"I'm just saying this is wild country and you can get turned around out there in the dark."

"Yes," Virginia agreed with a tight smile. "My father disappeared out there on a night a lot like this one."

"I don't want you disappearing, too," Jack said, only half-joking. "Also, there are rattlesnakes out there."

Josey glanced at his aunt as if to say, *And in here, too*.

"What is this about?" Jack asked his aunt, as Josey left.

"Why don't we step down the hall?" she said. "That awful woman might be listening. Both awful women," she added under her breath.

They stepped into the parlor. Virginia closed the door and spun around, clearly angry. "Okay, you can knock off the act."

"I beg your pardon?"

"You aren't Angus's son, and even if you are, you're not getting this ranch."

Jack had to smile. "Isn't it possible I'm just here to see my grandmother?"

His aunt scoffed. "You don't have to pretend with me. She can barely stand the sight of you. She isn't going to leave you a thing."

Jack was tempted to say that it seemed to him that Pepper Winchester couldn't stand the sight of anyone, maybe especially her daughter. "Frankly, I think she'll try to take it all with her before she leaves any of us a dime. But even if I'm wrong, I'm no threat to you."

Virginia looked skeptical. "*Please*. After that sympathy play you made at dinner? I see what you're doing, but it won't work. You're wasting your time."

"Is that why you pulled me in here? To tell me that?"

Virginia was tall like her mother, but without the grace. "Has my mother mentioned who else is coming to this gruesome reunion?"

"Your mother hasn't shared anything with me."

"Well, I'm worried." Her gaze bored into his. "I heard Enid and Alfred whispering between themselves. They seem to think Pepper might not be of sound mind. I'm betting they're thinking that they can somehow have her put away and take all her money."

Jack wasn't surprised to hear this. "God knows they've put up with her long enough. They probably deserve it." Enid acted as if she was the lady of the house, not Pepper. It surprised him that his obstinate grandmother put up with it.

"What Enid and Alfred Hoagland deserve is to be fired before they steal her blind," Virginia snapped. "What if they've somehow coerced her into making a new will and leaving everything to them?"

"I can't see Pepper doing that under any circumstances. Haven't you seen the way she looks at Enid? She detests the woman. And no one is going to have Pepper committed. It would require a mental evaluation, and I'd put my money on Pepper passing with flying colors."

"You'd put *your* money on it?" Virginia said. "As if you had any money. I know that's not your car parked out there." She gave him a satisfied look. "I have connections. I had the plates run. That Cadillac belongs to the Galaxy Corporation. I assume you're employed by them. Or did you steal the car?"

"I borrowed the Caddie with every intention of taking it back," Jack said, bristling. He hadn't expected this of his aunt.

"And your *wife?* Did you borrow her, as well?" Virginia asked with a laugh, then waved it off. "I was only joking. She's right up your alley. I've seen the way she looks around the lodge, as if she's putting a price tag on all the furnishings."

Jack bit back an angry retort. It was one thing to come after him, but it was another to go after his wife. Even his pretend wife.

The irony didn't escape him. He was defending a woman he'd picked up on the highway. A stranger he didn't know beans about. But then, neither did his aunt.

"Josey likes antiques and comes from money," he said, feeling that might be true. "I can assure you, she isn't interested in Grandmother's."

"You don't look anything like Angus," Virginia said, changing tactics.

Jack laughed, determined not to let his aunt get to him. "I'm not going to argue this with you. My grandmother knows the truth, that's all that matters."

"Your *grandmother* is the reason you're a bastard. She didn't think your mother was good enough for Angus."

He tried to rein in his temper, but Virginia had pushed him too far. "Pepper never approved of any of the women her sons fell in love with. Or her daughter, for that matter. She controlled you all with money and a cushy life on this ranch. All except Trace. Is that why you hated him so much because he couldn't be bought?"

The color had washed from Virginia's face. She stood trembling all over, her lips moving, but nothing coming out.

"But the truth is I wasn't the only bastard to come out of this house—was I, Aunt Virginia?"

JOSEY WALKED UP the narrow dirt road to a small hill before she stopped to look back at the sprawling lodge and the tall cottonwoods and the sparse pines that made the place look like an oasis in the desert.

The lodge was far enough off the main road that she felt relatively safe. From what she'd seen earlier, the main road got little use, not that the lodge could be seen by anyone just happening to drive past.

No one knew she was here. That was the beauty of it. So why couldn't she relax? Because her mother wouldn't be safe until she sent the money and got her moved.

Jack had said they would stay for the week, but Josey knew she couldn't make it that long. If there was just some way to send the money without having to leave here—or let anyone know where she was, she thought, as she walked back down the road in the diminishing daylight. It would be dark soon, and she had no desire to be caught out here alone.

But she wouldn't involve Jack any more than she had. She couldn't.

As she entered, she didn't hear a sound from down the hall. The door to the parlor was closed. She assumed Jack was still in there talking to his aunt, though she couldn't imagine what they might have to talk about. Unless Virginia was trying to talk him into doing away with Pepper and splitting the take.

They'd better cut Enid and Alfred in, Josey thought with a wry smile. The two gave her the creeps. If anyone was plotting to knock off Pepper it was one or both of them.

As she opened the door to the bedroom, Josey realized that Jack could have finished his talk with his aunt and be waiting here for her.

She was relieved to see the bedroom unoccupied. She closed the door behind her and stood looking at the large canopied bed. Playing married was one thing. But where was Jack planning to sleep?

The door opened behind her as if on cue. She turned to look at him, and he grinned as if he knew exactly what she'd been thinking.

"I'm sorry, where did you say you would be sleeping?" she asked.

"I was thinking we could negotiate something."

She smiled back at him. "Think again."

"I suppose sharing the bed is out of the question?"

"You suppose right."

"Don't you trust me?"

"Not as far as I can throw you."

"Now, honey," he said, reaching for her, "we can't let Enid catch us sleeping separately on our honeymoon."

Josey stepped away from him. "We can if we have a fight." She picked up a cheap vase from a nearby table, tossing it from hand to hand. "A lover's quarrel. You know newlyweds."

He was shaking his head, but still smiling. "No one will hear it if you break that."

"But Enid will see the broken glass in the morning when she comes with the coffee and catches you sleeping in that chair over there."

Jack launched himself at her and the vase, but he wasn't fast enough. The vase hit the floor and shattered like a gunshot. Jack's momentum drove them both back. They crashed into the bed and onto it, with Jack ending up on top.

"Now this is more like it," he said, grinning down at her.

Josey could feel the hard beat of his heart against her chest as she looked into those amazing blue eyes of his. The man really was adorable.

"I want to kiss you," he said quietly. He touched her cheek, his fingers warm.

She felt a small tremor. He could be so gentle that it made her ache.

"What will it cost me?"

"You want to pay for a kiss?" she asked, raising a brow, trying to hide her disappointment that he hadn't just kissed her.

"Is there any other way you'd let me kiss you?"

She hated that he made her sound cheap and mercenary. She'd only agreed to take his money for this week because it would have made him suspicious if she'd turned it down. Did he really think she was doing this for the money?

"I really—" The rest of her words caught in her throat as she realized he was untying her scarf. She grabbed for the ends to stop him—just not quickly enough.

"What the hell?" He pushed off her to a sitting position on the edge of the bed next to her, his expression one of shock and horror as he stared at her. "Josey... what—"

"It's nothing." She quickly sat up as she tried to retie the scarf to cover up the rope burn on her neck.

"Like hell," he said, reaching out to stop her as he took in the extent of her injury. "How did this happen?"

She didn't answer as she tried to take the ends of the scarf from him and retie them. "Please."

He held the scarf for a moment longer, his expression softening as he lifted his gaze to hers. "Who did this to you?" There was an edge to his voice, a fury.

"It has nothing to do with you." She pulled away, getting to her feet and turning her back to him as she clumsily tied the scarf with trembling fingers.

"This is why you were on the highway," he said, rising from the bed to come up behind her. "This is what you're running from."

She didn't deny it.

"I don't understand why—"

"No, you don't, so just forget it," she snapped. She finished tying the scarf and swung around to face him. "I took care of it."

He stared at her. "The only way to take care of it is to kill the person who did this to you."

Josey didn't dare speak into the dense silence that fell between them.

Jack seemed to be waiting for her to explain. When she didn't, he let out a curse.

She watched him grab one of the pillows and a quilt that had been folded up on the end of the bed. He brushed past her and dropped both the pillow and quilt onto the chair before leaving the room.

It was much later that she heard him return to the dark room and curl up in the chair across from her. She could hear him breathing softly and feel his gaze on her. She closed her eyes tight and told herself she didn't give a damn what Jack Winchester thought of her. It wasn't the first night she'd gone to sleep lying to herself.

She woke up just after two in the morning to find Jack gone.

Chapter Six

It was late by the time McCall reached her office in Whitehorse. She had brought evidence from the crime scene that needed to be sent to the lab in Missoula first thing in the morning.

Deputies had discovered a bullet on the outside of the car pulled from the river and in the headrest on the driver's side. Both were .38 slugs. Someone in camp had been armed. Deputies would continue their search in the morning for the weapon—and any more victims.

But McCall wasn't ruling out that at least one person had gotten away—possibly armed—from the crime scene.

"Any chance you'll be coming down to my place later?" Luke had asked as he rubbed the tension from her shoulders before she'd left the crime scene.

McCall had leaned into his strong hands, wanting nothing more than to spend the night with Luke in his small trailer curled against him. He was staying in the trailer out on his property until he completed their house. He planned to have it done before their Christmas wedding so they could move in together.

She couldn't believe how lucky she was that Luke had come back into her life.

"I'm sorry," she'd told him. "I'd better stay at my place near town tonight. This case—"

"I know." He'd turned her to smile at her, then kissed her.

He did know. He knew how much this job meant to her even though she'd fought taking the acting sheriff position. He'd encouraged her to run for sheriff when the time came.

"You sound like my grandmother," she'd said.

"Yeah? Well, we both know you aren't finished with your father's death, don't we?"

It was the first time he'd mentioned what he'd overheard the night he'd saved her life at her cabin. She hadn't had to answer, since there was no point. He was right. She wasn't finished, and she had a bad feeling her grandmother wasn't, either.

McCall pushed aside thoughts of her fiancé as she went to work.

George had assisted with taking their Jane Doe's prints. McCall entered them now into the system and waited. The chance of getting a match was slim at best. The Jane Doe would have had to been arrested, served in the military or had a job where her prints were required for security reasons.

That was why McCall was amazed when she got a match.

Her prints had come up from a prostitution charge. She'd served eight months and had only recently been released. Her name was Celeste Leigh of Palm City, California. No known address or place of employment. She was twenty-two and believed to be living on the streets.

McCall put in a call to Detective Diaz in Palm City

and wasn't surprised to find him still at work. Apparently he was getting a lot of pressure on the Ray Allan Evans Sr. murder because Evans had been the husband of Ella Vanderliner.

"I've got an ID on our Jane Doe," she said and proceeded to tell him about Celeste Leigh.

"Prostitution? I'm not surprised. From what we've discovered investigating his father's homicide, RJ was involved in a string of shady ventures that lost money, and his daddy had to bail him out. He was also known to frequent the lower end of town."

"Celeste was wearing a diamond engagement ring with a big rock on it. We found the receipt for it in the glove box of the car. It set RJ back a large chunk of change. Which might explain why her ring finger appeared to have been broken. I think RJ changed his mind about any upcoming nuptials."

Diaz swore. "The bastard broke her finger trying to take back the wedding ring? I guess I shouldn't be surprised given that he later hung her from a tree."

"Apparently, he'd been abusing her for some time."

"That fits with what we know about him. He'd been accused by other prostitutes of abuse, but they always dropped the charges. So what about the other noose?"

"We found Josephine Vanderliner's purse downriver from where RJ and Celeste were believed to have been camped. We'll continue dragging the river in the morning. Given the three sets of tracks, the two nooses and her purse, we're fairly certain Vanderliner was there with them."

"Keep me updated. I'll see if I can find some next of kin that need to be notified of Celeste Leigh's death."

McCall hung up and studied the photograph of Ray Allan Evans Jr. again. He was blond, blue-eyed, movie-star handsome, but there was something about him that unnerved her, and would have even if she hadn't known anything about him.

It was in the eyes, she thought, as she pushed away the photograph and looked instead at the copy she'd made of Josephine Vanderliner's photo.

Vanderliner was pretty in a startling way. In the photo, she had her long, ginger-colored hair pulled back and wound in a loose braid. Her eyes were aquamarine, and she was smiling into the camera as if she didn't have a care in the world.

That had apparently changed, McCall thought, as she sighed and made another copy of the photographs to take to the *Milk River Courier* office come morning.

If there was even a chance that either RJ Evans or Josephine Vanderliner were still in the area, then residents needed to know and be on the lookout for them.

If they were in Whitehorse, the town was small enough that any stranger stood out like a sore thumb—especially this time of year. During summer a few tourists would past through on what was known as the Hi-Line, Highway 2 across the top part of Montana. But it was a little early for tourist season.

As McCall locked up and headed for her cabin beside Milk River, she glanced at the vehicles parked diagonally at the curb in front of the bars. None from out of state. Only one from out of town.

She left the mostly sleeping little Western town and headed home, praying neither suspect was anywhere near Whitehorse, Montana.

WHERE WAS JACK? Josey felt a chill as she glanced around the empty room. The door to the bathroom was open, the room empty.

She sat up, listening. The house seemed unusually quiet. Eerily so. She had a sudden urge to get out of there while she had a chance. What was wrong with her?

From the open window next to the bed, she heard one of the horses whinny, then another. She threw her legs over the side of the bed and hurried to the window.

A wedge of moon and a zillion tiny stars lit the black night. She could make out the horses moving around the corral as if something had set them off. She waited for her eyes to adjust to the darkness, surprised that the floodlight near the barn was out.

It had been casting a golden glow over the ranch yard earlier when she'd gone to bed. Her pulse quickened.

A breeze rustled the leaves of the cottonwoods, casting eerie shadows in the direction of the lodge.

Among the shadows, something moved.

Jack.

He crept along the dark edge of the buildings like a man who didn't want to be seen. He had something in his hand that occasionally caught the moonlight. A crowbar?

Josey watched him reach the end of the far wing, the one she'd noticed was older than the rest and had boards over the windows and doors. He disappeared around the corner.

Where was he sneaking off to at this time of the night and why? Apparently, she wasn't the only one with secrets.

JOSEY WOKE THE next morning to the sound of running water. A few minutes later Jack came out of the bathroom wearing only his jeans and boots. His muscled chest was suntanned and glistening. He smelled of soap, his face was clean shaven, his blond hair was wet and dark against the nape of his neck.

She'd felt a wave of desire wash over her.

"Morning," he said, seeing she was awake. He seemed to avoid her gaze.

"Good morning." Well, if he wasn't going to say anything, then she was. "Jack—"

"I'll let you get ready and come down with you for breakfast," he said quickly. "Can you be ready in half an hour?"

She nodded, sensing the change in him. She'd hoped things would go back to the way they were yesterday, when he'd been playful and affectionate. It had been a game, this pretend marriage. But apparently yesterday had changed that after he'd seen the rope burn on her neck. Or did it have something to do with his late-night exploration?

She'd heard him come in just before daylight. He hadn't turned on a light. She'd listened to him stumbling around in the dark and caught a whiff of alcohol. Had he been drinking?

Now he didn't give her a second glance as he pulled on a Western shirt and left.

She lay in bed, hating this change in him. She knew he must be regretting picking her up on the highway, let alone proposing marriage, even a fake one. She touched the rope burn on her neck. What he must think of her.

If he only knew.

Well, what did he expect? she thought angrily, as she swung her legs over the side of the bed and headed for the bathroom. He didn't know a thing about her. He hadn't wanted to know a thing about her. All he wanted was a pretend wife to fool his grandmother. And she'd done her job just fine.

She took a quick bath and was ready when he returned.

He again gave her only a glance, his gaze pausing for a moment on the new scarf she had tied around her neck. She couldn't wait for her neck to heal enough that she could dispense with the scarves.

As they descended the stairs, Josey missed his warm hand on her back. She missed his touch almost as much as she missed the way he had looked at her.

Jack's grandmother glanced up as they entered the dining room, her gaze narrowing. The old gal didn't miss much. She must see that there was trouble in honeymoon paradise.

Josey felt uncomfortable, as if she was under scrutiny throughout breakfast. Even Virginia seemed to pick up on the fact that something was different between Josey and Jack.

"The two of you should take a horseback ride," Pepper Winchester said as they finished breakfast. "Show her the ranch, Jack. I know how you love to ride."

Josey started to say that wasn't necessary, that she didn't know how to ride, that the last thing the two of them needed was to be alone together, but Jack interrupted her before she could.

"I think that's a great idea," he said, getting to his feet. "I'll go saddle up two horses and meet you in the barn."

JACK WAS ALMOST surprised when he turned to find Josey framed in the barn doorway. He wondered how long she'd been standing there watching him. A while, from her expression.

He hated the way he'd been treating her since seeing what some bastard had done to her. He couldn't help his anger. He wanted to kill the son of a bitch.

A part of him also wanted to grab Josey and shake some sense into her. How could she have let something like this happen? Clearly, she'd gotten hooked up with the wrong guy. Why had he thought her too smart to fall for a man like that? He was disappointed in her.

But it only amplified the fact that he didn't know this woman. Apparently not at all.

"You've never ridden a horse before, have you?" he said now. "I saw your expression at breakfast."

"That had more to do with you than horses," she said, as she stepped into the barn. "I woke up last night and you were gone."

He finished cinching down the saddle and turned to her. "I went downstairs for a drink."

Her eyes narrowed. "Before or after you sneaked outside with a crowbar?" she asked. She started to turn away when he grabbed her arm and swung her back around to face him.

"What are you doing here with me?" he demanded.

She looked into his eyes, and he lost himself for a moment in that sea of green. "I didn't have anything better to do."

He let go of her arm, shaking his head. "So we're both lying to each other. Be honest with me and I'll be honest with you," he challenged. "What are you running from? Or should I say *who* are you running from?"

She took a step back. "Whatever you're doing here, it's none of my business."

He laughed. "Just like whoever is after you is none of my business?"

"It's better if you don't know."

He gave her an impatient look. "I'd like to know what has you so scared."

"No, you don't." With that she turned as if to leave, but collided with Alfred Hoagland, who was standing just outside.

"I came to see if you needed help saddling the horses," the old man said, his two large hands on each of her shoulders to steady her. "Change your mind about going for a ride?"

"No," she said, pulling free of him and stepping back into the barn.

"I've got it covered, Alfred," Jack said.

The old man stood in the doorway for a moment. "Fine with me," he said before turning away.

Jack stepped past Josey to make sure Alfred wasn't still standing outside listening.

"Do you think he heard what we were saying?" she whispered behind him.

"Don't worry about it." He turned his back to her.

"Look, if you've changed your mind about this marriage—"

"I haven't," he quickly interrupted. "I'm sorry about the way I've been acting. Coming back here…" He waved a hand through the air. "It's hard to explain. I have a lot of conflicting emotions going on right now. But I'm glad you're here with me. Come for a ride with me. It's a beautiful day, and Enid packed us a lunch so we can be gone until suppertime. You have to admit, that has its appeal."

IT DID. Just like Jack did when he smiled the way he was smiling at her now. Earlier, she'd stood quietly studying him from the barn doorway as he saddled the horses. He'd been unaware she was there and she hadn't said anything, enjoying watching him.

He'd spoken softly to each horse, touching and stroking the horses in such a gentle way that she'd found herself enthralled by this side of the man.

Now she eyed her horse, wondering what she'd gotten herself into. Her horse, like Jack's, was huge. She told herself she could handle this. After everything she'd been through, this should be easy.

But when she looked at Jack she didn't feel strong or tough. She felt scared and hurt. It was crazy that what he thought of her could hurt so much, and it scared her that she cared. She barely knew this man she was pretending to be wed to, and his sneaking away from their room last night proved it.

Worse, she couldn't help thinking about what his reaction would be if he knew the truth. She cringed at the thought.

"Ready?" Jack swung up into his saddle with a fluid, graceful motion that made her jealous. Everything seemed to come easy for him, making her wonder about the story he'd told at dinner last night.

Apparently, he'd had a hard life, and yet it didn't show on him. Unless his bruises were deeper than her own.

She concentrated on attempting to copy Jack's movements. She grabbed hold of the saddle horn and tried to pull herself up enough to get a foot in the stirrup.

She heard Jack chuckle and climb down from his horse.

"Here, let me help you." He didn't sound upset with her anymore. She wished that didn't make her as happy as it did. "Put your foot in my hands."

She looked into his face, overcome by the gentleness she saw there, and felt tears well in her eyes. She hurriedly put her booted foot into his clasped hands and, balancing herself with one hand on his shoulder, was lifted up and into the saddle.

The horse shuddered, and she grabbed the saddle horn with both hands, feeling way too high above the ground.

"Thank you," she said, furtively wiping at her tears. "You don't have to do this."

He misread the reason for her tears. She nodded, not looking at him. What was wrong with her? She hadn't shed a tear throughout her recent ordeal, and here she was fighting tears? She was letting Jack Winchester get to her. Big mistake.

"I want to do this." She could feel his gaze on her and was relieved when he walked around and climbed back on his horse.

As her horse followed Jack's out of the barn, she looked at the vast country and took a deep breath. Her father always told her she could do anything she set her mind to. But her father had been gone for years now, and her mother no longer knew her.

They rode through tall green grass across rolling prairie, the air smelling sweet with clover. In the distance, Josey could see the dark outline of a mountain range. Jack told her they were the Little Rockies.

They'd ridden from rocky dry land covered with nothing but cactus and sagebrush into this lush, pine-studded, beautiful country. It surprised her how quickly the landscape changed. Even the colors. They ran in shades of silken green to deep purple by the time they reached the horizon.

They stopped on a high ridge deep in the Missouri Breaks. She felt as if she was on top of the world, the land running wide-open to the horizons as clouds bobbed in a sea of blue overhead. "It's amazing up here," she said, taking an awed breath.

"It's still lonely country," he said. "There isn't anything for miles."

"Your grandmother doesn't run cattle or grow any crops?"

"She used to, back when the family all lived on the ranch, but I'm sure she sold off the herd after we all left," Jack said. "All she had was Enid and Alfred, and you can tell by the shape the place is in that they haven't been able to keep up with maintaining the house and barns. I'm surprised she kept the horses, but I suspect Alfred must ride. I wouldn't imagine my grandmother's been on a horse in years."

"You used to ride as a boy?" she guessed.

He nodded. "My mother and I rode down here. It was our favorite spot."

She heard a wistfulness in his voice that she hadn't heard since they'd been here, a love for this country and a sorrow for the mother he'd loved.

"You miss this," she said.

He chuckled.

She could almost feel the battle going on inside him. He'd come here to even a score with his grandmother in some way. But a part of him wanted this, not the money, but the land, and not just to own it, but to ranch it.

"What would you do if your grandmother asked you to stay?"

"She won't."

"How can you be so sure of that?"

"Because I know her."

"Maybe she's changed."

He chuckled again. "Right. Anyway, it's too late."

Was it ever too late? She thought of RJ. Maybe some people were too bitter, too sick, too hateful to ever change. Maybe Jack's grandmother was one of them.

She listened to the breeze blow through the boughs of the ponderosa pines and wished she and Jack never had to go back to civilization.

"I'd run cattle on it the way this ranch was when I was a kid," Jack said suddenly. "I'd get wheat growing up on those high benches and alfalfa and hay. I'd make it a working ranch again instead of..." His voice trailed off and he laughed, as if at his own foolishness. "Just talking," he said. "I came up here to say goodbye."

They ate the lunch Enid had packed them with a view of the lake where the Missouri River widened into Fort Peck Reservoir. The water looked like a sparkling blue jewel hidden in this untamed, uninhabited country.

"I'm sorry about the way I reacted last night," Jack said after they'd finished a sandwich and soda on a large flat rock.

She nodded, a lump in her throat. This was the last thing she wanted to talk about.

"I was just so angry at the person who did that to

you..." His voice trailed off. "And I took that anger out on you."

She understood more than he knew.

"Josey, I want to help."

She shook her head. "You don't know any more about me than I do you. I think it is best if we leave it that way."

"That's not true. You've met my family. You know where I was born. Hell, you practically know my whole life history."

"Just up to the age of six. I don't even know where you live now."

"Wyoming. Ten Sleep, Wyoming. How about you?"

She shook her head.

"Look, I know you're in trouble and it's because of a dangerous man." He raised his hand to keep her from interrupting him. Not that she was going to. So far he'd been dead-on. "All I'm saying is that maybe I can help."

Josey smiled, her eyes burning with tears again. She was touched and hated that she was. "Don't be so nice to me, okay?"

"I can't help myself." His gaze locked with hers.

She felt the heat in those eyes, the blue like a hot flame. Their thighs brushed as he moved, the touch sending a flurry of emotions racing through her.

Jack drew her into his arms before she could protest. His mouth dropped to hers as his strong arms encircled her.

His kiss was filled with passion and heat and, strangely enough, a gentleness like he'd shown with the horses, as if he knew to go easy with her because she would spook easily.

She did more than let him kiss her. She kissed him

back, matching his passion and his heat, if not his gentleness, until she came to her senses and drew back.

He was looking at her, his eyes filled with a soft tenderness.

It was as if a dam burst. All the tears she'd repressed for so long broke free. He pulled her back into his arms, holding her as she sobbed, his large hand rubbing her back as he whispered soothing words she could neither hear nor understand.

McCall stood outside the cold, sterile autopsy room waiting for George to come out and give her the results. The crime lab had flown in personnel to do the autopsy. George was assisting.

She'd had only a few hours' sleep before she'd called down to the Missouri River this morning to check with Luke. They were dragging the river and had been since daylight. So far, nothing.

George didn't look so hot as he came out of the autopsy room. "I figured you'd be waiting." He made her sound ghoulish. "The report should be typed up within an hour."

She shook her head. She didn't want to wait that long. "Just give me the highlights."

He sighed, looking exhausted and a little green around the gills. She figured he regretted taking this job and wondered how long he'd last.

"Could we at least sit down for minute?" he asked, and headed for the conference room.

She grabbed them both a cup of coffee from the machine and joined him.

"As you know, she had numerous signs of abuse," he said, as she handed him a cup of coffee and sat down.

"Scars, cuts and bruises, cigarette burns. She had either been with a long-time abuser or…"

"She got off on it," McCall guessed.

He grimaced.

"So maybe the hanging was a sexual thing."

George looked even more uncomfortable. "With two women? There were two places where ropes had been tied to the limb."

McCall thought about it for a few moments as she sipped her coffee. "Maybe we were wrong about there being another victim. Maybe he'd hung her up there before and the limb had held the first time. This time, it didn't."

"I guess. But how do you explain the car in the river?"

She shook her head. "I guess it would depend on whether or not they were alone at that camp. We've just assumed Vanderliner was with the other two because she was seen with her stepbrother leaving the scene of the murder and we found her purse."

McCall rubbed her temples. "Also there were at least three different sets of footprints found at the scene, two women's-size types of sneakers and tracks that matched the loafer we found stuck under the brake pedal of the car."

"You're thinking the victim on the slab could have had more than one pair of sneakers," George offered.

"Or the other prints could be those of the missing Josephine Vanderliner. It would explain the other noose, and we have three different hair samples from the car, which was only a couple of days old. We know Vanderliner was in the car at some point because of the eyewitness but we don't know for how long. He could have dumped her and kept her purse."

"So we don't know if Vanderliner made it as far as Montana."

McCall nodded thoughtfully. "I just have a bad feeling she's here. Either in that river or on the loose. I stopped by the newspaper office early this morning. They're running photographs of both RJ Evans and Josephine Vanderliner. If either of them got out of that river, then someone has to have seen them. They were going to need a ride since the only tracks we found were for the car in the river."

"Great," George said. "One of them abuses women for the fun of it and the other is wanted for murder." He shook his head. "I hope you put something in the paper to warn residents in case they come across them."

"Armed and dangerous and possibly traveling together."

Chapter Seven

RJ felt like hell. His shoulder had quit bleeding. Fortunately the bullet had only furrowed through his flesh and missed the bone, but it hurt like a son of a bitch. He knew he had to get some antibiotics. If it wasn't already infected.

But right now he was more concerned about the blow to his head. The double vision was driving him crazy. That and the killer headache. Bitches.

Celeste had almost drowned him. Josey had shot him. He'd been damned lucky to get out of that car. He wondered where Celeste was. The last he'd seen her she had been sucked out of the car by the current.

He'd gotten his foot caught under the brake pedal. When he'd finally freed himself, he'd come up downriver in time to see Josey getting away. He'd been bleeding like a stuck pig and was half-blind from the blow on his head, but even crazed as he was, he knew he had to catch her or everything he'd worked for would turn to a pile of crap.

How had things gone so wrong? Maybe Celeste was right. Maybe it had been when he'd lost his temper and strung her up from that tree limb. He hadn't meant to kill her, just shut her the hell up.

No, where things had really gone haywire was when he decided to string up Josey next to her. Should have known that limb couldn't hold both of them. Shouldn't have left the pistol lying on that log by the fire pit, either.

But who knew either of those women could move that fast? He hadn't been that surprised when Josey had shot him. He'd expected something like that from her, but he'd never seen it coming with Celeste. She'd been like a wild animal when she'd attacked him.

He'd tied the ropes to the bumper of the car and strung up both women. When the damned limb broke, he'd thrown the car in Reverse, thinking he could run them down. But then Josey had shot at him and Celeste had come flying in the driver-side window at him, the rope still around her neck and dragging in the dirt. She'd knocked the breath out of him.

And with her pummeling him he hadn't realized he was still in Reverse, the car still going backward toward the river. The next thing he knew the car was in the river and he was underwater and Celeste, that stupid whore, was still fighting him.

Shuddering now at the memory of how close he'd come to drowning, he stumbled and almost fell. He'd climbed out of the river and gone after Josey. He knew she'd make a run for it. No surprise, she'd taken the backpack with the money and his gun in it.

He'd climbed the hill back to the single-track dirt road. That was when he'd spotted her. She had shoes, so she had made better time than him. He'd lost both of his in the river, and he was shot and hurt, and with nothing but socks on his bare feet the ground felt rough.

He'd seen her on the highway halfway up the mountainside. Too far away to shoot her even if he'd had the pistol. Maybe with a rifle…

But then a pale yellow Cadillac convertible had roared across the bridge and up the other side, stopping three-quarters of the way up the mountain when the driver saw Josey standing beside the road.

RJ had picked up a rock and thrown it as hard as he could. It hit on the mountain below him and rolled down, starting a small avalanche. But of course it hadn't stopped Josey from disappearing in the Cadillac.

He didn't know how far he walked last night. He just knew he had to put some distance between him and the river. He'd finally laid down under a big pine tree and slept until daylight. The soles of his feet were bleeding through his socks.

He'd awakened this morning and realized he could see the highway from where he was on the side of the mountain and the cop cars. All that commotion. They must have found Celeste.

That was when he knew he was in trouble. He had to find Josey before the cops did. But he couldn't track her down in the shape he was in. He needed shoes, clothes, a vehicle, medicine and some drugs. He'd lost his stash in the car when it went into the water. He felt jittery and irritable. Soon his skin would be crawling as if there were bugs just under the surface.

He knew he couldn't get a ride. Not as bad as he looked. Not with cops and searchers crawling the area.

That's when he'd seen what appeared to be a roof in

the distance and remembered when he and his father had come to Montana for an elk hunt. There used to be a bar at what was called Mobridge. As he remembered, there was also a house. Was it possible someone still lived there?

JACK LEANED BACK, the rock warm, the view incredible, and studied Josey.

She stood on the edge of the ravine, staring out at the wild terrain.

They hadn't spoken since the kiss or her tears. He'd held her until she'd quit crying, then she'd stepped out of his arms, seeming embarrassed, and walked to the edge of the ridge.

He'd waited, giving her time and space. He knew better than to try to push her and yet he wanted desperately to know who had done those things to her and what had her running so scared. What the hell kind of trouble had she gotten herself into and how could he make it right?

Jack chuckled to himself, realizing he'd been wanting to make things right since he was a boy and he'd seen the pain his mother had suffered.

With Josey, it was more complicated. She didn't want to involve him. Didn't she realize he was already involved? He'd become involved the moment he'd picked her up on the highway. He'd only gotten in deeper by kissing her. He wanted to help her. And if that meant getting this bastard who'd done this to her…

She'd said she'd taken care of it. He didn't like the sound of that. Had she killed the man? Was that why she was so afraid? Why hadn't she gone to the police then? Between the rope burn around her neck and the bruises he'd only glimpsed, she would have had a good case for self-defense.

The breeze ruffled her short, dark curls. He watched her raise her hand to push it out of her eyes. She was so beautiful. So strong and yet so fragile.

He knew he shouldn't have kissed her. But he hadn't been able to help himself. And he couldn't even promise that he wouldn't do it again.

She turned to look back at him. "I'm sorry about that."

"I'm not. I'm used to women crying after I kiss them." Just as he'd hoped, she smiled. "I suppose we'd better head back. We have a long ride ahead of us. Can't have Aunt Virginia passing out from hunger if we're late for supper. She is such a delicate thing."

Josey chuckled. "She's a lot like your grandmother that way."

"Isn't she though." He handed Josey her reins and helped her into her saddle.

"I'm from California, an only child, my father is dead, my mother—" Her voice broke. "She was in a car accident and never fully recovered."

"I'm sorry."

"I probably shouldn't have even told you that," she said, looking toward the horizon. "The less you know about me, the better off you'll be once I'm gone."

WITH JACK AND JOSEY off on a horseback ride and Virginia napping, Pepper Winchester took advantage of being alone with Enid.

She'd managed to keep her housekeeper from drugging her for some time now by getting rid of the food or drink Enid gave her privately, but she had to put a stop to it. Pepper knew her only hesitation was that she didn't want to have to fire Enid and her husband.

Not because she felt any kind of loyalty to them. She'd been more than generous with the two over the years. They must have a nice little nest egg put away.

No, it was because she didn't like change. The last thing she wanted was strangers on the ranch. Enid and Alfred had been fixtures on the place since Pepper herself had come to the ranch as a new bride. Was it any wonder they felt they belonged here even more than she did?

But she couldn't let Enid run roughshod over her anymore. Nor could she trust the woman. Pepper was sure the two wondered what she was up to. They knew her well enough to know that getting her family back to the ranch hadn't been an act of sentiment.

She found Enid in the kitchen stirring something boiling on the stove. It was impossible to tell what she was cooking. The woman really was a horrible cook. When Call was alive and the kids were all on the ranch, they'd had a real cook and Enid had been the housekeeper.

Once everyone was gone, there had been no reason to keep on anyone else, although Pepper couldn't remember firing the rest of the staff.

She suspected Enid had done it, since Pepper had been so distraught that her housekeeper and caretaker had taken advantage of it.

"Please turn that off," she said now to Enid.

Enid turned slowly to stare at her as if she couldn't believe what she was seeing. Had it been that long since she'd been in this kitchen?

Enid turned off the burner, then crossed her arms

over her chest, leaning back against the counter next to the stove. "Well?"

Pepper bristled at Enid's insolent manner. She'd let this happen and had only herself to blame. In her grief, she'd given up control of her home and her life to this woman and her husband. She now saw what a mistake that had been.

"I'm going to have to let you and your husband go." Her words seemed to hang in the humid kitchen air, surprising them both.

She waited for Enid to put up an argument. When she didn't, Pepper added, "I'm sorry."

To her surprise, Enid began to laugh. "Alfred and I aren't going anywhere."

Pepper couldn't believe her ears. "I beg your pardon?"

"You best give it some thought," Enid said, and started to turn back to whatever she was cooking.

Pepper felt her temper rise. "I've made up my mind."

Enid sighed and turned back to her, eyes narrowing into menacing slits. "Do you know how long I've been on this ranch?"

"That doesn't have anything to—"

"I've been here since before Call brought you here. I've heard every argument, seen it all, *know* you better than you know yourself." She lowered her voice. "*I* know where all the bodies are buried."

"Are you threatening to blackmail me?" Pepper demanded, barely able to contain her rage.

"If I wanted to blackmail you I could have done it a long time ago." Enid smiled. "Even now I wonder what that new acting sheriff would think if I told her just half of what I know about her grandmother."

Pepper's stomach twisted into a knot at the mention of McCall. Her heart was pounding so hard in her ears she had to steady herself, her hand going to the kitchen counter for support.

"I'd hate to see you have to spend the rest of your golden years behind bars." Enid sounded so self-satisfied that Pepper had to restrain herself from picking up one of the kitchen knives and ending this right here.

She might have done just that, except then she couldn't finish what she'd started. But once she knew the truth about Trace's murder...

"So, to answer your question," Enid was saying, "of course I'm not blackmailing you. I'm just saying you might want to reconsider." Enid turned and picked up the spoon she'd laid down earlier. "Of course, if you saw fit to put a little something in your will for Alfred and me, that would be greatly appreciated. We *have* been loyal servants on the Winchester Ranch almost our whole lives. Call, bless his soul, always said he didn't know what he would have done without us."

Pepper's gaze bored into the woman's back like a bullet at the mention of Call's name. She felt powerless and hated the feeling, even knowing that it wouldn't be for long. The day would come when she would turn the tables on Enid and it would be soon if she had anything to do with it.

"Why don't you sit down and have some of this soup I made?" Enid said. "You can tell me what you're up to getting your family back here to the ranch." She glanced over her shoulder at Pepper. "I told you, I know you better than you know yourself."

If that were true, Pepper thought, then Enid would be terrified of her and what she had planned for her.

"You're mistaken about my motives," Pepper managed to say, and started to leave the room. "I just wanted to see my family."

She was almost to the door when Enid's words stopped her.

"Some people think you've already lost your mind, locking yourself up all these years in this old place," Enid was saying. "Wouldn't take much for someone to think you're not in your right mind. Now why don't you sit down and have a little soup. I made it special just for you. It will calm you right down."

Pepper turned back to watch Enid ladle out a cup of the soup and stir something into it before setting the cup on the kitchen table.

"You'll want to eat it while it's still hot."

She stared at the cup of watery-looking soup, Enid's threat still ringing in her ears as she stepped back into the room, sat down at the table and picked up her spoon.

"A little of my soup, that's all you need," Enid said, as she went back to work at the stove.

Pepper took a bite. She gagged a little, the bile rising in her throat. She took another bite and felt the warmth of the soup and the drugs take hold. She put down her spoon.

Enid took the rest of the cup of soup and dumped it down the drain. "You should lie down for a while. You look a little peaked. I'm sure you'll feel better after a nap."

DINNER WAS A solemn affair. Josey noticed that Jack's grandmother was especially quiet. Virginia drank her wine without incident, and Jack seemed lost in his own thoughts.

She was grateful he hadn't wanted to talk about what had happened on their ride. Josey was embarrassed. She never cried like that, especially in front of a stranger. And she needed to remember that was exactly what Jack was—a stranger.

As soon as dinner was over, she excused herself, saying she needed a little air, and went outside for a walk.

The air felt close. She was taken with the wild openness of this place. She could literally see for miles.

Josey thought about her mother and felt that old pain and frustration. For months she'd been trying to help her. Now she'd made things worse.

But once she got money wired to the new healthcare facility and knew for sure that her mother had been moved…

She hadn't realized how far she'd gone until she turned around to head back. The sky had darkened. Thunderheads hunkered on the horizon to the west, and the wind had picked up, sending dust swirling around her. She raised her hand to shield her eyes, squinting in the direction of the Winchester Ranch lodge.

Lights were on downstairs. Fortunately, as Josey was leaving the house, Pepper had grabbed Jack, insisting he come with her. Otherwise, Josey was sure Jack would have wanted to tag along. She knew he worried about her and, like her, he must worry that the trouble after her might somehow find her here.

As she neared the house, the first drops of rain began to fall. The Cadillac sat out front where they'd left it yesterday, the top down. She noticed the keys were in the ignition, opened the driver-side door and slid behind the wheel. She whirred the top up, snapping it into place, then put up the windows and sat for a moment in the warm quiet, listening to the rain patter on the canvas roof.

She looked toward the house and thought of Jack. Through the parlor window, she could see shadows moving around inside. Jack and his grandmother?

Feeling almost guilty, she reached over and opened the glove box and dug around inside until she found the car registration.

The car was registered to Galaxy Corporation. The address was a post office box in Ten Sleep, Wyoming.

What was the Galaxy Corporation? And did this car even belong to Jack Winchester?

Josey hurriedly put the registration back in the glove box along with the Montana map, then changed her mind and opened the map.

Just as she had suspected. The town of Whitehorse had been circled. She struggled to read what had been written off to the east of it. Winchester Ranch.

A sliver of worry burrowed under Josey's skin as she stuffed everything back into the glove box and closed it.

She sat in the car, listening to the patter of the rain, staring at the old Western ranch lodge and wondering who she was pretending to be married to.

JACK HADN'T WANTED to let Josey out of his sight, but he'd been cornered by his grandmother after dinner and had no choice.

A fire burned in the small rock fireplace. It crackled softly as Pepper Winchester motioned for him to sit opposite her in the matching leather chairs.

"I'm sorry I ambushed you the other day," she said. "I shouldn't have done that."

Pepper Winchester apologizing?

"I had hoped you might have remembered something from the day of Trace's birthday party."

What was it she wanted him to remember? he wondered. Or was it something she wanted to make sure he didn't remember?

Suddenly, the room felt cold as a chill ran the length of his spine.

"I foolishly thought that if I just asked you right out, you would tell me the truth," she was saying.

Jack smiled to himself. Now this was more like his grandmother. He said nothing, waiting for the barrage he knew would follow. What he wasn't ready for was the tears as his grandmother began to cry.

She quickly stopped herself, getting up awkwardly and leaning heavily on her cane as she moved to the fireplace, her back to him.

"Why don't you tell me what this is really about?" he suggested, determined not to be swayed by her tears.

"You're right, of course." She didn't turn around as she brushed at the tears, her back ramrod straight. "I have reason to believe that one of you saw something from the window up there. I thought if you had that you'd tell me. After all these years I'd assumed there would be no reason for any of you to keep the secret any longer. I foolishly assumed that one of you would want the truth to come out."

Her candor surprised him as much as her apology and her tears had. He didn't know what to say.

"I know it's possible that I'm wrong," she said, making it sound as if she didn't believe it. "Maybe none of you saw Trace being murdered." She turned to face him. "You see now why it is so important that I find out the truth. I don't believe the killer acted alone. I'm basing that assumption on where Trace was killed—within sight of the ranch. The killer got him to that spot, I believe, for a good reason. Because someone else was watching from the ranch that day. I believe that person didn't know that you children were in that third-floor room with a pair of binoculars."

Jack was stunned. "You're saying you think someone from the family was involved in Trace's murder?"

"Yes, I do."

So that was what this was about. He couldn't believe what he was hearing, and yet even as a small child he was aware of the jealousy among the siblings.

"I intend to find out who that person is if it takes my last dying breath."

Jack stared at her. "That's why you invited us all back."

She nodded. "I would be a foolish old woman to think that I could make up for the past at this late date." She shook her head. "I won't rest until I find out the truth. Will you help me?" Her voice broke and he felt something break in him, as well.

He reached inside himself for all the hatred he'd carried for this woman the past twenty-seven years, but that fire that had consumed him for so long had burned down to only a handful of red-hot embers.

His words surprised him, since he didn't feel he owed this woman anything given the hell she'd put his parents through. "We were in the room that morning."

His grandmother slumped down onto the hearth.

"We'd heard stories about the room and wanted to see it."

"Whose idea was it to go up there?" she asked in a voice fraught with emotion.

"I don't recall. All the adults were busy with Trace's birthday preparations for that afternoon."

Pepper's eyes shone brightly in the firelight as if remembering.

"I'm sorry, but I didn't see anything." He'd been busy reading what had been scratched into the walls.

Her disappointment was palpable. "Did one of your cousins have a pair of small binoculars?"

He felt a start as he remembered the binoculars.

"Which cousin?" she asked, witnessing his reaction.

"I… I really don't recall." He'd been distracted. By the writing on the walls. And the girl. Jack had wondered where she'd come from and why he hadn't seen her before. He gathered she shouldn't be there, that she'd sneaked in, ridden over from the only close ranch nearby, the McCormick Ranch. He'd forgotten until now, but there'd been another girl with her, a younger girl who they all ignored.

"I remember Cordell and Cyrus fighting over the binoculars." Showing off for the older girl. "I honestly can't remember which one of them ended up with the binoculars."

Jack wondered what his grandmother would say if he told her about the girls? He wasn't sure what held him back. Certainly not loyalty to his cousins or their friends. He wasn't even sure why he'd told his grandmother what he had. Just for a moment there, he'd felt sorry for her, he supposed.

She nodded slowly, as if sensing he was holding back something. "I would think that if anyone saw their uncle being murdered, that boy would have had a reaction. He might not have told me, but I would think he'd have told his cohorts."

"You have to remember, I was just the nanny's kid," Jack said, digging up some of that old pain to remind himself why he was here. "My so-called cousins weren't all that fond of me. So if they had secrets, they kept them to themselves."

She rose, but with effort. He started to help her, but she waved his hand away. "If you should think of anything that might help me…"

Did she really think he was here to help her?

He was glad when his grandmother called it a night and he could go look for Josey. He was relieved to find her alone, sitting in the tire swing under one of the massive cottonwood trees. A rain squall had blown through, but it was dry under the trees. He loved the smell after a rain almost as much as he loved the scent of Josey's damp hair.

"You all right?" Jack asked, as he gave her a push. The rope tied to the limb overhead creaked loudly.

Josey jumped off and turned as if he'd scared her.

He remembered the rope burn on her neck and mentally kicked himself for being so stupid. "I'm sorry, I—"

"No, it's just that I get motion sickness on swings."

Right. "Dinner was fun," he said sarcastically, to change the subject.

"Wasn't it." She stepped from under the canopy of cottonwood limbs and turned her face upward. "Have you ever seen so many stars?"

"You don't see many where you live?"

She didn't look at him. "No. I live in the city."

He found the Big Dipper, one of the few constellations he knew. He wanted to know more about Josey, but he knew better than to ask. Whoever had hurt her made her afraid to trust. He could understand that.

"How did your talk go with your grandmother?" Josey asked, afraid he was about to question her.

"She talked a lot about Trace, my uncle who was murdered."

"What was that she asked yesterday about some room that is off-limits?" Josey asked.

He turned to look back at the house and pointed. The room was barely visible from this angle, as it was on the far wing set back against the hillside—the wing that had been boarded up. It was an odd wing, she noticed. If had been built back into the side of a hill and appeared to be much older than the original structure. As an afterthought, a room had been added near the back.

"That's the room?" she asked.

"That's it."

"What's in it?"

"Nothing. A window." He shook his head. "Nothing else. It's soundproof."

"Soundproof?" She realized he'd been in the room, just as his grandmother had suspected. "Why is whether or not you were in the room such a big deal to your grandmother?"

Jack looked like he wished she hadn't asked. "Between you and me? She thinks one of us might have seen my uncle Trace murdered." He nodded at her surprised reaction. "There were a pair of binoculars in the room. I never touched them, but the others were looking through them. She thinks one of them witnessed the murder. The alleged murderer confessed, but was killed. My grandmother believes there was an accomplice, someone from the family, and that's why Trace was murdered within sight of the ranch."

"Well, if one of you kids had seen something, wouldn't you have told?"

"Maybe the kid did, and maybe whoever he told was the accomplice."

"That's horrible."

"It's also why she is getting us all back here, to interrogate us individually to get at the truth."

Josey jumped as she realized Enid was standing in the shadows off to the side.

"I guess you didn't hear me call to you," Enid said, stepping toward them. "I wanted to see if there was anything I could get you before I turned in."

"No," Josey and Jack said in unison.

"Well, fine then," the housekeeper said. She turned on her heel and headed for the house.

"That woman is the worst eavesdropper I've ever come across," Josey whispered. "I don't trust her."

"Me, either."

"The way she treats your grandmother, it makes me wonder."

Jack nodded solemnly. "It's almost as if she and her husband have something on Pepper, isn't it?"

Josey realized she was getting chilly. She started to head for the house when Jack touched her arm, stopping her.

"Thank you for being here. I mean that. No matter what, I'm not sorry."

"I hope you never are," she said, knowing he would be soon enough as they walked back to the house and their bedroom. Jack curled up in his chair. Josey thought she'd never be able to sleep, but, still tired from the long horseback ride that day, she dropped right off.

JACK WOKE TO a scream. He bolted upright in the chair, momentarily confused. The scream was coming from the bed.

He shot to his feet and stumbled in the dark over to the bed. "Josey." He shook her gently, feeling the perspiration on her bare arm. "Josey," he said, shaking her more forcefully.

The scream caught in her throat. She jerked away, coming up fighting. She swung at him, both arms flailing wildly.

"Josey!" he cried, grabbing her arms and pinning her down. "It's me, Jack. You were having a bad dream." He released one of her wrists to snap on the light beside the bed.

She squirmed under him, then seemed to focus on him. He felt the fight go out of her, but her face was still etched in fear and she was trembling under him, her body soaked in sweat.

He let go of her other wrist and eased off of her, sitting up on the edge of the bed next to her. He could hear her gasping for breath.

"That must have been some dream," he said quietly, thinking of the rope burn on her neck. Whatever had happened to her was enough to give anyone nightmares.

"I'm okay now."

He wasn't sure if she was trying to convince him or herself. "If you want to talk about it…" He reached over to push a lock of dank hair back from her face.

"I can't even remember what it was about." She shifted her gaze away.

"That's good," he said, going along with the lie. He stood. "If you want I can leave the light on."

She shook her head. "I'm sorry I woke you."

"No problem." He doubted he'd be able to go back to sleep, but he returned to his chair, glad Enid had put them at the end of the wing away from everyone, so no one else heard the screams.

Josey turned out the light. He heard her lie back down. The darkness settled in. He listened to her breathe and thought about how a man would go about killing a bastard like the one who'd given Josey such horrible nightmares.

He also thought about how a man might go about keeping Josey in his life.

IT WAS WHILE he was eating in the kitchen at the house at Mobridge that RJ spotted the phone hanging on the wall.

He'd had to break into the house and had been surprised to find that it appeared someone still lived here.

That was good and bad. The good part was that they weren't home and he'd been able to find some clean clothes, a warm coat, boots that were only a little too big and some drugs to tide him over.

He'd also been able to find food. Not much in the refrigerator so he suspected they'd gone into town to shop. He made himself some soup, ate the canned meat straight from the can along with the canned peaches he'd found, leaving the empty containers on the table. It wasn't like they wouldn't figure out someone had been here.

It appeared a man and woman lived in the house, both older from the clothing he'd found. He'd gone through the woman's jewelry box. Nothing worth stealing. But he'd managed to scare up almost a hundred dollars from a cookie jar in the kitchen and the man's sock drawer.

He got up, searched around for a phone book and finally found one in a drawer. It had doodles all over the front along with an assortment of numbers.

He pulled a chair over so he could sit and opened the phone book to Whitehorse, the town up the road in the direction the yellow Cadillac convertible had been heading when the driver picked up Josey. There were only a few pages, so it didn't take long to find the numbers he needed. He started with gas stations. With towns so few and far between up here, the driver of the Cadillac would have filled up before going any farther up the road.

Three gas stations. He called each, coming up with a story about trying to find his brother-in-law. The clerks were all friendly, that small-town trust that he had a growing appreciation for with each call.

No luck there. He began to call the motels on the chance that the Caddie driver had dropped Josey at one.

He got lucky on his fifth call.

"I remember seeing a yellow Cadillac," a clerk at one of the motels told him.

RJ tried not to sound too excited. "There at the motel?"

"No, over in front of the clothing store."

RJ frowned. "You saw the guy driving it? Was there a woman with him?"

"No. Just a man when I saw him and the car."

He was disappointed. Maybe the guy had already gotten rid of Josey. It just seemed odd the guy would be shopping for clothing, unless...

That damned Josey. She probably cried on the guy's

shoulder and suckered him in. RJ could understand being smitten with her. She was one good-looking woman. He'd wanted her himself.

Should have taken her, too, when he had the chance. He'd planned to, but Celeste had thrown a fit when he suggested the three of them get together. Once he'd given Celeste that engagement ring she was no fun anymore.

So let's say Josey got the driver of the Cadillac to buy her clothes. Then what else would she get him to do for her?

He tried the last motel, convinced he'd find Josey curled up watching television and thinking she'd gotten away.

"I saw the car," the male clerk said. "Sweet. One of those vintage restored jobs."

RJ couldn't have cared less about the work done on the Caddie. "So she's staying there at the motel?"

"The woman with him? No." The guy sounded confused. "I saw the *car* when I was getting gas at Packy's."

That was one of the numbers he'd already called. "Did you happen to notice if there was a woman with him? A woman with long, curly, reddish-blond hair, good-looking?"

The clerk had chuckled. "Good-looking, but she had short, curly, dark hair. And she wasn't with him then. I saw her in the car later."

"Wait a minute. So he didn't have her with him at the gas station, but you saw him with this woman later?"

"That's right. I passed the Cadillac. The cowboy was driving and the woman was in the passenger seat. I didn't get a really good look at her. She was kind of slumped down in the seat. But I saw she had short, curly, dark hair."

What? Slumped down in the seat? The answer came in a rush. Josey had changed her appearance. He wasn't sure how or when, but that had to be the explanation.

"Did you see which way they went when he drove out of town?"

"South."

"South?" Why would the driver go back the way he'd come? "On Highway 191 toward the river?"

"No, they took the Sun Prairie road. I was thinking I wouldn't take a car like that down that road."

RJ could only be thankful the cowboy hadn't been driving some nondescript sedan or this clerk would have never noticed him. "What's down that road besides Sun Prairie?"

The clerk laughed. "Well, there are some ranches, Fort Peck Reservoir, but they didn't look dressed for fishing. Mostly there's just a whole lot of open country."

RJ rubbed his temples. His head felt like it might explode. "So there is no way of knowing where he was going."

"Well, there wouldn't have been if he hadn't asked me for directions when we were both getting gas in our rigs."

This clerk was on RJ's last nerve, plucking it like an out-of-tune guitar string. If this discussion had been in person, that jackass would be breathing his last breath shortly. *"Directions?"*

"To the Winchester Ranch. Didn't I mention that?"

Chapter Eight

Josey woke a little after one in the morning to find Jack's chair empty.

She sat up, listening. A breeze stirred the limbs of the large cottonwood tree outside the window. Shadows played on the bedroom floor, the curtains billowing in and out like breath.

Where was Jack? She slipped out of bed and went to the window. For a moment, she didn't see him. But just as he had the night before, he moved stealthily along the edge of darkness, staying to the deep shadows. He was headed like before toward the closed wing of the lodge.

She frowned and realized it was time she found out what her "husband" was up to. She feared that, whatever it was, if his grandmother found out it would get them kicked off the ranch. She wasn't about to admit that she was worried about Jack.

Grabbing the robe Jack had bought her, she shrugged into it, failing to talk herself out of what she was about to do.

At her door, she listened. No sound. Opening it, she crept out, carrying her cowboy boots. At the top of the stairs, she stopped. A dim light shone downstairs. It seemed to be coming from the kitchen.

Josey listened but hearing no sound tiptoed down the stairs to the front door. Easing it open, she stepped out, closing it behind her.

She hesitated on the front step to pull on her boots. Then she followed the same path Jack had taken, keeping to the shadows until she reached the far wing of the lodge.

It was an odd wing, she noticed. It had been built back into the side of a hill and appeared to be much older than the original structure. The doors and windows had been boarded up, but someone—Jack?—had removed the boards from the doorway.

The breeze picked up, the door blowing open a little wider as she stepped into the darkness of the boarded-up wing. The air was much colder in here and smelled musky, as if the wing had been closed up for some time.

Josey waited for her eyes to adjust to the darkness. She didn't move, hardly breathed as she listened. The only light bled in from the doorway. She'd left the door open, thinking it might be the only way she could find her way back.

At first she heard nothing but the sound of the breeze in the trees outside. Then her ears picked up a fainter sound coming from inside, a scratching noise that could have been mice. Or something larger.

She hesitated. Was it that important she find out what Jack was up to?

The answer was yes, she realized. She moved toward the noise, feeling her way along the dark hallway until she saw the shaft of light coming from under one of the doors.

Mice didn't carry flashlights, she told herself. She moved cautiously forward, stopping in front of the door.

She listened to the scratching sound for a moment before she tried the cold knob.

It turned in her hand.

She took a breath. Was she sure she really wanted to know Jack's secrets? She eased the door open a few inches.

In the glow of his flashlight resting on one of the shelves, Josey saw Jack standing in front of a rock wall. Jack had a crowbar in his hand and was scraping mortar from between the stones.

The room appeared to be a root cellar with rows of shelves. There were dozens of old jars covered with dust, their contents blackened with age.

Jack worked feverishly, as if desperate to see what was on the other side of that wall.

Josey only had a moment to wonder about what she was seeing when a door slammed down the hall.

JACK FROZE, all his instincts on alert. Heavy footfalls echoed down the hall. The hall light flashed on. He swore under his breath and grabbed the flashlight, snapping it off as he turned to look toward the door.

The door was open. A figure was framed there. His heart caught in his throat. He knew that particular figure anywhere. Josey, dressed in only a robe and cowboy boots.

He started to take a step toward her, but she motioned him back as the heavy footfalls grew louder. Jack sank back into the dark shadows of the room, but there was no escape. He was caught. And so was Josey.

"What the hell are you doing in here?" boomed Alfred Hoagland's easily recognizable, raspy old voice.

Through the doorway, Jack saw Alfred grab Josey by the arm.

Without a thought, he stepped toward the door, going to her rescue.

A giggle, high and sweet like a child's stopped him cold. *What the hell?* It took Jack a moment to realize it had come out of Josey.

"Are you daft?" Alfred demanded, letting go of her and stumbling back.

Josey seemed to come awake with surprise. She stumbled back into the wall, closing the door partway as she caught herself. "What...where am I?" She sounded both surprised and scared.

"Something wrong with you?" Alfred demanded, sounding a little afraid himself.

Josey let out a sob. "I can't have been sleepwalking again." She began to cry, covering her face with her hands. Jack had seen her cry and wasn't fooled.

Alfred cleared his voice, visibly uncomfortable. "You should get back to bed."

"I don't know where—"

Alfred let out a curse. "I'll take you." Jack could hear him grumbling to himself all the way down the hall as he led Josey out.

Jack waited until he heard the door close before he turned on his flashlight again. He couldn't chance that Alfred might get suspicious and come back. Taking some of the boards from the cellar shelving, he covered the spot where he'd been working. With luck, Alfred wouldn't notice if he did come back.

Jack knew he had Josey to thank for covering for him tonight, but he was furious with her. She'd taken a hell of a chance. She had no idea how much danger she'd put herself in.

As angry as he was at her for following him and butting into his business, he was also grateful and more than a little awed. Who was this amazing woman? It made him wonder what he saved her from on the highway. Had she felt she owed him? Well, they were even. He'd make sure she wasn't that foolhardy again.

But even as he thought it, he realized his aunt was apparently right about one thing. He and Josey were definitely a pair.

JOSEY HAD BEEN in bed when Jack returned to the room. She pretended to be asleep, listening to him slip in and undress in the pitch blackness of the room.

Finally, he settled into the large chair.

She lay awake, listening to his breathing, knowing he, too, was still awake and just feet from her. She thought about rolling over and offering to share the bed with him. For the first time since they'd gotten "married," she felt they really were in this together.

But she remained mute, not daring to say the words because she knew right at that moment she was feeling scared and alone and would have given anything just to be held in his strong arms.

She knew, too, what would happen if she invited him into her bed.

"Josey?"

She froze, then said quietly, "Yes?"

"Don't ever follow me again."

She lay perfectly still, hearing the anger in his words and feeling her own fury race through her veins like liquid flames. She'd saved the bastard's bacon. "No need to thank me," she said sarcastically.

"We both have our secrets. Stay out of mine and I'll stay out of yours."

In the darkness, she touched the rope burn on her neck and felt the sting of tears. Sleep finally came as a godsend.

RJ DIPPED HIS FINGERS into the salve and touched it to his shoulder, grimacing with pain. He glared into the cheap mirror as if Josey was on the other side, relishing at the thought of the pain he would heap on her.

"I'm coming for you, bitch, and when I find you I'm going to hurt you in ways you never dreamed."

He opened one of the containers of prescription pills he'd found in the medicine cabinet. All of the pills were at least a year old, but if he took enough of them, he might be able to numb the pain, if not kill any infection.

Downing the pills, he took a drink and listened.

He felt better. His vision had cleared some and if he'd had a concussion, it seemed to be getting better. He'd turned on the radio, but hadn't heard any news, so he figured no news was good news.

Josey was smart. If he was right, she'd conned the driver of the Cadillac and was now on the Winchester Ranch miles from town. Hard to find, was what the clerk had said when RJ had made him give him the same directions he'd given the Cadillac driver.

Yeah, not that hard to find. He just hoped she stayed put. He figured she would. She'd feel safe. Her mistake.

He wanted to go after her right now. No holds barred. But even in his dazed state, he knew that would be stupid.

First, he had to take care of himself. Get his strength

back, patch up his wound. Hell, he wasn't going anywhere without a vehicle.

Josey always seemed to land on her feet. He hadn't been worried about her going to the cops—not with a murder rap hanging over her. She knew what would happen to her mother if she ended up behind bars. The thought made him frown. She had the money in the backpack. Would she try to get her mother moved out of the rest home his father had stuck her in?

Hell, yes. He stormed out of the bathroom, picked up the kitchen phone and called the nursing home.

"Just wanted to check on Ella Vanderliner. I mean Ella Evans," he said, when the night nurse answered.

"I'm sure she's asleep. May I ask who's calling?"

"Good. So she's still there?"

"I'm sorry, I didn't catch your name."

He hung up. Maybe he'd been wrong about Josey. Maybe her first thought had been to save her own skin without any thought to her mother.

He glanced in the bedroom at the soft-looking bed and thought about curling up for a while, but knew he couldn't chance it.

He'd gotten almost everything he'd needed here and he didn't want to push his luck. Now he just needed wheels. Unfortunately, all he'd found around this place was some old, broken-down, rusted farm equipment. No vehicle he could steal.

That meant he'd have to hit the road and hope someone stopped to give him a ride. But first he'd find a place to get some sleep in the pine trees again. His head would be clearer in the morning.

He wandered back into the bathroom, pocketed all the pills and a large bottle of aspirin. Pulling on the stolen coat, he took one last look around the kitchen, found some stale cookies and left Mobridge behind.

THE NEXT MORNING Josey woke to find Jack standing on the small balcony outside their room. He looked as if he had the weight of the world on his shoulders. For so long, she'd been so involved in her own problems that she'd been blind to anyone else's. That was what had gotten her into this trouble. Had she been paying attention—

She slid out of bed, wrapping her robe around her, and stepped out on the balcony next to him. Without giving it any thought, she put her arm around Jack as she joined him.

He glanced over at her, his smile shy, apologetic. "I'm sorry I snapped at you last night when I should have thanked you. But I was upset. You shouldn't have followed me."

She looked over at him, her eyes narrowing. "You mean the way you shouldn't have untied my scarf?"

He had the good sense to look chastised. "I wanted to help you."

"And why do you think I followed you last night?"

His gaze locked with hers. "You shouldn't be worrying about me. You have enough—"

"You can tell me what you're after," she said, lowering her voice. "I'll help you. You helped me by bringing me here." He started to argue the point. "Don't even bother to tell me you didn't know I was in some kind of trouble."

He smiled at her and touched her face. "Still," he said, shaking his head, "it's probably better that we don't know everything about each other."

His words cut like a knife, even though she agreed with him. They both had dark secrets, and yet living here pretending to be lovers was another kind of hell.

She pushed off the balcony railing and into the cool darkness of the bedroom, only to stop short at the sight of Enid standing in the middle of the room holding a stack of clean towels.

"I didn't think anyone was here," she said. Her expression left no doubt in Josey's mind that she'd heard everything.

JACK MENTALLY KICKED himself at the hurt expression on Josey's face as she'd left him on the balcony.

A moment later, he heard Enid's voice and swore. That damned sneaky woman. She'd probably heard everything. His fault. He should have been more careful.

Enid would take what she'd heard to his grandmother, sure as the devil.

But with a start, he realized he didn't care. Let her run to Pepper. Maybe it would be better if Pepper sent him packing. Hadn't he always known he might leave here empty-handed?

The bedroom door closed behind Enid, and he saw Josey standing in the middle of the room looking worried over what the woman had overheard. A wave of desire washed over him so strong, he thought it might drown him.

"She heard everything," Josey said, as he stepped into the bedroom, closing the French doors behind him.

He nodded, realizing he would have only one regret if he had to leave here—and it had nothing to do with what was or wasn't behind that rock wall in the closed wing.

"We should get down to breakfast," he said, his voice thick with emotion.

She didn't move as he stepped deeper into the room. "I think I'll skip breakfast," she said.

He started to talk her out of it, hating the thought of eating alone with just his grandmother and his aunt. But he saw the stubborn determination in the set of her jaw and decided to let it go.

They'd reached an impasse.

"I think I'll go for a horseback ride. Would you like—"

"No, thank you. I'll just stay in my room and read. I have a headache." Her words made it clear who'd given it to her.

"Should I have Enid send you up something to eat?"

Josey gave him a look of warning.

"I'll tell her not to disturb you, then." He stood for a moment, wanting to say all the things he felt, but unable to find the words. It was one thing to pretend they were husband and wife. It was another to get too close, and yet something like metal to magnet drew him to her. He wanted this woman. And not just for a week.

He had to fight every muscle within him not to reach for her.

As he descended the stairs, he found his grandmother waiting for him and groaned inwardly. Could this morning get any worse?

"Jack, may I speak with you?" Pepper led the way down to the parlor before he could answer.

The moment he stepped into the room, closing the door behind him as his grandmother instructed, she asked, "Why did you come here?"

Enid hadn't wasted any time. "Because you invited me and I wanted to see the ranch again."

His honest answer seemed to surprise his grandmother, who raised a brow. "I know you blame me for your unhappy childhood."

"My childhood wasn't unhappy."

"I kept your father from marrying your mother."

"Only until I was six. My father was an alcoholic and my mother spent her life trying to save him. Worse things happen to kids." He thought of his grandmother's children, that awful room on the third floor and what he'd seen scratched into the walls.

"I'm no fool," she snapped. "I know you want something from me, but I don't think it's my money."

As Josey said, the woman was sharp. "I have my own money, so it seems I came here to enjoy the ranch." He got to his feet. "Speaking of that, I'm going for a horseback ride."

"Alone?"

"Josey is resting. Please tell Enid she doesn't want to be disturbed."

Another raised brow. "Enid seemed to think that the two of you are going your separate ways when your week here is up."

"Enid should mind her own business." He saw that his grandmother had no intention of letting him leave it at that and sighed. "Josey and I, well, we think we might have acted in haste. Probably a little time apart would be good after we leave here," he said honestly.

Pepper's eyes narrowed, but when she spoke she said, "Enjoy your horseback ride. Don't go too far alone."

"Yes, I wouldn't want what happened to my grandfather to happen to me," he said, and saw his grand-mother's expression darken.

PEPPER TOLD HERSELF she didn't care one way or the other about Jack and Josey's marriage, and yet she found herself climbing the stairs to the far wing. She'd noticed there was trouble between the two of them, but things seemed to have been a little better after their horseback ride yesterday.

Now, though, something seemed to have happened to drive them apart again. It seemed odd to her that Jack would go off on a horseback ride by himself. It was the first time he'd left Josey alone.

"Jack said you were resting, but I wanted to check on you," she said when Josey answered her knock.

The young woman looked uncomfortable.

"He's gone for a horseback ride. I thought you and I might..." She looked past Josey into the bedroom. *Her* bedroom when Call was alive.

"Would you like to come in?" Josey asked with obvious reluctance.

Pepper stepped into the room, fighting off the memories that assailed her. She and Call had shared this room from the first night she'd come to the ranch. Had she ever been happy?

Yes, at first she'd been deliriously happy. Naive, foolish, blind with love, but happy. It had lasted at least a week. Maybe even a month before she'd realized what a controlling bastard she'd married.

And yet she'd stayed, believing that he would change. She silently scoffed at the thought now. There'd been a time when she really believed that love could conquer all. Why else had she not only stayed with him but also had five children with him?

"Would you like to sit down?" Josey offered.

Pepper smiled at the young woman. She was kind and thoughtful, clearly from a good family.

"Thank you, I think that would be nice." She took one of the chairs, noticing as Josey removed a folded blanket and pillow from the other chair.

Josey must have seen her expression and smiled ruefully. "I'm sure you've heard that Jack and I have been having our problems."

"Enid is a terrible old busybody," Pepper said, anxiously anticipating the day she would be able to get rid of the woman for good. Impulsively, she reached over and took Josey's hand. "I know you and Jack aren't legally married."

Josey opened her mouth as if to explain, but Pepper waved her off. "Jack thinks I'm an old fool. Of course I had my lawyer investigate. I like to know who is sleeping under my roof."

"I feel I should apologize for letting you believe—"

"Oh, don't look so aghast. I like you. I was truly sorry to find out the two of you *weren't* married. You're good for Jack, and from what I've seen, he's good for you, as well."

JOSEY DIDN'T KNOW what to say. She had to admit that Pepper Winchester had caught her completely off guard.

"Are you shocked that I'm not upset? Or that I actually care for my grandson?"

Again the woman had caught her flat-footed. Before Josey could speak, Pepper laughed, easing the tension in the room.

"I am capable of love and caring. I like Jack. I'm sorry I hurt him and his mother. But there is nothing I can do about that. You live to be this old, you, too, will have regrets. I unfortunately have more than my share."

"You are definitely a surprise," Josey finally said, relaxing a little.

Pepper smiled at that. "I just remember what it's like to be in love."

Josey started to protest that she wasn't in love with Jack, but stopped herself. Even if she and Jack weren't legally married, they were still supposed to be in love. And she did care about Jack. Too much.

"Jack seems to think that the reason you're asking your family back to the ranch is because you're not satisfied with the results of your son's murder investigation," Josey said, needing to change the subject.

"That's true."

"I thought someone confessed."

"Yes. Unfortunately, that person is dead, and I have reason to believe that there was a second person involved. I have no proof."

"You think Jack knows something?"

Pepper smiled secretively. "I guess time will tell. If there is any chance that the person responsible for Trace's death hasn't been brought to justice…" She shook her head. "It's something I need settled before I die."

"I can't believe it would be someone in your family."

"I've made a lot of mistakes in my life, but my greatest ones were with my children. Their father was a harsh disciplinarian. Too harsh. I didn't protect the older ones. But when Trace was born…" She cleared her throat.

"Would you like some water?" Josey asked. Pepper

nodded, and she stood and went into the bathroom, returning with a glass of cold water.

"I should have stopped Call sooner," Pepper said, after taking a sip. "I should have done so many things differently. By then my older children had no respect for me, and in my guilt I avoided them. That rift grew wider as Trace became my life, the only part I cared about."

Josey wondered why Jack's grandmother was confessing all this to her. Just minutes before she'd opened the door to Pepper, she'd promised herself that she wasn't going to get any more involved with this family. In fact, she'd been thinking that the best thing she could do was to make an excuse to leave sooner.

"If one of my older children had anything to do with Trace's death, then I am to blame for it." Pepper nodded, tears in her eyes. "But I still want justice and I will still get it."

Josey felt a chill at the woman's words as Pepper set down the glass on the end table and rose, picking up her cane.

"Thank you for listening to an old woman ramble," she said, seeming embarrassed. "I hope you don't think ill of me."

"No," Josey said. As she rose to escort Pepper out, she thought of her own father. He would have killed for her. He also would have demanded justice had anything happened to her. But he was gone, and there was no one to protect her or see that justice was done.

"Please don't give up on Jack," Pepper said. "He needs you. I don't think he realizes how much. He prides himself on his independence and taking on the world alone—but then you are a lot like that yourself, aren't you?"

Josey was startled that Pepper had realized that about her. "Sometimes we have to take on things alone because there isn't anyone else," she said, echoing her earlier thoughts.

"But you aren't alone anymore. You have Jack."

"Yes," she said, feeling guilty at how wrong Pepper was about that.

Chapter Nine

McCall had known that once the news hit the radio and newspaper the calls would start coming in. Most of them were from residents who'd seen someone suspicious hanging around the alley, heard a noise out back or thought someone had been in their house.

Her deputies were running themselves ragged checking on suspicious characters, only to find the suspect was a relative of a neighbor or nothing at all.

When she took the call from the dispatcher she was expecting just another bad lead.

"It's Frank Hanover down at Mobridge," a man said. "We just got home from Billings and found our house has been broken into."

"What's missing?" McCall asked, thinking Mobridge was near the Missouri River, near the crime scene.

"Clothes, some of my shirts and pants, a coat, as far as I can tell. Cleaned all the drugs out of the medicine cabinet, ate some food and left a mess."

She sat up straighter, remembering the house at Mobridge. It was back off the road, no other houses around.

"Took a pair of my boots," Frank was saying.

"What size do you wear?" she asked.

"Eleven." He seemed to hesitate. "Is that important?"

It was to her. Ray Allan Evans Jr. wore a size 10½ loafer. He could make do with a pair of size 11 cowboy boots real easy. "What else was taken?"

"About a hundred dollars in cash, the wife and I estimate. That's all that we've found missing so far."

"Did he take one of your vehicles?"

"Weren't none to take," Frank said.

So RJ was still on foot. "I'm sending a deputy. Please try not to touch anything that the intruder left. You said he made a mess in the kitchen? Please leave it."

"He used our phone, looks like since he left the phone book out and a chair pulled up to it. Probably ran up our long distance bill," Frank grumbled.

"What's your number out there?" McCall asked, and wrote it down. As soon as she hung up, she called the phone company and asked for the phone log on recently dialed numbers.

"I'm sorry, but we're going to need a warrant to do that or permission from the customer. We'll need those in writing. You're welcome to fax them to us. That would speed things up."

McCall cursed under her breath. "I'll get back to you." She then called Frank Hanover back, then called a deputy who was still in the area and sent him over to pick up the written permission slip from the Hanovers.

She wanted to know if Frank Hanover was right and RJ had called someone. She needed to know where he was headed. She'd called in extra officers to help search the area near Mobridge, even though she suspected he was long gone.

He would be looking to steal a vehicle. It was just a matter of time before he found one. She just prayed that no one would be driving it.

RJ DIDN'T KNOW how long he'd been walking up the dirt road when he heard the sound of an engine.

At first he thought he was hallucinating. It had been so long, and he'd been straining so hard to hear one. Praying for one, if he could call it praying. More like wishing on a curse.

He turned and saw what appeared to be a dark-colored pickup headed in his direction. RJ swallowed, his throat dry as he stuck out his thumb.

He'd cleaned up at the house, but he knew he still looked pretty rough. He feared no one would stop for him, so he was surprised when the driver slowed, then braked to a stop.

Sun glinted off the windshield, and it was a moment before he saw the lone driver, an old man dressed in a straw hat, flannel shirt and blue overalls.

He felt a wave of relief. One old farmer behind the wheel.

RJ would have shouted with glee if it wouldn't have made him look insane.

Both windows were already down on the old pickup. "Trouble?"

RJ stepped up to the open passenger-side window as dust settled around him. "Car broke down a good ways back by the river."

"You been walking this far in the wrong direction?" the farmer said with a laugh. "If you'd gone the other way, you have reached Highway 191 and gotten a ride a lot quicker than this."

As if RJ didn't know that. He'd opted for the less traveled dirt road for a very good reason. The highway was too visible. He couldn't take the chance since he knew the California police would have put out an APB on him and Josey by now.

"Well, hop in. I can take you as far as Winifred, that's where I'm headed."

RJ couldn't have cared less where Winifred was as he opened the pickup's door and climbed in. He wouldn't be going that far anyway.

The pickup smelled of hay and possibly manure. It didn't matter. RJ couldn't believe how good it felt not to be walking. The boots he'd borrowed had rubbed blisters on both feet. He leaned back as the old farmer got the rig rolling and watched the land slip by, a sea of undulating green.

The farmer made several attempts to make conversation before turning on the radio. He picked up a station in Whitehorse, Montana, that, according to the farmer, played a polka of the day at noon.

The news came on. Ray tensed as he heard first Josephine Vanderliner's name and description, then his own, followed by a warning that both were considered armed and dangerous. He wished he was armed as the farmer reached under his seat and pulled out a tire iron.

JOSEY WATCHED THE sun drop toward the dark outline of the Little Rockies in the distance. The spring day was hot and golden and held the promise of summer.

The prairie glowed under the heat. It was so beautiful and yet so alien. She wondered what this kind of isolation did to a person and thought of Pepper Winchester and the Hoaglands.

For the life of her she couldn't imagine what this ranch must have been like when all the Winchesters had lived and worked here. Children running up and down

the long hallways. The kitchen would have been bus-
tling with activity, the whole ranch alive with sounds.

Josey wished she could have seen it. She sighed and
looked to the road, anxious for Virginia to return from
town. Earlier, she'd caught Virginia as she was leaving.
The idea had come to her in a flash.

"Would you do me a huge favor?" Josey had asked
her and seen the woman's irritation. "I just need to get
some money wired to my mother's rest home."

Virginia's interest had picked up instantly. "Oh,
honey, your mother's in a rest home? Why, she can't
be very old. What's wrong with her?"

"Just give me a moment to get the money and the address." She'd run back up the stairs, telling herself this
was the only way. No one knew Virginia. And it wasn't
like involving Jack. Virginia couldn't get in trouble over
this since she really was an innocent bystander.

Josey had dug through the stacks of hundreds, choos-
ing bills free of blood. She'd already set up her mother's
transfer, planning to move her mother from the horrible
rest home where her stepfather had stuck her—to one
where he couldn't find her.

Virginia's eyebrow had shot up when she saw the
wad of money.

"I wasn't sure I could get a check cashed anywhere
up here, and everything with Jack happened so fast…"

His aunt had pursed her lips in disapproval. "Marry
in haste and… Well, you know." She seemed a little
upset that Josey hadn't satisfied her curiosity about her
mother.

"Here's the address. They're expecting the money. I
can't thank you enough for doing this."

Virginia had left then, promising to bring her a receipt and let her know that the money had arrived.

Neither Virginia nor Jack had returned and it was getting late. Josey got more restless by the moment. Tired of watching for both of them, she turned away from the window and went into the bathroom to bathe before supper, wondering if Jack would be back by then.

Her bruises were healing. So was the rope burn on her neck. Soon she wouldn't have to wear the scarves. But she would have to disappear. As long as she was free, her mother should be safe.

She closed her eyes as she slid down into the warm water filled with bubbles. Once her mother was safe and she was sure nothing could change, then she would deal with the fact that she was wanted for murder and she had no way to prove her innocence.

She opened her eyes and climbed out of the tub, wishing she could go to the police and just get it over with. As she toweled herself and pulled on the bathrobe, she told herself that maybe if the police knew what had happened—

No, RJ was right. She would fry, and what would happen to her mother?

She thought about the rest of the bloody money in the armoire and felt nauseous as she opened the bathroom door and stepped out. Either way, she would never see her mother again, she thought, as she looked through her clothes for something to wear to supper.

"Are you all right?"

She jumped as Jack touched her shoulder. She hadn't heard him return.

He looked so concerned, she was filled with guilt for dragging him into this, even if it had been his idea.

She'd only been thinking of herself. She hadn't considered the spot she was putting him in.

"You scared me."

"I'm sorry." He sounded as if he meant it. The last of the day's light shone on his face through the open French doors, accentuating the strong lines of his face. "Sorry about a lot of things."

"Sorry you brought me here?" She felt a little piece of her heart break off and fall

"No," he said. "No, you're wrong about that. If I've been distant it's just because…" He raised his hand, signaling to her to wait a moment, then walked over and locked the bedroom door. "Enid won't be coming back in without us knowing it," he said, as he dragged a straight-back chair from the small desk in the corner and wedged it under the doorknob.

"Jack?" Josey said. He turned to her, and she saw the look in his eyes. She'd noticed that he seemed different after his ride. More relaxed. More like the Jack she'd met on the highway.

"You want the truth?" he asked.

She swallowed as he moved toward her.

"I think it's time I was honest with you. I've been pushing you away because if I don't…"

JOSEY'S GREEN EYES widened in alarm—and something that seemed to simmer on the back burner as he moved toward her, his gaze locked with hers.

It had always been so easy to lose himself in that sea of green. He stopped just inches from her, saw her eyes fire as he reached for her robe sash and slowly untied it.

"Do you have any idea what you're doing?" she asked, her voice breaking.

He chuckled. "It's been a while, but I think I remember how it goes."

She placed her hand over his to stop him, her eyes searching his. "Jack—"

He knew all the reasons they shouldn't take this pretend marriage any further than they had. Hell, he'd listed them at length on his long horseback ride today.

"I want you. That, Josey, is the truth." He looked into her eyes, then he gently pushed her hand away and untied the robe sash. It fell open to expose bare flesh.

He slipped his hands around her slim, bare waist and felt desire spread through him, a fire rushing through his veins.

His gaze still locked with hers, he inched his hands up to cup her full breasts in each palm. She let out a sound and arched against him. He felt her nipples harden against his palms.

Slowly, his hands moved upward. He eased the robe off her slim shoulders. It dropped to the floor, and for a moment he was taken aback at how beautiful she was.

"I want to make love to you," he whispered.

Josey let out a soft moan and he felt something give inside him. He'd never wanted anything the way he wanted this woman.

His palms skimmed over her small waist to her hips. Cupping her perfect derriere in both hands, he dragged her to him, no longer able to stand another moment without kissing her again.

Her lips parted as his mouth dropped to hers. He heard her moan again and felt her working at the snaps of his Western shirt, and then his chest was pressed against her warm, full breasts, her nipples hard as stones, and he was carrying her to the canopied bed.

JOSEY WRAPPED THE ROBE around her and stepped to the window, the white sheer curtains billowing in on the evening breeze. She breathed in the unfamiliar scents as if only just now aware of them. Everything felt new and fresh, the day brighter. She hugged herself, smiling as she closed her eyes and turned her face up to the warmth of the sunset, reveling in the memory of making love with Jack.

Jack still lay on the bed behind her. She could feel his gaze on her. It heated her skin more than even the evening warmth. She would never forget the feel of his hands, his mouth, his body. His gentleness. His passion. He'd consumed her, filled her, fulfilled her.

"Come back to bed," he said softly. "We don't have much time. If we don't make an appearance at supper, I'm afraid there will be hell to pay."

She smiled to herself and was about to turn back when a flash of light caught her eye. The sun glinted off the bumper of a vehicle coming down the road toward them.

Josey froze, her pulse thundering in her ears.

"What is it?" Jack asked, sensing the sudden change in her. He pulled on his jeans and joined her on the balcony.

Her heart began to pound louder as she saw that there was something on top of the SUV roaring up the road. A light bar. And on the side of the vehicle a Sheriff's Department logo.

"It must be my cousin McCall Winchester," he said, as a woman with long, dark hair climbed out of the patrol car. Even from this distance Josey could tell she was wearing a sheriff's uniform.

"What do you think she wants?" Josey asked, fighting to keep the terror out of her voice. She'd thought she was safe here. That Jack was safe. She should never have involved him.

"My grandmother must have invited her for dinner," he said, as he drew Josey inside the bedroom and shut the French doors. "What's wrong?"

"Jack, I'm really not up to meeting her." She felt the heat of his gaze. He'd known she was in trouble. Now he knew it was with the law. "I should have told you—"

He touched a finger to her lips. "I'll take care of it." Jack's gaze locked with hers. "You're trembling. You should get back in bed."

"Jack—"

"It's going to be all right." He pulled her to him and kissed her. "You can meet my cousin some other time. Don't worry, I'll make apologies for you. I shouldn't have taken you on such a long horseback ride yesterday. I'd hate to think you're coming down with something."

She closed her eyes and wished they could just stay in this room forever. Become recluses just as his grandmother had done for twenty-seven years. No one had known for sure whether she was alive or dead. Nor had they cared.

She opened her eyes and grabbed for him as he started for the door. "I can't let you get in any deeper."

He took her in his arms, planted a kiss in her hair, then pulled back and smiled. "I'll be back as quick as I can. Lock the door behind me."

JACK LEFT JOSEY and went downstairs. He had known Josey was in trouble, but he'd just assumed it involved a man—not the law. As he descended the stairs, he had flashes of their lovemaking. He knew it had probably been a mistake, but even given what he now knew about his "wife," he couldn't regret it.

Enid opened the front door and Jack slowed on the stairs. He'd heard about McCall when the news had come about Trace Winchester's murder and the role Trace's daughter, a sheriff's deputy, had played in helping solve the crime—including almost getting herself killed.

So he'd been curious about his cousin the cop. He'd heard she'd been promoted to acting sheriff—their grandmother's doing, he would bet. Pepper Winchester might have been a recluse for the past twenty-seven years but she was still a force to be reckoned with, especially considering all the land she owned and the Winchester fortune. Which was surprising, given all the stories he'd heard about where that fortune had come from and at what cost.

He thought of the stories his mother had told him, and now he wondered how many of them were true. He had to remind himself that his mother had believed everything Angus Winchester had told her, and look where that had gotten her.

Still, he'd believed at least one of those stories was true. That's why he'd come here. Strange how long ago that seemed and, maybe more startling, how it had become less important.

McCall looked up as he came down the stairs. He couldn't hide his shock. She looked exactly like his grandmother had at that age.

She smiled at his surprise. "You must be Jack." She held out her hand. He stopped to shake it.

He found it amusing how wrong his grandmother had been. He recalled overhearing, when he was six,

Pepper saying her son Trace had eloped with a local tramp who was lying through her teeth about the baby she was carrying being her son's. Clearly, Ruby Bates hadn't been lying. McCall was a Winchester.

"Oh, I see you two have met," Pepper said, appearing from down the hall. "Where is your wife?" she asked Jack.

"She isn't feeling well. I think she might have picked up a bug. I shouldn't have taken her on such a long horseback ride, as hot out as it was yesterday."

His grandmother looked suspicious. "McCall was looking forward to meeting her."

He turned his attention to the acting sheriff. "I'm sure you'll get to meet her when she's feeling better. It isn't like we're going anywhere for a while."

RJ TURNED OFF the first side road he came to. Now that he had a ride, all he could think about was sleeping in a real bed tonight.

His shoulder hurt like hell, and he worried that it was infected. Wouldn't that be a kicker if he died from a stupid flesh wound?

He felt himself coming down from the rush of killing the farmer. He'd been glad when the old fart had pulled out the tire iron. Taking it away from him had almost been too easy. He'd smacked him a couple times with it, then reached over and opened the old man's door, shoving him out before sliding over behind the wheel to stop the pickup.

Once he'd gotten rid of the body, his head ached again but he knew he had to start thinking more clearly.

The pickup was old and dark colored, like a zillion others in this part of Montana. But he did stop and smear some mud on the license plate. He could camp out somewhere, hide the pickup, but he was counting on the farmer's body not being found for a while.

Eventually someone would call the sheriff's department to notify them that the old guy was missing. But in the meantime, RJ decided to press his luck.

He would drive to Billings, the largest city in Montana, where he could get what he needed—and not be noticed. It was out of his way by a few hours, but he couldn't chance going into Whitehorse. Too small. People noticed outsiders in that kind of town.

He shoved the farmer's hat down on his head and drove toward Highway 191. Tonight he would break into a pharmacy and steal the drugs and medical supplies he needed. He would sleep in a motel room bed, charging the room to the credit card he'd found in the old guy's wallet, and he'd have a nice meal.

Eventually, the cops would track the expenditures. But he would make sure they never connected it to him. Or at least make sure they couldn't prove it. Later tonight he would ditch the pickup and get himself a new ride, one no one in Whitehorse would recognize. Then he'd see about getting himself a gun.

Chapter Ten

Move! Josey grabbed her clothes and quickly got dressed, her mind racing. She found her backpack and opened the armoire, dumping the old clothing out and reaching for the money. Just touching it made her sick to her stomach.

But she couldn't leave it here, and she knew the day would come when she would need it to hire herself a good lawyer. In the bathroom, she retrieved the gun and dropped it on top of the money in the backpack.

Her gaze fell over the room, stopping on the canopy bed and the rumpled sheets. Her heart broke at the memory of the two of them making love there earlier. She'd given herself to Jack completely, surrendering in a way she'd never thought possible. He'd been so gentle, so loving. She thought of the passion that had arced between them. Had she been a romantic, she would have said they were made for each other.

But she was a realist, and because of that she knew making love with him had been a mistake. She was a woman wanted by the law. How could she have been so foolish to fall for Jack?

The realization struck her like a train. She'd let herself fall in love with this cowboy from Wyoming. Now there would always be this empty place inside her heart that only Jack Winchester could fill.

She took one last glance around the room. All she knew was that she had to get out of here, get away, far away. Once she knew her mother was safe…

Josey jumped at the sound of an engine turning over. Rushing to the window, she saw the sheriff's department car pulling away. Her hammering heart began to slow, then took off again as she heard the tap at the door.

"Josey, it's me."

She rushed to the door and into Jack's arms. All her plans to escape, to run far away, to keep her distance from this man went out the window the moment she saw the smile on his face.

"My cousin just stopped by because my grandmother had been nagging her to," Jack said. "She's on some big case and couldn't stay but a minute. She was disappointed, though, that she didn't get to meet my wife."

Relief made her weak as Jack locked the door, swept her up in arms and carried her back to the bed.

"All I could think about was getting back to you," he whispered against her hair. His mouth found hers.

She tried to speak, but he smothered her words with kisses. As he began to make love to her, all reason left her. There was no other place she wanted to be but in Jack's arms.

PEPPER WATCHED HER granddaughter drive away. The pride she felt surprised her, as did the guilt. She wished she'd known McCall sooner. She'd lost twenty-seven years of McCall's life. Her own fault.

She brushed angrily at the sudden tears that blurred her eyes, surprised by them and these feelings. She hadn't believed for a moment that the baby Ruby Bates had been carrying was her son Trace's. Because she hadn't wanted to.

But the two had produced McCall, and there was little doubt she was a Winchester. She hadn't even needed to see the DNA test. The young woman looked just like Pepper had at that age.

Trace had been her baby, her undeniable favorite, and she'd been sick with worry because she knew she was losing him. He'd married Ruby Bates because she'd been pregnant. Or maybe because he really had loved her. Pepper had never really known. Trace was dead, and maybe even Ruby didn't know the truth.

Not that it mattered. They had produced McCall, and she made up for everything.

It still amazed her that McCall seemed to have forgiven her for her past sins, unlike her children and even her other grandchildren. McCall knew that she'd tried everything to get Trace to dump Ruby and come back to the ranch.

So maybe Trace had loved McCall's mother. Loved McCall even though she hadn't been born before he was murdered. After all, according to McCall, it had been her father's idea to name her after her grandfather Call.

She wiped her tears as the dust from McCall's patrol car settled over the wild landscape, hating these sentimental emotions and wondering if she should have just left well enough alone and died in her sleep without ever getting her family back to the ranch.

"Mother?"

She turned to see Virginia standing in the doorway. She'd been so lost in thought, she hadn't heard her enter.

"I'm bored to tears. I'm going into town again. Can I get you anything?"

"No, but you should ask Enid if she needs any groceries, since you're going," Pepper said.

Virginia made a face. "She already gave me a long list. I hope to be back by supper. Enid wanted to know if you knew if Jack and his wife would be joining us. Apparently, they missed both breakfast and dinner."

A good sign, Pepper thought. "Tell Enid to plan on it. If they decide to skip another meal, that will be fine also."

Virginia didn't look happy about being asked to relay the message to Enid, but acquiesced. "Too bad Enid is such a horrible cook. I can't understand how you have survived eating her food all these years."

Her daughter had no idea.

As McCall drove back to Whitehorse, she thought about her relationship with her grandmother. She'd never even laid eyes on the woman until last month. But since that time her life had changed—and Pepper Winchester had had her hand in that.

She wasn't sure why she'd forgiven her grandmother for denying her existence for more than twenty-seven years. Maybe she saw herself in Pepper Winchester— and not just the fact that they resembled each other. Or maybe what had brought them together was the shared loss of a father and son. McCall had never gotten to know her father. Trace had been killed before she was born. Her grandmother's loss had been even greater because Trace had been her favorite, and losing him had made her lock herself away for the past twenty-seven years.

A call pulled McCall out of her reverie. "I've got Sharon Turnquist on the line. She says her husband is missing." Sharon farmed and ranched with her husband John south of the Breaks.

"Put her through."

"John left to go into Winifred and never got there," Sharon said, sounding worried and scared. "Neighbors are out looking for him, driving the road south, thinking he must have gone off somewhere along the way."

The Turnquist Ranch was a good fifteen miles from Mobridge on a narrow dirt road that wound through the rough badlands country. What were the chances this wasn't connected to Ray Allan Evans Jr.?

"I've got a deputy down that way," she said. "I'll have him help in the search. You let me know when you find him."

She hung up and called to make sure that the deputy she'd sent down to Mobridge had returned with a signed agreement from the Hanovers. Both had been faxed to the phone company, she was informed.

McCall hung up feeling antsy. She just hoped to hell that RJ hadn't stumbled across John Turnquist. She knew the elderly farmer and his wife. You couldn't ask for two nicer people.

Unfortunately, John was the kind of man who would stop and offer a ride to anyone walking along the road. This was rural Montana, where people still helped one another. Even strangers.

JACK AND JOSEY finally came up for air and realized they were both starving. They laughed and played in the huge clawfoot tub before getting dressed in time to go downstairs for supper.

There was an unspoken truce between them, Jack thought. It was as if they knew they didn't have much time together—although right now, feeling the way he did, he couldn't imagine a day without Josey in it.

He was surprised when Virginia was the one late for supper. She came into the lodge complaining about the road into Whitehorse, the dust, the distance, the rough road. She plopped down at the table, announcing she was starved as she distractedly thumbed through the newspaper she'd bought in town.

"Do you have to do that at the table during supper?" Pepper asked with no real heat behind it.

Jack had noticed that his grandmother didn't seem to be herself. She appeared even more distracted than even Virginia.

"I picked up the Whitehorse newspaper since everyone in town was talking about the front-page article," Virginia said, as if she hadn't heard her mother. "A car was found in the Missouri River south of town after a fisherman hooked into the body of a woman. You can't believe the rumors that are flying around town. What has everyone so worked up is a rumor that the woman was found with a noose around her neck. Someone had hung her!"

Josey's fork rattled to her plate.

Jack's gaze shot to Josey. All the color had drained from her face.

"Virginia!" her mother snapped. "We're *eating*."

"Why didn't McCall tell us about this?" Virginia demanded of her mother. "This must be the big case she is working on. Everyone is supposed to be on the lookout for possibly two individuals who might have been hitchhiking from somewhere near the Fred Robinson Bridge on the Missouri River crossing."

Jack heard all the air rush from Josey's lips. Her fingers gripped the table as if she were on a ship tossed at sea.

"They believe the driver of the vehicle got away after the car went into the water and that both suspects are believed to be armed and dangerous!" Virginia said, scanning through the story. "Apparently, they are both wanted for questioning in a murder case in California. The photos of them aren't very good in grainy black-and-white."

Josey stumbled to her feet. "I'm sorry, I—" She rushed out.

Pepper threw down her napkin, silverware clattering, and shoved back her chair. "Don't you ever know when to shut up, Virginia? Go after her, Jack. That woman could be the best thing that ever happened to you. Don't be like your father."

Jack was already on his feet before his grandmother had even spoken. He'd been so shocked by the news Virginia had brought home, it had taken him a few moments to move. He snatched the newspaper from Virginia's fingers.

"Oh, God, you don't think she's pregnant already, do you?" he heard his aunt say as he rushed from the room.

THE CALL CAME IN late that evening from the deputy Mc-Call had sent out to the Turnquist Ranch.

"One of the other ranchers spotted a body down in a gully," the deputy told her. "It's John Turnquist. I put in a call to the coroner. He's on his way out. Thought I'd better let you know. There's no sign of the pickup he was driving. His wallet's missing, as well. His wife said he didn't have much money in it, but did have several credit cards."

RJ. "Tell her not to cancel the credit cards just yet," McCall said. "We might be able to track him that way. We'll need numbers on the cards so we can work with the companies, and we're going to need a description of that pickup."

"There's something else," the deputy said. "Can't be sure until George gets here, but it looked like John was beaten with something before he was dumped out and rolled down into the gully."

She swore under her breath. "Well, at least now we know what Ray Allan Evans Jr. is driving. Let's find this bastard before he finds his next victim."

JOSEY RAN TO THEIR ROOM at the end of the empty wing, her heart pounding in her ears.

Celeste's body had been found. But the heart-stopping news: RJ was alive. He'd gotten away. She knew what that meant. He would be coming after her. Probably already was.

She stopped pacing to stand in the middle of the bedroom, her mind racing. She had to get out of here. She had to—

At the sound of the door opening behind her, she spun around.

"Talk to me," Jack said quietly, as he closed the door and locked it.

She shook her head and took a step back. "I need to get out of here."

"Josey, you have to tell me what all this has to do with you." His words were heavy with emotion as he put down the newspaper. "After what's happened between us, you owe me that."

She tried to swallow. Her stomach roiled. "I've already involved you. I can't—"

"Josey." He took a step to her, his big hands cupping her shoulders. "I can't help you if you don't tell me—"

"It's all too…" She waved a hand through the air, unable to even form words to describe what had happened to her. "You don't want any of this. Let me leave. Pretend you never picked me up on that highway."

"I can't do that." He sounded filled with anguish.

She stared at him in disbelief. "Aren't you just a little worried that I'm a murderer?"

His blue eyes lit with something akin to love as he took hold of the ends of the scarf around her neck and slowly began to untie it.

"Don't." The word came out a whisper.

"This is why I don't believe you're a killer," he said softly. "Someone did this to you. Just as someone did it to that woman they found."

She fought back the horrible memories. "You don't understand. You could be arrested for harboring a fugitive. Jack, everyone is looking for me, the police in California, the sheriff here in Montana, and…" Tears filled her eyes.

"And the person who hurt you. That's what has you so terrified." Jack thumbed at her tears, then kissed her. "But you're going to tell me because you know you can trust me."

She smiled at that. "The last man who told me to trust him almost killed me."

"I'm not that man."

No, Josey thought. Jack Winchester, whatever his secrets, was like no man she'd ever met. And right now, she suspected he might be the only person alive who'd believe her story.

AFTER BREAKING INTO a small older pharmacy and getting everything he needed, RJ had gone back to his motel and seen to his shoulder before going to sleep. He'd picked a Billings motel where he could park the pickup so the clerk couldn't see it. The clerk had been half-asleep when he'd checked in and hadn't paid any attention to him, anyway. He'd worn the hood up on the sweatshirt he'd taken from the Mobridge house just in case, though. No way could the man be able to make a positive ID of him.

He'd set his alarm for just after midnight and had come up with a way to get rid of all the evidence and the truck. Since hotwiring these damned new cars was next to impossible even if he knew how, he decided to take a more direct approach.

He drove around until he found a rundown bar on the south side of Billings. Then he crossed the river, and found an old abandoned farm house. Driving into the yard with his lights off, he parked the truck behind one of the out buildings.

He'd seen enough *CSI* to know exactly how arsonists set fires. With the pack of cigarettes he'd bought at a convenience mart and the extra gas in the back of the truck, he'd soaked the front seat and set the makeshift fuse.

He'd been about a half mile away, walking down the road, when the pickup blew. RJ smiled to himself as he walked the rest of the way to the bar. The back parking lot was cloaked in darkness. Ideal for what he had in mind.

The jukebox blared inside the bar, one of those serious drinkers' bars where patrons went to get falling-down drunk. There was a pile of junk behind the bar and a stand of pines.

Given the late hour, it wasn't long before a man came stumbling out of the bar, clearly three sheets to the wind. RJ stayed hidden in the dark behind one of the cars and waited until the man started to put his key into the door lock before he called to him.

"Harry?" RJ called, pretending to be drunk as he approached the man, the tire iron behind his back.

The man turned.

"Oh, sorry, I thought you were Harry Johnson." RJ was close now, close enough to smell the man's boozy breath.

"Nope, maybe he's still in the bar." The man turned back to his car, fumbling with the keys.

RJ hit him in the kidneys, then brought the tire iron down on the man's skull. He went down like a ton of bricks.

Unfortunately, the drunk was heavier than he looked, especially considering he was now dead weight. RJ dragged him behind the pile of junk and laid a scrap of sheet metal over him like a blanket.

He figured it would be a while before anyone found the guy and probably even longer before someone started searching for his vehicle.

Picking up the keys from the ground where the man had dropped them, RJ opened the car door and climbed into the large older model American-made car.

He swore. The man was a smoker, and the inside of the car reeked.

Well, beggars couldn't be choosers, as his father used to say. Just the thought of Ray Sr. made him grit his teeth. He wasn't the least bit sorry that old son of a bitch was dead.

RJ started the engine, turned on the radio, pulled away from the bar and headed for Whitehorse. Like the driver of the yellow Cadillac, he had the directions to the Winchester Ranch.

"It's out there and gone," the clerk had told him. "About as remote as it can get."

Josey didn't know it, but she'd chosen the perfect place to end this.

McCALL WASN'T SURPRISED to hear from Detective Diaz in Palm City, California. She figured he was calling for an update, and while she had little in hard evidence, when she finished telling him what they had so far, he came to the same conclusions she had.

"That sounds like him," the detective said. "RJ skated on more than a few run-ins with the law, from breaking and entering, theft and assault to allegations from prostitutes who claimed he'd abused them. None of them ever made trial. I'm sure his father paid the people off."

McCall heard something in his voice. "And Josephine Vanderliner?"

"She went through a wild time when she was younger, nothing big. Speeding, drinking, a couple of marijuana possession charges, but she's been out of trouble since her mother's accident."

"What about Ray Sr.?"

"Nothing on the books, but he was living pretty high on the hog and running out of money fast when he married Ella Vanderliner."

"What about her car accident?"

Diaz chuckled. "Like minds. There was some question since it was a single car rollover. She had been drinking. The daughter was convinced it was foul play, saying her mother never had more than a glass of wine."

McCall could almost hear him shrug. "You said the mother is in a nursing home? Have you checked it to see if Josephine has called or stopped by?"

Diaz cleared his voice. "Actually, that's why I called. The mother was apparently moved, but the home swears they have no idea where."

"Someone had to sign her out."

"Apparently her daughter had made arrangements before…" His voice trailed off.

"Then she must have known she was going to come into some money," McCall said.

"It does give her more motive for killing Ray Sr.," Diaz agreed. "The battle she was waging in court was for control of her mother, which means control of her mother's money."

"Ray Sr. wouldn't have wanted that to happen."

"Nope," Diaz agreed. "But then neither would his son, RJ."

Chapter Eleven

On the way to the Winchester Ranch, Ray popped some of the pills he'd stolen and realized he felt better than he had in days. He could hardly feel his shoulder and he was thinking clearly, maybe more clearly than he ever had.

He'd realized how crucial it was to his plan that he found Josey. He wanted the money in that backpack, but more important he needed to make sure she never surfaced.

Once she was dead, he would inherit his father's money—which was the Vanderliner money. His father had been broke when he married Ella Vanderliner. It had been a godsend when she'd gotten into that car wreck and he'd gained control over all her money—including Josephine's, as luck would have it.

RJ laughed, wondering if his old man had planned it that way. Maybe the acorn hadn't fallen that far from the tree after all. But if that was the case, Ray Sr. had been holding out on him all these years.

Worse, he'd had to put up with this father's lectures every time he'd gotten in trouble when it was possible his old man was just like him. Hell, wouldn't it be something if he'd gotten his predilection for rough sex from Ray Sr.? That would explain why his mother had taken off years ago and why his old man had paid to keep her in the style she'd become accustomed to, until she drowned in her fancy swimming pool.

RJ realized with a chill that his father might have been behind that accident, as well. But if true, then he really hadn't known his father at all.

He wheeled his train of thought back to his own problem: Josey Vanderliner. His fear now was that a judge would put Ella's care in Josey's hands. Unless Josey was arrested for murder, of course.

But RJ wasn't willing to put his life in the hands of a jury. He hated to think who would be more believable on the stand. That sweet-looking Josephine Vanderliner with the mother who was practically a vegetable. Or himself.

No, Josey had to disappear off the face of the earth. This was one body that could not be found.

Then he would surface and blame all of it on Josey. With her fingerprints on the weapon that had murdered his father, he didn't think he'd have that much trouble selling his story to the police. At least not in California.

It would be harder to explain the rest of what had happened. He thought he could sell the cops on a story that Josey had taken him and Celeste hostage. He had the bullet wound to prove that Josey had shot him. The rest he could say he didn't know anything about. He could say Josey had knocked him out and he came to underwater in the car. Let them try to prove he had anything to do with Celeste's death or that of the rancher.

Once he was cleared of any wrongdoing, he would be in charge of Josey's mother's care—and her money. He'd put the old lady in the cheapest rest home he could find, one that cost even less than the one his old man had stuck her in. She wouldn't know the difference anyway.

"TALK TO ME, JOSEY," Jack said. He took her hand and led her over to the bed. As he sat down on the edge, he pulled her down next to him.

"I should never have involved you in this."

"It's too late for that," he said quietly. "You knew this woman they found, didn't you?"

Josey closed her eyes for a moment. "Her name was Celeste. I didn't know her last name. I'd never laid eyes on her before a few days ago."

Jack could feel Josey trembling and see the terror in her eyes, the same terror he'd seen the day he'd picked her up on the highway. He tried hard to hide his own fear as he asked, "Did you have anything to do with what happened to her?"

"No," she said with a shudder. "But I was there. I saw RJ unraveling. I saw it coming and I knew what he was capable of. I'd seen him…" Her voice broke.

"Why don't you start at the beginning."

She stared into his eyes for a long moment, then nodded slowly. He waited while she collected herself.

"You aren't going to believe me. I hardly believe it myself."

He squeezed her hand. "Don't worry. I'll know if you're lying."

She smiled at that. "You think you know me that well?"

"Yeah," he said simply. "I do."

Josey took a breath and let it out slowly. "I guess it

starts with my family. My father was Joseph Vanderliner."

Jack's eyebrows shot up. "*The* Joseph Vanderliner of Vanderliner Oil?"

She nodded. "That's the reaction I've been getting all of my life."

"I knew you came from money, just not that much money," he said. "I read that your father died a few years ago, and your mother…"

"She took my father's death hard. She was never a strong woman. I hadn't realized how weak she was until she married my stepfather, Ray Allan Evans Sr."

"You didn't like him."

"At first I thought he was all right. Until my mother had a car accident. The police said she'd been drinking, but she didn't like alcohol. She never had more than a glass of wine and usually not even that."

"This accident. Was your mother…"

"She survived, but she suffered massive head trauma. She will never recover." Her voice broke again. "Ray Sr. put her in a nursing home and took over her finances, which included my own. My father had died suddenly and hadn't updated his will, so my inheritance was still tied up with my mother's. I had a job at Vanderliner Oil, but when Ray Sr. took over he had me fired. I sued him, because I desperately needed to get my hands on my inheritance so I could take my mother out of that horrible rest home he'd stuck her in and get her proper care."

Josey rubbed a hand over her forehead. "My father's will was just ambiguous enough that my stepfather had control over not only all of my mother's and my money, but Vanderliner Oil, too. And he was spending the money as if there was no tomorrow."

She let go of his hand and stood up, pacing in front of the bed. "I should have been suspicious when my stepfather called and said he wanted to settle out of court, no lawyers. He had arranged, he said, to give me part of my inheritance as a show of faith. All I could think was that if I could get my hands on enough money I could help my mother. I should have known it was a trap."

McCALL HUNG UP from her call to Detective Diaz and heard the fax machine buzz. She walked down the hall and checked. Sure enough, it was the phone logs she'd been waiting for from Frank Hanover's house.

Her gaze went to the most recent calls, her heart starting to pound. There were five calls made during the time Frank said he and his wife had been in Billings.

All but one of the calls had been to Whitehorse, Montana numbers. McCall took the list back to her office, picked up the phone and dialed the out-of-state number first. A rest home? Hadn't Detective Diaz told her that Josephine's mother was in a rest home?

After she'd established that Ella had been in that rest home, she hung up, wondering why RJ had called there.

McCall dialed the first Whitehorse number.

"Packy's," a woman answered.

Why would RJ call a convenience mart?

McCall hung up and checked the other numbers. A call to the other two convenience marts in town. The rest were to motels in town.

She stared at the list. RJ was looking for someone.

She called the next number and recognized the woman's voice who answered at the hotel. "Nancy, it's McCall Winchester. Did you get a call from someone inquiring about a woman?"

Nancy Snider laughed. "Is this a crank call?" she joked.

"I have two missing persons, both considered armed and dangerous, and it seems one of them is searching for the other one. Help me out here. According to my phone log, the call would have come into the motel at eight-forty last night."

"Sorry. Now that you mention it, I did get a call last night."

"Man or woman calling?"

"Man. He asked if his girlfriend was staying here."

"Did he describe her?"

"Long, red-blond hair, curly, carrying nothing more than a backpack. Said they were supposed to meet up, but she got mad at him. Said he was worried about her."

"What did you tell him?"

"Said I hadn't seen her. Then he asked about some guy driving a yellow Cadillac convertible. Said she might be with him."

"A yellow Cadillac convertible?"

"Said it was one of those old ones with the big fins," Nancy said. "Told him I hadn't seen it, either."

But McCall had.

JOSEY CONTINUED TO PACE the bedroom, too nervous and upset to sit still. "When I got to the house, my stepfather was waiting. I could tell at once that he'd been drinking." She hesitated.

"He made a pass at you."

She laughed nervously. "How did you—"

"I know people."

"I slapped him. He became angry. I picked up a bronze statue he had on his desk in his library. He backed off and went to the wall safe, opened it and showed me the stacks of money—*my* money."

"How much money are we talking?"

"A little over a million in the safe," she said, and saw Jack's eyes widen.

"And the rest of your inheritance?"

She'd known he would realize she had more than that coming. "He had a letter releasing the rest of my inheritance to me. It was…sizable." She swallowed. "Ray said, 'Come get it, then get out.' I was wary. I said, 'Do you have something I can put it in?' He'd laughed and called out, 'RJ, get the lady something to put her money in.'"

"RJ," Jack repeated.

"Ray Allan Evans Jr." She swallowed again, her throat dry. "He appeared and I realized he'd been waiting in the next room."

Jack swore under his breath. "The two of them had set you up."

"RJ brought in an old backpack. It's the one I had when you picked me up on the highway. He tossed me the empty backpack and I moved to the safe just wanting to get the money and get out of there."

Jack listened, holding his breath.

"As I started loading the money into the backpack, I heard Ray Sr. order his son to get him a drink."

She took a breath and let it out slowly, remembering how everything had happened so fast after that. "I saw RJ. He had gone to the bar but he'd come back with only a bar rag. His father had taken a step toward me, saying something I didn't hear or just don't remember because of what happened next."

She was breathing hard now, the memory making her

nauseous. "I had put the bronze statue back on Ray's desk. RJ walked past the desk, picked up the statue using the bar rag and struck his father in the back of the head. He hit him twice. I felt the spray of blood—" She was crying, remembering the way Ray Sr. had fallen at her feet.

Jack nodded as if he'd seen it coming. So why hadn't she? She'd known they were up to something, but she'd never dreamed...

"I must have been in shock. The rest is a blur. RJ was saying that his father never planned to let me leave with the money—or the legal document freeing up my inheritance. He shoved me aside. I was just standing there, staring down at Ray Sr. I could tell he wasn't breathing. The bronze statue was lying next to him covered with his blood. There was so much blood. RJ was frantically loading the money into the backpack. I saw it was splattered with Ray's blood."

"Let me guess. He wouldn't let you call the cops," Jack said.

"No. He said the only prints on the bronze statue were mine and that he would swear I'd killed his father for the money. Everyone knew about the legal battle I had been waging against my stepfather."

Jack swore. "They set you up and then he double-crossed his father."

Josey nodded. "I refused to go anywhere with him, but he pulled a gun and dragged me out of the house by gunpoint. When we got outside, he shoved me into the back of a car I had never seen before. That's when I saw that there was a woman in the car who'd been waiting for him."

"Celeste."

Josey nodded slowly. "She drove us to a secluded place while RJ held a gun on me. I thought they were going to kill me right there. I'd seen RJ kill his own father in cold blood. I knew he would shoot me without a moment's hesitation."

"Surely this Celeste woman—"

"She was excited, as if this was some great adventure. She didn't seem to notice the blood on RJ's clothing or that he had a gun. But he didn't kill me there. While he duct-taped my mouth, my wrists and ankles and shoved me into the trunk, she showed me the diamond ring RJ had bought her. He'd told her they were going to get married and then go on a long honeymoon."

"My God." Jack rose from the bed and took her in his arms.

"Oh, that was only the beginning," Josey said, as she leaned into his broad chest. "And now RJ is out there somewhere looking for me."

Chapter Twelve

RJ thought about taking a page out of Josey's play-book and drastically changing his appearance. But his last haircut and highlighting job had cost him a bundle and he wasn't about to ruin that with some disgusting dye job.

He decided he would just have to wear the farmer's straw hat to cover up most of his blond hair. His bigger concern was gasoline.

There was no way he could chance stopping at a station once he left Billings. There were only two towns between there and Whitehorse—Roundup and Grass Range, both small—and he'd heard on the radio that people were looking for him.

So he bought a gas can, put it in the trunk of the car he'd borrowed from behind the bar and filled it in Billings. Fortunately, the car had a large gas tank. The last thing he wanted to do was run out of gas before he found the Winchester Ranch.

His plan was to get to the ranch early enough that he could watch the comings and goings. He had no way of knowing how many people were on the place or how to find Josey. Once he had her, she would tell him where the backpack was with the money in it. At least the money better be in it, he thought.

There was always the chance that she wasn't even on the ranch anymore, but if the yellow Cadillac was there, then he would at least be able to find out where Josey had gone.

The drive was a lot longer than the clerk who'd given him the directions had led him to believe. This place was from hell and gone on miles of narrow dirt road. He was getting annoyed, the drugs he'd taken starting to wear off, when the right rear tire blew.

JACK COULD SEE how hard this was for Josey, but he had to know everything. It was the only way he was going to be able to help her. And no matter what she told him, he knew he would help her any way he could.

He'd never planned to let himself become emotionally involved with this woman, especially knowing from the get-go that she was in some kind of trouble.

But she'd brought out every protective instinct in him, and somewhere along the way he'd found himself falling for her.

"I realized he'd framed me for his father's murder, and the only reason he didn't dump me beside the road was because he needed to make it look as if I'd taken off with the money. I knew something else."

"He couldn't let you live," Jack said.

She nodded. "With his father dead and my mother unable to take care of herself, RJ would be in charge of everything my father had built. I knew he would destroy Vanderliner Oil, spend until he lost it. But I was more worried about what would happen to my mother.

"RJ was all drugged up, flying high, thinking he'd just pulled off the perfect crime. I had no idea how far he'd driven before he stopped. I thought he was going to kill me then, but he just let me out long enough to go to the bathroom, give me some water and a little something to eat. Apparently, he didn't want me dying in his car and smelling it up."

"He didn't give you any idea where you were headed?"

Josey shook her head. "I asked him to let me ride in the backseat and promised I wouldn't cause any trouble. I wanted to know where we were. I also didn't stand a chance of getting away bound up in the trunk. With my wrists taped behind me, what could I do anyway?"

"So he agreed."

"I think he did it because he was already over Celeste," Josey said. "She was complaining about everything, especially about having to guard me whenever we stopped for gas or he had to run in and get food. At one point, she told him she wasn't going any farther unless he dumped me."

Jack shook his head in disbelief. "She was as cold-blooded as he was."

"The money was part of the appeal. At one point, they thought I was sleeping, and I heard him explain to her that he had to make sure no one found my body and that was why they were going to a place he and his father had hunted in Montana."

"You had to be terrified."

"I watched for an opportunity to get away, but as drugged up as RJ was, he never let down his guard. He seemed ultraintuitive to even the slightest movement by me. By the time we reached Montana I realized he was going to get rid of not only me, but also Celeste. Unfortunately, she hadn't figured that out yet."

McCALL GOT THE CALL about a possible suspect sighting in Billings and hoped the recent incidents down there were RJ's doing only because it would mean he was nowhere near Whitehorse or the Winchester Ranch.

"We had a drugstore break-in," the cop on duty told her. "He sprayed something over the video camera, but missed a small spot. It was definitely a white male. Could be this Ray Allan Evans Jr. you're looking for."

"We believe he was injured at the scene and might be in need of medical supplies."

"Drugs and medical supplies were stolen. That same night a man was killed behind a bar and a pickup truck was set on fire near there. We also had a break-in at a house not far from the bar. A handgun was taken."

That sounded like her man. McCall made a note to see if Sharon Turnquist could get her the serial number on her husband's pickup. "What about the murdered man's car?"

"Missing." He rattled off the make and model and license plate number.

McCall was betting that RJ was now driving it.

After she hung up with the Billings police, she phoned the rest of the numbers that RJ had called. A few of the people who'd talked to him either hadn't come in yet for their shifts or had the day off. She asked for their numbers and tracked them down.

"Sure, I remember talking to him," the young male clerk at one of the motels told her. "He was trying to find his girlfriend. They'd gotten into a fight and she took off with some other guy. The guy did have a great car though. It was one of those Cadillacs with—"

"What kind of information did you give him?" Mc-Call interrupted.

"Pretty much the same as the other guy—directions to the Winchester Ranch."

"The other guy?"

"The cowboy driving the Cadillac convertible. He was getting gas at Packy's the same time I was."

"Was he traveling alone?"

The clerk laughed. "The second guy asked me the same thing. I told him about the woman I saw with the cowboy. Didn't match the description he gave me of her, but he sounded like she was the one he was looking for."

Didn't match the description? "What did the woman look like?"

"Pretty with short, curly, dark hair."

The same way her grandmother had described Jack's wife, Josey.

Josey. Josephine. The moment McCall hung up, she dialed her grandmother's number at the ranch. The phone rang and rang. Her grandmother didn't have voice mail, but she had an old answering machine. When it didn't pick up, McCall realized there could be only one reason why.

The phone line was out.

In the middle of winter it wouldn't have been unusual for the phone line to be down. But this time of year?

It seemed odd. RJ could have reached the ranch by now, but would he cut the phone cord in broad daylight? It was more likely he would watch the place and hit it tonight.

Without cell phone service anywhere near the ranch, there was no way to reach her grandmother to warn her.

McCall feared it was too late to warn any of them as she jumped in her patrol car and, lights and siren blaring, headed for the Winchester Ranch.

RJ SHOULDN'T HAVE been surprised to find no spare tire in the trunk. He pulled out the tire iron and beat the trunk lid until it looked like the craters on the moon. He felt a little bit better after that.

Back in the car, he downed a half-dozen pills, then drove until there was no rubber left on the tire and the rim buried itself in a rut. The car wasn't going any farther, he thought with a curse, then realized it was blocking the road to the ranch. With an embankment on one side and a ravine on the other, no one would be coming down this road tonight.

He studied the directions he'd been given under the dome light. If he was right, he could cut off some of the distance by going across country. He drank the last of the twelve-pack he'd bought in Billings. It was hot and tasted like crap, but he didn't want to get dehydrated and it helped the buzz he had going.

There was just enough gas left in the can in the trunk to soak the front seat pretty good. He lit the car and, taking the map, dropped off the side of the road and headed what he believed was southwest. The night was cloudy, but earlier he'd seen the moon coming up in the east.

He heard the *whoosh* as the car caught fire, and he was glad there wasn't much gas in the tank. Even if the car did explode, though, he doubted the sound would carry clear to the ranch. He'd hate for them to have even an inkling of what was coming.

As he topped a rise, he realized he couldn't be that far from the ranch. Pleased that maybe things were turning out as they were supposed to for once, he counted the minutes before he'd see his stepsister again.

IT HAD GOTTEN dark out. All Josey wanted to do was finish the story so Jack would understand why she had to get out of there. It was getting later, and the breeze coming in through the French doors was almost cold. She feared another storm was brewing on the horizon, and she worried about the road out of the ranch if there was a thunderstorm. She'd heard Enid say that when it rained here, parts of the road became impassible.

"When Celeste heard that we were going to camp, it was the last straw," she said. "We'd been eating fast food for thirty hours, sleeping in the car, and Celeste was ready for the good life RJ had been promising her. Also, he'd been popping a lot of pills so he could keep driving straight through, and he was acting oddly. When we reached the camp, RJ cut me free of the duct tape and tied me to a tree with part of the rope he'd brought along. I thought I might stand a chance since the rope was much less restricting than the tape.

"That night he and Celeste got into a huge argument. RJ demanded she give back the engagement ring. Celeste went ballistic and started hitting him. He grabbed her and tried to take the ring off her finger. The next thing, she was screaming that he'd broken her finger, howling with pain. He hit her and she went down."

Josey stepped to the open French doors to look out

into the darkness for a moment, hugging herself against the cold, against the thought of RJ and what he was capable of. "He'd been playing with the extra rope he'd brought. But it wasn't until then that I saw he'd fashioned two lengths with nooses at the ends. RJ was saying something about Montana being the last of the old West. He tied one end of the rope to the bumper of the car, threw the other end over a limb near the water and looped the noose over Celeste's neck and pulled it tight. He abused her all the time. It seemed to be their thing, but this was different. Then he came for me saying it was time to hang the bitches."

She looked back at Jack and saw the pain and fury in his face before hurrying on. "I fought him, but he was too strong for me."

"That's how you got all the bruises."

Josey nodded. "I must have passed out because when I woke up, RJ was in the car, the motor running and I was being dragged by my throat. Celeste had come to and she was screaming for him to stop. He kept going in the car until we were both hauled off our feet and were hanging from the tree limb. I remember gasping for breath. Then I heard this huge crack as the limb broke, and the next thing I knew I was falling. The moment my feet hit the ground, I tore the noose from my neck.

"I had seen where RJ had laid down the gun when he was hitting me. I ran for it. I grabbed the pistol and spun around. Celeste still had the noose around her neck, but she'd found RJ's knife he'd used to cut the rope earlier. RJ saw her and hit the gas in the car. She sliced through the ropes before they went taut again."

Josey closed the French doors and stepped back into

the room, still hugging herself against the memory—and the cold fear. "RJ threw the car into Reverse and headed right for her. I had the gun in my hand. I fired, but missed him, hitting the car instead. I fired again. I heard him cry out. I'll never forget the murderous look in his eye. Then he must have realized he was still in Reverse and headed for the river.

"It happened so fast. Celeste threw herself through the driver's-side open window. They were struggling as the car crashed into the river. Celeste had RJ in a head-lock. RJ was wounded and trying to fight her off. Neither seemed to notice or care that the car was sinking. I grabbed the backpack and ran, still holding the gun.

"When I finally did stop on a rise to look back, I didn't see either of them. By then I'd realized that if I had any hope of getting my mother out of that awful place Ray Sr. had put her in, I couldn't turn myself in. At least not before I wired the money to the facility I'd set up for her the night I met Ray Sr. to pick up the money. Now all I have to do is make sure my mother is safe, then go to the police and—"

"RJ is still out there," Jack broke in. "It's going to be your word against his, and as you said, your fingerprints are on the murder weapon. If you turn yourself in, you'll go to prison—and what will happen to your mother?"

"I hid her. He won't be able to find her." But even as she said the words, she knew her mother wouldn't be safe.

"And what happens when this money you have runs out?"

Josey raked a hand through her hair. "Don't you think these are the things I've been trying to figure out?"

"I know," he said, taking her in his arms. "That's

why we need to figure them out together. I can finish what I came to do tonight and we can get out of here."

She pulled back to look into his face. "Jack—"

"We're in this together now. I just need you to trust me and stay in this room," he said. "We'll leave first thing in the morning. I know of a place we can go until we can make sure your mother was moved and is safe. Then—"

"You're planning on going after RJ," she said. The thought of Jack being in danger terrified her more than RJ coming after her alone. "No. I can't let you do that."

He cupped her shoulders in his hands. "We can talk about this later. I need to go. There is something I have to do. It's from a promise I made a long time ago. I feel I have to do this. Stay here. I'll try not to be long. Keep the door locked." He touched her cheek, a tenderness warming his blue eyes. "I'm not going to let anything happen to you. Get packed and wait for me. I'll hurry."

IT WAS DARK when McCall came around the corner in her patrol SUV, and her headlights flashed on the burned vehicle in the middle of the road. She pulled up, grabbed her flashlight and got out, half hoping to find RJ's body in the car.

Instead, she found footprints and tracked them a short distance in her flashlight beam. They were headed southeast toward the Winchester Ranch.

RJ had a good walk ahead of him. As she climbed back into her SUV, she could only hope he stumbled across a rattlesnake or broke his leg in a prairie dog hole. Backing up, she turned around and returned to the main road. Unlike RJ, she knew another way to get to the ranch that would be faster than walking. She considered calling for backup, but changed her mind. From the single set of footprints, RJ was alone. McCall figured he was after Josey Vanderliner, also known as Mrs. Jack Winchester.

The only thing McCall didn't know was how her cousin Jack fit into this.

RJ LET OUT a low whistle under his breath when the saw the Winchester Ranch. It looked like a damned hotel. Who were *these* people?

With a sinking feeling, he realized he was screwed if all those rooms were full of people. He'd never be able to find Josey—let alone get her out of there. Even with the gun he'd stolen in Billings, he couldn't take on everyone in the place.

He reminded himself he had no choice. Getting rid of Josey had become more than just something he needed to do to seal the deal on his father's death. It had become personal, he thought, as he rubbed his shoulder. If it wasn't for the pills he kept popping, he would be in horrible pain. As it was, his shoulder was a constant reminder of why he had to find Josey and finish this.

He moved down the hillside in the dark to the back of the massive log structure. Finding the main phone line coming in was child's play, since the pole was right behind the house. There was even a yard light nearby, so he wouldn't have to use the small penlight he'd brought.

But when he reached the spot where the phone line entered the house, he found that someone had already beat him to it. What the hell? The cord had definitely been cut. A sense of dread raced through his veins like ice water. Who would have done this?

Suddenly he wasn't so sure about finishing this here. Maybe he should just cut his losses, steal one of the cars, take some back road across the Canadian border. But he knew he wasn't going anywhere without money.

Still, this felt all wrong.

He moved around to the front of the place, staying in the shadows, the fine hairs on his neck standing on end. He came to a window with a light behind it and crouched down to listen.

He could hear a radio playing and someone banging around in the pots and pans and mumbling under her breath. He took a peek through the crack between the curtains. A small, elderly woman appeared to be cleaning up the kitchen in angry bursts.

RJ waited to see if anyone else showed up. When no one did, he moved along the edge of the house, staying to the dark shadow of the building.

He heard more voices, saw another lighted window, and eased forward. The window was open a crack, and he could hear two women talking.

"Give me a reason to stay here, Mother."

"Virginia, you have to do whatever it is you need to do."

"Can't you just say you want me to stay? Is that so hard for you? Or say you want me to leave. If it doesn't make any difference to you, that's the same as telling me to leave."

The older-sounding woman sighed deeply. "Why does everything with you have to be so dramatic?

You've done nothing but complain since you got here. Why would you want to stay?"

RJ heard the younger one sniffle as if crying.

"Maybe I'd like to see my brothers and my nephews," she said, sounding hurt. "When are they arriving?"

"I don't know, Virginia. As you pointed out, they may not come to see me at all. I haven't heard from them. Or the rest of my grandchildren."

"I can't believe they won't."

"Perhaps they are less worried about their inheritance than you are," the older one said.

"You know, Mother, you deserve to die alone on this ranch with just Enid and Alfred here with you, both of them just waiting for you to breathe your last breath. I wouldn't be surprised if they helped that along one day."

He heard the scrape of a chair, then heavy footfalls and the slamming of a door. He listened but heard nothing more. Apparently, this place wasn't full. So far he'd only seen an old lady. But the daughter had mentioned two others, apparently caretakers.

As he started to move, he heard another sound, this one coming from outside the house. He pressed himself against the side of the house and stared out into the darkness.

Someone moved in the distance. Someone who seemed to be sneaking along the outside of the building—just as he had been doing.

The person who'd cut the phone line?

He waited until he saw the figure disappear inside a door at the far end of a separate wing of this monstrous place.

RJ waited for a moment, then followed.

IT DIDN'T TAKE Josey long to pack after Jack left, since she'd already started it earlier. She checked, though, to make sure she hadn't forgotten anything. Then she checked the gun she'd stuffed in the top of the backpack. She had only four bullets left. She hoped she wouldn't have to use them, but knew she would if they ran across RJ. As drugged up as he probably was, she wasn't sure it would be enough to stop him. The thought of killing him made her shudder. But she wouldn't let him hurt Jack, no matter what.

As she crossed in front of the French doors, she glanced out into the darkness, wondering where RJ was. Jack had said he wouldn't be able to find them on this ranch so far from everything. But Jack didn't know RJ.

Josey felt anxious, wishing Jack would hurry. They needed to get out of here, for their sakes and his grandmother's and Virginia's. She remembered Enid and Alfred. They seemed like they could take care of themselves.

She put the gun back into the top of the backpack and pulled the drawstring closed. Silently, she prayed that her mother had been moved to the new health-care facility and that RJ couldn't get his hands on her. That would be Josey's one weak spot, and RJ would capitalize on it if he thought of it.

With everything done, she turned out the lights and stepped to the window. She knew where Jack had gone. What she still didn't know was what was so important behind that rock wall. He'd said it was something he'd promised to do a long time ago. She knew Jack was the kind of man who stood by a promise no matter what.

What scared her was just that. He was risking his

life and hers. So what was behind that rock wall? Hidden treasure? The famous Winchester fortune Jack had told her about?

No, she thought. Knowing Jack it was something much more important.

Standing on the balcony in the darkness and cold, Josey wondered when the exact moment was that she'd fallen in love with Jack Winchester. Had it been that first kiss in the Cadillac? Or when he held her while she cried on that high ridge during their horseback ride? Or was it when he'd taken her in his arms and carried her over to the bed? Sometime over the past few days she'd begun to realize she was no longer pretending. She felt like his wife.

With a start, Josey realized that she'd just seen something move along the edge of the far building—the same one Jack was in right now. It couldn't be Jack. He'd left a long time ago. Unless something—or someone—had held him up.

She stared hard into the blackness at the edge of the building, fear gnawing at her insides. If not Jack, then—

Alfred. The old man was sneaking along the edge of the building. He must have seen Jack go into the closed wing earlier. Or suspected that's where he was headed. What would Alfred do when he caught Jack opening that old rock wall? Why would he care?

She thought about the other night when Alfred had caught her in that wing. Had he gone back to make sure no one had tampered with the wall? Then that would mean he knew something had been hidden behind it.

Her heart began to pound.

What was he up to?

As he stepped to the edge of the far wing, the moon slipped from behind the clouds. Her skin went clammy, fear closing her throat, as she saw what Alfred gripped in his hands. An ax.

Chapter Thirteen

Jack had made some progress on the rock wall the past two nights. He worked harder and faster tonight, anxious to get back to Josey. He didn't believe there was any way that her homicidal stepbrother could find her, and he'd made sure he had the Cadillac keys on him so she didn't do anything crazy like leave on her own.

He wished he could just let this go, but he'd promised his mother and himself years ago that he would see that Pepper Winchester got what she deserved. Today was that day. Then he could put this place and all that behind him.

But even as he thought it, Jack realized that something had changed in him. For years he'd been waiting for an opportunity to get back on this ranch and see what was behind this wall. It had always been there, that need to finish things in Montana. It hadn't mattered how well his life or his career had been going in Wyoming. There had always been this mission hanging over his head.

Now, though, his thoughts kept returning to Josey, and he realized just how much he'd changed since he'd met her. It was all he could do to keep chipping at the mortar. Did he really need to know what was behind this wall anymore?

The mortar in the wall was old, more than forty years. He chipped out another stone and set it aside. As he shone his flashlight into the space behind the wall, he could make out what looked like a large bundle wrapped in cloth.

His pulse kicked up a beat. Hurriedly, he removed another rock. There was definitely something in there. Something wrapped in what appeared to be an old canvas tarp.

For so long he hadn't been sure if his mother's story was even true. After all, she'd heard it from Angus Winchester, her lover, the man who'd lied to her for years.

Jack worked another rock out, and then another. Just a few more and he would be able to see what had been hidden for all these years behind this rock wall.

AFTER SEEING ALFRED with the ax headed for the wing where she knew Jack was working, Josey grabbed the gun out of the backpack and tore out of the room at a run. She heard someone call to her as she threw open the front door, but she didn't look back as she sprinted toward the closed wing.

The air chilled her to her bones. That and the fear that had her heart in her throat. There was no sign of Alfred as she ran the length of the building. She skidded to a stop as something moved out of the darkness just before she reached the door into the closed wing.

A low rumbling sound filled the air, and she froze as she saw the old dog. It blocked the way, the hair standing up on the back of its neck, a low growl coming out of its throat.

It took a step toward her. She raised the gun, but knew she wouldn't be able to shot it. "Nice dog," she whispered, and took a step away from it and the side of the building. The dog remained where it was. She took another step, then another, frowning. The old dog acted almost as if it was protecting something.

A bone? She squinted into the blackness at the edge of the building. Her blood suddenly ran cold. At first she thought it was a fawn deer or some other animal that the dog had killed and was only protecting its food.

But then she caught the glint of metal and saw that something was protruding out of the center of the dead animal. An ax.

"Oh, my God," she breathed as the moon broke free of the clouds, and she saw Alfred lying on his back, the ax buried in his chest.

Her mind whirled. Who would…? Jack! Where was Jack?

She turned and ran the last few steps to the door into the closed wing.

JACK REMOVED THE last rock in his way. Kneeling down, he picked up one end of the tarp. The canvas, rotten after all these years, disintegrated in his fingers.

The first thing he saw was what was left of a boot. He suddenly felt weak as he stared at what lay beyond the boot—a mummified body. Call Winchester.

Jack sat back on his haunches, surprised at the range of emotions that rushed through him like a wildfire. He'd dreamed of the day he would fulfill his promise to his mother. He'd expected revenge to taste sweet. Finally Pepper Winchester would get what she deserved.

But there was no sweetness, only a deep sorrow in

him as he looked at what he knew were his grandfather's remains. He'd spent his adult life working hard to succeed in business, waiting for the opportunity to break down this wall and show the world who Pepper Winchester really was. It was going to make it all that much sweeter that she was still alive and would know who uncovered her deadly secret.

Jack waited for the relief, the elation, the smug satisfaction. He finally had proof that his grandmother had killed her husband and hidden his body behind this rock wall, just as his mother had heard.

He'd gotten what he'd come for. He didn't give a damn about any inheritance. Now all he had to do was call his cousin the sheriff and let her take it from here. He could wash his hands of this place that had haunted him all these years.

But what he hadn't expected was to feel a connection to this ranch or this family. He hadn't expected to meet Josey or fall in love. Or feel anything for his grandmother, let alone a dead grandfather he'd never known.

Jack heard a sound behind him. Josey, he thought. Of course she wouldn't be able to stay in the room. She would be worried about him. She would— He turned and saw the figure framed in the doorway.

PEPPER WINCHESTER had been coming out of the parlor when she'd seen Josey racing down the stairs as if the devil himself were after her.

"Call the sheriff," Josey had cried. "I have to get to Jack."

She'd tried to stop the girl to make sense of what was happening, but Josey had rushed out without answering.

The fear in the young woman's face had sent an arrow of panic through Pepper's own heart.

"What is wrong with that girl?" Virginia demanded, coming out from her room at the back wing.

"Stay here. Call the sheriff. Tell McCall there's some kind of trouble."

Her daughter's eyes widened in alarm. "You're not going out there."

But Pepper was already following Josey. She couldn't move as quickly, and once outside it took her a few minutes for her old eyes to adjust to the dark. She caught a glimpse of Josey running toward the closed wing of the lodge.

That building was actually the first homestead. Call had workers add on to it, the lodge expanding, as his grandiose plans developed, into what it was today. But Pepper remembered his stories about his parents living in what people would call an old shotgun house. Long and narrow, the hall ran straight through every room to the back door. Only this one didn't have a back door. The house ended in an old root cellar tucked into the hillside.

She saw Josey stop, heard the old dog growling even from here. As she worked her way in that direction, Pepper realized it had been years since she'd ventured out of the house. She wasn't used to walking on uneven ground, even with her cane. She felt exposed out here and suddenly afraid as she saw Josey give the dog a wide berth before slipping past the dog and disappearing into the door of the wing Pepper had Alfred close off years ago.

She quickened her pace, gasping for breath, as she

realized that what she had feared for more than forty years was about to come true.

RJ WAS MOVING down the hallway toward a scratching sound and a sliver of light under one of the doors, when he heard someone come into the house behind him. He quickly stepped into one of the darkened rooms, pressing his back against the wall.

He'd heard the dog growling, heard someone trying to soothe it. He'd expected whoever it was to run back to the house screaming after seeing the old man's body with the ax buried in it.

Rubbing his wounded shoulder, RJ swore under his breath at the pain. He hadn't seen the old man until it was too late. He'd sensed someone behind him in time to avoid the brunt of the ax. But the wooden handle had hit his shoulder.

The ax had stuck in the side of the log house. As the old fool had tried to wrestle it free, RJ had hit him, knocking him backward. Then, close to blacking out from the pain of the blow on his already injured shoulder, RJ had furiously jerked the ax from the wall and swung it as hard as he could. It stuck with a suctioning sound.

RJ had looked around, but he hadn't seen anyone else. *One down,* he'd thought. Then he'd heard an odd noise coming from within the building. He'd looked for a way into this wing and found an old door where someone had removed the boards that had been tacked over it.

Someone was in there working at this hour? There was a chipping sound, then a scraping sound, as if something large was being moved across the floor.

He'd opened the door, listened, then stepped through,

and was partway down the hall when he'd heard someone come in behind him.

Now he held his breath, wondering what was going
on and why everyone was headed for this particular part
of the strangely built house. The only light was a faint
glow coming from under a door farther down the hallway. Where he stood there was total darkness. But he
could feel a draft and realized that the window across
from him, although partially boarded up, had a hole in
the glass between the boards the size of a small rock.

Tentative footsteps moved in his direction. RJ pulled
the gun he'd stolen from his jacket pocket, half wishing he'd brought the ax with him. He didn't dare fire
the weapon for fear of who it might attract. He'd have
to use it as a blunt force instrument. He'd had some experience with that.

As he listened to the footsteps growing closer
and closer, he heard something outside the building
that made his heart beat faster and his stomach drop.
Through the broken window came the whine of a car
engine in the distance.

It was headed toward the house, which meant there
was another road into the ranch.

McCall had turned off her lights and siren as soon as
she'd gotten out of town; she hadn't needed them because of the lack of traffic. Now she stopped in a low
spot and killed her headlights and engine. She reached
for her shotgun. She was already wearing the Kevlar
vest under her jacket and had her Glock in her holster.
Both the shotgun and the pistol were loaded and ready
to go.

Easing open the door, she slid out and started down

the road. Over the first rise, she saw the lodge sprawled against the mountainside. She could hear the wind in the cottonwoods as she neared the creek. The antique weather vane on the barn turned slowly.

She pulled up short as her eyes picked up movement in front of the house. Someone was walking toward the far wing. She heard the tap of a cane on the gravel. Her grandmother? Where was she going?

McCall began to run, hoping to hell her grandmother wasn't armed and would mistake her for a trespasser. But she wasn't about to call out and warn RJ that she was coming. She'd have to take her chances with her grandmother.

VIRGINIA PEERED OUT the window, seeing nothing. Where had her mother gone? The old fool. Well, she wasn't going out there after Josey, who'd probably just had a spat with her husband. Newlyweds!

She looked around, wondering where Enid and Alfred were. They lived in the wing opposite the kitchen and laundry rooms. Virginia realized she hadn't heard a peep out of either of them.

And it certainly wasn't like Enid to miss anything. Why hadn't she come out when Josey had come tearing through the house and both Virginia and her mother had raised their voices to call after her?

Virginia thought the whole thing ridiculous, but she stepped to the phone and began to dial 911 before she realized the line was dead.

She slowly put down the receiver. Her cell was useless out here; in fact, her grandmother didn't even own one and with good reason. Cell phone coverage was sketchy in this part of the county.

The huge old place seemed too quiet. She shivered and hugged herself, wishing her mother would come back and assure her there was a good reason the phone line was down.

Should she stay in here and wait, or should she go out and see what was going on herself? Maybe her mother needed her.

The thought actually made Virginia laugh out loud.

The wind buffeted the old glass at the window, making her jump. She'd been so busy listening to the house that she'd failed to realize how hard the wind was blowing. It thrashed the cottonwoods outside, sending leaves swirling across the yard.

She tried to convince herself that the wind had knocked down the phone line, just as it used to when she lived here. But she knew something was terribly wrong. She could feel it.

She eased open the front door and peered around the corner, hoping to see her mother. A gust of wind nearly wrested the door from her hands. She stared into the darkness. Was that Pepper headed for the old wing of the house?

She let out a small cry as ice-cold fingers bit into her upper arm. The door slipped from her fingers and swung open, banging against the wall as she swung around.

"What are you doing?" Enid demanded.

The elderly housekeeper looked odd. Or maybe it was the way the wind blew her hair back from her face in this dim light.

"You scared me half to death," Virginia snapped. "You have to quit sneaking up on people like that. You're going to give my mother a heart attack."

"It would take more than that to kill your mother." Enid glanced down the hallway in the direction of Pepper's room. "Where *is* your mother?"

"She's gone outside after Josey."

Enid pushed past her, fighting the wind to see.

Virginia heard her mother scream like a wounded animal, the sound getting caught up in the howl of the wind, as Enid began to run awkwardly in the direction Pepper had gone.

Virginia slammed the door, then hurried down to her room and locked herself inside.

RJ KNEW HE couldn't be seen where he was standing in dense shadow, and yet he'd almost blown it—he'd been so surprised to see Josey walk past the room where he was hiding in plain sight.

He wanted to laugh. Could his luck get any better than this? He felt he was on a roll. Nothing could go wrong.

The hardest part was waiting until he heard her footsteps stop. Still, he waited as he heard a door creak open. He started to take a step when he heard Josey speak—and a man answer.

Perfect. RJ took a cautious step out, then another. The door to the room down the hall was open now, a dim light spilling out. He could hear their voices, but couldn't make out what they were saying. Something in the tone, though, told him this was the driver of the Cadillac parked out front, the cowboy who'd saved Josey. Or thought he had, RJ thought with a smile.

He eased down the hallway, stopping as soon as he could hear what they were saying.

PEPPER TEETERED on her cane as McCall reached her.

"What is going on?" Pepper demanded, her voice warbling with emotion.

McCall steadied her for a moment, following her grandmother's gaze to the body lying in the shadow of the house and the old dog sitting next to it.

"It's Alfred," her grandmother said. "He has an ax in his chest."

McCall could see that. "What are you doing out here?"

"Josey rushed out of the house saying to call you because Jack was in trouble. I came out to find out what was wrong."

Josey, McCall thought, looking around the ranch yard. "I want you to go back to the house." At the sound of a sole crunching on the gravel, McCall swung around to see Enid. She had stopped short of where her husband lay dead next to the door. She had her hand over her mouth.

"Enid," McCall said, going over and taking hold of her arm. "I want you to take Pepper back into the house. Do you hear me?"

The ancient housekeeper nodded slowly.

"Now! Both of you, and stay there." McCall moved along the building, glancing back to see that neither old woman had moved. Damn it. She didn't have time to herd them back to the house. She reached the end of the building and saw where the boards had been removed.

The door into the old section of the house was open. Cautiously, she moved toward it.

FOR A MOMENT, Josey stood, her heart in her throat, afraid to breathe.

"Jack?" she whispered, as she stared into the dark room. The gun was in her hands, one finger on the trigger. She knew RJ might have already gotten to Jack. That if anyone was in the room it could be RJ, standing in the dark and laughing at her.

A light flashed on, the beam pointed at the floor.

Her finger brushed the trigger and jerked away. "Jack!" she cried. She lowered the gun and rushed to him. Her relief at seeing him unharmed made her throat swell with emotion. She could barely get the words out. "Alfred. He's dead. RJ—" The rest was choked off as she saw the hole in the wall and what lay just inside it. "Oh, my God. Who—?"

"My grandfather," he said, taking the gun from her and laying the flashlight on one of the shelves so the beam wasn't pointed at them. "My mother had heard stories from people who used to work on the ranch about Alfred rocking up a wall in the old wing the day Call Winchester disappeared."

The mention of Alfred brought back the horrible scene just outside. The words spilled out of her as she felt the urgency return. "I saw Alfred earlier carrying an ax and headed this way, so I came to warn you, but…" She shuddered as she met Jack's eyes. "He's dead. The ax is in…his chest. RJ's here."

Jack gripped her arm with one hand. He had the

gun he'd taken from her in the other. "Come on, let's get out of here."

They both seemed to hear the creak of a floorboard behind them at the same time. Turning toward the doorway, Jack stepped in front of her as they were suddenly blinded by a bright light.

JACK BLINKED, covering his eyes as he shielded Josey from the man standing in the doorway holding the gun on them.

"Drop the gun," the man ordered, and lowered the flashlight so it wasn't blinding Jack.

Jack knew he could get off at least one shot before RJ fired. He couldn't take the chance that Josey might be hit.

He had risked her life for revenge. He would never forgive himself. But he knew even if they'd left earlier, one day RJ would have caught up to them. This encounter had been inevitable.

Jack just would have liked to be more prepared.

He felt Josey behind him, heard the small sound she made and knew this was indeed her stepbrother, RJ Evans, the man who'd framed her, hurt her and planned to kill her.

In the diffused light from the flashlight in his hand, Jack saw that RJ was tall and blond, with eerie blue eyes. He looked strong and solid and armed. Jack had to believe that RJ wouldn't want to kill them here in this room, that he would get an opportunity to save Josey. It couldn't end like this. He would do anything to save Josey.

"I said drop the gun. Now!"

Jack dropped the gun to the floor at his feet.

RJ smiled. "Hey, Josey. Shocked to see me? I thought you might be surprised that you hadn't killed me." He sounded angry, his words slurring a little as if he might be drunk or on drugs. "Could you have hidden someplace more hard to get to?" His gaze shifted to Jack. "And you must be the guy with the Cadillac convertible. Nice ride. I think I'll take it when I leave here."

Behind him, Jack felt something hard and cold suddenly pushed against his back. The crowbar. Josey slipped it into the waistband of his jeans.

"Now kick the gun over here," RJ ordered.

JOSEY KNEW HOW this would end. She knew what RJ was capable of, his cruelty unmatched. He would make them both pay, Jack for helping her and putting RJ to all this trouble, and Josey—

She couldn't think about that or the fear would paralyze her. This had to end here. The last time she'd shot at RJ it had been to stop him from killing both her and Celeste. She'd sworn then that she would never fire another gun, especially at another person.

RJ stepped forward before Jack could kick the gun over to him in a swift movement that caught both her and Jack by surprise. He caught Jack in the side of the head with the butt of his weapon.

Jack started to go down and Josey saw her chance. She dropped to the floor, snatched up the gun Jack had dropped and fired blindly at RJ. The gunshots exploded in the small room, deafening her, as she saw RJ stumble backward toward the doorway. His flashlight clattered to the floor and went out, pitching the room in blackness.

The air had filled with five shots. Josey knew she'd had only four in the gun she was holding. That meant RJ had gotten a round off. Her heart leaped into her throat at the thought that Jack might have been hit. If the blow to the head from the butt of the gun hadn't killed him, then the shot could have.

"Jack?" For a moment, the silence was deafening. Then a chill skittered over her skin as she heard RJ chuckle. He knew there had only been six shots in the pistol. He knew she was no longer armed.

She could hear him feeling around in the dark for something. His gun? Had he lost it? Then her heart began to pound wildly as she heard him crawling toward her. "Jack?" No answer.

She was filled with agony and terror that Jack was dead. Her plan had backfired. Somehow Jack had gotten in the line of fire.

She scuttled backward from her sitting position on the floor until she hit the rock wall. Her fingers felt rocks and dried mortar. She felt around frantically for a rock small enough that she could use as a weapon, but found nothing.

Remembering the hole Jack had made in the wall, she felt around for it, thinking that if she could get through it—

As she tried to scramble to her feet, disoriented by the blackness, RJ's hand closed like a vise around her ankle. She screamed, grabbing a handful of dried mortar from the floor and throwing it where she thought his face should be.

He let out a scream of his own, clawing at her now

with both hands as she tried to fight him off. But RJ had always been too strong for her.

MCCALL HAD JUST stepped through the doorway and had started down the hall when she heard the five shots. She snapped on her flashlight. With her weapon drawn, she hurried down the hall.

She couldn't tell where the shots had come from. The sound had echoed through the wing. So she was forced to stop at each door, before moving forward again.

Behind her she heard a door open and spun around to see her grandmother standing in it, wide-eyed. Damn the stubborn woman. Hiding behind her was Enid.

McCall couldn't take the time to argue with them. She waved for them to stay back, knowing the effort was useless, as she moved forward down the hallway.

She hadn't gone far when the hallway light switched on. She swore. Her grandmother or Enid had just alerted whoever had fired those shots that they were no longer alone.

IN THE SUDDEN LIGHT, Josey saw that at least some of the four shots she'd fired had hit their mark. RJ had left a wide smear of blood on the floor as he'd crawled after her. He had pulled himself up into a sitting position and managed to get hold of her wrist, twisting it until she was sure he was going to break it, then pulled her facedown in front of him.

But when the lights had come on, her gaze had gone instantly to where she'd heard Jack fall. He lay just feet away. His eyes were closed and she could see that his shirt was soaked with blood. She stared at his chest, praying to see the rise and fall of his breath.

Please, God, let him be alive.

RJ let go of her wrist to grab a handful of her hair. He jerked her head up and slapped her almost senseless. "I'm talking to you, bitch. Look at me when I talk to you. I want you to be gazing into my eyes when I rip your heart out."

He'd already ripped her heart out if he'd killed Jack. She had fought RJ until he'd gotten her down on the floor. His face was scratched where she'd made contact, his eyes red and running tears, his cheeks gritty with mortar. He kept blinking and swearing as he tried to clear them.

But it was the way the front of his shirt blossomed with blood that gave her hope. "You're in no shape to rip my heart out," she said, meeting his gaze. She would fight this bastard to the death. "You're going to bleed to death on this dirty floor."

He laughed, a gurgling sound coming from his throat, that even gave him pause. A new cruelty came into his eyes. He wasn't going to die alone, the look said. He let go of her long enough to pull the knife from the sheath strapped to his leg.

Out of the corner of her eye, Josey caught movement. She wanted to cry in relief. She wanted to look in Jack's direction to make sure she hadn't just imagined it. But she did neither. She kept her gaze locked with RJ's, afraid of what he would do if he knew that Jack was alive.

Josey didn't move, didn't breathe, as RJ put the knife to her throat.

JACK CAME TO SLOWLY. The blow to his head had knocked him senseless. He lay perfectly still, listening to RJ threatening Josey. It was all he could do not to leap up and attack the man.

But first he had to be sure that RJ wasn't still holding a gun on her.

He moved his head as quietly as he could until he could see RJ sitting, leaning against the stack of rocks Jack had removed from the wall. He was turned slightly, so he wasn't facing Jack, but he didn't have his back to him, either.

Jack saw that RJ's shirt was soaked with blood. There was a wide trail of blood on the floor where it appeared RJ had crawled over to Josey. He now had hold of Josey's hair and was holding her in front of him at an odd angle.

The last thing Jack remembered was the sound of gunfire. At first he'd thought RJ had unloaded his weapon on Josey. But now he could see Josey's gun lying within her reach. He could only assume it was empty or RJ would have taken it from her. She didn't appear to be wounded, but Jack couldn't know that for sure until he got a better look at her.

Shifting just a little, he felt the crowbar at his back and eased it out behind him. He knew he would get only one chance if RJ was still armed. He would have to make it count.

"You know, RJ, you might have pulled it off," Josey was saying. Jack realized she was stalling, giving him time. "The way you set me up when you killed your father, that was brilliant."

"Thanks." RJ sounded touched that she thought so. "I hated that mean old son of a bitch. I don't know why I didn't kill him sooner."

Jack heard something in RJ's voice and the way he

was trying to catch his breath. He was bleeding badly and Jack suspected Josey had nicked a lung.

"Where you went wrong was taking Celeste along with you."

"Tell me," RJ agreed, struggling with each breath.

Josey had to have heard it, as well. She would be thinking that if she kept him talking...

Slowly, methodically, trying not to make a sound, Jack worked his way to a crouch. RJ's threats covered most any noise Jack had made.

"She was only after your money," Josey said. "I think you're better off without her."

"Uh-huh," RJ agreed. "You aren't going to suggest that I hook up with you, are you?" His laugh sounded as if he was underwater. "A woman who shot me not once, but twice?"

It wasn't until Jack was ready, the crowbar in his hand, that he saw a glint of metal and realized what RJ was holding to Josey's neck.

McCALL HEARD VOICES and followed the low rumble down the hallway, then stopped just outside the room. She heard a man's voice, threatening to kill someone. Not her cousin Jack's voice. RJ's? She could only assume so.

Then she heard a woman's voice, scared, but in control. Josey Vanderliner? Where was Jack? Hadn't her grandmother said something about Josey going after Jack?

Leading with the weapon, McCall swept it across the room, taking in the scene and making a decision in that split second.

She'd heard everything said within the room and

knew that RJ had some kind of weapon in his possession and planned to kill Josey. He sounded bad, but she knew that some men, especially those that took certain drugs, didn't die easily.

When she saw the knife RJ was holding to Josey's throat and her cousin Jack armed with a crowbar and ready to risk his life for this woman he called his wife, McCall didn't hesitate. She pulled the trigger.

Chapter Fourteen

It was chaos after that. Jack lunged forward even as RJ fell away from Josey, the shot to his head killing him instantly. Jack lunged, knocking the knife away from Josey's throat with the crowbar in the same instant Mc-Call fired.

McCall heard her grandmother and Enid behind her. Heard the gasps. Jack was cradling Josey in his arms. Past them, McCall saw the hole in the rock wall and what appeared to be a mummified body lying in what was left of an old canvas tarp.

"It's Call Winchester," Enid cried. "Just like Alfred said."

McCall rounded up everyone and got them all back to the house, but not before she'd seen the expression on her grandmother's face as she looked at the mummified body behind the wall.

"I'm going to need statements from all of you," Mc-Call announced after going to her patrol car and calling for backup, an ambulance and a coroner. "Starting with you. I assume you are Josey Vanderliner?"

Josey nodded.

"The rest of you just sit here quietly."

She took Josey down the hall to the first room Mc-

Call had ever seen in this house just a month ago. It had taken a while, but her grandmother had accepted her as a Winchester.

Now, though, McCall was wondering if that was such a good thing, as she turned on the small tape recorder she'd retrieved from the patrol SUV.

"Tell me what happened here tonight," she said to Josey, and listened to the horrific story the young woman told, beginning with the murder of Ray Allan Evans Sr. in Palm City, California, and finishing with RJ holding a knife to her throat.

"I heard him confess to the murder of his father," McCall said, when Josey finished.

"Jack didn't know anything."

McCall smiled, thinking that her cousin was a Winchester. He knew something was up with this woman he'd picked up on the road. He'd helped her disguise her looks and given her a place to hide out. But she kept those thoughts to herself, secretly admiring Jack. There would be no charges of harboring a criminal since Josey Vanderliner had been a victim herself.

After that, McCall talked to Jack. "You knew there was a body behind that rock wall?"

"I thought it might just be a rumor."

She nodded. "Do you believe Enid that her husband, Alfred, killed Call Winchester?"

Jack grinned. Even though he was blond and blue-eyed, McCall saw the Winchester shining through. "I would have no idea."

She laughed, shaking her head. "The old gal got to you, too."

"I don't know what you're talking about," Jack said.

Enid repeated the same story she'd told on the way to the house, swearing that Alfred had killed Call and that the only reason she'd kept silent all these years was that Alfred had threatened to kill her, as well.

McCall didn't believe a word of it.

Her grandmother looked pale by the time she came into the room. She sat down heavily, still holding her cane, appearing a little dazed.

"You must have wondered what happened to your husband," McCall said to her grandmother.

Pepper looked up, her eyes misting over. "I loved your grandfather. But it was a relief not to ever have to see him again because I *did* love him, and being around him hurt so badly, loving and hating him at the same time."

McCall was surprised at her grandmother's honesty. "What did you think happened to him?"

"You know this country. I thought eventually we'd find his body. I also thought he might have just taken off, put this life behind him. Your grandfather, well, he'd had other lives before I met him. I never knew where he got his money or how. But I did know that he liked the idea of reinventing himself. But to see him behind that wall…" Her voice broke. "Will the coroner be able to tell how he died?"

The question made the hair stand up on the back of her neck. "Probably not," McCall said slowly.

"I know what you're thinking, but I couldn't do that to him. I couldn't wall him up like that. Call was afraid of small spaces." She shuddered and wiped her eyes.

As McCall shut off the tape recorder, she didn't know if she believed her grandmother or not, but she wanted to.

JACK SANK DOWN into the bubbles, the water as warm and soothing as the feel of Josey's body tucked in front of him in the big clawfoot tub.

He pressed his face against hers, breathing in her scent, thanking God that she was all right.

They hadn't said much since McCall had allowed them to come upstairs and clean up. Their clothing would be taken as evidence, but since the acting sheriff had witnessed what had happened and had heard RJ confess to his father's murder, they had both been cleared.

"I thought I'd lost you," Jack said.

Josey cupped his face in her hands, her gaze taking him in as if memorizing every feature. "You aren't the only one. I was so worried that if the blow to the head didn't kill you then the one shot RJ got off did." There were tears in her eyes.

"You realize I'm not going to let you go."

She smiled almost ruefully. "Jack, we're virtually strangers."

"After what we've been through?" he scoffed, as he pulled her to him. "And we could have years to get to know each other better if you would say you'll really be my wife. I know this isn't much of a proposal—"

She touched her fingers to his lips. "This is the second best proposal I've ever had. The first was a few days ago on the highway."

He kissed her fingers, then removed them from his lips. "Well? Willing to take a chance with me?"

"One question. What is the Galaxy Corporation?" She looked chagrined. "I checked the registration in your car after you kept sneaking off in the middle of the night."

"It's a business I started that puts kids together with ranches. Oftentimes the kids are from the inner city or have been in trouble. I twist the arms of rich landowners, people who own large amounts of land but spend only a week or two actually at the ranch, to let the kids come work the place. Most ranch managers are fine with it as long as the kids are supervised. You can't believe what hard work and fresh air does for these kids."

She heard the love in his words for both ranching and kids. She should have known the Galaxy Corporation was something like that. "Did I mention how much I love you?"

"No." But his grin said he liked it. "I should tell you, though, I don't make any money doing this. Fortunately, it turns out that my mother's family had money. That helped get the corporation going so that now it is self-supporting."

Josey laughed. "I have a ton of money, more than I will ever spend. What?" she said, when she saw his expression.

"I don't like the idea of marrying someone who—"

"Can expand your kids-on-ranches program?" she asked.

He smiled at her. "Still—"

"The answer is yes. If you still want to marry me."

He looked into her beautiful green eyes and felt his heart soar like a hawk. "I don't want to spend another day away from you."

"You won't have to. My mother is safe. McCall checked for me. I will want to move her closer to wherever I'm going to be, that's all I need. Well, maybe not *all* I need." Desire sparked in her gaze. "I need you, Jack Winchester."

They made love in the tub, slowly, lovingly, a celebration of life. It wasn't until they were drying off that Jack broached the subject.

"My grandmother has asked me if I'd like to come back to the ranch at some point. I told her I would have to talk to you. I think everything that has happened has changed her. Well, at least a little. I know you probably have nothing but bad memories here and there is more than a good chance that my grandmother had something to do with my grandfather being put behind that stone wall, you know."

"Jack, you love this place and I love you."

"But after everything that's happened, not to mention the secrets that these walls have seen…"

She stepped to him, wondering at how fate and maybe a whole lot of luck had brought Jack Winchester into her life. She wanted to pinch herself. "I will be happy wherever you are."

He grinned as he reached for her, drawing her back into his arms. "I was thinking we should elope and go on a long honeymoon, then if you still mean it, maybe we'll come back here for McCall's wedding at Christmas and see how things go."

Josey kissed him, remembering that day on the highway when he'd come roaring up the hill in his old Cadillac convertible and had stopped for her. She remembered his handsome face beneath the brim of his Western hat. But what she remembered most was that boyish grin of his.

"Pepper said she would give me a section of land so we could build a house of our own," Jack said between kisses, as he carried her over to the bed. "We'll need lots of room for all those kids we're going to together. I'm thinking a half dozen."

Josey laughed as he lowered her to the bed. She pulled him down. "It is definitely something we can negotiate," she said.

"I love you, Josey," Jack said, grinning. "Taking you for a wife was the smartest thing I ever did."

* * * * *

SPECIAL EXCERPT FROM

Ⓗ **HARLEQUIN**

INTRIGUE

*Finding a baby on his doorstep is the last thing
Texas Ranger Eli Slater expects in the middle of the
night. Until he discovers that his ex, Ashlyn Darrow,
is the little girl's mother and the child was just
kidnapped from her. Now they have to figure out who's
behind this heinous crime while trying very hard to
keep their hands off each other…*

Keep reading for a sneak peek at
Settling an Old Score,
part of Longview Ridge Ranch,
from USA TODAY *bestselling author Delores Fossen.*

"Two cops broke into your house?" He didn't bother to take out the
skepticism. "Did they have a warrant? Did they ID themselves?"

Ashlyn shook her head. "They were wearing uniforms, badges
and all the gear that cops have. They used a stun gun on me." She
rubbed her fingers along the side of her arm, and the trembling got
worse. "They took Cora, but I heard them say they were working
for you."

Eli's groan was even louder than the one she made. "And you
believed them." The look he gave her was as flat as his tone. He
didn't spell out to her that she'd been gullible, but he was certain
Ashlyn had already picked up on that.

She squeezed her eyes shut a moment. "I panicked. Wasn't
thinking straight. As soon as I could move, I jumped in my car and
drove straight here."

The drive wouldn't have taken that long since Ashlyn's house
was only about ten miles away. She lived on a small ranch on the
other side of Longview Ridge that she'd inherited from her
grandparents, and she made a living training and boarding horses.

"Did the kidnappers make a ransom demand?" he pressed. "Or did they take anything else from your place?"

"No. They only took Cora. Who brought her here?" Ashlyn asked, her head whipping up. "Was it those cops?"

"Fake cops," Eli automatically corrected. "I didn't see who left her on my porch, but they weren't exactly quiet about it. She was probably out here no more than a minute or two before I went to the door and found her."

He paused, worked through the pieces that she'd just given him and it didn't take him long to come to a conclusion. A bad one. These fake cops hadn't hurt the child, hadn't asked for money or taken anything, but they had let Ashlyn believe they worked for him. There had to be a good reason for that. Well, "good" in their minds, anyway.

"This was some kind of sick game?" she asked.

It was looking that way. A game designed to send her after him.

"They wanted me to kill you?" Ashlyn added a moment later.

Before Eli answered that, he wanted to talk to his brother and get backup so he could take Ashlyn and the baby into Longview Ridge. First to the hospital to confirm they were okay and then to the sheriff's office so he could get an official statement from Ashlyn.

"You really had no part in this?" she pressed.

Eli huffed, not bothering to answer that. He took out his phone to make that call to Kellan, but he stopped when he saw the blur of motion on the other side of Ashlyn's car. He lifted his hand to silence her when Ashlyn started to speak, and he kept looking.

Waiting.

Then, he finally saw it. Or rather he saw them. Two men wearing uniforms, and they had guns aimed right at the house.

Don't miss
Settling an Old Score *by Delores Fossen,*
available August 2020 wherever
Harlequin Intrigue books and ebooks are sold.

Harlequin.com

H HARLEQUIN

INTRIGUE

SEEK THRILLS. SOLVE CRIMES.
JUSTICE SERVED.

Save **$1.00**

on the purchase of ANY
Harlequin Intrigue book!

Available wherever books are sold,
including most bookstores, supermarkets,
drugstores and discount stores.

- ✂

Save $1.00

on the purchase of ANY Harlequin Intrigue book.

Coupon valid until September 30, 2020.
Redeemable at participating outlets in the U.S. and Canada only.
Not redeemable at Barnes & Noble stores. Limit one coupon per customer.

52616828

Canadian Retailers: Harlequin Enterprises ULC will pay the face value of this coupon plus 10.25¢ if submitted by customer for this product only. Any other use constitutes fraud. Coupon is nonassignable. Void if taxed, prohibited or restricted by law. Consumer must pay any government taxes. Void if copied. Inmar Promotional Services ("IPS") customers submit coupons and proof of sales to Harlequin Enterprises ULC, P.O. Box 31000, Scarborough, ON M1R 0E7, Canada. Non-IPS retailer—for reimbursement submit coupons and proof of sales directly to Harlequin Enterprises ULC, Retail Marketing Department, Bay Adelaide Centre, East Tower, 22 Adelaide Street West, 40th Floor, Toronto, Ontario M5H 4E3, Canada.

5 65373 00076 2   (8100)0 12467

U.S. Retailers: Harlequin Enterprises ULC will pay the face value of this coupon plus 8¢ if submitted by customer for this product only. Any other use constitutes fraud. Coupon is nonassignable. Void if taxed, prohibited or restricted by law. Consumer must pay any government taxes. Void if copied. For reimbursement submit coupons and proof of sales directly to Harlequin Enterprises ULC 482, NCH Marketing Services, P.O. Box 880001, El Paso, TX 88588-0001, U.S.A. Cash value 1/100 cents.

® and ™ are trademarks owned by Harlequin Enterprises ULC.

© 2020 Harlequin Enterprises ULC

HICOUP21398

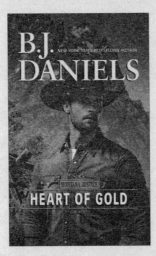

SPECIAL EXCERPT FROM

HQN

Charlie Farmington has blamed herself for her stepsister's unsolved murder for years. So when Charlie sees her—alive—she turns to the one person she can trust to help her: William "Shep" Shepherd, her first love.

Read on for a sneak preview of
Heart of Gold,
the third book in the Montana Justice series
by New York Times *bestselling author B.J. Daniels.*

Chapter One

"Jingle Bells" played loudly from a nearby store and a man jangled a bell looking for donations to his bucket as Charlie let her apartment door close behind her. Snow crystals drifted on the slight breeze, making downtown Bozeman, Montana, sparkle. Pine scented the air as shoppers rushed past, loaded down with bags and packages after snagging early morning deals.

Charlie had just stepped onto the sidewalk, when she saw a woman standing across the street under one of the city's Christmas decorations. Shock froze Charlie to the pavement, and she stared in disbelief. The woman, looking right at her, smiled that all-too-familiar smile—the one that had haunted Charlie's nightmares for years. Even as she told herself it wasn't possible, she felt the bright winter day begin to dim and go black.

Charlie woke lying on the icy sidewalk surrounded by people. She'd never fainted before in her life. But then she'd never seen a dead woman standing across the street from her apartment either.

As she lay there dazed, she realized that she probably wouldn't have even noticed the woman if it hadn't been for her horoscope that morning. It had warned that something bad was going to happen. Not in those exact words. But when she read it, she'd had a premonition she couldn't shake.

Not that she would admit checking her horoscope each morning. It wasn't that she believed it exactly. She just hated the thought of walking into a new day not knowing what to expect.

Earlier this morning she'd actually considered calling her boss and begging off work. She knew it was silly. But she hadn't been able to throw off the strange sense of dread she'd had after reading the prediction.

Unfortunately, she had a design project that was coming due before Christmas. She couldn't afford to miss work. So she'd dressed and left her apartment—against her instincts. If she hadn't been anxiously looking around, worried, she might not have seen the long-dead Lindy Parker standing across the street looking at her. And she wouldn't have dropped in a dead faint.

Becoming aware of the cold, icy sidewalk beneath her, she struggled up with some help from the onlookers. For a while, all sound had been muted. Now she heard the clanging bell again and the Christmas music from a nearby store. She could also feel a pain in her knees; she must have scraped them when she fell.

"Let me help you," an older man said, taking her arm so she could stand on her wobbly legs.

Her gaze shot to the spot where she'd seen Lindy. There was no one there. If there ever had been.

Charlie felt her face flush with embarrassment. Her foolish feeling was accompanied by nausea. She knew rationally that she couldn't have seen Lindy. Yet she couldn't stop quaking. She'd seen someone. Someone who looked enough like the dead woman to give her more than a start.

It didn't help that her rational mind argued against the chance that Lindy's doppelgänger had just happened to be standing across the street from her apartment smiling that evil smile of hers.

Don't miss
Heart of Gold *by B.J. Daniels,*
available September 2020 wherever
HQN Books and ebooks are sold.

HQNBooks.com